Dedicated to the memory of my good friend, neighbour and mentor, children's writer Geoffrey Trease (1909–1998), whose books I enjoyed as both child and adult. His play *The Dragon Who Was Different* is featured in this story.

Geoffrey Trease was an innovator who discarded the 'ho varlet' style of historical writing and instigated a new era of readable fiction for children. He was influential, forward-thinking, kindly, humorous and always ready to encourage young writers. And he thought of some wonderful titles!

With thanks also to Geoffrey's daughter, Jocelyn.

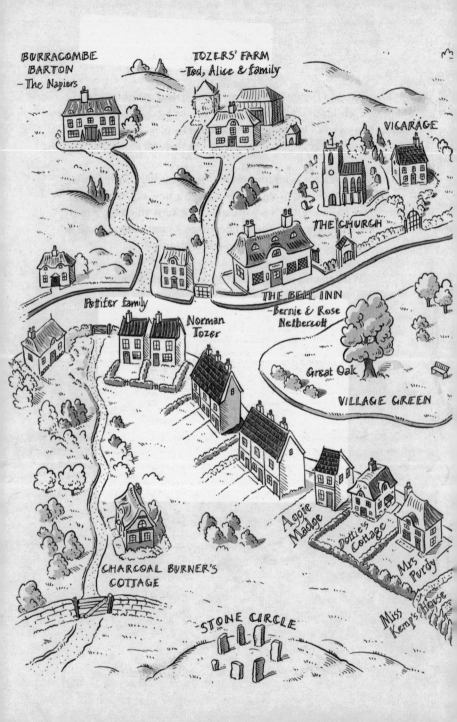

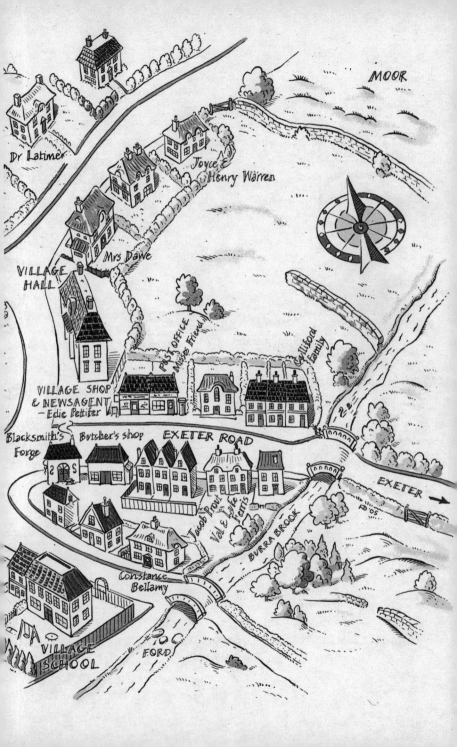

Chapter One

April 1955

'Well, would you credit it?' Alice Tozer spread Thursday's edition of the *Tavistock Gazette* out on the kitchen table, where her mother-in-law Minnie was peeling carrots for dinner, and gazed at the announcements page. 'Hilary Napier's got engaged to the new doctor!'

Joanna, her daughter-in-law, looked up from the farm papers she was trying to make sense of. 'That's not much of a surprise. Anyone could see how friendly they've been getting since he came to work with Dr Latimer.'

'I know,' Alice said, still gazing at the announcement. 'Everyone's noticed it. All the same, it seems a bit quick, considering he's only been here since New Year.'

'Didn't they know each other before?' Minnie asked, putting the last carrot into a saucepan of water. 'Our Val said something about them being in Egypt together during the war. And you remember Val already knew him from then too.'

Alice's lips tightened a little, as they always did when Val's time in Egypt as a nurse was mentioned, and Joanna looked at her with interest, wondering what it was that had happened to her sister-in-law to bring that expression to her mother's face. But all Alice said was 'Yes, I think that's right. He was an army doctor, wasn't he? I suppose they must have met each other then.' She turned over another page. 'Seems a bit of a coincidence, mind, that our Dr Latimer should have trained with Dr Hunter's father all those years ago and then asked him to come here as a partner. And then for him

1

and Hilary to get engaged almost at once ...'

'You reckon there's more to it than that, Mother?' Joanna asked, frowning over an invoice. 'You think there's been something going on we didn't know about?'

'And if there was,' Minnie said sharply, 'there's no reason why us should know anything about it! Miss Hilary's the Squire's daughter; her don't have to take people like us into her confidence. Besides, I don't see it's all that much of a coincidence that Dr Latimer should think of him when he was looking for a partner. I dare say he and Dr Hunter's father have kept in touch over the years, and both came round to thinking of retiring around the same time.'

'So why isn't this young Dr Hunter taking over his father's practice, then, up in Derby?' Alice demanded. 'You'd think that would be the usual way of things.' She turned the page again to read the letters.

'I suppose it's not the same for doctors as it is for farmers. Perhaps he just wanted a change.' Joanna sighed and picked up a receipt. 'Honestly, you'd think some of these people had never been to school. I can't make this writing out at all ... Can you see what it says, Gran?'

Minnie peered at the scrap of paper, decorated with stains that neither of them liked to enquire into. 'I think it's for hay. It's that old chap over to Penny Cross that Ted and Tom go over to help with the stooking. He's always six months behind with his paperwork. I dunno how he gets on with all these new-fangled regulations. Anyway, getting back to the young doctor, didn't Val say something about him not long having lost his wife? So there's not likely to have been anything going on as shouldn't, is there?'

Joanna smiled. 'I dare say you're right, Gran. Anyway, it's nice news and we all ought to be pleased about it. An Easter engagement. I expect they put it in the paper this week so that everyone would know about it by Sunday.' Her face saddened a little. Easter Day was not easy for Joanna, for it was only two years since her baby Suzanne had died in her pram on that day. But she was making a big effort this year not to allow grief to overtake her, if only for the sake of her son, Robin, and Suzanne's twin, Heather. 'I wonder when the wedding will be.'

'Not long, I reckon,' Alice said, folding up the newspaper.

'Hilary won't want to hang about, not at her age. She's past thirty now, getting late for starting a family.'

'Mother!' Joanna protested, laughing. 'She's barely got the engagement ring on her finger, let alone the wedding band, and you're looking for babies already! And there'll be heaps of things to do before the wedding – it's bound to be a big one, so there'll be a lot to plan. But at least they won't have to think about looking for a home. They'll live at the Barton, won't they?'

She looked down at the stack of forms and papers. 'You know, if the government sends us much more of this stuff, we'll have to have a proper office instead of just piling it all up on the dresser. Whatever do they do with all the information we send them? Tom reckons they just stuff it into a drawer and forget about it – and that's just what I'm going to do with it now.' She gathered up the papers and carried them over to the big kitchen dresser. 'It's Good Friday tomorrow and nobody up in London is going to do anything about any of it until next week. They've got enough to worry about with all these strikes to sort out, and a new prime minister to get used to. I'm going to give our bedroom a proper turnout, and then all the spring-cleaning's finished.'

'And I'm going to start the hot cross buns,' Minnie declared. 'It won't feel like Easter till we got the smell of they baking in the oven. I've got some nice fresh yeast in the larder ready. You've got the salt cod for tomorrow's tea, Alice, have you?'

'Val's going into Tavi this afternoon, she'll pick it up then. Salt cod and hot cross buns, and then roast lamb for Sunday dinner. And an engagement to celebrate. What more could you want for Easter?'

Most of the families in Burracombe were planning to celebrate Easter in much the same way – salted cod or smoked haddock or some other kind of fish on Good Friday, followed by hot cross buns from George Sweet's bakery; church or chapel and visits on Sunday morning, with a roast dinner around one o'clock and either a walk or a gossip (and maybe a snooze) in the afternoon, and then picnics or gardening on Easter Monday. A few chocolate Easter eggs had appeared in the shops, to the delight of the children, who had made do with cardboard ones for years, and Sunday breakfast was enlivened by boiled eggs of rainbow hues, cooked in water containing cochineal or other food colourings, or wrapped in onion skins.

Hilary Napier and David Hunter were doing all this. But they had something even more special to celebrate. They were busy planning the engagement party Hilary's father had insisted should be held on Easter Day, after church. Not the easiest time for a party, Hilary remarked ruefully as she and David staggered into the Burracombe Barton kitchen loaded with boxes of groceries, together with a few extra bottles of sherry just in case they ran out, but it was obviously the most appropriate. They heaved their shopping on to the big table and stood for a moment contemplating it.

'It's a good job meat came off ration last year,' Hilary observed. 'Bert Foster's let us have the biggest leg of lamb I've ever seen. Well, strictly I suppose it's mutton – by the time a lamb gets that big, it's a grown-up sheep.'

'And all the tastier for it,' said Mrs Curnow, the housekeeper, starting to unpack. 'You can't beat a joint of mutton, cooked nice and slow. I wish you'd let me come in to help, Miss Hilary. It's a lot for you to do on your own, what with going to church as well, and all the drinks to see to.'

'I shan't be on my own,' Hilary said with a smile at David. 'Patsy's coming in the morning to do the vegetables. David will see to the drinks, and Father will be fussing about making sure everyone has their glass topped up. And if the meat is ready to come out by half past twelve, I can just pop the potatoes in to roast and start the rest of the vegetables before going back to the party. Father's going to announce the engagement then – although everyone will know already – and probably propose at least two toasts, and I expect Dr Latimer will want to say something, and then I can just say that lunch is ready and make them all stop. You stay at home and enjoy Easter with your sister.'

'I'll do the trifle and the apple tart before I go on Saturday, then,' the Cornishwoman said. 'They'll be in the larder all ready for you. And if nobody else has done it yet, I'd like to be the first to give you my congratulations,' she added rather shyly.

It seemed to Hilary that dozens of people had already congratulated them, but she smiled and thanked the little woman before continuing to unpack. After a minute or two, Hilary's face grew pensive, and David glanced at her and said, 'Maybe we could leave this to Mrs Curnow and go and sit down with a cup of coffee. I'm only getting in the way, anyway.'

'You go and sit in the morning room,' the housekeeper nodded. 'I'll bring it in directly. The Colonel's out with Mr Kellaway, so you'll be nice and quiet.'

The tray appeared soon after they had settled themselves on the sofa in the big window. Hilary poured two cups and then turned to face the view outside. David watched her for a moment, then said quietly, 'What's worrying you, darling? Is it the party? You're not regretting the engagement already, I hope!'

Hilary smiled faintly at his tone. 'Of course not. After all this time? I just want to get to our wedding! No, it's this news from Cyprus, about EOKA. If they're starting a campaign to drive out the British, the services are the first people they'll attack. The RAF station, for a start.'

'And your brother Stephen's there.' He took her hand. 'Of course you're anxious. But it may come to nothing. It's only a few days since we heard the announcement, and the military bases will be well protected.'

'It's not just Stephen,' Hilary said in a wobbly voice. 'It's Maddy too. You've never met her, but she's such a dear, and life hasn't always been easy for her. She and her sister Stella were bombed out twice in Portsmouth, and lost their mother and baby brother the second time, and then they were separated when their father was lost at sea. They only found each other again a few years ago – here in Burracombe. Stella came as a teacher – well, you know that already – and she was here for months before she discovered that Maddy had actually lived here as a little girl. And then Maddy lost her first fiancé, Sammy. That was a dreadful time, and Stephen thought she'd never come back to him. He'd been in love with her for years.'

'And you're afraid of what might happen to them both out in Cyprus. But surely if there's any danger, the authorities will bring the families home.'

'Maddy will never come. She'll stay with Stephen if she possibly can.'

David sighed. He let go of her hand and picked up his cup. 'Well, there's nothing we can do about it. We just have to carry on with our own lives and hope for the best.'

'I know.' Hilary sipped her coffee. 'And I'm sure you're right – they'll be well protected. As you say, it's early days. I just hope Father doesn't get too worried about it. The thought of losing another son ...' She shivered.

David watched her for a moment, then said carefully, 'He seems to me to have more stamina than you give him credit for. He's ex-military himself – he knows the dangers. You can't protect him from those. But he also knows how to face them.'

'And he's getting older, and has had two heart attacks,' she replied swiftly. 'Oh, I'm sorry, David, I didn't mean to snap. You're right – he's a strong personality and that matters more than physical strength sometimes.' She sighed and picked up a sheet of paper. 'We really must get on with planning this engagement party. I've got a list of the guests here – let's work out the seating plan at the table. Luckily we've managed to keep it down to twelve. I think Father would have invited a cast of thousands if he'd had the chance.'

'He can do that for the wedding,' David said with a grin. 'Let him go to town on that, darling. You're the first daughter he's ever been able to marry off!'

'And the only one,' Hilary said, spreading the list out on the table. 'The next wedding from this house will be for someone not even born yet!'

6

Chapter Two

The news spread quickly through the rest of the village. Hilary was a popular figure, who had grown up at the Barton, gone away during the war to do her bit serving as an army driver, and lost her fiancé Henry, killed in action. Since then she hadn't found anyone to marry – hadn't looked, a lot of people reckoned – and had concentrated on managing the Burracombe estate. There had been some difficult moments when her father had insisted on appointing a manager, but Hilary and Travis Kellaway had finally shaken down well enough, and were now firm friends. The sudden appearance on the Barton doorstep of Robert Aucoin, the previously unknown son of Hilary's elder brother Baden, who had been lost at Dunkirk, had also threatened the stability of the estate, and indeed the village, but Colonel Napier had now accepted that the boy was more French than English and likely to make his home in the country of his upbringing, and Rob's mother, Marianne, had decided that until he finished his education, the boy should simply come for long visits during the summer holidays.

'Another big wedding in the village,' Edie Pettifer said to her shop full of customers that Maundy Thursday afternoon. 'Us'll have to get the bunting and flags out again, make a bit of a show. Not that it'll be for a few months – maybe even next year.'

'I wonder who she'll get to make her frock,' Jessie Friend said. She had popped in from the post office next door, leaving her sister Jeanie in charge. 'Someone up in London, I dare say. One of those posh designers.'

'Well, we can be sure it won't be your Dottie,' Ivy Sweet said nastily. 'For all she thinks she could make a dress fit for a queen. Anyway, Hilary Napier won't be wearing white, will she?'

The other customers rounded on her.

'Not wear white? Whatever be you insinuating, Ivy Sweet? Of course her'll wear white.'

'Oh, come on,' Ivy said scornfully. 'At her age? And after those years out in Egypt? There was plenty went on there a girl wouldn't tell her mother, wasn't there, Val?'

Val Ferris, who had just come in and heard the last few words, stopped and stared at her. 'Plenty went on where, Mrs Sweet?'

'Out in Egypt. You were there too – you'd know.'

Val caught her breath. Hot colour ran up her neck into her cheeks and then quickly receded, leaving her almost white. She looked round at the other women, and Aggie Madge, who was last in the queue, put out a hand to steady her.

'Here, Val, sit down for a minute. You look proper shook up.' She pulled forward the chair that Edie kept by the counter and turned angrily to Ivy, the baker's wife. 'I don't know what you think you'm doing, Ivy Sweet, passing remarks like that. And you're a fine one to talk anyway, seeing as what you got up to over in Horrabridge with all they Polish airmen.'

Ivy flared up at once. 'I never got up to nothing! You'll take that back, Aggie Madge.'

'And you take back what you said,' Edie said sharply. 'A lovely piece of news like Miss Hilary getting engaged, her that's always been so good to us all, and you have to start dragging her name in the dirt, just to get yourself noticed. Well you can go and get yourself noticed in Tavistock in future, because you're not welcome in this shop no more. Out you go.'

'You can't do that! I got all me Easter shopping to do.'

'I can and I have.' Edie began to come round the end of the counter, waving her arms. 'Go on! Be off with you! I don't want to see you in here no more.'

For a moment Ivy looked as if she were about to stand her ground, but a swift glance at the faces of the other customers showed that they were all on Edie's side, and with a snort and a toss of her head, for all the world like an angry Dartmoor pony, she gathered up her bags and departed, slamming the shop door behind her.

8

The others laughed.

'That told her, Edie,' Aggie said admiringly. 'Mind you, it isn't the first time you've banned her, is it?'

'No, but it's likely to be the last,' Edie said. She went into the back room and came out with a cup of water, which she handed to Val. 'Here you are, my dear. Drink that, and don't you take no notice of that woman with her spiteful tongue. I know Miss Hilary's a special friend of yours. You'm bound to be upset hearing such nasty talk.'

Val nodded and sipped the water. 'You've all heard about the engagement, then?'

'My stars, 'tis all round the village,' Aggie declared. 'And a better bit of news us haven't had in quite a while. It's time Miss Hilary found herself a nice man to settle down with. I suppose you already knew?' she asked artlessly, hoping to be told more, but Val just smiled.

'Only yesterday evening. I knew it was on the cards, but that's all. It's lovely that she won't have to move away. I know she was worried about leaving her father and the estate.'

'Well, with her intended doing so well in the village, there won't be no problem there,' Jessie said comfortably. 'He came to see our Billy when he had that bronchitis back in February and he were kindness itself. I know us don't want to lose dear old Dr Latimer, but if we got to, I reckon young Dr Hunter will suit us pretty well.'

'Dr Latimer won't be leaving just yet,' Val said. 'He wants to semi-retire for a year or two, once David – Dr Hunter – is settled in. He'll keep a lot of his patients.' She handed the cup back to Edie. 'Thank you, Edie. Now I'd better get on with my shopping.'

'And so had the rest of us,' Aggie Madge said, and turned back to the counter, consulting her list. 'I'll have a dozen eggs, please, Edie, and a pound of streaky bacon. I've got visitors in all over Easter, and they do like a proper cooked breakfast.'

Her shopping done, Val walked along the village street, pushing her baby Christopher's pram with the groceries packed at his feet. He was just over eighteen months old now and quite capable of walking short distances, but she still used the pram for longer trips out, and it was certainly useful for shopping. Today she intended to walk down to the ford by the humpbacked bridge and let him splash in the water.

'Hullo,' a voice hailed her as she rounded the corner. 'It's Mrs Ferris, isn't it?'

'Oh, hullo,' she said, pushing her hair back and smiling. 'You're Mr Raynor, the new teacher.'

'That's right. Not quite so new now – I've been here two terms. And this must be one of my prospective pupils.' He smiled at Christopher. 'But not for a while yet.'

'No, he's got a few more years before he starts school.' Val pushed the pram up the slope of the bridge and stood beside him. 'Isn't it a lovely morning?'

'It certainly is. And so peaceful – you'd never think there was so much unrest going on in other places. Firemen and railwaymen out on strike, no national newspapers for the past fortnight, a change in prime minister – and now the news from Cyprus.' He shook his head and took a pipe and some tobacco from his pocket.

'I suppose it's always the same really,' Val said slowly. 'We think Burracombe is a little backwater and none of those big events affect us, but they do. Stephen and Maddy Napier are in Cyprus, so Hilary and her father must be anxious about them, and with no papers to tell us what's happening ... I know we've got the news on the wireless, but it isn't quite the same somehow.'

'The papers must certainly be annoyed not to be able to report Winston Churchill's resignation,' he said. 'They would have really spread themselves over that – eighty years old, and all that he's done and been in that time. On the other hand, it has given us all a bit more time to get on with our own lives instead of feeling we must keep up with the news. I'd far rather be here, leaning over this lovely old bridge and watching the water tumble over the rocks, than sitting indoors reading a newspaper.'

Val laughed. 'Are you settled in here now?' she asked. 'Do you think you'll stay in Burracombe?'

'I hope so.' He dropped a small stick into the water, and Val quickly bent to pick up one of her own. She dropped it in, and they both automatically turned to watch them emerge under the other side of the bridge. They peered over the low wall and laughed as Val's stick came out just ahead. 'It's the perfect village for me, and the school is ideal. I know it's unusual to have a male teacher for the infants, but I like small children. And I get on very well with Frances – Miss Kemp.'

'We all like her. She's been here so long now, she's part of the village. And you have my little nephew in your class, too – Robin Tozer.'

'That's right, I do.' He found another stick and dropped it into the water. 'Nice little chap, and quite bright. He's got a sister, hasn't he, a little older than your boy here?'

'Heather.' Val debated whether to tell him that Heather's twin had died when they were in their pram together, but decided not to mention it. That was for Joanna or Tom to do if they chose, but Joanna didn't seem inclined to talk about it much to anyone. 'I suppose you only really get to know the people whose children are at school,' she observed. 'But as time goes on, you'll meet pretty well everyone. There's always something going on.'

She turned and unclipped Christopher's reins from the side of the pram, then lifted him to the ground. 'We came down for a paddle. He was too young last year and we've been looking forward to a splash, haven't we, Chris?'

'Isn't the water rather cold?' James Raynor asked dubiously, and Val smiled.

'He's got his wellingtons on. Show Mr Raynor your boots, Chris.' The toddler lifted his feet proudly, then scurried down the other side of the bridge to where the ford sloped into the water. Val ran after him, catching him just before he ran headlong into the stream.

James Raynor watched them for a few minutes, puffing on his pipe, then gave them a wave and turned to walk back towards the village.

James had spoken the truth when he said that Burracombe was the perfect village for him. After a war he had never wanted to go into robbed him of his wife and his home in the London Blitz, and part of his leg in action, he had felt he needed a complete change of direction and had given up his former work as a stockbroker and trained as a teacher. He had worked for some time as assistant housemaster at a boys' prep school, and then, finding the hours of duty too long and demanding, had applied for the position at Burracombe. He knew that the school governors – Basil Harvey, the vicar, Colonel

Napier and the elderly Constance Bellamy – had been doubtful at first about his appointment, but they'd given him a chance and he'd taken it. Now he hoped he would never have to leave. There was far too much to keep him here.

He reached the cottage he had been renting and was now in the process of buying, to find the school's headmistress, Miss Kemp, just turning away from the door.

'Hullo, Frances,' he said in surprise. 'I didn't expect to see you this morning.'

'I've just come back from Tavistock. I wondered if you'd like to come for supper tomorrow. It'll be fish, of course.'

'Of course. Thank you – I'd like to very much. And since you're here now, why not come in for a cup of coffee?' He unlocked the door. 'I've just been down to the bridge. I met Mrs Ferris there with her little boy.'

'Oh yes – Val. She's a nice young woman. You know her husband is Luke Ferris, the artist, don't you?' She followed him in.

'I do. I've seen some of his paintings in London. He's quite a rising star. But didn't someone tell me he teaches art in Tavistock?'

'He did for a while, but he's left now to concentrate on his painting. It means he has to go away quite often, but at least they're still living here. I think Alice Tozer – Val's mother – was afraid for a while they'd move away.'

'It does happen.' He led the way into the kitchen and put a kettle on the bandy-legged enamel gas stove. As in most of the cottages, the kitchen was large enough to be a dining room as well – in fact it had to be if you wanted the other downstairs room to be a sitting room. Some villagers still kept that room as their parlour, for formal occasions such as Sunday tea and Christmas, and lived most of their time in the one back room, but James had seen no point in depriving himself of space when there was so little to start with. 'Do you want to sit out here or go into the other room?'

'Oh, here, I think. You've made it very cosy.' Frances looked out through the stable door into the small back garden. 'In fact it's quite warm enough to sit outside. Look at all your bulbs! Crocuses and those lovely tiny daffodils, all mixed up together – they're a real tapestry of colour.'

'They've done very well, but they're not all mine – most would have been planted by the previous tenants. I didn't know what might come up so I poked a few more in here and there and it's turned into quite a display.' He carried a couple of cushions out and dropped them on an old wooden bench. 'I didn't really think they'd have much chance, being planted so late.' He went back indoors.

'Plants want to grow,' Frances said as he came out again with a tray and set it on a rather rickety little table. 'Give them the right conditions and they'll do their best to please.' She accepted her cup. 'And when you think about it, that applies to children as well.'

'It does. Plant them in the right soil of a good home, with plenty of nourishment for their bodies and their brains, and they'll flourish.' He raised his eyebrows at her. 'We're being very philosophical this morning!'

'It's because it's Easter. It's a time for reflection.' She paused for a moment, her head turned away, then looked back and asked more brightly, 'And what are you doing for the weekend? Will you be going away?'

James shook his head. 'Sunday's a busy day for the church choir, and we've got a wedding to sing for on Monday. Basil wouldn't agree to a Saturday wedding, of course, not during Holy Week.'

Frances Kemp nodded. 'It's not usual for a wedding to be held then,' she agreed. 'But Felix Copley held one last year, for Patsy Shillabeer and Terry Pettifer. It was rather a hurried affair, and only the closest members of the two families were there. Her father more or less showed her the door.'

'A shotgun wedding?'

'Not exactly, and not a tactful simile when you think what happened to Percy Shillabeer last November, on the night the baby was born. You'll remember that – it was the evening of Mrs Warren's Extravaganza.' She gave him an apologetic glance. 'Don't be embarrassed – it's not your fault. It's all too easy to put one's foot in it when coming into a new community. I still do it myself, after all these years.'

'I do remember. Tragic.' They were both silent for a moment or two, sipping their coffee, then he said more briskly, 'As for how I plan to spend Easter, I have some news – if all goes well, I'll be painting and decorating.'

Frances lifted her head. 'Really? The purchase has gone through, then?'

'Completion on Wednesday.' He beamed at her. 'I shall be a bona fide local!'

Frances laughed. 'I doubt it! You need to be at least third generation before you can claim that. But I'm sure everyone will be very pleased to know you're staying. The school has had too many upheavals lately.'

'I hope I'll be appreciated for my other qualities too,' he said with a sidelong smile. 'That's if you can think of any.'

Frances gave him a headmistressy sort of look. 'I'm not sure if you think fishing for compliments is one of them,' she remarked drily. 'But I dare say if we look hard enough we'll find others.'

James chuckled. 'I should have known I wouldn't fool you! Well, I'll do my best to be a credit both to the school and to the village. I like it here and I want to stay. I want it to be my home.'

Frances smiled and reached out her hand. 'That's exactly how I feel about Burracombe too. I can't think of anywhere I'd rather live. I'm very pleased that you feel the same.'

They touched hands for a moment and then looked away, neither knowing quite what to say next. Then she smiled again and stood up, saying, 'I told you Easter makes us reflective! Thank you for the coffee, James. I'll see you tomorrow evening. About seven?'

'I'll be there.'

He saw her back through the cottage and then returned to the little garden to collect the tray. He picked it up and stood for a moment gazing at the tapestry of flowers.

Yes, he said to himself. Burracombe is home.

Chapter Three

'And did you get your broad beans planted on Friday as usual, Jacob?' Basil Harvey asked as the congregation filed past him after the Easter Day service. He always felt that this was really the best and most significant day of the church's calendar – the day of resurrection, of new life, the true beginning of Christianity. After the quiet period of Lent, and then a week of mourning, with no flowers, only a purple altar cloth and the three-hour-long service of Good Friday, it was a blessing to come to a church filled again with light and colour and the singing of joyous hymns. He tried no more successfully than usual to put away the thought that today's collection would by tradition be the congregation's gift to him, and held out his hand to Jacob Prout, sidesman, sexton, gravedigger and keeper of the churchyard as well as of most of the village hedges and ditches.

'I did, Vicar,' the old man confirmed. 'Always gets the beans in then. It's the full moon, you see – draws the water to their roots. Watch the moon when you'm growing veg, and you'll never go far wrong. And now I be off to have my dinner with Jennifer and Travis and my little Molly.'

'Molly? I thought her name was Mary – Mary Susan. At least that's how I baptised her!'

'Ah, but I took to calling her Molly, you see, and it sorta stuck. Dear little maid her be, and artful as a basketload of monkeys – just nine months old and been crawling a month already. But I dare say you've seen her for yourself.'

Basil nodded. 'I popped in a month or so ago, but at that age a child changes every week. Give them my regards, Jacob.'

'Travis was here ringing earlier on,' Jacob said vaguely, glancing round. 'I suppose he must have gone straight back.'

Basil smiled. Most of the bell-ringers had been in church, but he was quite accustomed to the fact that some of them always slipped away at the start of the service. He didn't blame them – many were involved in farming and had spared enough time anyway in ringing the bells, and some wouldn't have come to church at all if it hadn't been for their ringing. Some vicars objected to this and banned ringers who didn't also attend services, but Basil regarded it as a fact of life and thought it was better that they came to 'make joyful noises' than never came at all.

Joyce Warren was waiting rather impatiently to shake his hand, with her solicitor husband, Henry, at her shoulder. She was wearing what even Basil could see was a new hat, with a large brim covered in flowers.

'A very nice sermon, Basil, if I may say so. And you're quite sure you and Grace won't come for lunch? You'd be most welcome. We're having roast lamb, and there'll be plenty.'

The whole village must be having roast lamb today, Basil thought as he smiled at her. 'Thank you, Joyce, but I did explain that we've been invited to the Barton for the celebration.'

'Oh yes. Hilary's engagement to the new doctor. Quite a surprise after such a short time.'

'But a very pleasant one,' Basil said, wondering if she was offended not to have been invited herself. 'I'm sure we're all very happy for her.'

'Oh, of course. Delighted. Well, you must come soon for sherry – drop in this evening, or tomorrow.' She moved on, and Henry gave Basil a small grin and shook his hand, leaving Basil to greet the Tozers.

'I got to say, Vicar, that were a fine sermon you gave us this morning,' Ted Tozer began. 'Proper built us up, and us needs it with all this bad news in the world. It's been getting me down a bit, I don't mind telling you, but what you said this morning put it all in perspective. I feel better for coming to church, I really do.'

'Why Ted, that's wonderful to hear,' Basil said. 'It's been quite difficult to find anything good to talk about recently, and it's been a hard winter for you farmers, with all that snow and ice back in February. I hope the year's turned its corner for you now.'

'I'd like to see it turn its corner for the whole world,' Ted said, and moved on so that Alice could take his place. Basil looked at her a little anxiously.

'Is Minnie all right? She doesn't usually miss the Easter service.'

'I think so. She just felt a bit tired and said she'd stop home with Heather and look after the roast. The rest of the family's here, though.'

'So I see.' He smiled down at Robin, who was tagging along between his grandmother and mother, clad in a smart blue jumper. 'Have you had any Easter eggs, Robin?'

The boy nodded and beamed. 'One's chocolate, but I'm not allowed to eat it until this afternoon. Mummy says it will spoil my dinner if I have it in the morning.'

'My mother used to say that too,' Basil said. 'I never understood why.'

'Izzackly,' Robin said. 'I don't see how it can.'

Basil laughed. The rest of the congregation, eager to get home for their own dinners, moved more quickly now, and he was soon free to return to the tiny vestry and take off his surplice. The churchwardens had finished replacing the hymn and prayer books used by the few people who didn't have their own, and were counting the last few coins in the collection bags. Constance Bellamy poured them into a cloth bag and stumped forward to hand it over to him.

'There you are, Basil. A nice little Easter gift for you, and very well deserved. I take it you'll be going up to the Barton now for this engagement party?'

'I am indeed. And you'll be there too, I expect.'

'I've been bidden,' she said drily. 'Though why young people like Hilary and Dr Hunter should want an old crone like me there is beyond my understanding. If you ask me, it's more Gilbert's party than theirs.'

'Felix and Stella will be there,' he offered. 'But apart from them, I think you're probably right. David's parents have come down from Derby, of course, and the Latimers will be there, since Charles and David's father trained together. And Hilary and her father, with David himself. That's all I know.'

'That's twelve. I'm the odd woman.' She grinned, her walnut face splitting into a thousand tiny wrinkles. 'That explains it – though I hope young Hilary isn't trying to do a bit of matchmaking and setting me up with her father!'

'I imagine if there'd been any chance of that, you and he would have decided on it long ago,' Basil said. 'Thank you, Constance. I always feel a little guilty taking this money. Still, I know it's a tradition – and not just in Burracombe – and it's very kind of people to give so generously. Now we'd both better go and get ready for the lunch party. I'll see you there.'

As he went down the path to the lychgate, he saw Frances Kemp standing by the memorial cross that bore the names of those who had died during the two world wars. She looked up as he approached and moved away a little. He thought there was a hint of sadness in her eyes, and he paused beside her, looking at the engraved stone.

'All those young men,' he murmured, shaking his head. 'Even in a small place like Burracombe, there are far too many names on the memorial. So many local names, too ... Tozer, Friend, Ellacott ... And one or two I don't recognise. Families moved away or died out, I suppose. One wonders how different the village would be today if they hadn't all been taken from us.'

But Miss Kemp had already turned away and was walking briskly along the church path, as if she had not heard him. Basil looked again, and felt ashamed that he had not taken more notice of the names inset into the granite block. It had been there so long, years before he had come to the village, and he had grown too accustomed to it.

Tozer. Friend. Ellacott. Prout. All local names, still borne by many of the people he knew.

And Stannard. Not a local name at all, yet there amongst all the others.

Ralph Stannard. Killed in action 1918.

Who had he been? Basil wondered. He must have lived in the village. Yet where was his family now?

The churchgoers reached their homes in time to check on their roast lamb and remove it from the oven if it was deemed done. They put the joints on large plates, covered them with clean tea towels and slipped the roasting tins back in the oven to keep the fat hot, then started on the potatoes, putting them in cold water, bringing them to the boil, letting them cook for a few minutes, draining them and shaking them about in the pan to roughen their edges. Most then tipped them straight into the roasting pan, but a few had their own way of making sure of a perfect, golden and crunchy roast potato.

Alice Tozer's trick was to sprinkle the roughened vegetables with mustard powder before putting them in the hot fat, so that they turned golden brown at once. Where she had learned this she had no idea, but she'd always done it and had passed on this tip to Val and Joanna. She did it now, before sliding the tin back into the oven and turning her attention to the carrots and cabbage.

All the family would be round the table – all except for Jackie, Alice's youngest daughter, and Brian and his wife, of course. Jackie was back in America now, which Alice and Ted still weren't happy about, and Brian and Peggy – or Margrit, as they had been sharply reminded to call her – had left Devon to join one of Brian's army friends in starting up a new machinery manufacturing business in the Midlands. So there would be herself and Ted, Minnie, Tom, Joanna, Robin and Heather, and Val and Luke with Christopher. Alice sighed with satisfaction. There was nothing she liked better than to have her family around the big kitchen table for a hearty meal.

Dottie too was roasting potatoes. With no lodgers now that Stella and Maddy were both married, she had envisaged a rather lonely Easter Day until her cousins Jessie and Jeanie had invited her to share their Sunday roast. Dottie had immediately asked them to come to her instead.

'You needs your day of rest,' she'd told them. 'And I miss having folk to cook for. Bernie don't want me at the Bell, so you and Billy come along to me about one o'clock and us'll have a glass of sherry before us sits down, seeing as it's Easter.'

They arrived just as she was closing the oven door, their brother Billy, in his thirties now yet still with the mind of a child, carrying a bunch of primroses, his round face wreathed in smiles. Dottie, whose garden was filled with spring flowers, accepted them with expressions of delight and immediately found her prettiest vase to put them in. She gave him a glass of orange squash and poured out sherry for herself and the two sisters.

Henry Warren was pouring sherry at exactly the same moment. The Warrens' guests were friends from Tavistock – two members of the golf club, who played with Henry, with their wives and Henry's partner in the solicitors' firm. Joyce was wearing a new dress of floral polished cotton with a tightly fitted bodice and full circular skirt. She turned gracefully as she served canapés to go with the drinks, so that the skirt swirled around her.

'It's such good news that dear Hilary and the new doctor have announced their engagement,' she said, and the sentiment was echoed in almost every house and cottage in the village, the comments reflecting a variety of points of view.

'Time the maid found a man good enough for her.'

'Thought it was never going to happen, didden us!'

'And it'll keep the young doctor here, too. I thought he might take one look at Burracombe folk and get back up north as fast as his legs could carry him.'

'He don't seem too bad, for someone from upcountry. When my Maisie had the croup back in February ...'

'When d'you reckon the wedding will be? June's a nice month for weddings.'

'Back end of September, more like, when harvest is in. Or maybe even later – could be next year.'

Hilary and David were fielding the same kind of questions. In the Barton kitchen, too, all was ready for the meal – the joint was out on the table, resting, the potatoes were in the oven and the rest of the vegetables were gently simmering. Hilary had sent Patsy home and now, seeing that nothing else needed to be done, threw her tea cloth over the bar on the front of the stove and went back to the drawing room.

Everyone had arrived. David knew them all by now, of course, and was introducing his parents. Mrs Hunter was ensconced on the big window seat with Grace Harvey and Stella, discussing names for the baby Stella and Felix were expecting in September. Charles Latimer was telling Gilbert about some of the more disgraceful episodes of his and the senior Dr Hunter's training together, and Constance Bellamy was talking to Mary Latimer about their gardens. Felix held up the sherry bottle enquiringly and, at Hilary's nod, went round topping up glasses. The conversation was a cheerful, muted hum. Hilary dropped on to a small sofa beside David, and he smiled at her and took her hand. She smiled back, happy that at last they could be open about their love, and relaxed.

Gilbert started to talk about the strikes and the situation in Cyprus. Hilary watched him a little anxiously, then turned her head, suddenly uneasy, listening.

'What's that?'

The others stopped talking and looked at her, surprised by her tone. She got up quickly.

'I can't hear anything,' Mary Latimer said doubtfully. 'What did you think—'

Hilary raised a hand. 'Something's wrong.'

'Imagining things,' her father said robustly. 'Sit down and enjoy your sherry, girl.'

'No. There's something ...' She went to the door and opened it, half running down the passageway. They heard her open the kitchen door, then cry out and slam it shut. They looked at each other in alarm and began to get to their feet.

In that instant, before the door slammed, they had all heard the roar of flames.

Chapter Four

'Give Tom a call, Joanna,' Alice said, lifting the big enamel dish of roast potatoes on to the top of the cupboard beside the sink. 'These are just right now and all the other veg are ready. I don't know why men always need to go to the lavvy the minute dinner's going on the table, I really don't,' she grumbled. 'Ted's just the same. Tell him to hurry up, or us'll start without him.'

Joanna grinned and went to the door. There was a bathroom in the house and a separate lavatory, but they were upstairs and the men generally used the one outside, a few steps from the back door. She stood for a moment sniffing, then banged on the door.

'Tom! Come on, your mother wants to start serving.' He came out and she looked at him with a frown. 'Can you smell smoke?'

'It's probably someone burning their dinner,' he said with a shrug. Then he sniffed more carefully. 'Here, you're right – that's a bit more than the carrots caught.' He moved further out into the yard, lifting his head to gauge the direction of the smell, then his eyes widened. 'My stars – it's the Barton! The Barton's on fire!'

'*What?*' Joanna ran to join him and together they stared at the plume of smoke rising from the Barton, barely a quarter of a mile away. 'Oh my God! Oh *Tom!*'

'We must call the fire brigade,' he exclaimed, heading for the house. He ran through the open back door to the kitchen, where Alice was spooning the potatoes into her big willow-pattern dish. She looked up in astonishment and began to remonstrate, but he cut her off. 'Never mind that. The Barton's on fire. We need to phone for the fire engine.'

'The fire engine? The Barton?' she stammered, and the rest of the family came to their feet. 'But how can it be ... They've got that party there – the doctor and the new doctor, and Miss Bellamy and—'

'That don't stop the house catching fire.' Tom was at the phone, dialling 999. Then he slammed it down again. 'I've just remembered – the firemen are on strike! They wouldn't come out for the Queen herself.'

'But Tavistock's are retained firemen,' Val said. 'Are they in the strike too? And aren't they sending out soldiers instead?'

'I don't know.' Tom was halfway out of the door again. 'We'll have to go over. We're nearest – the rest of the village probably don't even know. Jo, you try 999 again, see if they'll come out. Dad and Luke and me'll go over and see what we can do.'

'I'll come too,' Val said. 'Chris'll be all right with you, won't he, Mother? They'll need all the hands we've got.'

'I'll follow you,' Joanna said, and spoke into the phone. 'Fire! It's a house on fire, in Burracombe ... Yes ... Oh, please ...'

They heard no more. Pausing only to pull on boots, the three men and Val ran out of the house. Tom grabbed a couple of buckets as he ran, and Ted dashed into the milking parlour and came out with some more. Carrying two each, they raced across to the gate.

'Go the short cut,' Ted panted. 'Us don't have time to use the drive.'

Tom was already unfastening the field gate that led to the meadow separating Tozer farmland from the big gardens surrounding the Barton. As they sprinted across the grass, a few cows ambled towards them, curious about the sudden activity, and by the time they reached the far gate, they had a crowd of inquisitive beasts on their heels.

'Go *away*, you stupid creatures!' Val shouted, waving her buckets at them, and the ones in front backed off a little, blowing down their noses with astonishment. Joanna, who had already caught up, stamped her foot and scrambled through the gate, fastening it behind her.

'Oh, just look at that smoke,' she moaned. 'And flames, too. The whole place is going up. We'll never be able to put it out all by ourselves, never.'

'Are the firemen coming?' Tom asked as they raced across the wide lawns.

She shook her head. 'I don't know! I'm not even sure the operator understood what I was saying. Mother's trying again. Oh Tom, look at it. It's terrible.'

Dark grey smoke streaked with yellow and orange flames billowed from the big house, rising above the roof in a huge dirty cloud. The roar could be heard quite plainly now, and as the Tozers stared, they could hear the shouts of other people. They turned to see Ted's cousin Norman panting up the drive, followed by the whole of the Pettifer family, even Patsy, carrying her baby Rosie.

'Is anyone inside?' Norman shouted, and Ted shook his head.

'Us don't know yet. Seems to be round the back – the kitchen, likely as not. Some of you go round the front and see if the door's open. They might have got out by now. Rest of you, come round the back with me.'

Val and Joanna looked at each other and ran round the terrace to the front of the house. To their relief, they saw a small knot of people by the front steps and hurried towards them.

'Hilary! Are you all right? What happened? Is everyone out?'

Hilary, white as a sheet, started towards them.

'Oh, thank God someone's come. We tried to ring the fire brigade but the phone isn't working. It started in the kitchen. I'm afraid the whole house is going to go.'

'It's all right. People are coming.' Val glanced down the drive. Groups of men and women, many carrying buckets, were running towards the house. She waved them round the side. 'Can they get water?'

'There's a garden tap. And the stables, of course, but they're so far away. Oh *Val* ...' Hilary began to tremble, and Val took her in a firm grip.

'It's all right. It's going to be all right. The main thing is, is everyone out? Nobody hurt?'

Hilary shook her head. 'No. I found it before ... before ... David got them all out.' She turned, and Val followed her glance to the group on the terrace. Gilbert Napier was there, sitting on a bench with Charles Latimer beside him, while Constance Bellamy, Stella Copley and Mary Latimer were on another. Basil and Grace Harvey and a couple Val took to be David Hunter's parents were in earnest discussion, while David himself was just emerging from the front door with Felix, both smeared with smoke.

'David! You haven't been in?'

'It's all right,' he said, coming quickly over and giving Val a brief nod. 'I've closed all the doors and turned off the electricity. It's a good thing the doors are so thick and heavy, especially the kitchen one – with luck, the fire should be contained.' He looked at Val again. 'Has anyone telephoned the fire brigade, d'you know?'

'We tried, but they're on strike, aren't they! At least, we're not sure about Tavistock, but I don't know how long they'd take to get here – they're retained firemen so they're not there unless they're called out. Oh dear ...' Val gripped her hands together frantically. 'Look, the whole village is coming to help – if you're sure every-one's all right here ...'

David gave a quick glance round. 'I think so. Dad and Charles will cope. Come on, Felix, let's see what we can do round the back.'

The two men ran off, and Hilary and Val looked at each other.

'I'm going too,' Val said, a little shakily. 'The more hands, the better.'

By the kitchen door there was a crowd of people jostling each other for position, but even as Val and Hilary rounded the build-ing, they could see a queue forming and buckets passing from hand to hand from the garden tap to the open door. Inside, the flames were a mass of vicious yellow, streaked with black smoke, and as Val watched, she saw a line of fire flash along one wall, as swiftly as a snake's tongue, and set light to the curtains over one of the windows. In an instant the fabric was a sheet of flame and the win-dow blackened, cracked and scattered a million burning fragments across the ground, making those nearest leap back.

'Oh my God ...' Hilary whispered, and then: 'What's all that noise? It sounds like gunfire.'

Ted Tozer heard her and said briefly, 'Bottles and cans explod-ing. It must be like a bloody furnace in there.' He turned away and shouted to the chain of water-carriers: 'There's another tap, over to the stables. Some of you get over there ... It looks like the whole of

Burracombe's here,' he added more quietly. 'And just as well, with no firemen to help. What about garden hoses?'

'In the shed.' Hilary set off at a run towards the big shed where the gardeners stored their tools. 'Oh *hell* – it's locked! And the key's in the kitchen!' Her voice rose and broke, but Ted shoved her aside and set his heavy boot at the hinges on the door. Two kicks and it hung from its lock. Norman, close behind him, dragged the door fully open and pushed inside to find the hoses wound in neat coils on their nails. He pulled one off and raced away with it, while Ted hauled at the other.

Hilary felt a hand grip her shoulder. She turned quickly and found Travis behind her, his face taut with anxiety. He saw what Ted was doing and stepped quickly out of his way.

'What in God's name is going on? Hilary – are you all right?'

Hilary stared at him. 'Travis! How did you get here? How did you know—'

'Alice Tozer rang me. Jacob's here too, helping the water chain. For God's sake, Hilary, what happened? Is anyone hurt?'

'No,' she said through a sudden storm of tears. 'No one's hurt. We all got out, and David ... David ...' She broke down completely and he pulled her into his arms. 'Oh *Travis*!'

Val said, 'It seems to have been in the kitchen. David and Felix closed all the doors so it wouldn't spread, so they were in there, but they're all right.' Her voice trembled a little. 'Everyone seems to be here, trying to put it out, but I don't know ... I think ...' Her voice quivered to a stop.

Travis gave her a swift look. 'I'm going to help. Get Hilary away from here. Where's her father?'

'He's round at the front of the house with Dr Latimer and the others. But—'

'I'm not going anywhere.' Hilary dragged herself out of Travis's arms and stood up. 'I trained for this sort of thing during the war, and so did Val. We've seen fire before and we can help too. Come on, Val.'

Travis hesitated, but the two women were already heading for the long line of bucket-carriers, and he raced off to the head of the line, where Ted and Norman were already wielding the two garden hoses. The stream of water seemed weak and pitiful in comparison with the gush from the hoses firemen would have used, but there was a hissing sound as it penetrated the billowing smoke, and you could almost believe the fire was dying down already. Luckily, there were several taps around the garden and stables, so the transfer of water by bucket was not impeded. Val and Hilary both joined in, one line sending full buckets and one returning the empties, and they found themselves working as swiftly and smoothly as if the village practised every week for such emergencies.

At the Warrens' house, lunch had not been delayed at all. Joyce, who had been drifting round her guests with dishes of tiny biscuits decorated with swirls of cream cheese or scraps of smoked salmon twisted into fancy shapes, had heard nothing of what was going on in the village. The house stood on the side of the lane that wound uphill between the last of the houses, raised above the road and hidden behind a tall laurel hedge. The main reception rooms looked out towards the back, across the moor, and only Henry's study and a small sitting room referred to as the snug were at the front. To look out across the village you had to go upstairs to the main landing or the front bedrooms, and there was no occasion to do this, as Joyce and Henry entertained their guests in the drawing room and then took them through to the dining room, where the mahogany table, polished to within an inch of its life and laid with gleaming cutlery and glasses, stood ready.

Henry carved the lamb and filled the wine glasses, while Joyce served vegetables on her beautiful Wedgwood dinner service. They all ate and drank, praising their hostess and talking about golf and bridge and the holidays they hoped to have now that foreign travel was easier again and you could take a hundred pounds instead of the fifty that had been allowed up till now.

'We're thinking of going to the South of France,' one of the golfing wives observed. 'But it's such a long time since one was able to go where one liked, it's rather hard to choose.'

'One still can't go *just* where one likes,' her husband said. 'Large parts of Eastern Europe—' But his wife flapped her fingers at him, as if to say that one would hardly be likely to think of going there, and he subsided.

'Well, Henry and I haven't given it a lot of thought,' Joyce said, offering the roast potatoes to another of the men. 'Do take some, I'm sure you can manage another ... We do have a rather important wedding coming up in the village sometime this year, you know, and we must be here for that.'

'Oh yes, the Napier daughter. You mentioned her earlier. It's good that she's found a man at last.'

'Well, it's not quite like that,' Joyce said a little stiffly. 'I don't think she's been looking, particularly. She's been very busy taking care of her father and running the estate. And—'

She stopped as a sudden commotion sounded at the back door. Someone was banging on it and calling out, and Joyce and her husband looked at each other in alarm.

'Whoever is that?' Joyce asked. 'Henry, go and see – it sounds as if someone's in trouble.' She set down the jug of gravy she'd been holding. 'No, please don't all get up. I'm sure Henry can deal with it. You carry on eating – I'll just go and ...'

She hurried out after her husband and found him talking to Arthur Culliford. Arthur was red in the face and panting, but before either he or Joyce could say anything, Henry turned to her.

'It's the Barton! It's on fire!'

Chapter Five

The Cullifords, in their cottage at the end of the village, had known nothing of the drama until Micky Coker and Henry Bennetts, cycling home from Peter Tavy, where they had joined the local ringers to ring the bells for the Easter Day service, had seen the fire engine charging through the lanes. They had arrived at the Barton too late to be involved with the buckets or hoses so had had to content themselves with watching for a while, and had then continued on to the village to spread the news to anyone who didn't already know. Neither their own parents nor the Cullifords had heard about it, and Arthur set straight off for the Warrens' house on the rather dubious excuse that his daughter Brenda had worked for Joyce, while Mrs Bennetts thought that both the schoolteachers ought to know. She knocked on Miss Kemp's door first, since she was headmistress, and finding nobody in, went on to the cottage Mr Raynor had just bought. To her surprise, both teachers were there, clad in old clothes stained liberally with pale green distemper, and holding brushes. Miss Kemp even had distemper in her hair.

'My goodness, you look busy,' Mrs Bennetts said, taken aback. 'I knocked on your door, Miss Kemp, but I thought when you didn't answer . . .'

'You didn't think I'd be painting and decorating,' Miss Kemp said, smiling. 'Well, I had nothing else to do, so I thought I'd give Mr Raynor a hand.' She took in Mrs Bennetts' flustered appearance. 'Is anything wrong?'

'I just wondered if you knew.' Mrs Bennetts, who wasn't really a local, not being Burracombe born and bred – she and her account-ant husband, William, had moved out here from Tavistock just before the war – felt suddenly awkward, as if she'd taken more on herself than she should. 'It's the Barton – there's a fire …'

'A *fire*?' James Raynor appeared in the little passageway. 'Good God – is anyone hurt? How serious is it?'

'I don't really know. Henry and Micky just came in with the news. There are fire engines there now, apparently, and half the village passing buckets of water. I don't mean to be a busybody, Miss Kemp, only I thought you'd want to know.'

'Of course.' The headmistress turned to her assistant. 'We should go at once. There may be something we can do. Oh, what a terrible thing – the Barton on fire.' She stripped off her apron as she spoke and turned to snatch a jacket from the hooks behind the front door. 'Has your husband gone along?'

Mrs Bennetts nodded. 'And Arthur Culliford. He said he'd been to the Warrens – they were in the middle of their lunch. Well, so were we to tell you the truth – I dare say most people were.' She found herself hurrying along the path with the two teachers.

Out in the lane, a flurry of people who had only just heard were also on their way, chattering breathlessly as they went. 'A terrible thing … just when Miss Hilary was looking so happy, too … and what about the Squire, how will he stand up to it?' And, over and over again: 'I hope to goodness no one's hurt …'

'What's that noise?' Hilary panted, heaving another bucket of water along the line. Everyone paused, and Val lifted her head.

'It's a bell! A fire engine's bell! Hilary, they've come, the firemen have come! They're here – oh, thank God, thank *God*!'

The scarlet engine clanged its way up the drive and was waved round to the back almost as if it were a tradesman delivering goods. The lines of bucket-carriers scattered as it thundered amongst them, and the firemen tumbled out, already unwinding their big hoses. With relief, Hilary indicated the nearest tap, but the chief fireman shook his head and she remembered the fire hydrant, put in a few years ago and never used. She pointed, and he directed two of the men over, unwinding the reel as they went.

'There'll be more pressure there,' he said briefly. 'Kitchen fire, is it?'

Hilary nodded. 'I don't know how it started – I just suddenly realised something was wrong, and when I went to look—'

'Anyone inside?'

'No, we all got out. Nobody was hurt.'

'Anyone inhale any smoke?'

'No. Thank you so much for coming – I thought with the strike on ...'

'We'm Tavi men,' he said tersely. 'Retained. Us does what us chooses, and when 'tis a house fire and there might be lives in danger ... Over there, lads,' he called. 'And get that other reel out smartish.' He was gone, leaving the two women standing alone. The other bucket-carriers hesitated, uncertain what to do next, but the fire chief turned his attention to organising them. 'You can still bring the water up but us'll take over from there. You done a good job.' He headed for the kitchen, and Hilary and Val moved back to their places in the line.

Roy Pettifer stepped out towards them. 'You go back to your dad, Miss Hilary. There's enough of us to manage now the brigade's arrived, and I reckon he'll be worrying about you. It's been a shock, this has, and you don't need to do no more here.'

'He's right, Hil,' Val said. 'There are plenty of men here to help now. Let's go back to the others.'

'But what are we going to *do* with them?' Hilary wailed. 'We can't go back indoors, and – and, oh Val, the dinner will be *ruined*!'

Val laughed a little hysterically. 'Well so will a lot of other dinners in Burracombe today! But there'll be plenty to eat at the farm. Let's take your father and Miss Bellamy back there. The Latimers can go home and take Dr Hunter and his wife with them; I'm sure Mary Latimer will be able to rustle something up. David and Felix will probably want to stay here. Stella can come with us – we've got to take care of her too, remember.'

'Stella!' Hilary's hand flew to her mouth. 'The baby! Oh Val – suppose the shock brings on a miscarriage? If anything happens to Stella now, I'll never forgive myself.'

'Nothing's going to happen,' Val said firmly, taking her arm and steering her round to the front of the house. 'She's over the first three months and she's perfectly all right. But let's get her away from this, somewhere where she can rest and have a cup of tea and something to eat. My mother will look after her.'

There was, however, no need for Alice Tozer to look after Stella. News of the fire had spread through the village almost as swiftly as fire itself, and reached Dottie Friend's cottage. She and her cousins abandoned their Sunday lunch and scurried as fast as they could through the streets, gathering other villagers as they ran. By the time they arrived, however, there was little to be done.

The men had immediately joined the crowd around the back of the house, where the firemen were poking about in the ashes, while the women gathered at the foot of the steps, seeing that the little group from the Barton had three doctors with them, as well as Basil Harvey. Dottie, however, marched straight up the steps to Stella and folded her in her arms.

'Are you all right, my bird? Whatever happened? You'm not hurt, I hope?'

'I'm all right, Dottie,' Stella said, but her face crumpled a little. 'No, really I am. Nobody's hurt.' It seemed to be a mantra that everyone had to repeat. 'I – it's just been a shock. I feel a bit shaky, that's all.'

'You'm coming straight home with me,' Dottie said firmly. 'And I don't want you walking there neither, not in your condition. Can somebody with a car take me and Stella back to my cottage?' she asked, raising her voice, and Charles Latimer hurried over.

'I will. We came by car. I'll take you home as well if you like, Constance,' he added a little doubtfully, 'and then come back for the others.'

Hilary had followed Dottie up the steps. 'Val's offered to take Miss Bellamy and my father back to the farm, and I think that's a good idea. Alice Tozer will look after them, and Minnie knows Miss Bellamy well. But it's probably just as well if the rest of you go home now.'

Charles shook his head. 'The more doctors on hand here the better, just in case. I'll take you to the Tozers', though, to make sure your father and Constance are all right. And I'll come in to your cottage to have a look at Stella,' he added to Dottie, making his way down the steps. 'Come along, we can just about squeeze you all in.'

Hilary refused to leave the house, but her father, who seemed more shaken than he had been at first, went willingly enough, and so did old Miss Bellamy. Dottie and Stella got into the back with her, and the big car bowled away down the drive, while Val set off across the field to warn her mother that they were on their way.

'My dear soul!' Alice exclaimed, her hand over her heart as Val explained what had happened. 'What a terrible thing. And with all they people there so happy and excited, and dinner nearly ready ... What a mercy nobody was hurt.'

'The Squire's coming here, you say?' Minnie said, getting out of her chair to start tidying the kitchen. 'And Miss Constance?' Minnie had been Constance Bellamy's nursemaid over seventy years ago, and had never quite got used to the fact that her charge had grown up. 'And all these papers and stuff lying about that Joanna's been working on again. Her usually puts them in the dresser ...' She swept the papers, which Joanna had carefully sorted into piles, into a heap and stuffed them into a drawer. 'Robin and Heather, you'd better put your toys away, we don't want anyone falling over. At least there's enough potatoes to go round. Squire'd better have my rocking chair. Or maybe Miss Constance ...'

'Don't worry, Gran,' Val said. 'You sit down. Colonel Napier and Miss Bellamy can have Mum and Dad's chairs. They'll probably want a cup of tea more than anything else. Or perhaps something stronger,' she added with a frown. 'Do you have any brandy, Mother?'

'In the cupboard.' Alice was at the window, gazing anxiously out at the yard. 'Here they come now, in the doctor's car. Oh, what a to-do. It's to be hoped it don't set the Squire back again. Do you think we ought to put them in the parlour?'

'We'll just make sure he rests,' Val said, getting out the brandy and two glasses. 'That's the best thing for him. And I'm sure they'd rather be here, in the warm kitchen. Come on, Christopher, into your high chair.' She lifted the toddler into the wooden high chair that had been used for Tozer babies ever since Brian had been born, and went to the door, where Charles was bringing the two older people in from the car. 'Come in, Colonel Napier. Miss Bellamy, you look cold, come and sit here by the range. It's nice and warm and this is a very comfortable chair. Now, would you like a cup of tea, or would you rather have a brandy?'

33

'Very kind of you,' Gilbert Napier said, sinking into Ted's big wooden armchair, amply furnished with cushions. 'A brandy would be very welcome.'

'I'd like a cup of tea, please,' Miss Bellamy said. 'Or maybe a small brandy. I do feel a bit shaky.'

Charles came over and took her wrist between his fingers. 'You've had a shock. We all have. A very unpleasant experience. But rest is the best thing, and later on we'll be able to see what the damage is. To the house, I mean,' he added hastily. 'I don't think there's any damage to yourselves, thank the Lord.' He went over to check on Gilbert as well. 'I'll look in again later on, before you go home, but if either of you feels at all unwell, you're to call me immediately.' He looked at Alice and Val. 'I'm sure you'll keep an eye on them both.'

'We certainly will,' Alice said firmly. 'And us'll make sure they've got a good dinner inside them, too. I know t'others won't be here just yet, but what I'm going to do is serve up now and put theirs on plates to keep warm in the bottom oven. Those potatoes are going to be done to a crisp if they don't come out soon.' She glanced at Gilbert a little shyly. 'That's if you don't mind eating your dinner with us, Squire.'

'Not in the least,' he said, finishing his brandy. 'Very kind of you.' He got up and came to the table, to the chair Val drew out for him, while Alice brought out another for Miss Bellamy. 'As long as we don't eat you out of house and home.'

'I don't think you'll do that,' Alice said with a smile. She took a huge roasting tin out of the oven and displayed an array of potatoes, roasted to a perfect golden brown and kept hot in the oven. The rest of the vegetables were in the big willow-pattern dishes with their lids on, and the leg of lamb stood at the side. 'Val, you'd better carve this since your father's not here. I'll do up some plates for the rest of them.'

At that moment the door opened and Luke came in. He looked tired and dirty, his face and hands black with smoke, his eyes rimmed with red. Val dropped the carving knife back on the sideboard and went to him.

'Luke! You look dreadful. Are you all right?'

'Don't touch me!' he said with a grin that showed white in his blackened face. 'You'll get soot all over you. I just came to say I'm going home to wash and change and then I'll be back, so if there's any dinner left by then, I'll be ready for it.'

'Of course there will be. Mum's doing plates for everybody. But are you really all right?'

'Of course I am – just filthy dirty and starving hungry. I'll be back as quick as I can.' He was halfway out of the door again when Gilbert spoke.

'What about the Barton? How much damage is there?'

Luke turned back. 'I'm sorry, sir,' he said contritely. 'I should have said. Well, I don't know a lot, but I think there's quite a bit of damage in the kitchen but not much anywhere else. And it could be mostly smoke damage anyway. It's difficult to tell at present. The firemen won't let anyone in until they're sure it's safe, and of course it's still quite hot ... But the fire's pretty well out now, and didn't spread to the rest of the house. And nobody was hurt, that's the main thing.' He hesitated, and Val gave him a little push.

'You go home now and have a good wash. There'll be some dinner ready when you come back. What about the others?'

'They'll be along pretty soon, I think.' He gave her a crooked grin and they looked at one another for a moment. Val felt a sudden lump in her throat as she thought what might have happened. She gave him another gentle push.

'Go on, darling. The sooner you go, the sooner you'll be back.'

He nodded and closed the door. Val went over to the sink to wash her hands, then returned to her task of carving the meat. She and Alice served the children their portions, and within a few minutes they were all sitting down and starting to eat.

Ted and Tom arrived soon afterwards, with Joanna. Like Luke, they were black with soot and smoke, and Alice jumped up again and ran upstairs to fetch some clean clothes and a bar of Fairy soap.

'Joanna can wash upstairs,' she told them at the door, 'but you two had better go out to the milking parlour and use the tap there. You can't wash down here in the kitchen with Miss Bellamy and the Squire eating their dinner a few feet away.'

Joanna reappeared first and sat down beside Heather, gratefully accepting one of the plates from the bottom oven.

'That's my new Easter frock ruined,' she said ruefully. 'I don't think that black will ever wash out.'

35

'Why were you so dirty, Mummy?' Robin asked, holding up his fork as if it were a conductor's baton. 'You had all your best clothes on.'

'I know, love. It's because there was a lot of smoke.'

'Why was there a lot of smoke? Was there a fire?'

'There certainly was,' Tom said cheerfully, coming into the kitchen with his father just behind him. 'You know what they say, no smoke without fire.'

Robin gazed at him solemnly. 'But there *was* smoke.'

'Yes, but it's all gone now. All washed away.' Tom and Ted sat down at the table and took their plates, generously heaped with slices of roast lamb, from Alice.

Robin leaned his arms on the table. 'Was there a fire engine?'

'Yes.' Tom ladled carrots on to his plate while Ted helped himself to cabbage. 'The fire engine came from Tavistock.'

'Thank goodness for that,' Alice said. 'Lord above knows what would have happened if it hadn't.'

'I wish I could have seen the fire engine,' Robin said, his eyes fixed accusingly on his father. 'Why didn't you come and get me?'

'There wasn't time. Now you get on with your dinner.' Tom spooned mint sauce over his meat and began to eat hungrily.

Gilbert Napier laid his knife and fork down and said, 'That was excellent, Mrs Tozer. Thank you very much.'

'Yes, very good indeed,' Miss Bellamy said. She had left some of hers. 'I'm sorry I couldn't finish it. Appetite of a bird these days.'

'It's the shock,' Minnie said, thinking that years ago she would have made young Miss Constance sit there until her plate was clean. 'You probably need to go home and put your feet up, with a nice cup of tea.'

'I'll take you back as soon as we've finished,' Val told her. 'I expect you'll be able to manage a bit of Mother's plum crumble, won't you? They're your own plums, that you gave us last autumn – Mother bottled them.'

'Just a spoonful, perhaps, with some custard. Poor Hilary,' the old woman said. 'All her lunch ruined. And her engagement party, too. What a start for them both.'

'Hilary never seems to have much luck,' Gilbert said. 'But young David seems to be made of the right stuff. He'll look after her.'

The talk turned to Hilary and her engagement. Alice served plum crumble with a choice of either custard, clotted cream of her own making, or junket, and Constance managed a little of the crumble and quite a lot of junket. At last every scrap was gone and they leaned back in their chairs.

'A very fine repast,' Gilbert said. 'My thanks again, Mrs Tozer. Most kind of you. And now I think I should be getting back to the Barton, to see what's been going on.'

Alice offered tea, but the two visitors declined. Constance Bellamy was looking a little shaky again, and Minnie told her roundly that she needed to be at home on her rather battered sofa. Val got up and found her coat and led the old lady out to Ted's Morris Oxford, which was generally only used on high days and holidays, and Gilbert declared his intention of going too. Alice and Ted tried to dissuade him, saying that Hilary would come for him as soon as she was ready, but he was clearly anxious to be away, and they waved off the big car before going back inside to clear up.

'Well, that's an Easter Day us won't forget in a hurry!' Alice remarked, then caught herself up and gave Joanna a quick look of apology. 'I'm sorry, my dear. I know 'tis a hard day for you as it is.'

'It's all right, Mother. I have to get used to it, and it isn't the actual date Suzanne—' She stopped abruptly with a glance at Robin, and shooed him back to his toys. 'As a matter of fact,' she went on in a low voice, 'since the subject's come up, there's something I want to say to you all. I don't want little Suzanne talked about. I don't want Heather to know about her twin.'

Alice stared at her. 'Don't want Heather to know? But why ever not?'

'It's just a feeling I've got. You know the old saying about how if one twin dies the other follows? I know it's an old wives' tale, but' – her voice shook – 'I don't want to take the risk. And I don't want to have to answer a lot of questions either. You know what children are.'

'But what about Robin?' Minnie asked.

'I don't think he ever really understood what happened, and I'm sure he's forgotten about Suzanne now. He never mentions her. After all, he wasn't much more than a baby himself.' Joanna began to take dishes to the sink and turned on the hot tap. 'Anyway, that's what I've decided, and I've told Tom, so please don't let's talk about it any more. It's too upsetting.'

Alice and Minnie looked at each other but said no more. Alice took the plates outside to scrape any leftovers into the hens' bucket, and after a moment or two, Minnie joined her.

'What do you think of that, Mother?' Alice murmured.

The old woman shook her head. 'It seems a pity to me that the dear little mite should get forgotten, but if it's what Joanna wants ... She's their mother, after all, and she never proper got over it.'

'I suppose us'll get used to it,' Alice said. 'And she'll never be forgotten, Mother, the dear of her. Her'll always be there, tucked away in our hearts. And especially in Joanna's.'

Frances and James went back to his cottage, subdued and somehow not in the mood for painting any more.

'I'll leave it till tomorrow now,' James said, looking round at the buckets of distemper and the brushes they had hastily left behind. 'I think I'd rather get some fresh air. That burning smell ...' He shuddered, and Frances looked at him in alarm.

'You look as if you need it,' she said. 'Look, why don't we go for a walk by the river and then go back to the school house for some tea? You can stay for supper, too – I was going to ask you anyway. It's nothing much – just one of George Sweet's pork pies and some salad. Not the roast lunch we ought to have been having on Easter Sunday ...' She broke off. 'James, whatever is the matter?'

'Nothing,' he said, pulling himself together with an obvious effort. 'It's just – the smell of burning, and then thinking about roast meat ... It reminded me suddenly of the Blitz, and Dorothy ...' His voice faded. 'She would have been serving meals in that shelter. Not that it would have been likely to be roast lamb ... I'm sorry, Frances. I thought I'd got over all that.'

'There are some things we never get over,' she said quietly. 'Would you rather I left you alone?'

James turned and looked at her. His square, corrugated face was pale under the thick dark hair, but his gaze was as steady as ever. He smiled and shook his head.

'If it were anyone else but you,' he said, 'the answer to that would be yes. But if you'd like to come with me for a walk by the river, I would very much like your company.'

'And tea afterwards?' she asked. 'And George Sweet's pork pie?'

'Those too,' he said, and she was relieved to see his colour returning. 'Who could resist one of George Sweet's pork pies, after all? So, shall we go? We might even spot a kingfisher.'

Still in their paint-stained clothes, they left the cottage and walked down to the little bridge and the ford, turning to take the footpath beside the tumbling river where, over the generations, so many other couples had walked before them.

Chapter Six

Hilary and David stood hand in hand, gazing at the damaged kitchen.

'It's just dreadful,' Hilary said despondently. 'It's completely ruined. It'll have to be totally rebuilt.'

David gave her hand a squeeze.

'But that can be done, darling. I really don't think there's any serious structural damage.' He moved cautiously through the door and Hilary came with him. Everything in the room was either badly charred or wholly burned away. The big table she had grown up with, and spent so many hours preparing meals on or sitting at to eat them, was a blackened travesty of itself. The cupboard doors had been reduced to ash and their contents had either caught fire, exploded or been smashed. The floor was a morass of sooty mud, and plaster had lifted away from the walls to hang in great slabs, ready to fall at a touch.

'I can't bear it,' Hilary said, tears streaking the grime that, scrub as she might, still filmed her cheeks. It was in the very air, she thought, like an evil miasma. 'Our lovely kitchen.'

'And it will be again,' David said robustly. 'Look, sweetheart, this table—'

'It's ruined. And it was such a beautiful old table, too. It's been here for such a long time. It must have so many tales to tell.'

'But it's not ruined.' He touched it with a finger. 'Look, it's oak, isn't it? And very old. Oak doesn't burn easily – it can probably be scrubbed down and refurbished. It may not be as good as new, but it'll give good service for many more years and have even more tales to tell. And the range.' He went over to the cooker. 'It's hardly damaged at all. These iron ranges will stand up to almost anything. As for the rest of it ...' He glanced around. 'The walls can be re-plastered and the electrical wiring repaired – luckily the kitchen seems to have been on its own separate circuit, so the rest of the house is OK – and new cupboards can be put in. Honestly, darling, it's not as bad as it looks.'

'I suppose not.' Hilary came to stand beside him. 'And all the rest can be replaced – though we'll never find the same lovely old china that used to belong to my grandmother. And the insurance will cover most of it.'

'And nobody was hurt,' David added, repeating the words that had been spoken so many times already that day. 'That's the best thing of all. It could have been so much worse.' He led her back to the door and gazed around. 'I just wonder how it started.'

'It must have been me,' Hilary said as they walked round the side of the house to the front. 'I've been trying to think what I did when I popped out here that last time. I used a tea towel and I went to hang it on the rail on the range, but something distracted me and I think I just sort of threw it across. Perhaps an edge of it got caught on a hotplate. Oh David, it was all my fault.'

'Darling, you mustn't blame yourself. You don't know that was what happened, and even if it was ...' He took her in his arms. 'These things do happen. We all do things like that and nine times out of ten we get away with it. You were unlucky, that's all. Let's go back indoors and think what to do next. Your father will be wanting to come home, I expect.'

'Yes, he will. I hope this hasn't affected him. He really doesn't need any shocks.'

'I think he's a lot more resilient than you give him credit for,' David observed. 'I had a talk with Charles the other day – as doc-tors – and he says your father's made pretty nearly a full recovery. Anyway, we'll know soon enough because there's a car coming up the drive and I think that's him in the front seat!'

'It's Ted Tozer's car,' Hilary said. 'Val's bringing him home.' She moved quickly forward as the car drew to a halt. 'Dad! You shouldn't have come home so soon. There's been smoke every-where – the house is filthy.'

'Well, not completely,' David said, smiling as he opened the door for his future father-in-law. 'Hilary shut the kitchen door quickly enough to keep most of it out. I think there'll be a bit of extra work for poor Mrs Curnow and Patsy to do when they come back, though.'

'There won't,' Hilary said grimly. 'I shall do it all myself as a penance. Thanks for bringing him back, Val. Was he starting to be a nuisance?'

'Not at all,' Val laughed. 'We were glad to have him and Miss Bellamy to lunch, but they both wanted to be at home again. We took Miss Bellamy back first.'

'They've been very kind,' Gilbert said, leaning for a moment on Hilary's arm as she looked anxiously into his face. 'Fed us like fighting cocks. Owe them a debt of gratitude. Has everyone else gone?'

'Yes. Once the fire brigade were satisfied, I said we'd be better on our own to take stock. Travis is coming back later, but we can't really do any clearing up now until we've been in touch with the insurance company. And since tomorrow is Easter Monday and a bank holiday, that won't be until Tuesday, so goodness knows how long it will be before someone comes out to see it. And then we'll have to organise builders and so on.' She sighed and rubbed one hand across her forehead. 'I don't really know how we're going to manage without a kitchen.'

'Well, Mother says you're welcome to go to the farm for meals until you can get fixed up with a makeshift kitchen in one of the other rooms,' Val offered. 'I think you can hire cookers from the electricity showroom in Tavistock.' She reached into the back of the car. 'And we packed up a basket of things to keep you going for this evening at least – cold meat and bread and cheese, things that don't need cooking. And tea and milk, of course, and a good chunk of simnel cake! And look, here's a Primus stove for boiling a kettle. I didn't know if you already had one. We've put a kettle in too, and some cups and saucers and things.'

'Oh Val.' Tears came to Hilary's eyes again. 'That's so kind. Thank you very much.'

'Will you be all right here tonight?' Val asked anxiously. 'Because there's room at the farm for both of you, if you'd rather.'

Hilary opened her mouth, but David answered for her. 'It's all right, Val. I'll stay here tonight, and for as long as necessary. I'll slip over to Charles later on and collect a few things.' He grinned. 'That's if the village won't be scandalised by us being under the same roof!'

Val shot Hilary a quick glance and saw the colour rise in her friend's face. 'Oh, I don't think you need worry about that,' she said easily. 'After all, you're a respectably engaged couple now and the Colonel's here to chaperone you. And I think you should be going indoors,' she added to that gentleman. 'Take him in, Hilary, and give him a stiff gin and tonic. The sun's well over the yardarm, I'm sure. I'll give you a lift to the Latimers' house,' she added to David. 'And bring you back too. Seeing you walk through the village with a suitcase *might* cause a bit of talk!'

Hilary and her father went inside. The smoke damage was not as bad as Hilary had at first thought; only a few billows had escaped into the front of the house, and although some surfaces were grimy, the main rooms, whose doors had all been quickly closed, were clean. They went into the drawing room and Gilbert sank into his favourite armchair with a sigh of relief.

'That's better,' he said. 'The Tozers were very kind, but there's nowhere like your own place.' He fixed his gaze on Hilary's face. 'And now tell me how you are, my dear. You look exhausted.'

'I feel it,' she confessed, taking the sofa opposite him. 'It was such an awful shock, seeing the kitchen on fire like that. And it seemed to happen so quickly. I really thought we were going to lose the whole house. Oh *Dad* ...' And the tears that had been threatening all afternoon, which she had kept at bay with such determination, suddenly broke through, and she put her head in her hands and wept.

Gilbert got up. He came over and sat beside her, putting his arm about her shoulders. 'There, there. Don't let it upset you now. It's all over and it could have been a lot worse. After all,' he said, and Hilary, knowing exactly what he was going to say next, looked up, half laughing, half crying and dangerously close to hysteria, and spoke the words with him:

'Nobody was hurt ...'

*

The rest of Burracombe slowly settled back into their interrupted Easter Day. Almost every roast dinner had been abandoned, but in general the meat had already been taken out of the ovens to rest and could be eaten cold, and fresh vegetables could be cooked to replace those taken hurriedly off the heat half cooked. By six or seven o'clock, most people had eaten more or less what had been planned, albeit several hours late.

'That was a proper handsome dinner, Dottie,' Jessie Friend said, leaning back in her chair. 'You didn't have to go to all that trouble, not after what you been through today.'

'No, you didn't,' Stella said. She had managed most of the plateful Dottie had put in front of her but refused more than a small portion of steamed jam pudding. 'I could easily have gone home.'

'All by yourself in that great big vicarage, with no proper food ready for you!' Dottie exclaimed in outrage, offering more pudding round. 'I wouldn't hear of it. You'm eating for two now, remember. Anyway, Felix here still needs feeding. He was working like a Trojan with the other men, fetching water and so on.'

'He's not eating for two, though,' Jeanie said, accepting a second helping.

Stella laughed. 'Felix is always eating for two! Look how fat he's getting.'

They all looked at the young vicar, still as thin as a runner bean, and he rolled his eyes. 'I'm wasting away to nothing,' he said mournfully. 'It's Dottie's teas I miss most. I think we'll have to move back to Burracombe after all. Could you pass the custard, please, Jeanie?'

'You get plenty of teas given you in Little Burracombe,' his wife told him heartlessly. 'I know just what you'll have had from the people you've visited.' She held up her hands and counted on her fingers. 'Mrs Lillicrap – scones, jam and cream. Old Mrs Corner – Victoria sponge. Fred Brimacombe – his daughter's flapjacks, made with peanut butter. Mrs Lydiard – dainty little smoked salmon sandwiches, sponge fingers and Viennese whirls.'

The others stared at her. 'He don't really get through all that!' Jessie said in awe.

'Well, not in one afternoon, no,' she admitted. 'But he always manages to be somewhere just at teatime.'

'People have their tea at different times in the afternoon,' Felix said defensively. 'I can't help it if I happen to call in at just that moment. Anyway, it helps with our budget – you don't have to feed me then.'

'It doesn't help at all, because I wouldn't,' she retorted. 'Not all those things, anyway. When you are home for tea, it's fish-paste sandwiches and a bit of fruit cake left over from Sunday, if there is any.'

The others laughed. 'And you wonder why he goes scrounging round the village!' Dottie said. 'He's like a half-starved dog. I dare say it's all my fault anyway, when you come to think of it,' she added thoughtfully. 'I spoilt him when he was coming here courting you.'

Billy had been listening to the conversation. Now he leaned across the table, patted Felix on the arm and said, 'Can I come with you next time, Mr Copley? I like flapjacks and sponge cake.'

'Billy!' his sisters said reprovingly, but Felix smiled kindly at the man and said, 'I can't take you visiting with me, Billy, but you can come to tea with us at the vicarage one day – can't he, Stella?'

'Of course. And I'll make flapjacks and sponge cake specially.'

'I wonder how Miss Hilary's going to go on about cooking,' Dottie remarked. 'That kitchen won't be fit to be used for months.'

'I suppose they'll have to use one of the other rooms,' Felix said thoughtfully. 'There are several other kitchen- or scullery-type rooms, aren't there?'

'Yes, they'll be able to use one of those.' Stella glanced at the clock on Dottie's mantelpiece. 'Felix, we really ought to be going. You've got evensong at seven, and it's nearly six now.'

'My goodness, yes.' He jumped up and collected his jacket from the chair where he had dropped it when he came in. 'Get off, Albert,' he said to the cat, who had made himself comfortable on it. 'Look at all those hairs. Good job it's black. Dottie, thank you very much.' He kissed her cheek and smiled at the two sisters and Billy. 'It was good to sit down and have a proper chat. Billy, we won't forget you're coming to tea one day. And now I think you should all have a nice quiet evening. We've had plenty of excitement for one day.'

They were gone in a flurry of farewells, and Dottie went to fill the kettle and put it on the range.

'A cup of tea is what we all need now,' she said. 'And then I'm going to sit and listen to the wireless while I do a bit of sewing. You'm welcome to stop and listen with me if you'd like to. It's _Grand Hotel_ and _Sunday Half-Hour_, and I always think that sets me up for the week.'

Chapter Seven

Easter Monday being a bank holiday, quite a few Burracombe residents didn't have to go to work. It wasn't a bank holiday for farmers, of course, as Ted Tozer was fond of pointing out, but once the essential work of milking and feeding animals was done, they took the rest of the day off too.

'Not that us can have *all* day,' Ted warned the family at breakfast. 'Us still got afternoon milking.'

'Norman's doing that,' Tom said, his mouth full of fried mashed potato. 'I fixed it up with him at ringing yesterday. That's why he wasn't there this morning.'

'I thought I give him the whole day,' Ted said, carefully placing his egg on a slice of fried bread so that the yolk would soak into it.

'You did, but he said he wasn't doing anything special and he knows how much you like to have a day off with the family and take us all out somewhere really nice,' Tom said innocently. 'That's right, isn't it?'

Ted looked at him. 'I never said that.'

'No, but it's true. We always have a day out on Easter Monday.'

'Not always,' Joanna murmured beside him, and he flushed and looked down at his plate.

'No, not always.' Then he turned to her, speaking quietly. 'But look, Jo, we've got to decide which day we remember Suzanne – Easter, or the real date. And I reckon it ought to be the real date. We got two other tackers to think of as well. I don't want Easter to be miserable for them.'

'I don't want any date to be miserable for them,' Joanna said tightly, pushing away her empty plate. 'I've told you, I don't want it talked about at all. It's unlucky for Heather and it's too upsetting.'

Tom sighed. 'Then why bring it up now? Oh, I'm sorry, love. We can't just forget it, I know. We'll do whatever you want. As long as it don't stop us giving the little ones a good Easter.'

'It won't,' Ted said firmly. 'You'm right, Tom, Easter Monday is a day for the family, and it's the first day of the year that's fine enough for a proper outing. I'll tell you what us'll do. Us'll take the lorry and all go out somewhere. What about Widecombe?'

'A picnic up on Hound Tor,' Alice said, her eyes shining as she turned away from the range with a slice of toast held firmly in the wire toaster. She opened it and dropped the toast on Joanna's plate, then inserted another slice of bread between the two halves and clasped them together. 'Ted, that's a handsome idea. I wonder if Val and Luke would like to come.'

'They were talking about walking over to the reservoir and having a picnic up in the bluebell woods,' Joanna said, pushing away her sadness and spreading butter on the toast. 'But I tell you who would like to come. Some of the Culliford kiddies. They don't get many outings, and I saw Maggie yesterday and she looked really washed out. I reckon she'd be glad of a bit of peace and quiet. She hasn't got over what happened, not by a long way.'

The Tozers were silent for a moment, thinking of the family at the other end of the village who never quite seemed to be able to hold their lives together. Since Arthur's recent imprisonment for poaching, with the repercussions on his family, followed by Maggie's loss of their twin babies at birth, the village had rallied round and given them a lot more help. Joanna in particular, having also lost a young baby, seemed to have struck up a rapport with the slovenly Maggie. But to take the children on a family picnic ... Ted looked doubtful and Alice uncertain.

'Come on, Dad,' Tom urged. 'It's only a day out, and there's plenty of room in the lorry. We'll put some hay bales in the back and I'll sit with them. We can sing campfire songs. Starting with "Widecombe Fair", of course!'

Joanna gave him a grateful look and poured more tea into his cup. 'It'll be good for Robin, too. He and Billy Culliford are great friends, aren't you, Robbie?'

Robin, who had been steadily working his way through a breakfast nearly as big as his father's, looked up. 'Is Billy coming on our picnic?'

'I don't know. You'll have to ask Grandad.'

'That's blackmail!' Ted said, but he was laughing. 'All right, as long as your grandmother don't mind, but you'll have to help make the sandwiches, and I hope there's enough sausage rolls and hot cross buns left over. The only thing is,' and his voice grew sober again, 'I was wondering if us didn't ought to go over to the Barton and lend a hand clearing up. There's a master lot to do there, from what I saw yesterday.'

'Yes, but we can't do anything yet,' Tom said, accepting the second slice of toast. 'Thanks, Mum ... I spoke to Hilary yesterday and she says she thinks it ought to be left just as it is until the insurance people have seen it, and that could be days. Weeks, even.'

'Oh I hope not,' Alice said. 'It would be awful for them to have to live with all that mess, and how are they going to manage for a kitchen? Us ought to ask them over for their dinner at least. I did tell them they were welcome any time.'

'There'll be plenty of people wanting to invite them,' Ted said. 'I reckon you'm right, Tom – they're probably better left to themselves and their own folks for today. They've got Travis and Ernie Crocker and any amount of estate workers. Me and you'll walk over tomorrow and see what's what. And now, if everyone's finished their breakfast, I reckon it's time we started to get ready for this day out. I'll see that the outside chores are all done while you women get the food ready, and Joanna, you'd better walk down to the Cullifords and see if any of them want to come along. All present and correct in an hour's time, all right?'

The family cheered, and there was a flurry of getting up from the table, clearing away dishes, and assembling a fresh loaf of bread, a ham Alice had baked for cold meat, sausage rolls made by Minnie, and various cakes and buns that had been hidden away in tins in the larder. The two big thermos flasks were found and filled with tea, and two or three bottles with squash. Old enamel mugs and plates, kept specially for picnics, were hauled out of their hiding place at the back of a big cupboard, and the whole lot was shoved into haversacks and baskets, with half a dozen old blankets stuffed into Tom's wartime kitbag.

By the time this was done, and the sandwiches made, Joanna was back to say that Shirley, Betty, Jeanie and Billy Culliford were coming with them. Freddie was still only two years old so would stay at home, and the two older ones, Jimmy and Brenda, had other things to do. What Jimmy proposed, nobody quite knew – 'Some sort of mischief, you can be sure,' Ted said darkly – but Brenda was helping Joyce Warren to clear up after her lunch party the day before.

'That's five young 'uns,' Alice said, trying to keep track of them as they swarmed about the yard. 'I hope you can keep them under control in the lorry, Tom. Us don't want no one falling out.'

'Don't worry,' he said cheerfully, throwing his kitbag into the back of the open truck along with the hay bales. 'We'll be snug as bugs in rugs. Jo and I'll make sure they behave, won't we, love?'

They climbed aboard and Ted fastened the tailgate. The children beamed down at him, thrilled to be so high up and able to look around them at the countryside. It struck him suddenly that the Cullifords had never been on a trip like this before. Most of them had never even been out of the village, unless to Tavistock to see the goose fair. He felt an unexpected ache in his throat and slapped his hand on the side of the lorry.

'You hold on tight now,' he ordered them a little gruffly. 'Us don't want to come home and have to tell your mother us lost one of you somewhere along the way. Do as Mr Tom and Mrs Joanna tells you, and us'll all have a good time.'

He went round to the front of the truck and climbed into the driving seat. Alice and Minnie were packed in beside him

'Right then,' he said, starting the engine. 'Let's go.'

The truck moved slowly out of the yard, down the farm track and along the village street towards the Exeter road. Widecombe was only a few miles away, but it was an adventure for the children, and the rocks of Hound Tor and the broken walls of the ancient village just below it would make a fine playground. Ted turned to his wife and grinned.

'I reckon this was a good idea of mine,' he said. 'I always did say Easter Monday's a day to take the family out somewhere special!'

*

Maggie and Arthur Culliford waved as the truck went past with the children and Tom perched on hay bales in the open back, already singing their hearts out to songs Tom had learned in his days as a Boy Scout. They watched the merry load out of sight, then looked at each other.

'That's real good of the Tozers to take our tackers along,' Maggie said. 'They'll have a proper day out. Burracombe folk have got good hearts, you got to admit that.'

'Some of 'em, anyway,' he agreed. 'There's still one or two that sticks their noses in the air when us walks past. That Ivy Sweet, for one, and *she* got no call to look down on other folk.'

'I don't take no notice of her,' Maggie said, which wasn't entirely true as the two women often crossed swords if they met in one of the village shops, and Maggie wasn't one to take insults lying down. 'Anyway, never mind that. What are we going to do with ourselves?'

'We still got young Fred,' he said doubtfully. 'Us can't do much with he tagging along. To tell you the truth, I thought I'd walk up to the Barton, see if they needs a hand up there. Squire been good to me; it's only fitting I should offer a bit of help clearing up.'

'And if they don't,' Maggie said, looking at the garden, which the villagers had cleared while she was in hospital but which was now gradually filling up with rubbish again, 'you could do some clearing up here. The grass'll be starting to grow again soon and I wants a nice bit of lawn for the little ones to play on.'

'Seems to me you got some fancy ideas since our Brenda started working for Mrs Warren,' he said with a grin. 'And now she's up at the Barton, you'll be even worse. You'll be wanting a clean white tablecloth for every meal next, and posh plates and glasses like Bren says they got there.'

'Chance'll be a fine thing,' she said, giving him a push. 'Go on, then, Arthur. You go over to the Barton. And I shan't say anything if you happens to call in at the Bell on the way back, only don't have more than one pint, see? I don't want you snoring the afternoon away just when us got a bit of time to ourselves.'

He gave her a wicked grin, pulled her against him and delivered a smacking kiss. 'I can think of summat better than snoring to do on an Easter Monday afternoon,' he said. 'You make sure our Fred's ready for a bit of a rest himself, all right? I'll be back d'rectly.'

Maggie shook her head and watched him go, then turned back to the cottage. Now would be a good chance to tidy up the back room. Since the big clear-out and redecoration her neighbours had done while she was in hospital the previous summer, when she had lost her baby twins, she had made a real effort to keep the place clean. Some of them, like Dottie Friend and Aggie Madge, had popped in and out after she had come home, ordering her to rest while they swept round and cooked meals for the children and Arthur. Maggie had watched and learned, and with the tuition Joyce Warren had given, had felt more confident in her housekeeping.

She looked at the old clock, which had been her mother's and still kept good time, as long as you wound it up while the little ones were at Sunday school each week. Arthur would be gone for a couple of hours now. There was time for a Woodbine and a read of the *Western Morning News* before she needed to start work. It was, after all, a bank holiday.

Joyce and Henry Warren were also on their way to the Barton. They had been there yesterday, of course, rushing through the village as soon as they heard the news, but found the fire brigade in charge and little for them to do. Joyce's offer of taking the Squire and Constance back to her home had not been needed, and they'd left again feeling rather redundant. This morning she was determined to be of help.

'So dreadful for you, my dear,' she said to Hilary, turning away from the devastated kitchen. 'However are you going to manage?'

'Well, we've rescued some old camping equipment from one of the barns – a couple of Primus stoves, as well as one Val Ferris gave us, and some pots and pans left over from when my brothers and I used to make camps – and I managed to cook quite a decent breakfast this morning. Alice Tozer sent over some bread and a big jug of milk and some eggs and bacon. But I believe we can hire an electric cooker from the electricity company in Tavistock, so we'll do that tomorrow. Everywhere's shut today, of course.'

'But you've all today to get through first,' Joyce said. 'And I want you to come to us for lunch at least. No, I won't take no for an answer! It will only be cold meat and pickles and jacket potatoes, I'm afraid, but I can make a hot meal for this evening and—'

'That's really kind of you,' Hilary broke in, 'but the Latimers have asked us for tonight. We'd love to come to lunch, though,' she added, seeing the woman's disappointment. 'And cold meat and pickles sounds ideal.'

Joyce's face lit up. 'I'll make some soup as well,' she promised. 'And do bring your fiancé, won't you? We've not really had a chance to meet him socially yet. Oh, and I'll make up a box of groceries so that when you get your cooker, you can set up a little kitchen somewhere for your housekeeper to work in.'

'We've already had a box,' Hilary said. 'Underwood's sent one up early this morning. They must have heard about the fire and opened the shop specially. There's enough to tide us over for several days – wasn't that kind?'

'Very kind indeed,' Joyce said. 'I always did say they were the best shop in town. Apart from Creber's, of course. Well, let me know if there's anything else you need, won't you?'

'I will,' Hilary promised, and saw the couple out. As usual, Henry had said very little – she often wondered if he got much chance to talk at home – but he gave her a warm smile and held her hand as he shook it, and said that Joyce was right and they must say at once if there was anything they needed.

'Legal advice too,' he added. 'You'll probably find the insurance company quite fair, but if you have any problems, any at all, you must come and see me at once. You know where my office is in Tavistock – Plymouth Road, not far from the church. I'll be very glad to do anything I can.'

'That's very good of you,' Hilary said, reflecting that it was particularly kind of Henry because he wasn't her father's solicitor in the normal way – his legal affairs were dealt with by John Wolstencroft in Exeter. But it might be useful to have a local man too, she thought, closing the door after them.

David appeared from the kitchen regions covered in sooty grime. He dusted his hands together, creating a small storm of black flecks, and gave her a rueful grimace.

'It's completely gutted. We'll need to strip it back to the stone walls and rebuild the whole lot. I'm afraid it's going to be a big job, darling.'

'Oh dear,' Hilary said, thinking how inadequate a phrase it was. 'And we were going to plan our wedding, too. Now goodness knows when it will be ...'

Chapter Eight

Patsy and Terry Pettifer were also having a day out – one that a year ago nobody could have dreamed might happen.

'Who'd have thought we'd be able to go and see my mother, taking little Rosie with us, all open and above board like this?' Patsy said as they walked over the Clam, the old footbridge crossing the tumbling Burra Brook and linking Burracombe itself with its sister village – and arch-rival – Little Burracombe. 'It seems wicked to say it, seeing as he was my father, but everything do seem so much easier now he's gone. I'm sorry it had to be the way it was, though.'

They paused for a moment as they always did, gazing down at the swirling water and thinking of that terrible November night when Patsy's father had been drowned at this very spot. Yet there had been joy as well, for Rosie had been born then and it wasn't until later that they had learned of the tragedy.

'It's over now,' Terry said gently, taking her arm. 'Whatever torment he went through while he was living, he's at peace now. Let me have a carry of the baby, sweetheart.'

'He wasn't a bad man,' Patsy said, handing over the bundle of blankets and shawls. 'I know he had some funny ideas, especially after he got mixed up with the Exclusives, but he always tried to do good, in his way. He was very religious, you know.'

'I know,' Terry said a trifle grimly, thinking of Percy Shillabeer's stick and heavy fists, and the way he wasn't afraid to use them against his wife and daughter, and the way he'd threatened Terry himself with his shotgun that last night. 'He just got things all twisted up in his mind.'

He knew that both Patsy and her mother would continue to make excuses for Percy, rebuilding the fierce, angry religious fanatic they'd known into someone who was good at heart, maybe even gentle if you could get right through to the core of the man. Terry had his doubts about that, but perhaps it was better that they should remember him that way. The bare truth was too harsh, too painful to carry through life.

They walked on up the steep, rocky track that led to Little Burracombe, and came to the church and the first few cottages. The vicarage was next door to the church and Stella was in the garden. She saw them approaching and came over to the low hedge.

'Hello, you two. On your way to visit your mother, Patsy? Oh, and little Rosie too – let me have a look.' She scurried along the other side of the hedge and out through the garden gate. 'Oh, what a darling. And fast asleep too. How old is she now – five months?'

'Just,' Patsy said proudly. 'She'll be waking up any minute, wanting her feed. She's so greedy!'

The baby stirred and opened her eyes. They were as blue as cornflowers and looked straight into Stella's face. There was a flicker of bewilderment, and then a broad, beaming smile broke out and Stella made a small sound of delight.

'She is absolutely beautiful. You must be so proud.'

'We are,' Patsy said. 'I hope you'll be as proud of yours when it's born. How much longer is it now?'

'Not for ages – four months, at least. Either the end of August or the beginning of September, Dr Latimer isn't quite sure. It seems like a lifetime, anyway.'

'It'll pass,' Patsy said with all the wisdom of an experienced young mother. 'Anyway, us'd better get on. Mother's waiting.'

Stella nodded and gave the baby's cheek a final stroke, then watched them go on their way. How different it was now from the days when Patsy had had to come over in secret, terrified that her father would find out, and Stella herself had been involved in a chain of people watching out for him, so that she could be warned of his unexpected return.

She sighed and went back to the garden. However idyllic village life might be, she thought, there would always be a darker side, and you would never really know which cottage hid unhappiness, misery and even tragedy behind its ancient walls.

There was, however, no misery within the walls of the Shillabeer farm these days. The doors and windows were open wide, letting in fresh air and sunlight that seemed to cleanse the bitter unhappiness that had tainted its rooms for so long. The children ran in and out, going about their own small tasks of feeding the hens, cleaning out their coops and changing the water in the geese's bowl, and playing in the yard when they were done. They all ate at the same table again, the dark days of their banishment to the inner scullery, when their father refused to allow them to eat with him, a memory they thrust away from them. They listened to the wireless, even on Sundays, rocking with laughter at the jokes on *Educating Archie* or *The Clitheroe Kid*. They went to church on Sunday morning, scrubbed until they shone and dressed in their best clothes, but the rest of the day was theirs.

They ran now to greet their eldest sister and her husband, clamouring to see their baby niece, still hardly able to believe that they themselves could be uncles and aunts while they were still at school.

'Can I hold her? Can I hold Rosie first?'

'When we get indoors,' Patsy said. 'I don't want her dropped in this mucky yard. And you'll take turns nicely.'

'I wish I could give her her bottle,' Iris said wistfully. 'Could I?'

'She only has water in it,' Patsy said. 'But you can give it to her when she's thirsty.'

'Can *I*? Can *I* give her her bottle?' Milly and Denny clamoured at once, and Patsy raised both hands in the air.

'If she wants it. She's not a toy. There'll be plenty of other chances, anyway. Let me and Terry get inside the house, for goodness' sake.'

They parted before her like a wave, and Ann came to meet them, wiping her hands on her apron. She held out her arms and Patsy went into them, hugging her mother. It was always the same in that first moment of meeting: a rush of thankfulness that now Patsy could come openly to the house, bringing her husband and baby with her, knowing there would be no retribution. It was followed by a swift pang of remorse that they could feel like this over a tragic death, and then, as they drew apart, by the reassurance they gave

57

each other with their eyes. Felix Copley had spent hours with them both, coaxing and persuading them that they need feel no guilt. Percy had been a sick man, he said, and was to be pitied, but he was safe now and they could move freely into the rest of their lives.

'Dinner's nearly ready,' Ann said after she had hugged Terry as well and was rocking her granddaughter in her arms. 'It's a nice shepherd's pie, and there's cabbage to go with it and stewed plums for afters. And when us've had it, there's something I want to talk to you both about.'

'What's that then, Mum?' Patsy shooed the children out of the kitchen and unbuttoned her blouse. 'I'm just going to give Rosie her dinner before we has ours,' she told them. 'Then she'll be quiet while we eat and after that you can all have a turn at giving her water.'

'I'll tell you after,' Ann said firmly, going to the range. 'And you can tell me about the fire I've heard they had at the Barton. I hope it weren't nothing to do with you.'

'Of course it wasn't! What do you take me for?' Patsy cuddled the baby against her and Rosie took her nipple in her mouth and began to suck with concentration. 'Anyway, I wasn't even there. I'd done the veg and gone home ages before. We went up as soon as we heard, though, didn't we, Terry? It's awful. I've never seen such a mess. The whole kitchen is just black with burned plaster and stuff. I don't think there's anything left at all. It's a wonder the ceiling never fell down.'

Ann put a pan of water on the range to boil for the cabbage. 'What about the rest of the house? Is that all right?'

Patsy nodded. 'Miss Hilary shut all the doors as soon as she realised what was happening. They said if she hadn't done that, the whole house could have gone up.'

'Terrible,' Ann said, shaking her head. 'That lovely house ... Thank goodness it didn't come to that.'

'I tell you what, mind,' Terry said suddenly from the chair Percy used to sit in. 'They say it's an ill wind don't blow nobody no good, don't they? Well I reckon there'll be some work there for Bob and me when they starts to rebuild it. All that electrical wiring will want doing again, and they might even do the whole house while they'm at it.'

The two women stared at him.

'That's an awful way to think about it,' Patsy said at last.

'It's not. I got a living to earn, don't forget. There'll be a master lot of work wanting doing up there, and me and Bob did all that wiring last year, if you remember.' He glinted a look at her, for it was while he was working at the Barton with his brother that he and Patsy had fallen in love. 'They'm bound to ask us again.'

'He's right, maid,' Ann said, standing with her back to them as she tipped cabbage into the pan. 'You got to be practical about these things. We all got to make an honest living, one way or another.' But there was an odd note in her voice and Patsy glanced at her doubtfully.

They talked of other things then as Patsy fed the baby. Finally she seemed replete and fell asleep in mid-suck, and Patsy eased her gently away and laid her in the old cradle Ann had brought in from one of the barns and cleaned and polished for her. They called the children in and gathered round the table.

'And now,' Patsy said, when the cheerful meal was finished and the washing-up done, 'what was it you wanted to talk to us about?'

Ann sat down in her own chair. Patsy was now in her father's, with Terry on a stool beside her. Rosie had been transferred to the old pram last used by Milly and taken out for a walk, with Iris proudly pushing and Ben walking a yard or so away, giving elder-brother advice. Denny and Milly skipped ahead with strings tied round their waists and fastened to the pram, being horses in harness.

Ann looked down at her lap. 'Now it's come to it,' she said, 'I don't rightly know how to begin. Especially after what Terry said about there being plenty of work up at the Barton. But that's not going to last for ever, is it, and who knows what work there'll be when it's done? And once all the houses round about are wired up, maybe there won't be so much call for electricians.'

'Of course there will be, Mother,' Terry said. 'There'll always be new houses built and other work needing doing. Electricity's not going to go away. There'll be work and plenty of it, enough to keep me and Bob going until us is old men.'

'Well maybe,' she said. 'But is it work you'll be happy doing until you'm an old man?'

Patsy leaned over and put her hand over her mother's anxiously twisting fingers.

'What is it, Mother? What are you trying to say?'

Ann lifted her eyes and looked at her daughter, then spoke quickly, as if afraid she might lose her nerve.

'I been wondering if you could see your way to coming over here, that's what,' she said in a rush. 'You and Terry and the baby, coming to live here and help me with the farm.'

Patsy and Terry turned to look at each other, then back at Ann. Terry rubbed his forehead.

'Come and live here?' he said at last.

'That's right. There's plenty of room – two bedrooms us never uses, and the big front parlour you could have to yourselves of an evening. I don't want us tripping over each other. Den and Milly will be company for Rosie as she grows up – why, they'll be more like brother and sister to her than uncle and aunt. And Patsy knows how things go here; she'd slip back in as easy as putting on an old shoe. What do you say?' She gazed at them eagerly.

Terry shook his head and looked at Patsy. 'I dunno what to say, Mother. It's come as a bit of a surprise. Me and Patsy never thought ...'

'You can't stop along with your mother and father for ever,' Ann said. 'I know how cramped you must be in that little old cottage.'

'It's not all that little ...'

'It's not all that big, neither.' She turned to her daughter. 'You'm a bit quiet, Patsy. Don't you have no thoughts about it?'

'Of course I do, Mother. But it's like Terry says – it's a bit sudden. We can't make a snap decision just like that. We need to talk it over.'

'Isn't that what we'm doing now?' Ann asked, her voice edged with impatience.

Patsy looked at Terry again. 'No, it's not, not really. I mean, me and Terry need to talk it over ourselves, as well as with you. There's a lot to think about. And what you were saying before – do you really want Terry to give up being an electrician? Is that what you were getting at?'

'Well, he couldn't be a farmer *and* an electrician.' Ann got up and went to fill the kettle. Her hands were shaking. Patsy gave her an anxious glance and caught her husband's eye. She shook her head very slightly.

'So that's something we'd have to think about, and it can't be decided all in a hurry. Terry's a bound apprentice. He's got nearly three more years to go. He can't just walk out on that.'

'I could pay for him ...'

'No, Mother. One thing Terry and me have made up our minds on, and that's to be independent. Or as independent as we can be, till he gets his indentures. And he wants to get qualified, don't you, love?'

'I do. I always wanted to be an electrician and work with our Bob.' He faced his mother-in-law. 'I'm sorry, Mother, I just never thought of being a farmer. I'm not sure I'd be any good at it.'

'Our Patsy would be.' Ann slid the kettle from the side of the range, where it had been simmering, and lifted down the brown teapot. 'Grown up with it, she has. It's in her blood.' She took cups down from the dresser and put them on the table. 'So what you'm saying is that you won't even countenance the idea. You'll leave me here to manage on my own.'

'No!' Patsy and Terry spoke together. Then he sat back to let Patsy talk to her mother in the way she knew best. 'What we're saying is that we need time to think about it, and talk about it, and look at it all ways before we makes a decision. Like Terry said, it's come as a surprise, that's all. And it's very good of you to think about it, Mum,' she added. 'Don't think we don't appreciate it.'

Ann sniffed. The kettle had come to the boil, and she poured some water into the teapot, swilled it round and tipped it down the sink. She spooned in tea from the old caddy and poured boiling water over it, then went to get a jug of milk from the larder.

'I'm sorry,' she said, sitting down again. 'I'm just a bit disappointed, that's all. It come to me in the middle of the night, and I was so excited thinking about us all here together, and little Rosie growing up on the farm with the others, just one big happy family. It would be like I always wanted. And it seemed like a good chance for you, too. I never thought for a minute you might say no.'

Patsy crossed the space between the chairs and knelt beside her mother, taking both hands in hers.

'We haven't said no, Mother,' she said gently. 'We just need time, that's all. I'm not making no promises, mind,' she added quickly as Ann's face brightened again. 'There's Terry's apprenticeship to think about, apart from anything else. And his National Service. He'll have to do that as well.'

'Not if he comes into farming,' Ann said eagerly. 'I heard someone talking about it the other day when I was in the shop. You can be exempted if you work on a farm for eight years. He wouldn't have to go at all if you came here.'

'I thought you said it only come to you last night?' Patsy said.

'It did. It was hearing that that made me think about it, I suppose. See, it would work out all ways. You can't really want to go away now you'm married and got a little girl,' she said to Terry. 'I can't see there's all that much to discuss.'

Patsy sighed. 'We've still got to have a bit of time, Mother. You can't spring it on us and expect us to say yes all in five minutes. I'm not saying we won't help out. You've got Clem Hathaway and Jim Pretty, haven't you? I know they got more work to do now that ... that Father's not here, but we can always come over and give a hand when you need it. I can milk, and Terry can learn, can't you, Terry?'

'I dare say I can,' he said, not mentioning that he didn't much like cows. 'I don't mind helping out any time. I don't work Saturday afternoons or Sundays.'

'No, but you got your own things to do then. You got a babby, and I don't suppose Jack and Nancy want you off out somewhere else all the time. You got to pitch in and do your bit there too.' Ann sighed. 'I suppose I did come out with it a bit sudden, but you know what it's like, you get an idea and it seems like the answer to all your prayers. It's never that easy when you get down to it.'

'Well, we can work it out,' Patsy said peaceably. 'Do you reckon that tea's drawn enough now?'

'My stars, it'll be like cocoa!' Ann jumped up and poured it out. 'There, my bird. And there's a nice Victoria sponge in the tin to go with it. I'll get some plates. And you forget about my old silliness. Talk about it together, like a husband and wife should, and take as much time as you like. I shan't mention it again until you do.'

'She will, though,' Patsy said later as they walked back across the Clam. 'She might not actually say anything, but she'll look at us every time we go over there now, hoping we're going to say yes. What are we going to do, Terry?'

'We'm going to do exactly what we said,' he replied, tucking her hand into the crook of his arm as he carried Rosie firmly against his chest. 'We'll think about it and talk about it, and we'll take our time. We won't be rushed into this, Patsy. That farm's going to be there a long time yet, and you and me's not even twenty years old. There's a lifetime ahead of us, and one way or another we're going to make the most of it.'

Chapter Nine

After a more dramatic Easter than anyone had expected, Burracombe settled back into its usual routine. Only those working on the estate found their lives disrupted. Arthur Culliford told Maggie that Hilary had said not much could be done until the insurance assessor had been, so he and the other staff were to continue with normal estate work, but once they knew what they could do, they would be glad of help in clearing up the mess.

'And that'll be a mucky job,' he observed. 'Filthy, it is. I reckon I'll have to be hosed down in the yard every day before I can even come home.'

'You'd better take a change of clothes with you then,' Maggie said. 'Hose the dirty ones down too and hang 'em up to dry somewhere. It'll save me a lot of washing and scrubbing.'

When the assessor came, he told Hilary he would need a complete list of what had been lost, and three quotes from local builders for repairs. She chose two from Tavistock and one from a neighbouring village. They arrived separately, whistled through their teeth when they saw the damage, and spent hours measuring and doing sums on old envelopes. They went away promising their estimates soon, while Hilary, Patsy and Mrs Curnow sat at the table in the breakfast room with sheets of paper before them, trying to remember what had been in the big kitchen, the scullery and the boot room, which had all been burned out.

'There was so much,' Hilary said in despair. 'And I'm sure they're not going to believe us. Who in their right mind keeps an old parrot cage in the corner of a kitchen?'

64

'Well I thought it looked nice there,' Patsy said. 'With that lovely big plant growing in it. Can you put that down too?'

'How can I? I've no idea what it was worth. It was only a small plant when I got it. I don't even know what a parrot's cage is worth! It must have been at least a hundred years old. It belonged to my grandmother, and the parrot was supposed to have been seventy when he died. And that was back in 1920 or thereabouts, before I was born.'

'It was an antique, then,' Mrs Curnow said. 'It could have been valuable.'

'And it could have been worthless. I think that's what the insurance company will say, anyway. I don't think I'll even mention it.' Hilary drew a line through the item. 'Let's think about the china. At least we know what that was.'

'All that beautiful Wedgwood,' Mrs Curnow mourned. 'I always loved the willow pattern. I heard the story of it once. It was about two young sweethearts who wanted to marry, only the girl's father wouldn't hear of it and he chased them across this little bridge ...' She caught Patsy's eye and put her hand to her mouth. 'Oh, I'm sorry, my bird! But it just goes to show, some things never change.'

'It's all right,' Patsy said. 'I don't suppose me and Terry will ever be put on dinner plates anyway. There was a full set, wasn't there, Miss Hilary? Twelve of each?'

'Twelve of everything,' Hilary said despondently. 'It was my grandmother's ... Well, it's no use thinking like that. It's gone, and that's all there is to it.'

'And you and Dr Hunter will be able to buy all new for your-selves,' Patsy said comfortingly. 'There's some really lovely things in the shops now. Me and Terry were down in Plymouth last week and we went into Dingles, just to look of course, because we could never afford anything in there, and you wouldn't believe the beautiful patterns there are now. It's nice to have things your granny used,' she chattered on, 'and there's a lot of my granny's china still at the farm, but I do think it's lovely to be able to choose for yourself.'

'Yes, it is,' Hilary agreed with a smile, thinking how different Patsy was now from the little mouse who had come with her father to apply for the job of housemaid. She'd had hardly a word to say for herself then, but then he'd barely given her a chance to speak anyway. Now, having asserted herself and married the boy she loved and had her first baby, she was a confident young woman. 'But let's get on with this first. The Wedgwood dinner service – I've no idea what that would be worth. I'll have to consult someone about it. An antique dealer, or an auctioneer, I suppose. There were quite a few things like that, so I'll use a separate sheet of paper for those.'

The task went on, but even when they thought they'd remembered everything, one or another would suddenly recall another item. Hilary's old riding boots – they wouldn't be worth much, in fact they ought to have been thrown away when she got a new pair, but they had to be counted – and even Baden's favourite crop, which nobody had ever had the heart to get rid of. Tears came to Hilary's eyes as she thought of this, but she blinked them away and firmly wrote it on the list. At last she threw down her pencil.

'I can't write another thing. We've cudgelled our brains to pulp. It's nearly lunchtime; let's have something to eat. That soup smells delicious, Mrs Curnow.'

'It's been simmering all morning.' The breakfast room had been turned into a makeshift kitchen, with an electric cooker from the Electricity Board showroom temporarily wired in, and tables and cupboards brought in from various parts of the house to act as worktops. Travis had cut a huge sheet of plywood to go over the top of the big table, and Mrs Curnow had covered it with a double sheet. When Patsy saw it, she thought it looked quite smart.

'Did you say the Colonel wouldn't be in for lunch?' Mrs Curnow asked, ladling onion soup into bowls lent by Alice Tozer while Hilary tidied up the papers and Patsy set out some cutlery, also borrowed from neighbours. The best cutlery, silver and glass had all been in the dining room sideboard so had not been damaged, and a Royal Doulton tea service had also escaped, but Hilary was reluctant to use those for everyday meals and was grateful for the loans.

'Yes, he's gone to Miss Bellamy. Everybody's been so good, inviting us to meals. We would have had to live on bread and cheese these past few days without their generosity.'

'That's Burracombe for you.' Mrs Curnow brought the bowls to the table. 'Look how everyone rallied round to help the Cullifords a few months back, and you can't say they ever did much for the village! Not like you and the Squire.'

'Well, that's our job.' Hilary picked up her spoon. 'And how is your mother getting along, Patsy?' she enquired. 'It must be hard for her, managing the farm on her own.'

To her surprise, Patsy coloured, but her answer came readily enough. 'She do have Clem Hathaway and Jim Pretty to do the heavy work. She do need another man about the place, though, and there's the marketing, and deciding which animals to keep and which to send, and all that sort of thing. Clem and Jim can't really do that.'

Hilary nodded understandingly. In running the Burracombe estate, she knew very well what was involved in farming, and often helped her own tenants to make such decisions. 'Well, if there's anything we can do ... I could go over myself if she'd like me to, or get Travis Kellaway to spare an hour or so now and then. Ask her if that would be any help.'

'Oh, I'm sure it would be,' Patsy said gratefully. She took a piece of the bread Mrs Curnow had placed on the table and smiled her thanks. 'But you'll surely never have the time, not with all you've got to do here, and your wedding to think about.' She hesitated, then said, 'As a matter of fact, she's asked Terry and me if us would go over there to live.'

Hilary paused with her spoon halfway to her mouth and stared at her. 'Over to the farm? Well that's an idea, isn't it? There must be plenty of room. Would you like that? What does Terry think?'

Patsy looked uncomfortable. 'He's not really that struck, to tell you the truth. You see, she don't just want us to live there – she wants us to help run the farm.'

Mrs Curnow looked at her in surprise. 'Run the farm? But Terry's an electrician – and still an apprentice. How can he run a farm? I'm not saying he haven't got the brains, mind,' she added hastily, 'but he's never lived on a farm. And he's not a big chap, is he, not really.'

'He's quite tall,' Hilary said a little doubtfully, thinking of the lanky, rather gangling young man who had been at the Barton the year before, helping his brother Bob with the wiring. 'And he's sure to fill out.'

'Yes, but Mrs Curnow's right,' Patsy said. 'He's never done more than help his mother with a few hens, and he've got to finish his apprenticeship anyway, and then there's National Service. And the thing is, he've always wanted to be an electrician and work with Bob. They got plans to set up in business together.'

'I should think they'd do very well, too,' Hilary said thoughtfully. 'Get themselves a little van, work in the villages ... It's a big thing to ask him to give that up, and there's Bob to consider too.'

'I know.' Patsy took another spoonful of soup. 'Us haven't even mentioned it to Bob yet. Well, 'twas only Easter Monday when Mother asked us.'

'And you have to think about her as well,' Hilary said. 'She must be anxious about how she's going to manage.'

'Couldn't you just go and live there with her without Terry having to give up his work?' Mrs Curnow asked. 'There's more soup if you want it, by the way.'

'I'll have some, please.' Hilary handed over her bowl. 'Yes, how would that be, Patsy? You need somewhere to live, after all. I know you're all getting on well in the Pettifers' cottage, but it must be a bit cramped, and as Rosie gets bigger ...'

'It would be fine. Me and Mother get on well enough, and the little ones love Rosie. I'd like her to grow up on the farm, too. And I could help quite a bit. But I couldn't do all the heavy stuff that Father did. We'd still need another man, and he'd have to be paid. And Terry needs his wage, too.'

The other two women nodded as Mrs Curnow ladled more soup into each bowl. When they'd finished that, she brought a bowl of apples over. They were the last of the autumn's Cox's and russets, their skins wrinkled and their flesh at its sweetest. They ate in silence, pondering Patsy's dilemma.

'Well, my offer stands anyway,' Hilary said at last. 'I'm willing to go over one day and see what I can do, or I could ask Travis. I dare say we could spare a worker from the estate to give some help now and then with the farm work. Arthur Culliford, perhaps – we use him to go wherever a hand is needed, and he knows most farming jobs. Would your mother have any objection to him?'

'I don't know. I could ask her.' Patsy's face glimmered with a smile. 'Father would have done, I know that!'

Hilary smiled back. 'He wouldn't have been alone. But I really do think Arthur is a reformed character these days. What happened last year was a shock for him and he hasn't forgotten it. I don't think he'll ever be perfect, mind you, but he's a good enough worker when he puts his mind to it.'

They finished their apples and Patsy gathered together the bowls and plates. Washing up was another makeshift affair these days, generally done in the downstairs cloakroom. It was lucky, Hilary thought, that they didn't have elaborate meals to clear up after – the simpler everything was now, the better.

'If you don't want us for anything else,' Mrs Curnow said, 'Patsy and me will do the bedrooms. They haven't had a proper clean since before Easter, and Patsy will need to be getting home soon to see to Rosie.'

'That's fine, Mrs Curnow. I think we've broken the back of this job.' Hilary scooped up the papers. 'I've had enough of it anyway. I'll put them away now and get them organised and sent off tomorrow. I'm going to do some work outside now and get some fresh air. The smell of the fire seems to have got all through the house.'

She went out to find a jacket, for the spring days still had a bite of coolness to them, and stood for a moment on the terrace, breathing the clean air and thinking of the smell of smoke and fire pervading the house. Keeping the windows open seemed to be helping, but she thought they would probably need to have all the carpets and curtains cleaned to get rid of it completely. She sighed.

Who would have thought that just carelessly throwing down a tea towel could cause such havoc?

In the privacy of their bedroom, and at any other time when they could snatch a few moments together, Patsy and Terry had continued to discuss Ann Shillabeer's proposal. When Patsy went home that afternoon, her head was still full of it, the problem circling endlessly in her mind until she thought they would never find a solution. It would have been better if her mother had never mentioned it, she thought despairingly, and then felt guilty because she knew that Ann really did need the help.

Rosie was awake in her pram, propped up against the pillows, and crowed with delight as she saw Patsy come in. She held out her arms, and Patsy picked her up and nuzzled her neck.

'Here I am, my pretty. And have you been a good girl for Granny? Did she take all her bottle, Mother?'

Nancy nodded. 'You must have plenty of milk, Patsy, to be able to take it off the way Lucy Dodd showed you, after a full feed and all. It's nice to be able to give the little dear her own mother's milk instead of that dried stuff. I can't see how that can be as good, whatever anyone says.' She watched Patsy cuddling her daughter and smiled. She and Jack had been as displeased as any parent would be when they'd found that Patsy was pregnant – and even more so when they discovered it had been deliberate – but there was no denying that, young as they were, she and Terry made good parents, and they really did seem to love each other. Just lately, however, Nancy had felt a little worried about the two of them. There was something wrong, she was sure, and although she'd told herself she would never interfere, a careful question or two wouldn't do any harm, especially if it was something she could help sort out.

'I've made a cup of tea, and there's a batch of flapjacks not long out of the oven,' she said, testing one to see if it was crisp yet. 'We've got a bit of time before anyone else gets home, so let's have a few minutes' peace and quiet together.'

Patsy sat down, still cradling the baby, and Nancy set a cup of tea beside her and handed her a plate with a flapjack on it. She sat down opposite and took a sip of tea.

'So how is everything up at the Barton?' she enquired. 'There'll be quite a bit of work for you there, getting it all sorted out. And our Bob reckons there'll be a deal of building and electrical work, too.'

'I'm not sure Miss Hilary will be able to decide who does that,' Patsy said, taking a bite of flapjack and picking a crumb or two of oats from Rosie's cardigan. 'She's got to get quotations from three different builders, and 'tis the insurance company that decides who gets the job. Squire's not too pleased about that, but apparently that's the rules.'

'Yes, I reckon it is.' Nancy was silent for a moment, then she said casually, 'And how about you and Terry? Everything still all right with you two, is it?'

Patsy looked at her in surprise. 'Why, yes, Mother. Why shouldn't it be?'

'No reason at all. I just like to be sure. Only ...' Nancy hesitated, aware that she was now straying dangerously close to interfering. 'Only I thought you both seemed a bit worried about summat lately, and you know if there's anything me and Jack can do to help any time ... If you'm feeling cramped in that room now you've got the cot in there, or if you need to be more private, well ...'

'I don't know what you could do if we were,' Patsy said with a smile. 'You can't magic another room up out of thin air! Honestly, everything's all right. We're really grateful to you for letting us stop here at all.' She looked down at the baby, as flowerlike as her name. 'My own father wouldn't have,' she added in a low voice.

'Oh, my dear,' Nancy said warmly. 'I'm sorry. I shouldn't be reminding you ... Forget I mentioned it. But if there *is* anything, you only got to say, remember.'

Patsy was silent for a minute or two. Then she lifted her head and her grey eyes looked into her mother-in-law's. 'There is something,' she said at last. 'It's nothing to do with us being here, though. Me and Terry have talked and talked about it and us just can't see the way forward. And I told Miss Hilary about it today, so I reckon 'tis only fair you should know too. But I ought to talk to Terry first, see what he says.'

'Of course you should. That's what Jack and me always does, set aside an evening to sit and thrash through any problem we got, and ten to one we got it sorted by the time us goes to bed. You have a word with Terry, and when you'm ready, we'll send our Bob off to that skiffle group of his and have an evening to ourselves. I'd just like to know one thing first, to stop me worrying.' Her face was grave. 'You're not going to tell us you'm sorry you and Terry got married, are you? Because I'm certain sure *he's* not sorry.'

'No! I told you, it's nothing like that.' Patsy would have jumped up if she had not had the baby in her arms. Instead she reached

71

across and patted her mother-in-law's arm. 'I love Terry more than ever, and I know he loves me. It's nothing like that – nothing at all.'

'In that case,' Nancy said firmly, wiping away a tear, 'it's nothing that can't be sorted out. What I've always found is that as long as a couple stand firm together, facing the same way and holding each other's hands, then nothing can come between them.'

Chapter Ten

By the time the school term was about to start, James Raynor's cottage was like a new pin, completely redecorated throughout and with all his furniture in place. He hadn't had much of his own before, he told Miss Kemp; his home in London had been destroyed in the Blitz, during the same raid that had killed his wife, and as he'd never had a proper home after that, he'd never needed to buy furniture.

'I did buy myself this desk when I was at the prep school,' he said, displaying it proudly. He had turned his front room into a study, and the newly fitted bookshelves set off the antique roll-top desk to perfection. 'We had new furniture in our first home – it was what Dorothy wanted, and we both rather liked the art deco styles of the twenties – but I didn't want that again, and after the war there was only utility for a long time.'

'Nasty stuff,' Frances agreed with a shudder. 'All plywood and veneer. This is much nicer.'

'Yes, that's what I thought.' He took her through to the back room with its little kitchen added on. Unlike a lot of the cottages in the village, it was a two-storey extension, and the room above was a tiny bathroom with a lavatory beside it. 'So as I liked the desk, I decided to continue with antiques – or at least older furniture. It's not all a hundred years old.'

'No, but it's nice. And good quality.' Frances admired the cherrywood dining table. 'All my furniture is plain cottage style – you could find similar dressers and tables and chairs in almost every house in the village.'

'Yes, but it's good quality, as you say, and the kind of style that will last. It suits your nice little school house. I sometimes wonder if mine hasn't turned out to be a little pretentious.'

'Oh, not at all. I admit it's a surprise – your study would be just as much at home in the Barton! But you haven't overdone it, and nothing is too big for the room it's in. And this room is lovely and cosy.' She looked around at the deep, soft sofa and the single armchair, and the round dining table with its leaves folded and a chair at each end. There were bookshelves in here too. 'You do have a lot of books, don't you? Were they rescued from the house?'

'No, a lot of them belonged to my parents. They were in storage during the war – my mother died just before it started – and survived. Otherwise the shelves would look pitifully empty. I have collected a lot since,' he added. 'And my boyhood favourites are all there – Rudyard Kipling, H. G. Wells, Jules Verne, Stevenson, Conrad.'

'*Treasure Island*,' Frances said, taking the well-thumbed copy from the shelf. 'I love that story. I think Blind Pew is one of the most sinister characters in fiction. That *tap-tap* ... *tap-tap* ... It used to give me nightmares!'

'What about the Vicar of Altarnun, in *Jamaica Inn*?' James suggested. 'He still makes my flesh creep.'

'Oh yes, I love that book too. I like all that Daphne du Maurier writes.' Frances looked again at the book in her hand. 'You know, I've always thought this would be a good story to read to my older children, but it needs a man's voice. You could do it. We could bring the infants into my classroom with the seven-to-nine-year-olds, and you could have the nine-to-elevens one afternoon a week. What do you think?'

'I think it's an excellent idea.' He took the book and opened it at random, reading aloud in a sinister tone and a very creditable Devonshire accent: '*Come away, Hawkins, come and have a yarn with John. Nobody more welcome than yourself, my son. Sit down and hear the news ...*'

'My spine is tingling already,' Frances said with a laugh. 'Even the Crocker twins would be terrified of that. Unfortunately, they're still in the younger class.'

'I'm sure we can find something suitably frightening for them,'

74

he said. 'Now, I'm going to make some tea, and we'll have our discussion about the other ideas for the summer term. I'm looking forward to something special to follow the pageants you've held, and the performance of *A Midsummer Night's Dream* I've heard so much about from Mrs Warren.'

He went into the little kitchen and filled the kettle, setting it on the stove and turning to take cups and saucers from the dresser.

'The highlight of her career,' Frances agreed with a smile. 'But she really is a rather good teacher, as we discovered when she helped us out last year. It's a shame she had to give up so young, but the rules about married women not working are so strict. She's missed years of useful work and a lot of children have missed benefiting from her skills.'

'And instead she's become rather a village busybody,' he said. 'When all she's looking for is an outlet.'

Frances went to the larder to fetch a jug of milk. Since helping him to redecorate, she had become very much at home in the little house. She spoke thoughtfully.

'I was hoping that those rules would change after the war. Women did so much then – married or not, they went into factories, drove buses, did all kinds of work that only men did before. I thought perhaps some, at least, would be able to carry on, having proved that women could do these jobs. But instead they seem to have been driven back to the kitchen sink, and only unmarried women like myself are allowed to continue.'

'To be fair,' he said, 'the men returning from the war were quite entitled to expect their jobs back. It would have been very unfair if not.'

'I know. And I don't think married women have ever been barred from more menial tasks, like factory work or cleaning. But there ought to have been a change in the law to allow them to work in professional jobs like teaching or the civil service. And they should be paid the same as a man, too, if they're doing the same work. Equal work deserves equal pay!'

'My goodness,' he said. 'What a firebrand you are! You'll be marching on Parliament next.'

'And that wouldn't be the first time,' she retorted. 'Where do you imagine I was when we were fighting for the right to vote?'

75

The kettle began to sing, and James poured hot water into the teapot, then swilled it out and replaced the kettle to come to the boil. He spooned tea into the pot.

'I can see I still have a lot to learn about you,' he said, and Frances was glad his back was turned so that he didn't see her colour rise. 'But there's plenty of time. I don't anticipate moving away from Burracombe for a very long time. If ever.'

Frances carried the tray of cups and milk into the living room and set it on a low table.

'That's good,' she said, without turning round, 'because neither do I.'

The children were loud in apparent disappointment that the holidays had come to an end, but when they gathered in the playground on the first morning, they seemed cheerful enough. They clustered in little groups, swapping stories about the Easter eggs they had been given and the outings they had enjoyed on Easter Monday. For most of the holiday they had been left more or less to their own devices and had roamed the village and the moors, but those who lived on farms were expected to give a hand with the work.

'Us did some swaling,' Edward Crocker boasted. He was wearing a green jersey with the name George knitted into the front, while his twin wore the one marked Edward. 'Us beat out the flames with big rubber spades. Farmer said he couldn't have managed without us.'

'No he didn't,' Joe Culliford contradicted. 'He said he'd have managed *better* without you. I was there and I heard him. And you got the wrong jumpers on,' he added.

The twins stared at him. 'No we haven't,' Edward said, but George asked, 'How d'you know that?' and everyone laughed.

'You just told us, stupid! You'll have to change back now or us'll tell Mr Raynor.'

'Tell-tale-tit!' George said indignantly, but he pulled off his jumper and handed it to his brother. Without speaking or even looking at each other, they both knew that they would find some private moment during the day when they would change back. Their likeness to each other had been a bane to their teachers ever since they had started school. Short of suggesting different haircuts,

Miss Kemp had never been able to think of a solution. And Mrs Crocker had flatly refused to have her sons' physical appearance changed; the jumpers had been as far as she was prepared to go.

'They like looking like each other. It would upset them if they didn't.'

Privately, Miss Kemp thought that this would be no bad thing, but she kept that reflection to herself. She was supposed to be a caring and compassionate teacher, she reminded herself – even if, just occasionally, she couldn't help being human too.

As yet, it had to be admitted, the Crocker twins had caused no serious havoc in the school. Cheeky they might be, mischievous they often were, and certainly ready to take advantage of their similarity, but there was a chirpy likeability about them that you couldn't help smiling at. It was a pity that one or two of the other children couldn't take a leaf out of their book – most notably Barry Sweet.

Barry was the red-haired son of George and Ivy Sweet, the village baker and his wife. The red hair seemed to have come out of the blue, for George had had dark hair before he went bald, and Ivy's had been brown until about six months before Barry was born in March 1945. More than one person had commented on the friend-ships Ivy had enjoyed with some of the Polish and Czechoslovakian pilots from Harrowbeer aerodrome, who frequented the pub in Horrabridge where she worked.

Frances Kemp tried not to let the gossip influence her, but she couldn't help knowing about it, and she thought there was probably some foundation for it. All the same, it mustn't be allowed to af-fect her attitude towards Barry. If he was going through a difficult period, she should do her best to help him, but somehow he seemed resistant to help. It was as if he had built a shell around himself. Perhaps, she thought, James might be able to succeed. His reading of *Treasure Island* might be just the thing to appeal to the boy.

The trouble was that Ivy spoiled him. George, the schoolmistress reflected, was a good father – sensible, doing his best to exert a proper discipline, taking an interest in the boy – but Ivy seemed resentful of anything he did, keeping the child to herself, almost flaunting him in George's face. If the rumours were true, Frances Kemp thought, she ought to be grateful that her husband gave the child – and indeed herself – a home and his own name. But Ivy Sweet was not the sort to show, or even feel, gratitude. And Barry seemed to take after her.

Frances sighed. This was Barry's last year in Burracombe school; after this term, he would go on to St Rumon's, the secondary modern school in Tavistock. He could easily have passed the 11-plus examination and been accepted for the grammar school, but he had refused to take any interest in his lessons and had shrugged his way through the exams. Frances was genuinely worried about his future once he was away from the village and subject to wider influences. She decided to talk to James about him.

She found herself talking to James about school matters more and more these days. She had always discussed them with Stella, of course, if not with the unpleasant Miss Watkins who had caused such distress to them all by accusing an innocent child of crimes she had committed herself, but with James it was different. They talked on equal terms. Perhaps it was because of his army experience, but it seemed more than that, because they could talk about so many other matters in the same way. It was, she thought, trying to find words to express it, as if their minds met.

Slightly disturbed by this thought, Frances went into the school to fetch the bell. Perhaps we're seeing too much of each other, she thought. All that painting and decorating during the holidays – I enjoyed helping him, but should I really have done it? And the little suppers we cook for each other – are they a good idea? It can't be right for a head teacher to become too friendly with her assistant. Perhaps I ought to keep a little more distance between us.

It was a sad thought, but as she came out again and began to ring the bell to summon the children in for their first lesson of the summer term, she knew that she was right.

Ivy Sweet had seen her son off to school in a bad temper. She'd almost had to force him to wear a clean white shirt and new grey flannel shorts, and had very nearly marched him through the village with a hand on his shoulder. It was only this threat that had finally persuaded him to go at all.

'It's a waste of time. I don't learn nothing there.'

'That's because you don't try,' Ivy snapped. 'You ought to have passed that exam for the grammar school, but you didn't. And why not? Because you never try, that's why not. You'm an idle little toad, Barry Sweet, and you won't never come to nothing in this world by being idle.'

Like many mothers who overindulged their children, Ivy had a breaking point, and the grammar school examination had been hers. Since the results had come out, there had not been a moment's peace in the Sweet household. Even George, who would do almost anything for a quiet life – and had already done more than many men would have done – had rebelled.

'Leave him alone, Ivy. The boy'll do all right at St Rumon's. I went there, and I ain't done so bad.'

'A village baker!' Ivy said contemptuously. 'I want something better for him than that.'

'It's a good, honest trade,' George retorted. 'And it's kept you comfortable enough all these years.'

'Oh, and I've done nothing, have I? Going over to Horrabridge night after night to work in the pub, that didn't bring in any money, did it?'

George looked at her. It was on the tip of his tongue to say that her time working in the pub during the war had brought in more than money, but he held back. He and Ivy never referred to that subject. He had made his decision years ago not to ask the truth, whatever he might suspect; as far as he was concerned, Barry was his son and that was the end of the matter. Dimly he knew that it would be dangerous to go any further. Uneasy though his marriage might be, it was all he had, and it was better than some.

Ivy knew perfectly well what was in his mind and she gave him a look that dared him to say it. Then she turned away and began to fuss with Barry's red curls, brushing them unnecessarily in a futile attempt to make them lie flat. They never did and they never would, but Ivy still kept trying.

'Leave me alone, Mum,' Barry protested, trying to squirm free. 'Anyway, I don't see why I got to wear all this new stuff. Nobody else does.'

'You'll have to wear it when you go to big school,' she told him. 'You'll have a proper uniform then. Anyway, I like you to look smart, you know that.'

79

'I look like a namby-pamby,' he muttered. 'I'll only get it dirty, and then you'll be fed up about that.'

'Don't get it dirty, then.'

'I can't help it! I got to be able to play football and that. Us all gets dirty.'

'He's right,' George said. 'Boys got to be able to muck about, Ive, you knows that. Let him wear his old shirts and save the good ones for when he goes to Tavi school.'

Ivy sighed and gave in. She produced a grey flannel shirt and allowed Barry to put it on, but she wouldn't let him change his shorts. 'Those old ones got almost no seat to the trousers, they'm worn so thin. I don't know what you done to them, but don't do it to these or you'll feel the back of my hand.'

Barry had gone off to school, still sulky, and Ivy folded his shirt, her lips pressed tightly against each other. George, who had been up since three o'clock baking bread and wanted some sleep, looked at her.

'What's the matter, Ive? You've been out of sorts for the past week or two now. You feeling all right?'

'Of course I am. Nothing's the matter.' Her voice was terse. 'I dunno why you should think that.'

'Well you don't usually go on at our Barry like that, and I've never heard you threaten to take the back of your hand to him before.'

'Maybe I should have done. He's getting altogether too cheeky lately. I tell you what it is, George, he needs a father's discipline, and that's just what he don't get.'

Again George opened his mouth to say something but bit the words off before they could be spoken. 'You never wanted me to interfere with him. You always said you'd bring him up your way.'

'When he was a little boy, maybe, but he's getting too big for a mother's control. It's a father's authority he needs now.'

'All right,' George said mildly. 'I'll do what I can, but if you ask me, it's been left too late. I don't reckon he'll take it from me now. And I'm not sure that's what's really the matter with you neither. Come on, Ive. There's something, I know.' He hesitated, then said delicately, 'It's nothing to do with – you know – your time of life, is it?'

'My time of life?' Ivy stared at him. 'Whatever be you on about, George Sweet? Of course it's not my time of life!'

'Well all right, I only wondered. I don't know much about it. I just heard some of the blokes talking about it in the pub one day, and Norman Tozer said it do make women go a bit funny in the head, like, and—'

'*Funny in the head?*' Ivy took a step towards him and George backed away hurriedly. 'Are you calling me barmy, George Sweet?'

'No, of course I'm not.' He put up both hands. 'Look, I'm sorry I said anything. I didn't mean it. I just been a bit worried about you, that's all. Like I said, you've seemed a bit under the weather, and if there's anything I can do to help—'

'The best thing you can do,' Ivy said in a tight voice, 'is take yourself off to bed and get some sleep. I'll open the shop. It seems to me *you'm* the one out of sorts.'

George hesitated, then with an air of resignation turned away. He opened the door to the staircase and went up the narrow steps. After a few moments Ivy heard the bed creak as he got into it, and she closed the door after him and went through to the shop.

'Time of life!' she muttered to herself. 'Time of life indeed!'

But George was right. There was something amiss in Ivy's life these days, and she really didn't know what to do about it.

Chapter Eleven

T he insurance company had finally agreed to Hilary's first choice of local builder to carry out the rebuilding work at the Barton. The Tavistock firm of E. L. Greening were a family outfit with a good reputation and a son coming into the business once he'd finished his National Service, and Hilary had confidence in them.

'It's good to have someone you know and trust,' she said to David when he called in for tea after finishing his rounds. 'And they'll be a real help in deciding how to plan the new kitchen. Actually, now that we're getting sorted out, it's quite exciting!'

'We can plan it together,' he said, buttering a scone. 'Just like any other newly-weds planning their own home.'

Hilary looked at him anxiously. 'Is that what you'd rather be doing, David? Planning a whole new home for us, I mean, instead of just a bit – and not even the bit that you'll be most interested in yourself!'

'Not at all,' he said, putting down the scone and taking her hand. 'I'm too happy about getting married to you to worry about where we live. In fact I think I'd live in a cardboard box with you if that were all that was available, and the Barton's a great improvement on that!'

She laughed. 'It looked very nearly as if it might have to be a cardboard box when that awful fire was burning. But I don't want you to feel – well, beholden or put upon in any way.'

'I won't. I understand the position completely and I think I am very lucky. There is just one thing, though.' He finished spreading his scone, then said, 'It's about when Charles finally retires.'

Hilary's forehead creased a little. 'What do you mean? He's not thinking of full retirement yet, is he?'

'No, but it will come, probably in the next three to five years, and then he and Mary will be free to live wherever they like. They may decide to travel. They might even move away from Burracombe –'

'Oh, I do hope not!'

'– but whatever they decide, it's unlikely they'll stay in the same house. Their daughters will all have left home by then – even Tessa's hardly ever there now – and it's a big house for two retired people.'

'Yes, that's true, but I don't see ...'

'The surgery,' he said patiently. 'Whether they stay there or sell up, it won't really be possible to continue running the surgery from the house.'

'Oh,' Hilary said. She poured him a second cup of tea 'Yes, I see what you mean. So what will you do?'

'Well, it's something we'll have to think about, and there's plenty of time to do that, but we do need at least to be aware of the situation. Because when it arises, I shall need to find a new surgery.'

'You could have it here,' Hilary said. 'We've got more than enough rooms. There's the small sitting room by the front door that would do as a waiting room, and you could have your surgery in the room behind it. It's hardly ever used. We could put a door through—'

'And how would your father feel about that? A constant troop of villagers up and down the drive every day, coming into the Barton through his own front door, with all their aches and pains and coughs and sneezes? Crying babies, lame old men, grumbling women – not all of them will be in a good mood – all staring round his hallway. His peace and privacy would be destroyed, because even if we didn't use the rooms you suggest, even if we used rooms at the back of the house and nobody came near the front, he couldn't fail to be aware of them. I'm not sure he would be at all keen.' He helped himself to a slice of fruit cake.

'No, he wouldn't,' Hilary said thoughtfully. 'Well, forewarned is forearmed, and we do have time to think about it. Meanwhile, we've got to think about the kitchen. I want you to look at these plans Mr

Greening has drawn up. And there's a new range to consider, and cupboards, and—'

'I'll leave those to you,' David said with a grin. 'You and Mrs Curnow will have a far better idea about such things. But I'd like to see the plans, if your father doesn't mind, and we can talk about them together.' He stroked her hand. 'There's something else we need to talk about and decide, just you and I.'

Hilary met his eyes and felt suddenly breathless. There had been so much to do in the past two or three weeks that they'd barely had time to think about their own concerns. She felt a twinge of guilt. David was a patient man, she thought, but even he had his limits.

'I know. Our wedding.'

'When is it to be?' he asked. 'It's almost a year now since Sybil died. I want to wait until that anniversary has passed, in June, but after that I shall consider myself free to move on to a new life – with you. Just name the day.'

Hilary gave a little laugh. 'Oh David, I haven't thought! It's been so good having you here, and being engaged ... Even with the fire, it's been the happiest time of my life. I've just been enjoying that.'

'And so have I,' he said. 'But I don't want to go on enjoying it for too long. I mean – well, you know what I mean. Stop giggling.'

'Sorry,' she said, taking a deep breath. 'All right. We'll look at the calendar together and decide on the best time. Although it might be better to wait until all the rebuilding's done, don't you think?'

'And when might that be?'

'I think Mr Greening said about three months. That takes us to the end of August. Except that Stella's baby's due just about then,' she remembered, 'and she said she didn't want to be either like a balloon or actually in childbirth when we get married. Halfway through September? Or maybe early October, to be sure everything's done.'

'It sounds an eternity away,' he said gloomily, 'but I dare say it will do. As long as it doesn't interfere with harvest festival or the whist club's fur and feather drive or some other immovable village activity. Honestly, it's much easier living in a city – there's not nearly so much going on!'

Hilary laughed. 'That's why I said we should look at the calendar.

But I think the second half of September and early October are fairly clear. And it would be a lovely time for our honeymoon.'

'And where would you like to go for that?' he asked, dusting crumbs from his fingers. 'I've got one or two ideas of my own, but let's see where you favour.'

'Venice,' she said promptly. 'And I hope it's one of your ideas too. I've always wanted to go there, and for a honeymoon I think it must be the most romantic place in the world.'

'Venice it will be,' he said, and pulled her towards him for a kiss. 'An early autumn wedding, and then Venice. I can't wait.'

Stella and Felix were looking forward to the autumn too. They were busy at the Little Burracombe vicarage, redecorating the bedroom next to theirs for the baby, and planning what they would need to buy. A cot, a baby bath, a nursing chair, some furniture – both were agreed that the rather heavy, old-fashioned furniture left by Mrs Berry, wife of the previous vicar, was not at all suitable – and some pretty curtains. The perennial dilemma over colour was resolved by using yellow.

'It's a lovely sunshiny colour,' Stella said, 'and it will suit either a boy or a girl. Yellow check curtains and that brown and yellow rug from the spare bedroom for the floor, and yellow cot blankets. And when the baby's born and we know what it is, we'll buy a little eiderdown to go on top.'

'I'm not sure about pink and yellow,' Felix said dubiously from halfway up a stepladder. 'Do they really go together?'

'No, not really. It had better be a boy, then. Or maybe we should wait until it's born before we do the curtains. Dottie could make them while I'm in hospital. And we could just have cream blankets.'

'That's a bit dull. I think we should wait for all those things. I can buy them in Sweets in Tavistock before you come out of the maternity home. But at least we can go on painting the walls yellow. The curtains don't have to be *very* pink, do they? Pass me that brush, darling.'

'They don't *have* to be any colour,' Stella said, handing him the paintbrush. 'They could be brown or dark red if we wanted. In fact, I'm not all that keen on pink anyway. I think the yellow check would be quite all right. We'll keep to that for the nursery and just have blue or pink for baby clothes. Nobody expects a baby to have any colour sense anyway.'

'Especially if it's my baby,' he said. 'My sisters used to say it was a pity I wasn't colour blind. At least I'd have had some excuse.'

Stella giggled. 'They probably had a fit when you told them we were having a rainbow wedding! But it was lovely, wasn't it? And it meant we could have all those bridesmaids without people being knocked out by a solid wall of one colour going up the aisle.'

'All those bridesmaids!' he said with a wicked grin, dipping the brush into the pot of paint and slapping it on the wall. 'You didn't want any, if I remember rightly. Or only Maddy, anyway.'

'I know, but I hadn't realised then about all the little girls in your family who'd want to be part of it, and some from the school. I couldn't hurt all their feelings. And once I'd got used to the idea, I did like it. It was very special.' She paused in the midst of measuring the window. 'Felix, I'm really worried about Maddy.'

Felix looked at her. He came down the ladder, carefully replaced his brush in a spare tin and put his arms round her. 'I know, darling. It's not good news about Cyprus, is it.'

'It's these EOKA people,' she said, looking up at him with tears trembling in her lashes. 'They're starting riots in the towns, and ambushing service vehicles on the roads. There's talk of them attacking military installations. Suppose they attack the airfield where Stephen is? Suppose Maddy's in town one day, shopping, and she gets caught up in a riot? It doesn't bear thinking of.'

'I'm sure she'll be careful not to go where it's dangerous—' he began, but she cut him off.

'How can she know where it *is* dangerous? That's the whole point of terrorism – they strike places people think are safe, so that they're frightened to go there, and in the end they're frightened to go anywhere. And then the terrorists have won.'

'Well they can't be allowed to win,' Felix said firmly. 'People must show them they won't be frightened out of going where they want to. Show them it's just not worth making trouble.'

'And how many people have to die before that happens?' she asked. 'One of them could be Maddy.' She turned away from him.

'It's all very well being brave and refusing to be frightened of them here in a peaceful Devon village. It's not so easy when you think there might be a terrorist with a gun or a bomb hiding round every corner.'

'No,' he said quietly. 'You're right. And I'm not going to say don't worry, because you can't help worrying. I'm worried too. I just can't see what we can do about it. The only hope is that they'll send the military families home.'

'Maddy will never come. Not without Stephen.'

'She may have no choice.' He picked up his paintbrush again and put one foot on the bottom step of the ladder. 'And if she does, we'll need to have a bedroom ready for her, so let's get on with the nursery and then think about decorating the east bedroom for Maddy. I think that's the one she'd like best.'

'Yes, it is. She always loves to wake with the sun shining through the curtains.' Stella went back to measuring the window. 'And there'll be no problem about the colour scheme, because she likes green sunlight, like we used to get through the curtains in the bedroom at Dottie's. She said it made her feel as if she was at the bottom of the sea. So we can use that pretty green sprigged material we found in the box Mrs Berry left behind. It's never been made up and I'm sure there's enough.' She wrote down the measurements she had taken on a scrap of paper. 'It would be lovely to have her here, but I hope it doesn't come to that. She was so looking forward to her time in Cyprus with Stephen, and it would be a shame if she was robbed of that.'

The Tozers too were concerned about a member of the family who was abroad.

'I don't know what that girl's thinking of,' Alice said, sitting at the kitchen table and staring at Jackie's latest letter. 'Talking about going off to California now, she is! And her engaged to that chap in Corning. What do *he* think about it, I wonder?'

'He probably knows enough about our Jackie by now to know what a headstrong, self-willed maid she be,' Ted said. He sat down opposite Alice and fumbled in his jacket pocket for the reading glasses he had finally been persuaded to wear. 'Give us the letter, Alice. Let's see what she says.'

'I've already told you what she says,' Alice grumbled, but she passed the flimsy blue airmail sheet over and he ran his eye down the closely written lines. 'Not that she says all that much, for all the writing she does. 'Tis all about what she thinks she's going to do, and not a word about why, or how she's going to pay for it all. And what's your Joe thinking of, letting her gad off to the other side of America?' she demanded. 'Didn't he promise to look after the maid and treat her like one of his own daughters? Did he ever let *them* go off like that, all on their own, before they were even twenty-one? I tell you, Ted, America's turned her head, just like us always knew it would, and heaven above knows what will happen to her out there in the west, all by herself.'

'We don't know as she is going to be by herself,' Ted pointed out. 'It might be that this fiancé of hers is going too.'

'And would that be any better? An unmarried girl, travelling around and staying in hotels and such, with a man she've only known a few months? Engaged they might be – or think they might be, since nobody's ever asked *our* permission – but that don't make it right. Anyway, why *is* she going? I tell you what I think it is. Hollywood's in California, isn't it? She thinks she's going to be a film star!' Alice's tone showed just what she thought of this possibility. 'It's given her ideas, this trip has. *Silly* ideas.'

'I know, my bird, but what can us do about it?' Ted laid the letter down and gazed across the table at his wife, then took off his glasses. 'I can't see proper with these things on,' he complained. 'They'm only any good for reading.'

'Well that's because they'm reading glasses,' she said impatiently. 'What can us do about it? I don't know, do I? Short of going over there ourselves, and she wouldn't take no more notice of us if we did that than she did in the first place.' Her face crumpled suddenly and she felt for a hanky and put it to her eyes. 'You know what's happened, Ted, don't you? We've lost her. Our last baby, our little girl, and we've lost her.'

Ted stared at her in dismay. He put out his hand and took hold of her wrist, rubbing her arm as she blew her nose. He started to utter whatever words of comfort he could find, then faltered into silence. At last, in a heavy, despondent tone, he said, 'I think you're right, Alice my dear. Not that we've lost her, I don't mean. But there's nothing us can do about her. She'll go her own way, just like she always have done, and all us can do is hope she'll tread the paths we always showed her as a little maid. She knows right from wrong and I don't think she'll forget it. All us can do is hold on to that.'

Chapter Twelve

'Well now,' Nancy Pettifer said as the four of them sat round the empty fireplace. After the bitter winter, April had ended with a few warm days, and May looked like keeping it up, for a while at any rate. 'You know me and your father don't want to interfere in your lives – you'm a married couple and got the right to make your own decisions – but that don't mean we can't help chew over any problems you might have, and being older, we might see things a bit straighter. But only if you want us to, mind. That's right, isn't it, Jack?'

'It is,' he said, drawing on the pipe he had just lit. 'I know there were times I was glad of a bit of advice from my mother and father. And there was times I took no notice, too. So you tell us whatever it is you wants us to know, and see for yourselves if we got anything useful to say.'

'The main thing we'm concerned about,' Nancy went on, 'is that you'm not in any sort of trouble, and that everything's all right between the two of you. And with the baby, the dear of her.'

'Well we can set your minds right on all those things,' Terry said. He and Patsy were sitting on two kitchen chairs by the table, while Jack and Nancy were in their accustomed easy chairs, one each side of the fireplace. 'You know there's nothing wrong with Rosie, and me and Patsy are as happy being married as ever we thought we would be. More, even.' He grinned at his young wife, who blushed and looked down at her hands. 'And we're not in any trouble. More the other way, a lot of people would say.'

Jack and Nancy waited while he and Patsy seemed to search for words. At last Jack said, 'Well spit it out then, boy, or do us have to start pulling out your fingernails?'

Terry grinned, and Patsy laughed. She said, 'It's my mother. She wants us to go and live over there on the farm.'

Jack and Nancy looked at each other. Then Nancy said carefully, 'I can't say I'm surprised. She's got the room and you'd be a help to each other – she could look after Rosie while you go to the Barton, and you could help her with the other children. I'm not saying we wouldn't miss you here, of course we would, but us always knew it wouldn't last for ever. I take it you've said yes?'

'No, we haven't,' Terry said. 'That's the problem. It's not just living there – she wants us to help on the farm.'

'Well you couldn't live there without helping out a bit, could you,' Jack said. 'Stands to reason. I know you've never done much farm work as such, apart from a bit of swaling and joining in with the harvest up at Tozers', but you could give a hand at weekends and in the evenings in summer.' He looked at Patsy. 'What about you? Would you give up your job at the Barton? You'd have to eventually, if more little ones come along.'

'Miss Hilary's getting more help anyway, now she's getting married,' Patsy said. 'Brenda Culliford seems to be settling in all right. Mrs Warren gave her a job during the summer holidays, but she didn't want her permanent, and she's given her a good training.'

'You don't understand,' Terry said before the discussion could veer towards Brenda Culliford's suitability to work at the Barton. 'She wants us *both* to give up our jobs. She wants us to take over the farm. Not just yet, but eventually. She wants me to work full time – be a farmer.'

The older couple were nonplussed. They looked at Terry and at Patsy, and then at each other. At last Nancy found her voice.

'But Terry, you're an electrician!'

'And an indentured apprentice at that. You got another three years at least to run before you can leave. They could have you up in a court of law if you tried.'

'They might agree to let me go,' Terry said, and his father snorted.

'At a price! Where are you going to get the money to buy yourself off? And what about our Bob? It wouldn't reflect well on him when he did so much to get you the place to start with.'

'I didn't say I *wanted* to do it,' Terry protested. 'But I've had to *think* about it.'

'Come on, Jack,' Nancy said. 'The boy's right. He's been asked and he's had to give it some thought. 'Tis no use you working yourself up into a state of indignation when us haven't even started to talk about it.'

Jack subsided. 'No, all right. You'd better tell us a bit more, then.'

'There's not much more to tell,' Terry said, a little sullenly. 'Patsy's mother's finding it hard to manage the farm on her own and she needs someone to help her, that's all. Seems natural to turn to her own folk first, I'd have thought.'

'All right, all right,' his father said. 'You don't need to get on *your* high horse, neither. If we'm going to be any help to you, we got to talk it over sensibly. I'm sorry I flew off at you. But what about the men she got working for her? Clem Hathaway and Jim Pretty, isn't it? They're decent chaps, they'll be doing the heavy work.'

'But there used to be three men doing that,' Patsy said. 'Mother's right, she do need a bit more help about the place.'

They were all silent for a moment, thinking of Percy Shillabeer's end. For all his faults and his temper, he'd been a good farmer, working all hours to provide for his family. He left a big gap in that way, if in no other.

'Our Terry couldn't do what your dad did, though,' Jack said. 'I mean, look at him.' They all turned their eyes to the lanky young man in question. His bony face turned crimson.

'You don't need to stare like that, as if you never seen me before. Anyway, I don't know what you're on about, Father. I'm not a seven-stone weakling like in those Charles Atlas adverts. I'd soon put on a bit more muscle.'

'It's not just the heavy farm work,' Patsy said. 'It's the paper-work. The accounts, and the government forms farmers got to fill in, all that sort of thing. And the stock. Father knew all about the breeding, and which animals to send to market and which to keep. He knew about the feed, so that they'd produce more milk. He was a *farmer*. It's not just about lifting bales of hay or doing the milking twice a day.'

'Seems to me you'd be more use to your mother than our Terry,'

Jack said after a moment. 'I reckon you got a pretty good idea about all that yourself.'

'I used to help him a bit,' she admitted. 'I reckon I could soon pick it up.'

Jack stared at the fireplace for a moment. Then he said, 'What about your National Service? They'll want you for that, soon as you finish your apprenticeship, don't forget.'

'Not if I was a farmer,' Terry said. 'And anyway, I'm not sure they'll still be doing it by the time I finish my apprenticeship. They're talking about phasing it out by around 1957.'

There was a short silence. Then Nancy said, 'What about the money side of it? I don't want to poke my nose in, but how would you manage that? You haven't got much money coming in as it is – just Patsy's thirty-five shillings a week from the Barton, and Terry's pay as an apprentice.'

'Two pounds five bob,' he said. 'If you didn't let us live here rent-free, we wouldn't be able to manage. We know that.'

'Well, you'd be living rent-free on the farm, I take it,' she said thoughtfully. 'And all found as far as food goes. But you still got to think of clothes and that, especially for the baby. She's almost grown out of her second things already. You need to have the money sorted out between you.'

'You're talking as if it's all settled,' Jack objected. 'There's still the matter of young Terry's indentures, in case you've forgotten. And I'm not even sure at the minute if he and Patsy *want* to do this. I thought he was set on being an electrician and starting up in business with his brother. And that's another thing,' he added, warming up again. 'What's our Bob going to say when he finds out you'm letting him down?'

'Who said I was letting him down?' Terry demanded. 'I told you, we haven't decided yet.' He turned to Patsy, who was looking distressed. 'I said it would be like this. I knew it was no good trying to talk about it. They still think I'm a little tacker in short trousers.'

'No, we don't.' Nancy frowned across the fireplace at her husband. 'Calm down a bit, Jack. It won't do no good getting aeriated about it. We said we'd talk it over sensible between us, and that's what we got to do.'

'Well all right,' he muttered. 'But all these things got to be considered.'

'And we *have* considered them,' Terry told him. 'We've thought about all of it, but we don't seem to get no further. It's like we come up against a brick wall whichever way we look at it.'

Nancy got up out of her chair.

'I'm going to make a cup of tea,' she said decisively. 'We can all have a quiet think while I'm doing that, and then we'll start again. And if we haven't come to a conclusion by nine o'clock, we'll stop. Otherwise we'll be going round in circles till midnight.'

'*The Prince and the Pauper*,' Miss Kemp said thoughtfully as she and James Raynor tidied the classrooms at the end of the afternoon. 'You know, that's a very interesting idea. Is there a script available, suitable for children?'

'I don't know, but we can probably find one,' James said eagerly. 'If not, we'll knock one out ourselves. It's such a good story, and since we've got the principal actors – the Crocker twins – it would be a shame not to make use of their likeness.'

Frances smiled at his enthusiasm. 'It would, but they'll be with us for a few years yet. Don't you think they're a little young at present? They'd be better able to take on such big parts at the age of ten or eleven. Maybe nine, at a stretch.'

'I suppose they would,' he admitted, pinning that day's artwork on the wall. 'But I was trying to think of something to occupy their minds now. I've always found small boys much easier to deal with if they've got something definite to do. Learning their lines and taking part in rehearsals would leave them very little time or energy for mischief.'

'It would, but they're barely six years old and I really think it would be too demanding. I suggest we keep the idea for a couple of years and think of something more suitable for their age now. Aren't there any other twin stories we could use?' Frances looked along the shelf where the school's reading books were kept.

'Offhand I can only think of *Twelfth Night*,' he said gloomily. 'And one of them would have to dress as a girl. I can't see either George or Edward agreeing to that.'

'Not for long. Viola pretends to be a boy for most of the play.'

'A eunuch, actually,' he corrected her. 'But we don't need to go into that ... Anyway, I was rather hoping to get away from Shakespeare.'

'That's a pity, because I was just going to mention *A Comedy of Errors*! But I agree, it would be nice to do something the children can relate to a little more. What about Tweedledum and Tweedledee?'

'I always find them rather sinister,' James said thoughtfully. 'To tell the truth, I find both the *Alice* books sinister. There seem to be so many unpleasant undertones. Well, it seemed a good idea, but I think you're right. We should keep *The Prince and the Pauper* until they're nearer the age of the boys in the book.'

'We still have to think of something for the children to do at the summer fair, though,' Frances said, putting away her pencils and papers. 'It seems to have become a fixture since the pageant, and the success of *Dream*. And I do agree with you about the twins. It's a shame not to use them, and it would be good for them too. Although I'm not sure we'd be wise to make too much of them. I usually try to bring out the children who have *less* self-confidence, rather than those who have plenty already!'

She closed her desk and took a final look round the classroom. It was neat and tidy, ready for the next day. She would spend the evening planning her lessons, listening to the wireless – *Ignorance is Bliss* would be on the Light Programme, she remembered, followed by *Much-Binding-in-the-Marsh* – and reading the Eden Phillpotts novel she had brought home from Tavistock library last Saturday, and then have an early night.

'Would you like to come for supper later on?' James asked, breaking into her reverie. 'Arthur Culliford brought me a couple of trout this morning.'

'Did he indeed?' she asked, diverted. 'I hope that doesn't mean he's going back to his bad old ways.'

'I don't think so. He's allowed to fish that stretch just below the bridge, isn't he? I understand most of the villagers go there at some time or other.'

'Yes, he is. Hilary persuaded her father to make it free for the village a few years ago. I should imagine that Arthur's more likely to have tickled them than stand on the bank for hours, though. I'm sure there's gipsy somewhere in that man.'

'I wouldn't be at all surprised. What do you say, then? About seven?' He gave her a persuasive smile. 'I'm going to grill them with almonds and boil a few of my own new potatoes to go with them, with some salad.'

Frances hesitated. Grilled trout in James's company suddenly seemed more attractive than the solitary evening she had planned, and she almost said yes. Then she remembered her doubts about their relationship and her vow not to let it go too far.

'It sounds lovely,' she said politely. 'But I've got quite a lot to do this evening. Another time, perhaps.'

At his look of disappointment, she almost retracted her words, but it was too late now. She regretted her distant tone, too. She might have been replying to some chance acquaintance who had presumed too much. She bit her lip and said, 'James, I—'

'It's quite all right,' he said quickly, his tone as polite as hers had been. 'I quite understand. I expect the other trout will keep until tomorrow.' He turned towards the door. 'Well, I won't detain you any longer. Perhaps sometime we could talk again about the summer fair.'

He limped out and Frances watched him go. I've hurt him, she thought remorsefully. I didn't have to do that. I could have gone to supper and come away early. We could have had a pleasant evening together and been none the worse.

Except ... except that every pleasant evening, every happy hour spent together took them further along a road she had made up her mind never to travel again.

James walked slowly back to his cottage. For the first time since he had come to Burracombe, he felt dispirited and lonely. I said something wrong there, he thought, but go over the conversation again in his mind as he would, he could not think what it might have been. His suggestions for the children's summer play? She had seemed as interested and enthusiastic as he. Perhaps he shouldn't have corrected her over Viola's masquerading as a eunuch – could that have offended her? But for heaven's sake, Frances was no prim Victorian miss; she was a woman in her fifties who had lived through two world wars. And she had never shown any sign of prudishness before.

It was when I invited her to supper, he thought. Perhaps she didn't believe him when he said that Arthur Culliford had come by the trout honestly. Perhaps she even thought he had poached them himself. No – that was ridiculous. She'd even laughed about Culliford having some gipsy in him. And yet that did seem to be the moment when she had begun to withdraw. And her voice had been distinctly cool when she declined his invitation.

But *why*? They'd visited each other in their cottages often enough in the past few months. They'd cooked several meals for each other. She had even spent part of her Easter helping him to redecorate. They were *friends*.

At least, he'd thought they were. Perhaps he was wrong. Perhaps she'd just been friendly towards her new assistant, wanting him to settle happily into the village. Perhaps she had never intended it to develop into real friendship. Perhaps he had presumed too much.

James let himself into the cottage and stood inside, looking around at the freshly distempered walls, the pictures they had hung together, the books they had discussed with such enjoyment. He thought of Frances sitting at the small dining table as he brought plates and dishes for their meal. He thought of her relaxing in one of the armchairs as they listened to music together or laughed at some silly, amusing radio programme.

I took too much for granted, he thought sadly. I thought we had a friendship that would endure. I even hoped it might ripen into something more, something deeper.

For the first time he admitted to himself that he had begun to see in Frances Kemp the possibility of love; something he had thought never to feel again.

There had been a warmth in his life since he had come to Burracombe, a warmth that had driven out the ice that had been in his heart ever since Dorothy had been killed. But now it had gone, and the familiar chill was creeping back, like a slowly freezing hand that caught him and would not let him go.

He wondered how Frances had been feeling during these past weeks, seeing and understanding how his feelings for her were beginning to develop. For surely she must have known. He did not see how she could have failed to know.

She must have wondered how to tell him, how to let him down

gently before it all went too far. She must have worried about it. And now, at last, she had done it, as kindly as she could, simply by refusing a meal. I hope she isn't upset at having hurt me, he thought. I don't want her to be upset.

He made up his mind that he would not let her see that she had hurt him. He would not presume on their relationship any more. From now on, he would remain strictly formal, as befitted an assistant teacher with his superior.

He went into the kitchen to prepare his supper.

Chapter Thirteen

'And if you asks me,' Jacob Prout declaimed, standing at the counter in the village shop while Edie Pettifer weighed out a bag of sugar for him, 'that new young doctor and Miss Hilary are well suited. I hope they gets married soon and makes sure of each other.'

Dottie, waiting her turn to be served, laughed at him. 'You reckon one of them's going to get away, then? It don't look to me like either's trying very hard to do that.'

'Nor to me. Proper pair of lovebirds they be,' Edie said sentimentally. 'I saw them down by the river the other evening when I was out walking with Bert. I said to him it was lovely to see two young people so wrapped up in each other. There'll be another wedding in Burracombe this side of Christmas, I wouldn't wonder.'

'And what did Bert say?' Jacob enquired. 'Didn't take the hint and say it could be yours, did he?'

Edie flushed and said sharply, 'Of course he didn't! Don't talk more foolish than you have to, Jacob Prout. You know there's nothing of that sort between me and Bert. Just friends, that's all we be.'

Jacob grinned. 'If you say so, Edie, and mind that sugar, it'll overflow the bag if you'm not careful. But you been friends for such a long time, I wonder Bert don't make an honest woman of you.'

'I don't know what you think you mean by that,' she said, sounding really angry this time. 'But if you don't take it back this minute, you'll find yourself banned from this shop.'

'Come on, Edie,' he said, surprised. 'You know I didn't mean nothing. It was just a joke, that's all. Anyway, you already banned

Ivy Sweet just before Easter. You can't afford to shut too many of your customers out.'

'I know what I can and can't afford,' she told him. 'Now, are you going to apologise or not?'

'You better had,' Dottie said. 'You don't want to find yourself going on the Tavi bus with Ivy to do your shopping.'

Jacob shrugged. 'I'm sorry, Edie. I never meant it serious and I didn't say it to upset you. You and Bert got a good friendship and I wish you luck. I wouldn't mind a nice little woman living next door to me to have a cup of tea and a game of crib with, and that's a fact.'

'You can come in to me for that if you feel a bit down any time,' Dottie said. 'So long as it don't start any talk in the village.'

'I might take you up on that.' Jacob took his bag of sugar from Edie and put it with the rest of his groceries. 'Until that brother of Ted Tozer's comes back and whisks you off to America, anyway.'

'And *that's* something that's not going to happen,' Dottie retorted, flushing as deeply as Edie had done. 'I reckon it's time you took yourself out of here, Jacob. You'm in a frisky mood this morning with all these insinuations about respectable women. I don't know what's got into you, I really don't.'

Jacob grinned. 'Must be spring in the air,' he said. 'You know what they says, don't you – "In the spring, a young man's fancy …"'

'Go on with you and your young man's fancy!' Dottie said, laughing in spite of herself. 'It's many a long year since you were a young man. Go back to your dog and cat, and leave us all in peace.'

Jacob chuckled and went out. The women shook their heads at each other and Dottie took Jacob's place at the counter. 'I'll have a pound of butter, please, Edie, and two pounds of plain flour. Stella and Felix are coming over to tea and I want to make some scones.' She watched as Edie took a slab of butter and cut off exactly a pound. 'You're still not letting Ivy Sweet in, then?'

'She can come in if she wants to,' Edie said carelessly. 'I told George the other day the ban was off. It's up to her where she does her shopping now. Mind you, she went past the other day and to my mind she don't look well. There's a pinched look to her face.'

'I thought that too,' Dottie agreed. 'I saw her getting on the bus this morning and she looked real down in the mouth. Not that she's ever been the cheeriest person in Burracombe.'

'Well, I can't say I've ever got on all that well with Ivy Sweet,' Edie said, 'but I don't wish her any harm. I hope whatever it is that's wrong, it's nothing serious, if only for poor George's sake.'

The subject of their discussion was at that moment dawdling along the main street in Tavistock, her shopping basket over her arm. She had been into International Stores for her groceries and Woolworths for other bits and pieces, and had half an hour to kill before catching the bus back to the village. George had told her that Edie had lifted the ban, so she didn't really need to come into Tavistock at all, but she wasn't going to demean herself by going straight back to Edie Pettifer's shop, as if she was desperate. She'd go in a week or two, but only for a few oddments, and then slowly resume doing her main shopping there. It would do Edie good to think she'd lost Ivy's custom for good.

She walked through the big square to the bridge and then down the slope to the path that led alongside the river. Might as well have a sit-down here on the bench and watch the ducks swimming below the weir. You could see salmon jump here too, if you caught the right moment. Not that Ivy was particularly interested in either ducks or fish, unless they were on a plate, but she and George had come here once or twice in their courting days to see the sight. And quite a sight it had been – shoals of bright silver fish, their scales glinting in the sunlight, flying upwards over the sparkling foam of breaking water. George had got quite excited. He'd been an excitable sort of chap in his youth, she thought, not at all like the quiet, placid man he was now. Mind you, a lot of things had happened since those days. A lot of water had passed under the bridge, she thought, scarcely noticing the aptness of the thought.

It wasn't so much what *had* happened, though, as what hadn't. Kiddies, for instance. They'd both looked forward to a family – two of each, George used to say, so that everyone gets a brother and a sister. Ivy hadn't been quite so sure about giving birth that many times, especially since she'd happened to be present when her Aunt Nellie had had her third a month before it was due, in the middle of Christmas dinner, but there was plenty of time to convince him when she decided she'd had enough. As things turned out, however, she'd never needed to convince him, because until Barry had come along, it looked as if they'd never have any children at all. And there'd never been any sign of another child after Barry, either.

Ivy sighed. She knew perfectly well what the village thought about Barry. They didn't take it out on him, but they looked down their noses at Ivy, thinking they knew the truth when in fact they didn't know a thing. They pitied George, too. And it was so unfair – just as if none of them had ever made a mistake, just as if they were all perfect. And the worst of all were those like Val Ferris and Hilary Napier, and that young hussy Patsy Shillabeer as was. Acting as if they were better than other people, when they'd been no better than they should be, as the saying went. Acting as if they were better than Ivy Sweet, when they knew nothing – nothing at all.

The water broke over the weir in a shower of glittering drops and the ducks floated in the pools below as serenely as white lilies, but Ivy Sweet scarcely saw them. If a thousand salmon had suddenly leapt from the water and flown up over the shimmering river, she would not even have noticed. The bitterness that filled her heart, and the disappointment of her life, left no room for beauty.

Joanna Tozer noticed Ivy sitting on the bench as she walked along the river path with Heather, coming back from the Meadows to finish her shopping and catch the bus back to Burracombe. She hesitated, but unless she turned back and walked through the wharf area, with its warehouses and men working, there was no way of avoiding the other woman, so she shrugged and continued. She was as likely to run into the baker's wife any day in the village anyway, so why try to avoid her now?

Ivy saw her coming and saw the hesitation, guessing correctly what it meant. Fresh bitterness rose in her like sour bile. Who were those Tozers anyway, setting themselves up to be better than anyone else in the village? Joanna wasn't even a local girl – she'd come from Hampshire as a Land Girl during the war and caught the eye of young Tom when he'd been demobbed from the army afterwards. She met Joanna's gaze and held it firmly, determined not to be ignored.

'Hello, Mrs Sweet,' Joanna said as she drew near. 'Heather, say hello to Mrs Sweet.'

The little girl, walking beside her pushchair, said a shy hello and Joanna sat down on the bench beside Ivy. 'You've been shopping, I see.'

'Since that Edie Pettifer won't have me in the village shop, I got to, haven't I,' Ivy retorted. 'Mind you, she's regretting it now, so my George told me. Says I'm welcome back any time I want, but I've got used to coming into Tavi now, so I reckon I'll go on doing it for a bit.'

'I suppose you can get more variety here,' Joanna said vaguely. 'I came in for some fish. Granny fancied a herring for her tea, and she's been off her food a bit lately so we like to give her something to enjoy.'

'Old Mrs Tozer?' Ivy asked, interested. 'Not feeling well, is she?'

'Just a bit off colour,' Joanna said. 'Nothing to worry about, Mother says.'

'Still, she's a good age. Getting on for ninety, isn't she?'

'Next birthday,' Joanna said proudly. 'She really is a marvel. Still helps with the cooking, making cakes and pastry, and it's only these past few months we've been able to persuade her to have a lay-down in the afternoons. You wouldn't think she was anywhere near that age.'

'All the same, nobody lasts for ever,' Ivy persisted. 'She's bound to start failing soon. Or it might come sudden, at that age. I dare say her'll pass away in her sleep one night, just like—' She stopped abruptly, then went on, 'Just like old Zeb Endacott did, over to Horndon.'

Joanna's face was white. 'That wasn't what you were going to say. You were going to say like my baby Suzanne.'

'No, I wasn't! I wasn't going to say that at all. You shouldn't be so quick to jump to conclusions.' Ivy's voice was high and indignant, a little too indignant to ring true. Joanna rose to her feet.

'I'm sorry, Mrs Sweet, but I don't believe you. I'll go now, if you don't mind. I don't want to miss the bus.'

She stalked off up the slope to the road and Ivy watched her with fury boiling in her breast. I never even thought about her baby, she told herself angrily. I was going to say something quite different. I couldn't remember Zeb's name, that's what it was. Nothing to do with her precious baby.

After a few minutes she realised that she was in danger of missing the bus herself. She dragged herself to her feet and picked up her basket. She'd make sure she didn't sit anywhere near Joanna Tozer, anyway.

The bitterness that had been growing in Ivy Sweet for so long became even sharper.

Chapter Fourteen

Joanna had time to walk down to the bus station, so she was on the bus first. She sat near the back, hoping that Ivy Sweet would take the hint and choose one of the seats at the front. To her relief, she saw the frizzy dyed ginger hair amongst the little group waiting by the churchyard wall, and a moment later the baker's wife climbed aboard, took a quick look round and sat down just behind the driver. The other shoppers distributed themselves and their shopping bags and baskets around the bus, near enough to continue their gossip, and the cheerful chatter accompanied them all the way back to Burracombe.

Joanna sat looking out of the window, feeling rather ashamed. She had no real reason to believe that Ivy had been going to mention her lost baby, and even if she had, she'd had the sensitivity to stop herself. There'd been no need to jump down her throat like that.

The trouble was, she still hadn't got over Suzanne's sudden death. She probably never would, not completely. How could you? It might not have been so bad if the baby had been ill, if it had been expected, but when Joanna had laid the twins in their double-ended pram on that Easter Sunday and wheeled them out into the garden, both had been as healthy as any two babies could be. They'd done so well, too, after their premature birth, when it really had seemed to be touch and go for both of them. But once they were over those early weeks, they'd blossomed. And look at Heather now – as rosy-cheeked and lively as the next toddler. That was what Suzanne should have been like, and no doctor had ever been able to tell Joanna why she had died. And that was the worst part, for Joanna would never know if it was because of something she had done, or not done.

'You'm just punishing yourself,' her mother-in-law told her. 'It happens sometimes, for no reason anyone can tell. 'Tis no fault of yours – you're a wonderful mother.'

'But suppose it happens to Heather as well,' Joanna had cried in anguish. 'I couldn't bear to lose them both, Mother. I just feel that if Heather doesn't even know she had a twin, maybe that will keep her safe. I know it doesn't make sense to anyone else, but it's the way I feel.'

She knew that Alice didn't agree with her over that. Neither did Ted, nor Tom, nor Minnie, nor any of the family. But she had been adamant, and after a while they respected her feelings and Suzanne was never mentioned.

Would other people be as sensitive, though? she wondered. People like Ivy Sweet, who had so nearly spoken her name by the river only half an hour ago. Could Joanna really protect her remaining daughter for the whole of her life?

The bus arrived in Burracombe and everyone got off. They were all in a hurry now, with dinners to cook for men who came home from the fields and children home from school. Joanna hoped that Ivy would have gone by the time she helped Heather down and unfolded the pushchair, but the ginger-haired woman had stopped to speak to Aggie Madge. They stepped aside to give Joanna room, and Aggie gave her a nod and a smile and set off for her own cottage.

Ivy looked coldly at Joanna and turned away, but Joanna put out a hand to stop her. Ivy's face tightened.

'I wasn't going to say what you thought,' she said abruptly, and glanced down at Heather, now strapped into her pushchair. 'I know you don't like it mentioned. But there, it's no use me saying nothing. You'll think what you like, and with you Tozers, 'tis always the worst.'

'I'm sorry,' Joanna said, biting back a retort. Really, the woman didn't help matters! 'I just wanted to say I'm sorry. For taking you up so quick,' she added, seeing the surprise on the other woman's face. 'It just upsets me so much. You're a mother yourself, I'm sure you understand. It's not something you ever get over.'

Ivy hesitated. The tight look softened slightly, although her downturned mouth never looked exactly cheerful. She nodded. 'I don't reckon it is. I was as sorry as anyone when I heard about it, don't think I wasn't. But it don't make it easy for others when they got to watch every word they says.'

'I know,' Joanna said. 'I'm sorry.'

Again Ivy hesitated, and it occurred to Joanna that the woman was probably not used to apologies. A lot of people were sharp with her as a matter of course, and although she wasn't exactly friendless, she certainly wasn't popular. Joanna felt a little ashamed, and then reminded herself that it was probably Ivy's own doing. She didn't set out to be friendly.

'Well, we'd better go now anyway,' she said, bending to check that Heather's straps were secure. 'Mother's waiting for things for dinner. Goodbye, Mrs Sweet.'

She walked rapidly away along the road, unsure whether she had done any good by apologising. Ivy was just as likely to think she'd won some sort of battle and go off feeling triumphant. Even more so because Joanna was a Tozer. For some reason, Ivy had always detested them – and especially Alice. The two could never meet without exchanging sarcastic words.

Still, not everyone had to get along, Joanna thought, and in a village it showed more than anywhere else. There were bound to be a few people who rubbed each other up the wrong way. And Ivy Sweet was one who seemed to have that effect on nearly everyone. Perhaps she'd always been like that, even as a little girl. Or perhaps something had happened, long ago, to spoil life for her.

It was a sad way to live, though, and Joanna was uncomfortably aware that she could go the same way herself if she wasn't careful. Keep snapping at people because they don't happen to say the words you want them to say, she told herself, and they'll stop speaking to you at all. And it wasn't just Ivy Sweet – who would be no loss – it was her own friends and even her family.

'Flowers, Mummy,' Heather said, breaking into her thoughts. 'Flowers for Granny.'

Joanna looked down at her daughter, stretching her hands out towards the primroses in the hedgerows, and felt tears sting her eyes. She bent to let Heather out on to the lane.

'Let's pick some to take back,' she said. 'Look, these are easy to reach. Pick them low to the ground so they have nice long stems, and Granny will put them in a jar of water.'

Alice's garden was full of primroses, but the gift of a few, their stems half crushed in a small fist, would be dearer to her than a whole bed of them outside the kitchen door.

'A jar of primroses on the table and fresh herring for tea,' Minnie said, coming down from her afternoon rest later. 'Who could want for any more than that?'

Alice laughed. 'You'm easy to please, Mother! 'Tis a pity not everyone's as content with life as you be.'

'It's the secret of a long life, contentment is,' Minnie observed, settling into her rocking chair. 'You ought to remember that yourself, Alice, instead of worrying yourself sick over our Jackie. She's a young woman now and she'll go her own way, and there's nothing you can do about it, specially with her being thousands of miles away.'

'But that's just it,' Alice said, getting out an enamel canister of oatmeal and sprinkling some on the marble slab beside the range. 'She's thousands of miles away, and her ways seem less and less like ours all the time. Look how she was when she came home – flaunting herself in those slacks, doing her hair up like some film star, smothering her face with make-up. And she's even beginning to sound like an American! I tell you, Mother, us have lost her, and I worry about what's going to happen to her. Us ought never to have let her go, and if your Joe hadn't promised to look after her, Ted and me would have put our foot down.' She rolled the herrings in the oatmeal and got out the big, heavy frying pan. 'We should never have taken notice of him.'

'Joe's done his best,' Minnie began. 'But Jackie's a headstrong girl, always has been.'

'So it's our fault, is it? Ted and me haven't brought her up right, is that what you'm saying?' Alice felt angry tears come to her eyes and brushed them away. 'I don't know what else we could have done. The others all turned out all right.' Even as she said it, she couldn't help remembering Brian and the way he'd upset them all during his recent visit home, and Val, whose behaviour in Egypt had been so disappointing. Only Tom seemed to have gone the way she and Ted had hoped. Maybe that was all you could expect – one out of four. Somehow, she'd imagined better than that.

'Of course I'm not saying that,' Minnie said sharply. 'But some folk are naturally more self-willed than others and got to go their own way. My Joe was one, and your Jackie's another. They see greener grass over the other side of the fence and they got to go and try it out.'

'And what about when they find it's no greener than it is at home?'

'Well, then they come back.' But Minnie knew it was a weak argument and Alice took her up on it immediately.

'Your Joe never came back! Twice you've seen him in all the years since he went away. You've never seen his children, apart from Russell, and you won't see his grandchildren. And that's what Ted and me are so afraid is going to happen with Jackie. She'll marry this man she've got herself engaged to and they'll stop over there and have a family and we'll be lucky if we sets eyes on them once in ten years. How do you think that makes us feel?' She took a handkerchief out of her apron pocket and mopped her eyes.

'I know how it makes you feel,' Minnie said quietly. 'I went through it all myself.'

Alice blew her nose. 'I know, Mother. I'm sorry. It's just that you never showed it much. You just said he'd got to make his own way and 'twasn't for you and Father to interfere. I was never sure how much it really affected you.'

'Well you can be sure now,' Minnie said tightly, 'because it was much the same as how this is affecting you. I almost broke my heart over it, thinking I'd never see him again. I used to lay awake at night imagining him being chased by those Red Indians or eaten alive by bears, and I didn't know how I could carry on. But I had to, didn't I? We were just getting over the First World War. People had lost their sons – you can see their names on the war memorial by the church gate. And anyone that didn't get killed in that went down with that terrible flu. How could I complain? My son was alive and well, even if he had gone off to the other side of the world.' She paused for a moment, her eyes misted with old memories, then added quietly, 'And our Jackie's alive and well too, and you and

Ted have brought her up right, so now what you got to do is let her go. And trust her. Stop thinking of what might happen for the worst. It probably won't.' She smiled suddenly. 'After all, our Joe never did get chased by wild Indians or eaten by a bear, did he?'

Alice smiled too, though her smile was rather wobbly. 'Well not yet, anyway,' she said. 'There's still time!'

They laughed a little shakily, and Joanna came in through the back door with Robin and Heather. 'Hullo, what's the joke?'

'Nothing worth repeating,' Alice said, and went back to her work with the herrings. 'There's some mashed potato in that pan, left over from dinner time. You might make a few potato cakes with it. I always think they go nice with herring.'

Joanna nodded and went to the larder for some flour. She poured a cup of water for each of the children and settled them on the rag rug with Robin's farmyard set. Then she sifted some flour into a mixing bowl and began to work in the mashed potato, with some butter. After a few moments she said, 'I saw Ivy Sweet in Tavi. She looks ever so miserable these days.'

'I don't remember a time when she didn't,' Alice said. 'Born a misery that one was.'

'I don't think that's true,' Minnie said thoughtfully. 'I remember her as a kiddie and a young girl ... Used to come here quite a bit to see our Ted – in fact my hubby thought they'd make a go of it, though I got to admit I wasn't that keen myself. But when she and George were first married, they were happy as larks.'

'Ivy Sweet as happy as a lark?' Joanna said. 'I'd like to have seen that!'

'You remember her,' Minnie said to Alice. 'I know you hadn't been in the village all that long, but she was here your first Christmas with us, and all you young ones used to go to the village hops together. You must have seen quite a bit of her.'

'No more than I could help,' Alice said tersely. 'Me and Ivy never did hit it off. She was always a high-and-mighty sort and thought I was beneath her, being a maid-of-all-work on the farm.'

'Well you soon put her right over that, marrying the farmer's son!' Joanna said with a laugh that stopped short as she caught Alice's eye on her. 'There's no need to look like that. I didn't mean anything by it.'

'Maybe you didn't, but it's not something I like to hear you say. It makes me sound like a gold-digger.'

'That's just ridiculous!' Minnie said sharply. 'Nobody would ever say that. You've made Ted a fine wife and you've been a fine mother, and if you ask me, I think us ought to drop the subject now. Seems as if everyone's a bit on edge this afternoon, and I want to enjoy my herring.'

'And so you shall,' Joanna declared. 'We all will. It's nearly time for the men to come in, so we'd better stop talking and start cooking.'

Ivy had also come home from Tavistock with fish. She had bought three pieces of cod, and when Barry came in from school, she was slicing potatoes to make chips. He went past her without a word, going through to the shop and coming back with a doughnut.

'Don't you go spoiling your tea,' Ivy warned him. 'Anyway, doughnuts are no good in the afternoon, they go stale too quick. Morning goods, that's what they are.'

'I'm starving.' He bit into it, and jam oozed out and ran down his chin. He wiped it into his mouth with a grimy hand.

'Barry! Look at the filth you're putting in your mouth. Go and wash yourself before you take another bite. What have you been doing, anyway?'

'Nothing.' He lifted the doughnut to his mouth again and Ivy slapped it away. It fell on the floor and rolled a few inches, leaving a trail of jam.

'Look at that on my clean floor! Well you can clear it up and then go and have a wash, and don't go through to the shop again. We're having cod and chips for tea and I don't want you stuffing yourself with chips and leaving the fish.'

'I don't *like* fish,' he complained, taking the cloth she handed him and making a few sulky passes at the spilt jam. 'Can I have a biscuit, then?'

'No you can't, and that floor needs more wiping than that. It's all sticky. You'll have to use hot water.' Ivy sighed impatiently. 'Oh give it here, I'll do it meself. Have you got any homework?'

'A bit. Sums mostly.' Miss Kemp didn't believe in homework for the younger children, but she felt that those in the top two years should have the discipline of some, to prepare them for secondary school. Arithmetic in particular was a subject they needed to practise at home, to make sure that they'd understood what they'd been taught in class, and it was good for them to write essays for English, or draw maps for geography, or make lists of kings and queens with their dates for history.

'Well you go and do that before we has our tea, and then we can listen to the wireless together. It's *Meet the Huggetts* tonight.'

'I wanted to listen to *Children's Hour*.'

'Well that doesn't start till five, so you can if you get on with your homework now. Go on, Barry. I'm busy.'

'Can't I just have a biscuit?' he whined. 'School dinner was horrible today. I couldn't eat any of it.'

Ivy doubted that. School dinners were prepared in the school kitchen by Mrs Purdy, and she was an excellent cook. Ivy had often thought the school would do well to open up as a restaurant. Half the village would be there for their dinner.

'There's no need for you to have your dinner there if you don't want to,' she told her son. 'It's meant for children who can't go home. You could come home easy.'

He scowled. 'I wouldn't get time to play.'

'Well, it's your choice. Go on then, you can have a biscuit. Just one, mind. And then go and do your sums, and make sure you do them properly. I don't want Miss Kemp calling me in and saying you'm not trying.'

'It don't matter, do it,' he muttered. 'I won't be there much longer. I'll be in big school.'

'Yes, and you'll find it a bit different there, my handsome. You'll have to toe the line a lot more than you do in Burracombe. They got teachers there who eat tackers like you for breakfast and don't even spit out the lumps. Now get out from under my feet, for pity's sake.'

Barry departed with a biscuit between his teeth and another half concealed in his hand. Ivy thought about telling him she'd seen it but decided to let it go. She was too tired to argue any more.

She rinsed the chips and put them into a pan of cold water. The fat that stayed in the big chip pan, going solid after each use, was heating on the stove, and by the time the water was boiling, it was ready. She drained the chips and dried them on a tea towel, then tipped them into the hot fat and listened to the satisfying sizzle. She already had more fat heating in another pan, and she dipped the cod into a bowl of batter and then put them in the pan. As they cooked, she laid the kitchen table and filled the kettle for tea.

Ivy had carried out these tasks so often that she could do them without really thinking about them. As she worked, her mind was occupied with the problem that was looming larger and larger these days. I'll have to decide what to do soon, she thought, and felt the familiar mixture of fear and guilt settle in a heavy load on her shoulders. It was like being between the devil and the deep blue sea, and she really didn't know what she should do.

Chapter Fifteen

For weeks now, the general election had occupied attention everywhere – in the newspapers, which had finally begun to appear again at the end of April after their month-long silence, on the wireless and on television. Quite a few families in Burracombe now had sets – the Warrens, of course, the Latimers, Basil and Grace Harvey and even Jessie and Jeanie Friend, who thought it would be nice for Billy to watch cowboy films. They invited their cousin Dottie in to see it sometimes, but she wasn't keen. She said it was like having strangers in your living room who wanted everyone to listen to them all the time and weren't a bit interested in you, or in village affairs. Edie Pettifer liked it, though, and said Bert Foster was thinking of getting one, so they could watch it together on Saturday evenings.

'I thought he always came in to you for supper on Saturdays,' Jeanie said, handing her a cup of tea as *Come Dancing* began. 'Don't you play cards or something? You won't want to sit staring at a box all night.'

'He might come to me on a different evening, then,' Edie said. 'Us don't have to make it just once a week, do us? Anyway, he's not sure he's getting one. You have to have a licence or something. I don't know how you go about getting that.'

'Mr Beckerleg would tell you,' Jessie said. 'He's selling television sets in his shop, corner of King Street in Tavi. He rents 'em out too, if people don't want to buy. I reckon that'd be the best way to do it, then if you don't go much on it you can send it back.'

'I'd be sending it back soon enough if it went on being election broadcasts all the time,' Edie commented. 'Did you see the one Mr Eden did the other night? Half an hour long it was, so Mrs Warren was saying in the shop, and all about politicians arguing the toss with the newspaper editors. Mind you, that strike did put a lot of people out. They couldn't even tell us about him being made prime minister after Mr Churchill stepped down. I like a bit of entertainment, not men up in London who don't even know Burracombe exists going on about how to run the country.'

'They'll stop once they've had the election,' Jessie said, helping herself to a ginger biscuit. 'They'll go back to their offices and Parliament and us won't hear anything much of them.'

'I don't know so much,' Jeanie said thoughtfully. 'I think they'll be on television as much as they can manage. It's a good way of getting votes, and that's all they're interested in, when it comes down to it. And it could be better than the newspapers for telling us what's going on in the world. Like having Pathé Pictorial.' She gazed at the screen. 'Look at the lovely dress that girl's wearing! And the man just said she and her mum sewed on all those hundreds of sequins themselves. They must have been working on it for months.' She sighed. 'I wish we could see the colour, but I don't suppose they'll ever manage to do that.'

The general election was held on 26 May. Everyone went to the village hall to vote. The member for Tavistock was Henry Studholme, who had been in since 1942 and was expected to retain his seat easily – indeed, as Ted Tozer remarked as he and Alice walked down to cast their vote, it was so certain, it was hardly worth anyone going.

'If we didn't, he wouldn't get in,' Alice began, then noticed the look Ted always had on his face when he was pulling someone's leg, and gave his arm a shake. 'Oh you!'

Not everyone wanted the Conservatives to win. Terry and Bob, both members of the electricians' union, which had played a large part in bringing about the newspaper strike, were hoping that Clem Attlee would be the next prime minister. But Labour had been split by Aneurin Bevan into two factions – the Bevanites and the Gaitskellites – and a split party was weakened. 'United we stand, divided we fall,' Bob intoned gloomily. Not that Terry could vote anyway, being under twenty-one.

'Daft, I call it,' he grumbled. 'Here I am, married and got a baby, and old enough to go and fight in the army, but I can't put a cross on a bit of paper and say who's going to tell me what to do. Well, old Studholme had better look out at the next election, that's all, because I'll be voting then all right.'

He and Patsy were still thinking hard about whether to take up Ann's offer. One day they said yes, they would, and the next they couldn't think of anything worse. In the end, they told Ann they would go over for Sunday dinner the weekend after the election and give her their answer. To take their minds off it, they left Rosie with Nancy and went to the Carlton cinema in Tavistock on Saturday night to see the new film *The Dam Busters*. The next day, with the powerful music still in their heads, they walked across the Clam and up the lane towards the Shillabeer farm.

They met Ann Shillabeer coming out of church with the rest of her family. Ben, who would be starting at big school in Tavistock after the summer holidays, was wearing the new blazer and grey shorts that had been bought as school uniform, although Ann hadn't yet sewn the school badge on his blazer pocket. Iris and Milly were dressed in flowery cotton frocks that Ann had made from the end of a roll of material she'd bought cheap in the market, and Denny was in grey shorts like his brother's and a yellow Aertex shirt with a grey cardigan over the top. Their hair had been brushed and their faces scrubbed till they shone.

'Hello, Mum,' Patsy said, giving her mother a kiss. 'Was it a nice service?'

'It was. Mr Copley gave us a lovely sermon, all about trees and flowers and birds. And how's my pretty little bird, then?' she asked, bending into the pram. 'Look at you, sitting up so strong and smiling round at everything. The dear of her!'

They walked on together, discussing the general election. Henry Studholme had got in again, as expected, and Mr Eden was forming a new Conservative government, again as expected. That said, there didn't seem to be much else to say. Things would probably go on in the same old way, some better and some worse, and nothing anyone in Burracombe might do would alter that. Village affairs were much more interesting.

'How are they getting on at the Barton?' Ann asked. 'Sorting things out, are they?'

'They're planning a new kitchen. It's going to be lovely – all modern, with nice cupboards and a big new refrigerator as well as the larder, and a washing machine, and Miss Hilary's even talking about a machine that washes dishes! Mrs Curnow won't know herself. She's half afraid she'll be out of a job.'

'And what about young Brenda Culliford, is she doing a proper job? You never know with they Cullifords.'

'Yes, she's a good little worker and it means I can go part-time. I still take Rosie, of course. She sits in her pram in the hallway and she's no trouble at all. Once the kitchen's finished, there'll be plenty of space there for her.'

'She'll be crawling by then,' Ann observed. 'That won't be so easy.'

Terry, who had been listening to Ben's talk of the village cricket match held the day before, said, 'Mother says I was crawling by the time I was eight months old. Into everything, she says I was.'

'There you are then,' Ann said. 'It won't be so easy taking her to the Barton when her gets to that stage.'

They walked on towards the farm, passing the little birch wood where Patsy used to play as a child. It was full of bluebells, lit to a deep sea-blue by the sun as it shone down through the pale green tracery of the trees and fading to a soft blue-green mist as you looked through the silver trunks. There were still patches of primroses and violets between the carpet of bluebells, and Patsy laughed as a family of baby rabbits, grazing at the side of the lane ahead, sat up suddenly, their ears quivering, and then scampered across the lane and into the high Devon bank ahead.

'It's lovely to be able to come here like this, all of us together,' she said. 'Burracombe's a good village, with all the shops and everything, but it's so much bigger, you hardly ever see rabbits in the hedgerows. Not till you get past the cottages, anyway.'

'I don't know that you see them in the middle of Little Burracombe, where the post office and the village shop and the hall are, come to that,' Ann said, as if trying to be fair, but there was a note of hope in her voice and she cast her daughter a quick glance.

'But if it's seeing rabbits out and about that you want, you couldn't come to a better place. All over the farm they are – your father never stopped complaining about them.'

The smell of roast lamb greeted them as they came to the farm-house door. Ann went immediately to the kitchen, tying a pinafore round her waist, to see that it wasn't overcooked, and put the potatoes on to parboil. Patsy shooed the children upstairs to change out of their Sunday clothes and Terry went to the back kitchen to draw himself a glass of cider from the cask Ann now kept there.

'I've made a plum crumble for afters,' she said to Patsy. 'There's a couple of jars left from those I bottled last year need using up before the next crop comes along. You could do the custard, if you don't mind, and get Iris down to lay the table. She's bound to have her nose stuck in a book, and if there's one thing I can't abide, it's reading when there's so many jobs to be done.'

Patsy smiled and went to root her sister out from the bedroom she and Milly shared. As Ann had suspected, Patsy's sister was lying on her bed with a book open on the pillow in front of her. Patsy went over and looked at it.

'*The Wind in the Willows*. I always liked that book too. I read it over and over again. I liked the bit where they find Mole's home best, when the carol-singers come and they have a party.'

Iris rolled over and looked up at her. 'Are you and Terry and Rosie going to come and live here?'

'That's what we've come to talk to Mum about,' Patsy said. 'What do you think about it?'

'I think it would be nice. Me and Milly could help look after Rosie all the time then.'

'What about Ben and Denny? D'you think they want another girl living here?'

'Course they do! It's our Rosie! She *belongs* here.'

Patsy looked at her thoughtfully. 'It might not be that easy.'

'Don't see why not,' Iris said, and turned back to her book.

Patsy reached out and closed it. 'Mum wants you to come and lay the table. Come on now – the sooner we have dinner, the sooner me and Terry can talk to her and decide, and then we can tell you.'

'Can't I help decide?'

'No, you can't. You can take the others out to play while we talk.'
It struck Patsy suddenly that not so long ago she had thought of
herself as one of the older children, along with Iris and Ben. Now
she had become a grown-up, making grown-up decisions and sending the little ones outside. For a moment she felt frightened by the
change, which had come so swiftly. And all because I'm a mother
myself now, she thought. All because me and Terry fell in love and
Father wouldn't let us see each other. If he had, I'd still be living
here now, walking out with my young man on Sundays, going to
the pictures or the local village hop on Saturdays and not thinking
of marriage or babies for years.

Instead, she was about to make a decision that would affect all
their lives.

Stella had noticed Patsy and Terry coming along the lane as she
left the church to hurry back to the vicarage to prepare her own
Sunday dinner. Felix, still standing at the door chatting to members of the congregation, would be at least another half-hour. She'd
smiled and waved, but, seeing Ann and the children with them, had
not stopped to talk. Their family time was precious to them, she
thought, after all they had been through, and she wondered if Patsy
and Terry had come to any decision about their future. Patsy had
told her about Ann's proposition a week or so ago, when Stella had
called at the Barton to see Hilary, and she thought that it would be
a good thing for the family to be together, provided that the new
arrangement suited Terry himself.

Her own future with Felix seemed to be rosy at the moment,
although no one knew better than Stella how life could change in an
instant. She had tried hard to forget that terrible night when Felix's
car had run into some ponies on the moor. It had been dark and
icy, and the ponies almost invisible as he met them on the Devil's
Elbow bend near Princetown. Devil's Elbow was a good name for
it, she thought with a shudder. It was almost as if Felix had been
given a sharp nudge as he drove, sending him into a skid that killed
one pony and almost killed her as well. The weeks and months that
had followed were a murky period of pain and fear – fear that she
might never walk again, fear that she could never be a true wife to

Felix. I almost drove him away, she thought as she went into the vicarage kitchen. I almost lost everything.

But it was all over now, leaving her with only a slight limp, and they were here in their own home, awaiting the birth of their first child. It seemed as if nothing could go wrong ever again – but Stella was on guard now against complacency. You never knew what was around the corner, she thought as she peeped into the oven to see that the beef was roasting nicely, and began to mix the batter for Yorkshire puddings. The important thing was to take each day as a blessed gift.

Felix arrived just as she was laying the table. Most of the week they ate in the kitchen, with the door open to the garden in summer and the warmth of the big range cooker in winter, but on Sundays she felt they ought to use the dining room. She didn't like it much – it was large and rather gloomy, its walls papered with a tangled pattern of overblown chrysanthemums (not Stella's favourite flower) in shades of dirty brown, and its windows looking out into an overgrown part of the shrubbery. Felix had cut back some of the bushes, which seemed determined to get into the house, but it really needed more ruthless attention. Perhaps I could tackle it once the baby's born, Stella thought, and we might redecorate the room then, with something lighter and prettier.

'Let me do that,' he said, taking the bundle of knives and forks from her hand. 'You ought to be resting.'

'I can't rest all the time,' she said, relinquishing the cutlery. 'I've got a meal to cook. I'll put my feet up after dinner. Anyway,' she added wickedly, 'I had a nice sleep during your sermon.'

'What an example to my parishioners,' he said. 'I'll shout louder next week. There'll be no more dozing off in my church. Now, would you like a glass of elderflower before we eat?'

'Yes please. And you have your sherry.' This had been their weekly treat – a sherry before Sunday dinner – but Stella had given it up as soon as she knew she was pregnant. 'Isn't it lovely to have lunch on our own at home for once? Usually we're either invited somewhere else or Dottie's here. Not that I don't love having Dottie, but it is nice to be by ourselves once in a while.'

'I know. Mrs Lydiard tried very hard to get us to go to them, but I managed to fend her off. We won't have all that many more Sundays before the baby's born, and then everything's going to be different.'

'It is,' she agreed, and as they turned to go back to the kitchen, Felix slipped his arm around her waist.

'Different – and wonderful.'

Chapter Sixteen

'So what's it to be?' Ann asked when at last dinner was over, the dishes done and the children sent out to play. 'Have you made up your minds?'

Her voice was tense and a little abrupt. Patsy, who was making a pot of tea, gave Terry a small warning frown. 'She don't mean to sound like that,' she whispered as he came out of the pantry with a jug of milk. 'She's just worried.'

'Let's hope she's not more worried when we've told her,' he muttered, and put the jug on Ann's old tin tray with the cups and saucers to carry it through to the living room. Patsy followed with the teapot and set it down in the hearth to draw, then brought the pram through from the kitchen.

'Well?' Ann asked again. 'You promised you'd tell me today.'

'And so us will,' Patsy assured her. 'But let's get a cup of tea in our hands first. And I'll have to give Rosie her afternoon feed soon, too. But we can talk while I'm doing that. Oh, Terry, I've forgotten the strainer – go and fetch it for me, would you?'

She poured milk into the cups and, when Terry brought the strainer, added the tea. Ann accepted her cup and waited with barely concealed impatience while Patsy peeped at the baby and then picked up her own cup and sat down.

'I'm sorry, I'm all on edge. Only I've been tossing and turning all night, wondering what you'd decided.' Ann's eyes were fixed on her daughter's face. 'For pity's sake, put me out of my misery!'

Patsy laughed a little. 'Come on, Mother, it's not that bad. You'm not in a court of law, you know! But there's been a lot for me and Terry to weigh up. Us couldn't make up our minds all at once.'

'But you have now?' Ann's voice was edged with anxiety.

Patsy glanced at her husband. 'Go on, Terry.'

Terry cleared his throat, then took a gulp of tea. He sent Patsy an imploring look and she nodded encouragingly. As if marching to his doom, he set his cup on a small table beside his chair and began. 'It's like Patsy says, Mrs Shilla— I mean, Mother. There's been a lot to think about. I still got my apprenticeship to finish, and then there's National Service, if they'm still doing it by then. I couldn't do full-time farm work for at least three years, maybe five or six. Seems to me you need someone now.'

'That's right, I do. Miss Napier's been sending Arthur Culliford over three days a week or so to help out, but that's out of the kindness of her heart – she must want him on one of her own farms. And like I said, you can never be sure of they Cullifords. Not that he hasn't put himself into it while he's been here – tell you the truth, I've been pleasantly surprised – but it's someone permanent I need. And it's not just the help round the farm, it's our Patsy here, she knows what's what with the animals and crops and such. I always hoped her'd stop home anyway to help her father out in that way, and I reckon he did too. And since the two of you and dear little Rosie need somewhere to live – well, it seemed ideal to me. I still can't properly see what there is to think about.'

'I told you,' Terry said patiently. 'There's my apprenticeship and National Service, if I has to do it. But it's not just that.' He paused. 'The thing is, I don't see I'm cut out to be a farmer. I've never really wanted it. I like being an electrician, I really do. It's interesting. And me and our Bob – well, us have been talking for a long time about setting up on our own in a few years' time. It's been pretty well settled between us. I don't want to let him down and I don't want to give up the idea anyway.'

Ann stared at him. Her lips quivered a little and her eyes moistened. She turned to Patsy.

'So you'm saying no, then?'

'No, Mother, we're not – don't look like that. Terry's just telling you what we've had to consider. And there's other things too.' She paused. 'There's Ben, and Denny. They might want to take it on theirselves when they'm older. It don't seem right for me and Terry to come in over their heads.'

'Ben's barely twelve years old.'

'But he'll be seventeen by the time Terry's finished his apprenticeship and done his National Service, if he has to do it, and he'll probably be leaving school at fifteen. It's not so far away, Mother.'

Ann sighed and chewed her lip. 'So what *are* you saying?' she asked at last.

Patsy leaned forward a little. 'Suppose we come to live here, like you want. I'll help you with everything and I'll do the farm accounts and all the other things you want me to do. Terry can go on with his apprenticeship and all that, and if he and Bob still want to set up their business together in a few years, they can do that, but us'll stay here and be a family if you still want us.'

'Of course I still want you. I want it more than anything. But it means Terry won't be helping round the farm, and we need that too. I need someone full-time, Patsy.'

'Have Arthur Culliford, then,' Patsy said. 'Look, if Terry's bringing in some money and the farm's doing well, we'll be able to afford it. You're paying Arthur three days a week as it is. Another two and a half isn't going to break us.'

'No ...' Ann pressed her lips tightly together, her face doubtful. 'I don't know, Patsy ...'

'Why not give it a try?' Patsy suggested. 'We'd *like* to live here, wouldn't we, Terry? You're right about Jack and Nancy's cottage – it's too small for us all, especially now we got Rosie.' As if she had heard her name, the baby murmured in her pram. 'And Terry'd help round the place when he's at home. He's not going to sit about letting other folk do the work, he's not that sort. You never know, you might make a farmer of him yet!'

'And the other boys are growing too,' Ann said slowly, as if she was coming round to the idea. 'You'm right, Ben's getting quite handy now he's bigger. Well, all right, if that's the way you want it, that's the way it had better be.' Her smile belied her apparently grudging agreement. 'I must say, it'll be a real joy to have you all here, and that's the truth.'

'Oh Mother!' Patsy jumped up, almost knocking over the little table, and knelt beside her mother to throw her arms around her.

For a moment they clung together, both weeping a little, then she drew back and laughed. 'Look at us! You'd think we'd had bad news. Are you really sure you want us?'

'Of course I do! And the little'ns will be tickled pink. Shall we call them in and tell them?' Ann's face was glowing now and her eyes bright. She began to get up.

'Let's finish our tea first. And Rosie wants hers too.' The murmurs from the pram were beginning to develop into complaints. 'There's plenty of time, and there's still a lot to decide – like when we'll move over, and what we're going to do about bedrooms and things. But if you're really happy about it, I don't see why it can't be quite soon.'

'The sooner the better,' Ann declared, pouring more tea. 'Oh Patsy, I can't tell you how happy you've made me. I've been so worried. And you too, Terry.' She got up and went over to kiss him. 'It'll be a real pleasure to have you here. And I've just thought of something else, too.'

'What's that, Mother?'

'The electric light bulb in the back kitchen has blown,' she said. 'I meant to put a new one in, but I forgot. But now I've got a real live electrician on the premises, I don't need to bother!'

'You reckon they really have decided to go over to the Shillabeer place then?' Bob asked his parents as they sat at their Sunday dinner. 'You sure that's what our Terry meant?'

Nancy nodded. 'He wouldn't say straight out, said they ought to talk it over with Ann Shillabeer first to be sure she were happy about it all, but that's what it sounded like to me. You'll be able to have your bedroom back, Bob.'

He grunted. 'I'm not so worried about that as about what Terry's going to do about his apprenticeship. And what happens after that. You know him and me wanted to set up together in a few years.'

'He'll have to finish his apprenticeship,' Jack observed, helping himself to more roast potatoes. 'I don't think you got cause to worry, Bob. He's not cut out to be a farmer.'

'But if they'm going to *live* over there ... He can't stay idle when there's work to be done around the place. Next thing, he'll be helping out with the milking, and then he'll be telling me he can't do

125

his electrical work because they got a cow sick or summat.' Bob stared dismally at his plate. 'Tell you what, I reckon I'd better start looking round for another partner.'

'Don't do that, Bob!' Nancy said sharply. 'You don't know what he's got in mind. Wait till they've had their talk with Mrs Shillabeer. He'll tell us all about it then.'

'And why couldn't he tell us before?' Bob burst out. 'Don't we matter too? Don't *I* matter? I got him that apprenticeship. It's my reputation he's playing about with, as well as his. If old man Wedderburn gets the idea he's going to be let down by our Terry, he'll not trust me neither. And look at the trouble it'll cause if he tries to get out of it early. I'm beginning to wish I'd never bothered.'

'You're being very unfair,' his mother told him. 'You don't know what Terry's going to do, but whatever he does, he won't be letting anyone down. And he'll tell us all the minute it's decided. It's not as if he hasn't talked it over with us; we've gone over and over it till we're all blue in the face. But 'tis his decision, his and Patsy's, and us got to respect that. Now eat up your food before it goes cold.'

They ate in silence for a few minutes. Nancy collected up the plates and took them to the little scullery, then brought in a large dish of queen of puddings. It was one of Bob's favourites, but even the sight of the crispy meringue topping failed to light his eyes up now.

'Come on, Bob, stop worrying,' Nancy said, spooning out a large helping and handing Jack his bowl. 'You'll know soon enough. Are the others coming round for a skiffle practice this afternoon?' She gave Bob a bowl of pudding too and he poked his spoon in and lifted it to his mouth.

'Supposed to be. We're playing at a dance over at Mary Tavy next Saturday, and we're practising for the summer fair as well.'

'Well, that's good. You're doing quite well with your bits and pieces of old tea-chests and washboards and stuff. Who'd have ever thought folk could make music with a lot of rubbish their mothers were chucking out?'

'That's if you call it music,' Jack said, hoping to get some kind of response from his son, even if it was only an indignant one.

'I dunno,' Bob said, still playing with his pudding rather than eating it. 'It might all fold up before the summer fair anyway. Roy

Nethercott's got a girl now, over to Little Burracombe, and he don't seem so keen any more.'

He still spoke in a gloomy tone and his mother shook her head in exasperation.

'Well, if you'm determined to look on the black side, there's nothing we can do about it. Jack, you'll have some seconds, won't you?'

'I thought you'd never ask.' He held out his bowl. 'And then if you boys are going to be turning me out of my own shed for the afternoon, I reckon I'll go over to the new teacher's place. He wants me and Jacob Prout to help him put some new fencing posts in.'

'He seems to be settling in pretty well, don't he?' Nancy said. 'Making that little cottage look like a new pin, so they tell me. Quite friendly with Miss Kemp too, so I hear.'

'I dunno about that. I was round the school house on Friday, cutting back the hedge a bit, and he came to bring her some papers about the school. I thought they were a bit cool with each other.'

'Lovers' tiff!' Nancy said with a laugh, and Bob snorted.

'Lovers! Two teachers their age? Don't be daft.'

'And don't you be cheeky,' she told him. 'Miss Kemp's not that old. About my age, I reckon, and he's no older. People still have feelings even at that age, young man.'

Bob shrugged. 'All right, no need to bite my head off. Don't seem as if I can say a thing right round here. I've had enough to eat, Mother, so if you don't mind I'll go down the shed now and do a bit of practising on me own before the others come.'

He got up and walked out. Jack and Nancy looked at each other and shook their heads.

'He must be really upset,' Nancy said. 'Look, he never even finished his pudding. I tell you, Jack, it's time our Terry put us all out of our misery. Until he does, none of us is going to have any peace.'

Chapter Seventeen

Frances Kemp was spending the afternoon in her garden. The azaleas were just breaking their buds and would soon be a blaze of lemon, crimson and pink, like a day-long sunset in her hedge. The apple tree was smothered in snowy rose-tinged blossom and the border beside her lawn was filled with pansies and primulas of all colours, like a kaleidoscope to dazzle the eyes.

Frances had just finished weeding. Her policy was to cram as many flowers as possible into every space, leaving no room for weeds, but still some managed to get through and she fought a constant battle again the hairy bittercress that seemed able to fire its seeds off like a machine gun and spread everywhere. Jacob Prout had told her once that you could eat it and she should treat it as a crop, but Frances had never quite been able to do that.

She fetched a deckchair from the garden shed and then went indoors to pour a glass of water and pick up her library book. It was *The Heart of the Family* by one of her favourite authors, Elizabeth Goudge, the third of a trilogy about a family living near Buckler's Hard in the New Forest. Frances remembered the area from her childhood, and she settled in her deckchair, hoping that she would soon be lost in that magical place with the family she now felt she knew so well.

But for once Damerosehay and the Eliot family failed to hold her. After a while, feeling that she was wasting the pleasure the book ought to be giving her, she laid it down and lifted her face to the sun, closing her eyes so that she could see the pink light that had so fascinated her as a child.

The past seemed to be all around her. It had been like this ever since she had come out of church this morning and paused by the war memorial beside the gate. She never walked past without giving it at least a glance, but this morning there had been nobody near her at that moment and she had stopped to look at the names. At one name in particular.

Ralph Stannard. Died 1918.

Ralph, she thought, with a sudden, familiar wave of longing. Oh Ralph ...

It was Ralph's photograph that she looked at every night before she got into bed, touching his face with a gentle forefinger. Ralph for whom she had waited as a young girl, deeply in love for the first and only time. Ralph for whom she sometimes thought she still waited.

Suppose he hadn't been killed at all?

Died, the telegram had said. Died of his wounds, 25 March 1918. But there was always that tiny doubt, that nagging question, that a mistake had been made, that it might not have been him, that he might somehow have escaped and still be alive somewhere. Perhaps wandering still, a bewildered tramp who had lost his way amidst the battlefields of France; perhaps taken in by some compassionate family, tended and looked after and persuaded to stay ...

No, he would never have done that. Not the Ralph she knew, her upright cousin who would never cheat in the smallest way at any game, who was as brave as a lion, who had endured so much in that terrible war.

No. If he had survived, he would have come back to her as he had promised. She knew that it was her own yearning that caused the occasional doubt; she knew he had been killed.

So why did she still wait?

There are thousands of women like me, she thought. Probably millions, who lost their man during that war and never found another. Some of them married someone else, it was true, and most of those probably lived and were still living happy, fulfilled lives. But there just weren't enough young men for all the women who had waited. So few had come home, and of those the influenza epidemic had taken even more. The surplus women, women without sweetheart or husband and without much hope of ever finding one, far outnumbered the men available. So many of them had remained single, either from choice or from lack of opportunity, and Frances Kemp was one of them.

Sitting in the garden on that late May afternoon, listening to the birds as they flew busily about their nests, she thought of the vow she had made all those years ago, a girl of nineteen at the threshold of life, engaged to marry her cousin – not a first cousin, for it was their fathers who had been cousins – and then losing him so near the end of that cruel, brutal war. Not that she had known then that it would end in a few months; as far as she could see, it would drag on for another four or five years, killing more and more young men until there were none left anywhere to kill. Until there were only old men sitting at home staring at the destruction their quarrels had caused, and still harbouring bitterness in their hearts.

She remembered her outburst when Ralph had tried to make her see that he must join up. 'Everyone wants us to win this war,' he'd said, 'and the only way it can be done is by every man possible going to fight.'

'But it shouldn't be like that!' she had cried passionately, turning so quickly that she swayed and he caught her against him. 'Why do all the men – all the *young* men – have to be killed to satisfy a quarrel they have no part in? It's such a waste! All the work they would have done, the lives they would have lived ... Men like you and Johnny, men like Herbert, with your lives just ripped away as if they don't matter ... As if *you* don't matter ...' She stepped away into the darkness, then turned swiftly and returned to beat her fists against him. 'Don't they realise, all those politicians who decide these things, what they're throwing away? It's our future – the children we'll never have, the grandchildren who will never be born. There won't be anyone left to run the country and look after us all. Everything's being taken away – everything will be gone.'

She had not known then how true her words would turn out to be. Ralph, her brother Johnny, their friend Herbert, who had marched away so blithely to be a hero – all dead. She remembered wondering, over and over again, what it must have been like for Ralph, for Herbert, for all those men whose lives had been taken over by a war they barely understood and had no real part in, other than to kill and be killed. To become, she had thought, nothing but numbers, so that one day other men could sit down and count those left alive and decide who had been the winner. Like a boys' game of soldiers, played on the carpet on a rainy afternoon, until it was time for tea.

Except that for hundreds of thousands of those men, it would never again be time for tea.

Since then, Frances had seen another world war. She had seen more young men march off to fight, never to return; more girls left behind to wait and hope and, all too often, to mourn. She knew now that it had all been far more complex than her simple view of it as a young girl, but the tragedy, the pity of, it was still almost impossible to absorb. There must be a better way.

Instead, it seemed there was a worse. Since the Second World War had been finally ended by the atomic bombs over Hiroshima and Nagasaki, the world had lived under an even more terrible threat. Today, in peaceful Burracombe, it seemed inconceivable that such events could take place here, yet with the seemingly endless Cold War existing between America and Russia, the whole world could be drawn into a third and even more devastating war, and once again there would be nothing that ordinary people – those who were ultimately most affected – could do about it.

We should make the most of the lives we have, Frances thought, opening her eyes to look at the tender blue of the sky, the fresh green of the grass and the hawthorn hedge, the vivid colours of the azalea buds and the creamy blossom of the apple tree. And she wondered, suddenly – have I done that?

She had made a vow, on that Easter Day in 1918, that she would return to Burracombe, to live and work as she and Ralph had planned. Had she kept her vow?

I came back, she thought, closing her eyes again. I came back at the first opportunity, even though your family had left by then and few of the villagers remembered me as the young girl who used to come for holidays. I've lived and worked here, as we said we would. But have I lived my life as you would have wanted? Have I been as frozen as the two countries who cannot forget their differences and have prevented the world from living in peace?

'Frances.'

The voice seemed to come directly from the past. A deep shiver ran through her entire body. The world seemed to tilt dangerously and she felt as if all time was spread out beneath her and she was swinging back thirty-seven years. Almost afraid of what – or whom – she might see, she slowly opened her eyes and looked into the dark brown eyes of James Raynor.

'I'm sorry,' he said. 'Were you asleep? I shouldn't have disturbed you.'

Frances stared at him. The world straightened itself and she found herself safely back in her deckchair, in her own small garden. She shook her head a little and struggled to sit up.

'Don't worry,' he said, putting out a hand. 'I'll go – I shouldn't have come bothering you on a Sunday afternoon. You must have been sound asleep; you look completely bemused.'

'No.' Frances brushed her hand across her hair. 'I don't think I was asleep. Just thinking. But perhaps I was beginning to dream a little.'

'Pleasant dreams, I hope.'

She looked at him. 'Not very pleasant, no. Not the sort one ought to dream on such a lovely afternoon.' She sat up straight. 'Don't go, James. I'll fetch another chair and make a cup of tea, or some lemonade. And I baked some rock buns an hour or so ago – they'll be just right now.'

'I'll sit here,' he said, indicating the garden bench Jacob Prout had made her once out of the trunk of a fallen tree. 'But let me help you first.'

'No – there's hardly anything to do.'

She went into the cool kitchen, needing time to come fully to her senses. She had been so lost in her memories and her thoughts that she felt as if she had been transported to the past and that Ralph was close beside her. She really had expected to see his face when she had heard her name spoken and opened her eyes.

Instead, it had been James Raynor. And a different sensation had clutched her heart.

'Mother wanted us to stay to tea as well,' Patsy said as the family gathered round the table again. 'But we thought you were expecting us back here.'

'So we were,' Nancy said, coming in with the big brown teapot.

132

'Make room in the middle there, someone. I don't know who moved those scones after I'd left a gap specially.'

'Sorry, Mother, that was me.' Terry lifted the plate of scones, still warm from the oven, and inserted them between a pile of bread and butter and a fruit cake. 'Only they look so good, I thought I'd have one to start.'

'Oh did you now? And how many times have I told you to start your tea with bread and fish paste, or Marmite? Anyway, there's a bit of ham salad to begin with, so you can have that. Here, Patsy, pass the plates round, if you don't mind.'

They settled down to their tea. Jack began to talk about the help he'd been giving James Raynor that afternoon, and Bob, when pressed, mumbled a few words about the skiffle group. The fence hadn't taken more than an hour with three of them working on it, and Jack had gone back with Jacob Prout to inspect his roses, which looked like doing well this summer, while Mr Raynor had gone off for a walk. Bob, in his turn, admitted that the afternoon's skiffle practice had gone quite well and they had mastered a new song that Roy had written. Between them they'd hammered out a passable sort of tune and Brenda had made a good job of singing it. It might even, he said with reluctant pride, be a bit of a hit.

'What, in Tin Pan Alley?' Terry asked with a grin, but when Bob gave him a scowl, he added in an injured tone, 'What's the matter? What did I say wrong?'

'It's not what you've said,' Bob told him. 'It's what you haven't said. Sitting there like a blooming Buddha.'

'A *Buddha*? Whatever be you talking about?'

'All smug and smiling, like you know the secrets of the world and the rest of us got to find out by ourselves. Come on, out with it. Can't you see we'm all waiting? What have you and Patsy decided to do about the farm?'

'Well, I dunno nothing about Buddhas,' Terry said. 'I didn't know you did, neither. But as to what me and Patsy have decided – well, we reckon it makes sense to do what Ann asked us and go over there to live.' He glanced apologetically at his mother. 'I'm sorry, Mum, I know you like having Rosie here, but there isn't really room for two families. Us would have had to move out sometime,

133

and this way we get a nice big farmhouse to live in and other kiddies for Rosie to play with and—'

'And a job for life as a farmer,' Bob cut in. 'All handed to you on a plate. Well I wish you joy of it, Terry. And you don't need to worry about the plans we had, you and me, because I'll have no trouble finding someone else to set up with. There's plenty of young blokes who'll jump at the chance.' He began to get up. 'I won't have no cake, Mother. I've lost me appetite all of a sudden.'

'Bob!' Nancy said sharply, as Terry stared in astonishment. 'Sit down. Terry's only told us half of it so far. The least you can do is hear him out.'

'I don't need to,' he growled, doing his mother's bidding nevertheless. 'I know what he's going to say.'

'And that's where you're wrong,' Patsy said. 'Tell him, Terry.'

In a few short sentences, Terry outlined the conclusions he, Patsy and Ann had come to that afternoon. 'So you see, I won't be giving up me trade and I won't be giving up any idea of setting up with you. We got to make sure Arthur Culliford's interested in full-time work and Miss Hilary don't have no objection to letting him go—'

'Objection?' Jack butted in. 'Her'll be over the moon! Only took him on out of the kindness of her heart. Mind you, he do seem to have turned over a new leaf, so he might do all right for you.'

'Well, even if he don't want to work for us, we won't have much problem finding someone else. But you and me can go on just as we planned, once I've done me time.'

There was a short silence. Bob gave his brother a searching look and Terry met his eyes squarely. Then he turned to Patsy.

'And that's all right with you too? You'll be happy with our Terry carrying on as an electrician?'

'Course I am. I'm proud of him, and I'll be even prouder when you and him are driving round in a little van with *Pettifer Electrics* painted on the side.'

Bob blinked. 'Blimey, I haven't got that far yet.'

'Well, you'll have to. If you'm setting up in business, you got to have a proper vehicle and a proper name. You'll need someone to do your books too – accounts and that.' She smiled. 'Since I'll be doing all that for the farm, I might as well do yours too.'

'There you are, Bob,' Nancy said. 'That's the best offer you'll

134

get today, and I got to say I'm pleased it's all turned out this way, aren't you, Jack?'

'I am,' he said. 'Looks like you two have got your heads screwed on the right way after all. As long as Ann's happy, I reckon we all are.'

'And now, Bob,' Nancy said, turning to her elder son, 'you can stop sitting there like the cat's got your tongue and have a piece of my fruit cake. I dare say you've got your appetite back now, haven't you?'

'I reckon I have, at that,' he said, accepting a large slice. 'I reckon I feel more hungry now than I have for weeks.'

'I really shouldn't have bothered you on a Sunday afternoon,' James apologised again as Frances came out with the tea and rock buns. 'I just wanted to leave this script with you. I thought it might do as the play we were talking about for the children to perform at the summer fair.'

Frances set the tray down on her garden table and took the little book he was holding out. '*The Dragon Who Was Different*. Oh, it's by Geoffrey Trease – one of my favourite children's authors. This would be ideal – but does it have twins in it? I know you were keen for the Crocker boys to take part.'

'No, it doesn't have twins,' he admitted. 'But I think you're right – it's too soon for them to take a major part. We'll save them for *The Prince and the Pauper* when they're older. I have thought of another way in which we could make use of their likeness, though.' He picked up his cup. 'We give them one part to share.'

'To share? You mean they both play the same character?'

'That's right. They'd be dressed alike, of course, and play alternate scenes. It would give them both something to do, and if either of them became ill or broke a leg falling out of a tree or something, we'd have a ready-made understudy!'

Frances laughed. 'That's positively Machiavellian. You're not going to arrange this broken leg, are you?'

'The very idea!' He grinned. 'Mind you, it's quite tempting ... But what do you think about the play? It's all in verse, which the children find easier to learn, and it's quite a simple story, the usual sort of thing: a king collecting taxes from his subjects – a dragon tax, in this case – and a bold young hero called Peter who is too poor to pay. The king gives him a choice of prison or trying to kill the dragon. But when Peter meets the dragon, he turns out to be rather nice – he's a vegetarian and has never met the king, nor demanded a tax. He also objects to having to speak in verse. Peter returns to the city and incites the townsfolk to rebellion. The king arrests him, and condemns him to execution without trial, which of course is very unfair. Peter is saved when the dragon arrives and breathes peppermint over the king and his court, who all faint.' He glanced at her apologetically. 'It sounds nonsense told like that, but it could be fun and the children will enjoy it.'

'I think it's perfect. The children listen to Geoffrey Trease's plays and serials on *Children's Hour* and love them. He ranks almost as high as Jennings!'

'And that really is an accolade. Having worked in a boys' prep school, I can vouch for the authenticity of the Jennings stories. Not that I laughed as much at the antics our boys got up to – I'm afraid I was more of a bewildered Mr Wilkins than a tolerant Mr Carter.'

'I'm sure that's not true,' Frances said. 'Are you ready for more tea?'

He drained his cup, then held it out. 'Thank you. You make very good tea, Frances.' He hesitated, then said, 'To tell you the truth, I did have another reason for coming this afternoon.'

'Did you?' Frances, busy pouring tea, spoke casually. 'Well, you don't really have to have a reason at all. You're welcome to drop in.'

'That's just it.' He paused again. 'Just lately – well, I haven't been so sure that I would be. Welcome, I mean.'

'Oh.' Frances put down the teapot and looked at him. Her colour rose a little. 'I'm sorry you've felt that, James.'

'I was right, though, wasn't I?' he said quietly. 'Things have been a little awkward between us lately. I haven't been imagining it.'

There was a small silence. Then she said, 'No, you haven't. And it was all my fault, I'm afraid. I – well, I don't know quite how to put this, but I haven't had all that many men friends, and ...' She looked away, her colour deeper.

'I find that difficult to believe,' he said. 'Unless you chose not to, perhaps.'

Frances turned her head quickly and looked back at him. 'Oh no!

Well – not in the way I think you mean. Perhaps I should say that life hasn't sent them my way.'

'None at all?' he asked gently, and she looked down at her hands.

'Not many, anyway. In fact' – she raised her eyes again – 'only one. There might have been more, perhaps, but I haven't noticed them. Perhaps, as you say, I chose not to.'

There was another short silence. Frances dropped her eyes again. There was a trill of song from a robin in the azalea hedge and the distant sound of voices in the lane. Presently, James said, 'You don't have to tell me anything, Frances. I don't want to pry. And I think I understand at least one reason why you might have chosen not to notice, because I've been very much the same since Dorothy died.'

He waited a moment or two, but Frances said nothing. He reached across and touched her hand. 'Frances? Are you all right? Would you like me to go?'

'No! No, I'm quite all right. I just didn't know quite what to say.' Again she raised her eyes. 'I'm really sorry about your wife, James.'

'I know. And for a long time I felt that I would never find anyone else to share my life. I was choosing not to notice too. But one can still have friends. Friendship is different.' He paused again. 'I thought we were becoming friends, Frances, and then suddenly it seemed as if we weren't. I wondered what I had done wrong. I wish you would tell me. I'll put it right, if I can. I need friends in Burracombe.'

'And you have them!' she exclaimed. 'You're well liked here, James, and with good reason. And – yes, I thought we were becoming friends too. But suddenly – well, I can only say I felt afraid. It sounds stupid, I know.'

'It's not stupid at all,' he said. 'But there's nothing to be afraid of. Not where friendship is concerned. Not where *our* friendship is concerned.'

'It sounds so good,' she said a little wistfully.

'And it can be good. It *is* good.' He took her hand in both of his. 'Let's start again, shall we? I've missed our meals together, our walks, our friendly companionship. Let's begin again, in good, true, simple friendship. Is it a pact?'

Frances smiled. 'It's a pact.'

137

Chapter Eighteen

'This Cyprus business,' Gilbert Napier said, looking up from his copy of the *Times*. 'It's beginning to look grave. There's a report here about another police station being attacked, and it won't be long before they start on the British services. There's serious hostility towards the men now.'

Hilary spooned scrambled eggs on to his plate and added bacon and tomatoes. 'I know. David was talking about it yesterday.' It still gave her a little thrill of pleasure to be able to mention his name openly. 'I was thinking of going over to see Stella today. She must be worried about Maddy.'

'I'm worried about the pair of them,' her father stated. 'I never liked the idea of Stephen going into the RAF. It's not natural, flying around in aeroplanes. The army's the place for Napiers, on the ground where you can see what you're doing.'

Hilary smiled. Gilbert had made his feelings about the RAF very clear as soon as Stephen had first told them that was where he would be doing his National Service. He had been bitterly disappointed that his younger son had been unwilling to follow in either his own or his elder son Baden's footsteps and enter the army. But Stephen had always gone his own way, perhaps because he knew he would never be able to live up to his brother's measure – and even more so after Baden had been killed in the retreat from Dunkirk. It was impossible to compete with the dead, he'd once told Hilary, so he might as well be himself.

And he hadn't done so badly after all, she thought. Gilbert had slowly come to recognise and appreciate Stephen's own qualities.

His marriage to Maddy Forsyth had helped, of course - Gilbert had always had a soft spot for Maddy. And it had turned out well in the end, Maddy was very happy with Stephen and had been almost childishly excited at the thought of accompanying him to Cyprus. But now, as her father had said, the situation with EOKA, the guerrilla force that wanted Cyprus to remain with Greece rather than Turkey, was becoming grave, and it was impossible not to worry about her.

'Do you think they'll bring the wives home?' she asked, beginning her own breakfast.

'Wouldn't be surprised. They shouldn't have let them go out there in the first place. Anyone could see there was trouble brewing. Grivas is a clever man, and I dare say he's got guerrillas in every village. And Archbishop Makarios is involved too, as likely as not, though he plays his cards close to his chest. If you ask me, there's not much to choose between EOKA and Enosis.'

'I'm not sure what the difference is between them,' Hilary admitted, pouring more coffee into his cup.

'In their aim, which is to get the British out of Cyprus and unite with Greece, not much. But EOKA seem to have a more violent method in mind, and nobody's quite sure whether Makarios is in agreement or not. He certainly doesn't seem to be in *dis*agreement. That's why the situation is so uncertain, and so volatile.' He frowned at his plate. 'I'd like young Maddy out of there, and if Stephen had any sense, he'd send her home.'

Hilary sighed. 'I'm sure we'd all be happier to see her safe. Not to mention Steve himself! I'll definitely go over to Little Burracombe and find out if Stella's had any news. I want to see Ann Shillabeer about Arthur Culliford anyway. I'll ride over on Beau – he needs some exercise.'

She took the breakfast dishes through to the makeshift kitchen, where Patsy had just arrived for work. She and Brenda had settled into a comfortable routine now, with Patsy working mostly in the kitchen, preparing meals and looking after the laundry, and Brenda helping with the housework. Considering the home she came from, Hilary thought with amusement, Brenda was turning into a thoroughly dependable worker, and paid great attention to her dusting and scrubbing.

'And how are your plans getting on?' she enquired as Patsy began to wash up. 'When do you think you'll move over to the farm?'

'Next week, we hope.' Patsy rubbed at a plate with a dishcloth. 'Mother's some pleased, I can tell you, and the children can't wait to have Rosie there – even the boys. But we're doing a bit of painting and decorating in the bedrooms first. The little one where Rosie's going to sleep hasn't been used for years.'

'That sounds like a lot of work.'

'Bob's helping us. He's so thankful Terry's not going to let him down, he's even given up skiffle practice. Mind you, I suspect it's because he'll get his own bedroom back sooner,' she added with a grin.

Hilary laughed. 'I'm glad it's going so well for you. I thought when you told me last week what had been decided that you looked a lot happier.'

'I am. It's not that I don't like living with Terry's mother and father, and they've been real kind to me, but it wasn't meant to last for ever. There's much more room at the farm, and Mother and me have always got along well. We can help each other in lots of ways. And she's letting me and Terry have the big room downstairs for ourselves, so we can be private if we want to.'

'Our dad's looking forward to working over there too,' Brenda said, coming in halfway through the conversation. 'He's starting next week. He's going to buy Mr Foster's old bike so he can get over there quicker. And Mum's going to be pleased. She's getting over what happened last year now.'

'Next week's not going to be easy for her, though,' Hilary observed. 'It was early July when she lost the twins, wasn't it?'

'Yes, it was,' Brenda said soberly. 'And we all thought we were going to lose her too. I reckon it gave our dad a real shock. That and being sent to prison for poaching. He's turned over a new leaf since then anyway.'

Hilary left the kitchen feeling that life was turning a corner for many people. Patsy and Terry settling down on the farm, Maggie Culliford recovering from the blow of losing two babies at once, Arthur Culliford with a real job at last – for he had been a floating workman on the estate for the past few months, going from farm to farm to help out wherever an extra hand was needed – and herself and David planning their wedding. Even the renovation of the kitchen was coming along well now, with Mr Greening overseeing the building work. Hilary and Mrs Curnow had pored over plans for hours, with occasional help from David, who had some good ideas, and hindrance from Gilbert, who thought everything should be exactly as it was before. With luck, she thought, it would all be completed before the wedding.

The date had been set at last for 17 September. Stella should have had her baby and be out and about by then, and the weather should still be pleasant for their honeymoon. They had decided to spend the first week in Venice and then go on to Verona. Following in Shakespeare's footsteps, David had said with a smile, although it seemed unlikely that the Bard had ever been to either place.

'I'll read both plays before we go,' Hilary said, 'and drag you round all the sights he mentions. It will be very educational.'

'It's the first time I've ever thought of a honeymoon being educational,' he observed solemnly. 'Not in the Shakespearean sense, anyway.'

'David, really!' But she had laughed, and she smiled again now as she remembered it. She decided to go over to Little Burracombe straight away, and popped her head round the door of the study, where her father had gone to read through some of the estate papers. Although Hilary and Travis now did almost all the work between them, he still liked to know exactly what was happening and make his own contribution. And why should he not? she thought as he glanced up and nodded a goodbye. He's perfectly fit now, as long as he's sensible, and he's only in his sixties after all. There's no reason why he should be pushed into a retirement he doesn't want.

Saddling her horse, Hilary was also aware that marriage would bring fresh responsibilities and new demands on her time. Just because David would be living at the Barton and working with Charles Latimer did not mean that her own life would go on in just the same way. They would want time together to enjoy their new life, to support each other, to grow to know each other. This must inevitably mean less time available for the estate, and for the first time Hilary found herself entirely thankful that they had Travis as estate manager. From her outright resistance when her father had first insisted on appointing him, to her eventual respect for him and now their genuine friendship, she had never completely accepted that she could not run the estate alone.

It wasn't just David either, she thought as she swung herself on to Beau's broad back. God willing, there'd be children too. A family to fill the Barton with noise and laughter again. And they couldn't wait too long for that – she was over thirty now.

She rode down the track leading to the Clam and dismounted to lead Beau across the narrow wooden bridge. The waters of the Burra Brook were peaceful today, running clear and shallow over smooth rocks, with just a few gentle sprays of foam. Hilary thought of what the river had been like that night in November when Percy Shillabeer had lost his life here, and shivered. It could rise so swiftly and so dangerously, creating whirlpools and eddies that could wrench even a strong man into their clutches and hold him there, helpless against the water that poured without mercy into his lungs. One of the most horrible of deaths, Hilary thought, and yet to look at the river now you would have thought it too innocent ever to carry out such a deadly act.

The spring flowers were over now, and the high Devon banks were pink with campion and rosebay willowherb. Dog roses twined their stems in the hedges, their delicately tinged pink faces peeping shyly from amongst the hawthorn and beech leaves. Gold and apricot tendrils of honeysuckle wound themselves about them, competing for space, and the scent of a natural bouquet drifted about her in the warm July air.

I must remember it's Val's birthday on Monday, she thought. I expect there are some nice cards in the village shop, and I'll buy her a box of chocolates too. Val and Luke seemed to have settled into the routine of his spending one week a month in London. She was glad they were staying in Burracombe; she'd have missed them dreadfully if they'd moved.

The track up from the Clam was too steep for Beau to carry her, so they walked together up the deeply sunken lane between banks the height of two or even three men. It must be a very ancient track, she thought, trying to imagine the people who would have taken this way between the two villages over many centuries. And had there always been a rivalry, partly friendly and partly hostile, between the two Burracombes? Probably there had. It was the age-old story of 'us and them', the white rose and the red, the Montagues and the Capulets. Nowadays it was more jokey than serious, but it still raised its head whenever there was a whiff of competition between them.

She was on Beau's back again by the time she reached the vicarage, and feeling at peace with the world and with herself. Life was good after all, she thought. After years of feeling on the sidelines, looking on at other people's joys, she was a part of it all herself. And the best was yet to come.

'There,' she said to Beau, dismounting near the front door. 'I'll just loop your reins round this post Felix has so thoughtfully provided, and see if Stella's got a carrot for you. Now stand nicely, there's a good boy, and don't scrape holes in the path with your hooves. There's Stella now – she must have seen us coming. Stella, I just popped over to see if—'

'Hilary!' the younger woman cried, flinging the front door wide and starting down the steps. 'You've heard too! Felix and I were just coming over to Burracombe to see what we could do. Felix,' she called over her shoulder. 'Hilary's here.'

'Heard what?' Hilary asked, a cold hand clutching at her heart. 'Stella, whatever's wrong? What's happened?'

'You haven't heard?' Stella's brown eyes were wide and anxious. 'You don't know anything about it?'

'I don't know what you're talking about. Is it Stephen? Maddy? Are they all right?'

Felix came down the steps and took his wife's arm. 'Come inside, darling. You ought to be sitting down. Hilary, come into the living room. There's some coffee there. We'll tell you then.'

He led them back indoors and through to the big, slightly untidy living room with its comfortable old sofa and armchairs and French windows leading to the garden. They stood wide open, letting in the fresh morning air, and Hilary could see the bright colours of the roses Stella took such pleasure in. But she wasn't interested in the garden. She waited impatiently while Felix saw his wife solicitously to an armchair, then burst out, 'For heaven's sake, tell me! What's *happened*?'

'It's Dottie,' Stella said, and Hilary was so astonished that she could only stare. 'She's been taken to hospital. Dr Latimer thinks she's had a stroke.'

Chapter Nineteen

'**I** couldn't believe it when Stella told me,' Hilary said later, as she sat drinking coffee in Val's tiny living room. 'I'd gone over there with my mind so full of worries about Stephen and Maddy and the situation in Cyprus that I couldn't take it in at first. It was so unexpected.' Her voice shook a little. 'Dottie Friend, of all people! I don't think she's ever had a day's illness in all the years I've known her. And she's not even sixty yet.'

'It was a shock to everyone,' Val agreed. 'It was George Sweet who raised the alarm. Dottie had promised him some of her butterfly cakes for this morning, and when she hadn't arrived by ten o'clock he thought he'd better go and see if she was all right. He knocked on the front door and then went round to the back and knocked there, without any answer, so he pushed it open and went in. And there she was, lying on the floor. He nearly had a heart attack himself!'

'I'm not surprised. So did he call Charles straight away?'

'No, he came round to me and I went to see what I could do while he went to the doctor's house. It's lucky it's so close to the middle of the village. There wasn't much I could do, though. I got her into a better position and made her as comfortable as I could, but I was afraid to do too much in case there were any injuries. She might have banged her head or broken some ribs, or anything. You just can't tell when someone's unconscious.'

'Poor Dottie,' Hilary said. She fiddled with her teaspoon. 'I suppose Jessie and Jeanie know, do they?'

'Yes, Jessie's at the hospital now. They couldn't both go because of Billy. He knows she's ill, of course, and he's upset and frightened. They can't leave him alone. I offered to have him here but they said he'd be better at home with one of them.'

Hilary nodded. She finished her coffee and stood up. 'Well, I'd better go home myself. Father will want to know what's going on. I came straight over as soon as I left Stella. She's terribly upset – Dottie was like a mother to her and Maddy. She wanted Felix to take her to the hospital, but we persuaded her that it was better to wait until Dottie recovers consciousness.' Val was silent, and Hilary gave her a sharp look. 'She – she *will* regain consciousness, won't she?'

'I hope so,' Val said soberly. 'But nobody knows yet how bad the stroke was or if there are any injuries. And until she does come round, we won't know what her chances of recovery are.'

'I know,' Hilary said. 'Oh *Val* ...' And to her own surprise as much as her friend's, she sat down again abruptly and burst into tears.

'Hilary!' Val came over and knelt beside her, putting her arms round her shoulders. 'Hilary, don't cry. There's every chance she'll be all right. It was probably just a slight stroke and there's nothing else wrong at all. I'm sorry, I shouldn't have been so gloomy.'

Hilary shook her head and felt for her hanky. 'It's not that, Val. It's not your fault. I just ... well I can't help remembering Sybil – David's wife. She never came round from her stroke, and she died. And she was no older than I am.'

'But that was a much worse stroke,' Val said. 'They aren't all like that.'

'But Dottie's older than Sybil was. And you said yourself we don't know how bad it was. We don't know how long she was lying there before George found her. It could have been hours. It could have been all night.'

'Hil, listen to me. It's no good torturing yourself. Whatever happened to Dottie, she's in good hands now, and there's nothing any of us can do about it.' She looked closely at her friend. 'It's not just that, though, is it? There's something else.'

'Yes, there is,' Hilary said miserably. She wiped her eyes and blew her nose. 'It's brought it all back – that awful time when Sybil had her stroke and nobody knew whether she'd live or die. And how it seemed possible that she could live for years, nothing more than a vegetable.' She raised anguished eyes. 'I thought I'd lost David then. I knew he could never leave her in that state. And I felt so selfish, because she was in a living hell and he was having to cope with it, and all I could think about was myself and how much I wanted him. It was so awful. And here I am, being selfish all over again, or even worse, because this time it's Dottie and I'm *still* thinking about myself ... I really am the most horrible person, Val. I'm surprised you want to be my friend. I'm surprised *anyone* does.'

'Oh *Hilary*!' Val shook her gently by the shoulders. 'Stop being so dramatic! You're behaving like Maddy used to before she grew up. You're not horrible at all, as it happens, and I do want to be your friend and so do lots of other people. What you're going through is quite normal. You've had a very difficult time these past few years, especially recently, and however happy you are now, none of that is very far away. It's normal for it to come bubbling up when something reminds you. But you don't have to let it weigh on you. You're strong enough to cope with it. What happened to Sybil is over – nobody can change that, and it wasn't your fault anyway. It's what's happening now that we have to concentrate on, and what's going to happen next.'

'Dottie.'

'Yes, Dottie, and Stella who is so fond of her and needs help now. And Maddy – someone will have to tell Maddy.'

'Goodness me, yes. I hadn't thought of that. I'm sure Stella and Felix will have done, though. And it was worrying about Maddy that sent me over to see Stella in the first place. Father and I were discussing this EOKA business at breakfast. He says they've started attacking police stations, and servicemen are being abused in the streets. The whole situation is getting ugly. He thinks they ought to send the wives home.'

'Would Maddy come?'

'She wouldn't have any choice if they were ordered home. To be honest, Val, I wish that would happen. I know she'd hate it, but we want to see her safe. And it can't be any fun, living where you might be attacked at any moment. All their trips to the beach and into the countryside and so on must have been stopped by now, I should think.'

'So did you go to see if Stella had any news?'

'Yes. And in all the shock of hearing about Dottie, I clean forgot to ask. But I'm sure she would have told me if she'd heard anything.'

Val was silent for a moment. Then she said, 'It seems to me that's another thing we can't do anything about. It's sit-and-wait time all round, Hilary.'

'And that,' Hilary said miserably, 'is just what I find so hard to do. I can't even talk to David – not yet, anyway. He'll have been in surgery all morning and then out on his rounds. It'll be teatime before he has any time at all, and then he'll be doing evening surgery until six.'

'You wouldn't think there were so many sick people in Burracombe,' Val remarked wryly, and Hilary laughed a little.

'There aren't so many really. He just likes to give them all plenty of time, as Charles has always done. Often only two or three turn up in the evenings, and he uses the time to get some paperwork done.'

'Is he coming to you for supper? You'll be able to talk to him then. And we should have some news of Dottie by then, too.'

'He wasn't, but I'll call at the Latimers' and ask Mary to say we'd like to see him then. She won't mind not feeding him for once.' She blushed a little. 'We do try to see each other most days, but coming to us for supper tends to take all evening and it doesn't leave him much time for other work. It will be so much easier when we're married.'

'And that's not so long now. Less than three months.'

'It seems a lifetime to me,' Hilary said glumly, and Val smiled.

'It won't when you start making serious preparations! Have you decided on your dress yet?'

'No. I was going to ask Dottie—' Her hand flew to her mouth. 'Oh dear – I'll have to find someone else now. She'll never be fit enough to make a wedding dress by September.'

'You don't know that. I should wait until we know how she is before you give yourself something more to worry about. Anyway, it's not the end of the world if you have to find someone else. To be honest, I'm surprised you're not getting some smart London dressmaker to do it for you.'

'Why ever should I do that when we've got Dottie on our

doorstep? Anyone who spent years in the theatre making wonderful costumes can run up a wedding dress in no time. The one she made for you was beautiful.'

'Yes, it was. And if she can't do it and you can't find anyone else, you could borrow that. But I'm sure you'd rather have one of your own.'

'Well, probably.' Hilary stood up again. 'I'd better go. I ought to let Father know what's happened, and I'm going to see Mary Latimer first, and pop into Mr Foster's for some extra chops for David ...' She rubbed her forehead. 'Mary might have some news about Dottie too ... Sorry, Val – this seems to have knocked me all of a heap. Dottie's one of those people you think will go on for ever. It's made me think how fragile we all are. I just feel as if the whole world is shifting under me.'

'I know.' Val watched her sympathetically. 'Look, Hil, don't you think you ought to take things a bit more easily for a while? You've had such a lot on your plate over the past few years. Your father's illness, having to agree to a manager coming in, all that business with Marianne and Rob, then meeting David again and not knowing what was going to happen, and Sybil dying, not to mention the fire, and now worrying about Stephen and Maddy *and* trying to organise your own wedding ... Nobody could have coped with all of that without showing some signs of strain.'

Hilary gazed at her. 'But it's Dottie that seems to have upset me the most somehow. I don't understand why. I mean, I'm fond of Dottie, just as we all are, but ...'

'Because it seems like the last straw,' Val said. 'It's often just one thing that makes us crack. Look, isn't there something you can give up for a while – hand over to someone else? Because if you don't, I'm afraid you'll be the next one to be ill.'

'I don't have time to be ill!' Hilary said with a short laugh.

'People don't have that choice. Being ill happens whether you've got time or not. I mean it, Hilary, and I'm sure Dr Latimer would say the same. You've got to hand over some of your responsibilities.'

'And which ones do you suggest?' Hilary asked sardonically.

'That's your decision. The ones that someone else can manage on your behalf, I should think. You've got plenty of people around you – a competent estate manager, more help in the house than you've had for years, a fiancé who would jump over the moon for you, a father who is pretty much back to full health ... You don't have to take on *every* burden yourself. And Dottie definitely doesn't have to be one. Not for you. No matter how fond of her you are.'

Hilary stared at her. 'You make me sound like Joyce Warren. A village busybody. Finger in every pie, wants to run everything, won't let go.'

'You're not a bit like Joyce Warren and you know it. You've just got yourself into a bit of a state, and no wonder. All I'm saying is step back a bit and look around. If there's someone who can help, let them. Then you can concentrate on the things you really have to do yourself.'

'Like wedding dresses,' Hilary said wryly.

'Yes, like wedding dresses. Nice things, things that are exciting and happy – things that are only going to happen to you once.' Val leaned forward. 'Don't let them pass you by, Hil. Don't let them go to waste.'

'I'm not wasting anything,' Hilary said, a little uncertainly.

'That's all right then. As long as you're sure.'

There was a short silence. Then Hilary said, 'I really must go. Thank you for the coffee, Val. And you will let me know if you hear anything, won't you?'

'Of course I will. And you let *me* know too.' Val rose and went with her friend to the door. It had been standing open, letting in the warm air and the scent of Jacob Prout's roses in his garden next door.

As Hilary was going out, she turned and gave Val an impulsive kiss on the cheek.

'Thanks, Val. You're a good friend to me, and I promise I'll think about what you've said. I probably do try to do too much myself. It's this awful Napier arrogance – we all think we're better at things than anyone else could be! I've always said it about Father, and now I think I'm just as bad.'

Val gave her a wicked grin. 'Get away! Not that I'm saying a word, of course ...'

'Oh, *you* ...' Hilary said, and aimed a punch at her shoulder.

*

'She'll pull through all right,' David said as they sat round the dining table at the Barton that evening. 'She came round quite quickly and it seems she was pretty lucid – knew what day of the week it is, and who's prime minister and so on. There's some weakness on one side, but with the right exercises she should get her strength back in time. She's been very lucky.'

'Oh, thank goodness,' Hilary said with relief. 'I've been worrying about her all day. Stella will be so glad. Has anyone told her?'

'Charles rang her as soon as we heard, but I thought you might like to stroll over to see her after supper. It's a lovely evening for a walk.'

'That's a good idea. I still want to talk to her about Maddy and Stephen. I never got a chance this morning. You won't mind if we leave you on your own, will you, Father?'

'Not a bit. I'd like to know what young Felix thinks about the situation in Cyprus. In fact, I'd come with you if I didn't think I'd be spoiling love's young dream.' Gilbert gave a bark of laughter at his daughter's astonished expression. 'It's all right! You don't have to worry. I was young once myself.'

'You're not so very old now, Colonel Napier,' David remarked, accepting a bowl of strawberries from Hilary. 'Perfectly capable of walking over to Little Burracombe – in fact it would probably do you good – and you'd be very welcome. Wouldn't he, darling?'

'Yes, of course,' Hilary said, a little startled. Without David to make the suggestion, it would not have occurred to her to invite her father to go with them. She wondered when they had last gone for a walk together, and felt rather guilty. I've got too used to treating him like an invalid, she thought, when really he's almost back to normal. Val was right – she could easily hand over some of the estate management to him. He'd always fretted at being left out, even though it was his idea to bring in a manager, but he and Travis could manage very well without her a lot of the time.

At the same time, she knew that it would be difficult for her to relinquish any of her duties. I just want to be in control of everything, she thought wryly, that's my trouble. Val must have thought that but was too polite to say so!

'Do come with us, Dad,' she said impulsively. 'It's a lovely evening and it won't be dark till gone ten. We can walk back in the dimpsy light.'

'I love that expression,' David said with a smile. 'It's as Devon as clotted cream. It makes me think of rosy-cheeked milkmaids and bowls of strawberries and hedges full of honeysuckle and black-berries.'

'Not all at the same time,' Hilary said. 'But you're right. It has a sort of flavour, doesn't it. What do you say, Father? Are you coming with us?'

'Do you know, I think I will,' he said. 'We'll go as soon as we've finished these strawberries. We won't bother about coffee – young Stella will probably offer us some. Let's make the most of the fine weather while we've got it!'

Stella was almost as surprised as Hilary when she opened the door to find the Colonel standing on her doorstep. She invited them in and showed them into the living room. The scent of fresh-cut grass wafted in through the French doors, which stood open, as they had that morning. Felix was outside, mowing the lawn, the soft purr of the blades an accompaniment to the evening song of the blackbird that had been nesting in the hedge.

'We can sit outside if you like,' she offered. 'It's still warm enough, and it seems a shame to be indoors on an evening like this. I'll ask Felix to fetch some more chairs.'

'I can do that,' David said, and under her direction he carried out some chairs from the small summer house in the corner of the garden. Felix waved and called out that he would finish the lawn, and, as Gilbert had expected she would, Stella offered coffee.

'Let me help you,' Hilary said, following her back indoors. 'We heard that Dottie recovered consciousness this afternoon. You must be so relieved. Have you been in to see her?'

Stella filled the kettle and nodded. 'Felix took me at visiting time. She was still quite sleepy, but she knew us. Her smile's a bit lopsided, but the doctor said that will improve as she gets the use of her right side back. He said it wasn't a severe stroke, thank goodness.'

Her voice wobbled a little, and Hilary moved quickly to take her in her arms. 'It's been an awful shock for you. Why don't you sit down and let me make the coffee?'

'I don't know what's the matter with me,' Stella sniffed, doing as she was told. 'I didn't cry at all before I knew she was going to be all right, and now I can't seem to stop.'

'It's shock,' Hilary repeated. 'You kept going until you knew you could relax, and now reaction is setting in. You'll be fine again tomorrow.' She took some cups down from the hooks on the dresser and put them on a tray. 'Where are the coffee and sugar?'

'In that cupboard. I ought to be doing this, not you. You're a visitor.'

'I'm a friend,' Hilary said firmly. 'In fact, we're family now – your sister's married to my brother! As a matter of fact, that's why I came over to see you this morning.' She hesitated, looking at Stella and wondering whether she ought to bring any fresh worry to her mind, then decided that Stella and Felix must have been just as anxious as she and her father. 'Dad and I have been wondering about them – with this EOKA situation, you know.'

'Yes, so have we. The coffee pot's over there, on the windowsill.' Stella watched as Hilary fetched the pot, spooned in coffee and then poured in boiling water. 'Do you want cream or milk?'

'Father will like some cream, if you have it. David has his black.' Hilary went to the larder for a jug of cream and carried the tray out to the garden. Felix had finished his mowing and was sitting at the table with David and Gilbert. He jumped up and took the tray.

'Has she got you working? Honestly, this baby is having a bad effect on my wife. Everyone's her servant these days.'

'Quite right too,' Hilary said, and David added, 'You'll both be servants once the baby's born. You do realise how much your life is going to change, don't you, Felix?'

'But only for the better,' Felix said, pouring coffee into their cups, 'Do you know, if you'd asked me six months ago if my life could have got any better, I would have said no. Now I know it can!'

They sat silent for a few moments, sipping their coffee and listening to the blackbird. A song thrush had joined in from the branches of a cherry tree, and the two birds seemed to be competing for some 'Best Birdsong of the Year' contest. The twittering of smaller birds as they found their roosts or settled fledglings for the night was a soft accompaniment, and the sun spread a canopy of delicate pink high across the sky.

'It's such good news about Dottie,' Hilary said at last. 'But it will take her a while to recover, won't it, David?'

He nodded. 'Even though it wasn't a serious stroke, there will be after-effects. She may have difficulty walking and managing tasks such as dressing, doing up buttons and so on for a while.'

'Oh dear, poor Dottie,' Stella said in dismay. 'She's always been so clever with her hands. She spends all her time cooking or sewing. She'll hate not being able to do those things.'

'It's not easy for someone like her,' he agreed. 'We'll all have to make sure she doesn't get low in her spirits. But she has plenty of friends, from what I can gather, and if she keeps a cheerful outlook she should get better quite quickly.'

'And what about Maddy?' Hilary asked when they had talked a little more about Dottie. 'You're as concerned about her as we are, aren't you?'

Felix nodded soberly. 'It doesn't look good, does it. I shouldn't think Stephen is happy about Maddy going off the base without him.'

'I don't really know how close to the base the married quarters are,' Hilary said, and it transpired that Stella and Felix weren't sure either. 'They won't let the wives stay out there if there's any danger though, surely.'

'That's what Felix and I think,' Stella said. 'But Maddy won't want to come home without him.'

'What Maddy wants and doesn't want will have precious little to do with it,' Gilbert Napier said abruptly. 'She's there as a service wife, and if the government decides to bring the families home, they'll have to come. And I strongly suspect it will come to that. Even if it doesn't, Stephen ought to persuade her. He needs to be able to concentrate on his job without worrying about his wife. It's not as if she doesn't have a home to come to.'

'No, it's not,' Stella agreed. 'It's lucky we've got plenty of spare rooms in the vicarage.'

'The vicarage?' Gilbert echoed. 'Why, she'd be coming to the Barton, surely. That's her home now.'

There was a brief silence. Hilary glanced from her father to Stella and back again. This was something she hadn't foreseen.

'But I'm her sister,' Stella said at last. 'Of course I'd want her to stay with me.'

'For a visit, yes,' he said. 'But if Stephen were here, they'd be at the Barton. That is her home now.'

Hilary saw the tears gather in Stella's eyes and looked quickly at Felix. He leaned forward and took his wife's hand.

'Naturally we understand that, Colonel,' he said. 'But I'm sure you'd let us borrow her for a while, until Stephen does come back. Stella and Maddy have had such a lot of separation through their lives, and she'd be good company while we're waiting for the baby to arrive. Not to mention the help she'd be afterwards,' he added with a grin.

'In any case,' Hilary cut in before her father could reply, 'we don't know yet that Maddy *will* be coming home. It may all blow over. You know how these things are.'

She glanced up at the sky. The pale shell-pink had deepened to the apricot glow of early sunset, merging at the horizon to a coppery flame shot through with streaks of blue-green. The dimpsy light that she and David had spoken of was spreading its dusky blanket over the gardens and meadows of Little Burracombe, and soon it would become twilight and then full darkness.

'It's time we went. Thank you for the coffee, Stella.'

'I ought to be thanking you – you made it!' Stella struggled up out of her deckchair. 'I should know better than to sit in these things, the size I am now! I shall be stuck one of these days and Felix will have to call the fire brigade to prise me out. Thank you for coming. I'll write and tell Maddy what's happened and post it tomorrow, and maybe we'll have more news about what's going on out there when she writes back. Jeanie and Jessie are going in to see Dottie tomorrow afternoon. They're going to ring up when they get home and tell us how she is.'

Hilary nodded and kissed her. David and Felix shook hands, followed by Gilbert, and they began their walk back to the river.

'You won't insist on Maddy coming to us if she does come home, will you, Father?' Hilary asked presently. 'I think she'd probably like to be with Stella at first. She'll be over like a shot when Stephen's back.'

'I dare say,' he said. 'It's all right, Hilary. I know when I'm beaten, and the Barton is never going to be their real home anyway. To tell you the truth, I think I'm lucky to have you staying in the fold. There've been times when I thought you were going to leave and I'd be all alone in that great rambling place.'

Hilary smiled and squeezed his arm.

'I don't think that's likely to happen now, Father. And once David and I start to raise our own family, who knows – in a few years' time you'll probably be begging for some peace and quiet!'

Chapter Twenty

The news of Dottie's stroke spread rapidly round the village. Even Ivy Sweet, who had never got on all that well with her, said she wouldn't have wished it on her worst enemy when she came into the shop on Monday morning to find a group of people discussing the news. All eyes turned on her as she came in, and since it was her George who had found Dottie, she was for once the centre of attention.

'White as a ghost he said she was,' she told them. 'Thought for a minute 'twas all over for her. But he took that first aid course the St John's Ambulance Brigade ran in the village hall a year or two back, you remember, so he knew just what to do, and once he'd got her comfortable he dashed in next door for Val Ferris, and she took over while he went for the doctor. Dr Latimer said he'd done a proper job,' she added proudly. 'Saved her life, as like as not.'

'Poor Dottie,' Aggie Madge said feelingly, and turned to Jessie Friend. 'How was she when you saw her yesterday afternoon, Jess?'

'The hospital doctor says her's doing well,' Dottie's cousin answered dubiously. 'But I got to say, her still looks like a ghost. Her mouth's crooked on one side, and the eye that side's sort of dragged down and don't shut properly, and her can't talk much, not so you can understand her. To tell you the truth, it upset me and Jeanie to see her like that. Us can't help thinking about Mother. She died of a stroke, you know.'

'So she did! I'd forgotten that.' Aggie put her hand to her mouth in dismay. 'Does it run in families, then?'

'Well, if it do, it wouldn't run as far as Dottie,' Ivy told her. 'She wasn't no relation to Jessie's mother, except by marriage.'

'All right, no need to be sarcastic,' Aggie retorted, and Ivy's brief moment of glory abruptly faded. She sniffed and turned away to examine a display of tinned fruit that Edie had arranged on the counter.

Edie weighed out some broken biscuits for Maggie Culliford and said, 'I hear your Arthur's going to work over at Percy Shillabeer's place. That'll be one and three, please.'

Ivy turned back, her eyes snapping with curiosity, and Maggie nodded as she handed over a shilling and a sixpence.

'That's right. A proper full-time job. Not that Miss Hilary's not been good to him, giving him work about the estate, but he were never settled in one place. He'll have responsibilities now. Stockman, he's going to be, working alongside Jim Pretty and Clem Hathaway. He's knowed they since they was all tackers, so he'll get on all right there.'

'Let's hope so,' Ivy said. 'You don't want any repetition of what happened last year. I'll have one of these tins of pineapple chunks, Edie.'

Maggie turned a deep crimson and looked as if she were about to cry. She picked up her threepenny bit change and hurried out of the shop. Aggie Madge turned on the baker's wife.

'There wasn't no call for that. You know Maggie lost her twins, what with Arthur being in prison and her afraid they'd all end up in the workhouse. Downright nasty that was. I don't know what gets into you, Ivy Sweet, I honestly don't.'

Ivy flushed and mumbled something. In truth, she felt ashamed and shocked by her own behaviour. She paid quickly for the pineapple and left. As she walked rapidly back along the village street, she felt tears come to her eyes.

It wasn't my fault, she told herself. The whole village knows what the Cullifords are like, and I helped get them on their feet again same as everyone else did. And I was being sympathetic anyway, saying she wouldn't want to go through all that again. It was Aggie Madge's fault, taking it the wrong way.

But she knew that none of this was true. She *had* said it in a nasty way, and everyone had known it. The whole village knew what *she* was like. And she didn't know what got into her to make her say these things either. She hadn't meant to be nasty at all, not to start with. She'd gone into the shop to say how sorry she was about Dottie, even though the two of them had never been friends.

It was as if some spiteful little demon lurked inside her, waiting for a chance to leap out and snap someone's head off. Waiting for a chance to hurt.

I don't even get any pleasure from it, she thought as she opened her back door and went into the kitchen. It just makes me feel even more miserable.

She put the tin of pineapple on the table and stared at it. That wasn't what she'd gone out for. She'd meant to buy tea and sugar, and now they were out of both and she'd have to go back to Edie's shop and eat humble pie. And what were the odds that Maggie Culliford or Aggie Madge would be there again? Always in and out they were. She really didn't know if she could face them.

I'll send Barry when he comes home from school, she thought, and then her legs crumpled beneath her and she sank on to a kitchen chair. Leaning both arms on the table, she lowered her head on to them and began to cry.

Jessie Friend finished her shopping and returned to the post office, where her sister was in the back room working on some invoices. Billy was at Bert Foster's, helping to carry lamb carcasses into the butchery at the back, and Jeanie had the wireless on, playing *Music While You Work*. It was Tommy Kinsman and his dance orchestra, one of their favourites.

'Ivy Sweet's tongue's so sharp it's a wonder she don't cut herself,' Jeanie remarked when Jessie finished telling her what had happened. 'Fancy upsetting poor Maggie like that. She does her best, and it do look as if Arthur's turned over a new leaf.'

'Pity Ivy don't do the same,' Jessie said, putting the kettle on. 'Only thing is, if she turned over a new leaf there'd be something horrible crawling about underneath. Why do some people have to be so spiteful, Jeanie? Was she like it at school? You were in the same class as her.'

'I don't think she was as bad as she is now,' Jeanie said thoughtfully. 'She was always a bit quick to take umbrage, mind, but she was all right most of the time. Seemed to be something happened to her later on that made her like this, but I don't know what it was. Unless ...' She paused and looked at her sister.

'If you'm thinking the same as I'm thinking,' Jessie said, 'it's got something to do with when she started to dye her hair. And it don't take a lot of imagination to put your finger on what it could have been.'

'Nobody's ever really come right out and said it,' Jeanie said uneasily. 'And George Sweet won't hear a word about it.'

'All the same ...' Jessie made the tea and brought the cups to the table. 'Not that it gives her any excuse to take it out on everyone else. It's not our fault, whatever it was!' The shop bell rang and she took a quick sip and then hurried back though the door.

Jeanie drank her tea slowly. She'd quite liked Ivy at school. They hadn't been best friends, but they'd never really fallen out. It was a shame to see her like this, and it looked to Jeanie like she was getting worse. She seemed really down just lately.

Still, whatever it was, there was nothing she or Jessie, or indeed anyone else, could do about it. And they had more to worry about now, with Dottie lying ill in hospital and perhaps not able to look after herself when she came home. She dismissed Ivy Sweet from her thoughts and went back to her invoices.

'Ivy! Whatever be the matter with you, maid?' George Sweet, coming through from the bakery, stopped and stared in astonishment at his weeping wife. 'What's happened?' A terrible fear caught him. 'It's not Dottie, is it? She's not ...'

'Not that I know of.' Ivy raised her head. Her eyes were red and her nose running. She groped for a hanky and George quickly handed her his. He came over and sat in one of the other chairs and put his arm round her shoulders, looking into her blotchy face. 'What is it then, Ive? Is it our Barry?'

She shook her head. 'I dunno what it is, George. It's like everything's just too much for me lately. And it don't matter what I do, I seem to put people's backs up. I can't say anything without managing to rile someone, and I don't mean to. All I do is speak me mind.'

'Maybe it depends what's in your mind,' he suggested. 'What I'm getting at is if you'm miserable in yourself, then you're going to say miserable things. What's happened this morning to upset you?'

Ivy told him. 'I only said what was true about Dottie not being related to Jessie Friend's mother. She was Dottie's aunt by marriage, so it stands to reason their strokes weren't nothing to do with each other. But no, apparently that was being sarcastic, and when I said to Maggie Culliford that she wouldn't want a repetition of what happened last year, that was being cruel. You see what I mean? And I bet if it was anyone else that said those things – Aggie Madge or Jessie herself – nobody would have batted an eyelid. But because it's me, it's taken all wrong.'

'It could be the way you say it,' he offered diffidently, not wanting her to flare up again. 'You do sound a bit sharp at times, Ive, you got to admit that.'

She bridled a little and for a moment he feared that she was about to go into a huff. Then her shoulders sagged and she said again, 'I don't mean to. But when everyone's against you like they are me, you can't help being prickly. You got to stand up for yourself, haven't you, George?'

He felt helpless. He knew that Ivy wasn't happy inside, and hadn't been for a long time. If he thought about it, he had a fairly good idea why that might be, but he tried not to think about it too much. He'd always liked a quiet life, and it seemed to have worked well enough so far. But Ivy seemed to be in real trouble just lately, and he didn't know what to do about it.

The shop bell rang and he stood up. 'I'll have to go, Ive, but you put the kettle on and make a cup of tea. That'll make you feel better. I'll come back the minute I've got a chance.'

To his dismay, this innocent suggestion provoked a fresh outburst of crying. He stared down at his wife, torn between staying to comfort her and going to attend to his customers.

'Ivy, whatever is it now? What did I say wrong?'

'Tea!' she wept, and her voice rose almost to a howl that caused him to look nervously at the door. 'That's what I went to the shop for, and I was so upset I forgot to get any. I can't make tea, George – we haven't got none and *it's all my fault*!'

'Crying her eyes out, she was,' Jacob Prout said in the Bell Inn an hour or so later. 'Poor old George looked at his wits' end when he come out into the shop. We could all hear her, weeping and wailing and carrying on. Mabel Purdy reckoned she was hysterical.'

'But why?' Rose Nethercott asked as she filled his pewter tankard with beer and passed it across the bar. 'I never thought she and Dottie were all that thick with each other.'

'Don't reckon it was anything to do with Dottie,' Jacob answered shortly. 'If you ask me, anything Ivy Sweet's upset about is to do with Ivy Sweet and nobody else. And I'll tell you something else.' He glanced round the ring of faces, most of them only mildly interested in the baker's wife and her troubles. 'She were in a funny mood when she come in the shop before that. Made nasty remarks about Dottie and about Maggie Culliford, to her face and all!'

'Nasty remarks about Dottie, while she'm lying in a hospital bed?' Norman Tozer echoed. 'Well if that ain't Ivy Sweet all over! What did she say?'

'Maybe it weren't as terrible as all that, come to think of it,' Jacob admitted. 'It was more the way she said it, when Jessie Friend said her mother had died of a stroke. About them not being blood relatives, so it didn't seem likely that it could have run in the family ...' His voice trailed off and the others stared at him.

'That don't seem too bad,' Norman said doubtfully. 'Anyway, it's true. I reckon any one of us might have said that. So what did she say to Maggie Culliford, then?'

Jacob was beginning to wish he'd never mentioned this. 'Oh, just that it was good that Arthur's got a proper job at last and they wouldn't want what happened last year happening again.' He looked apologetically at his listeners. 'I know it don't sound much, but it was the way she said it. Anyway, it upset Maggie and she went out as red as a beetroot.'

'Ivy do have a sharp way of putting things,' Rose said thoughtfully. 'But I can't see why any of that should have made her go home crying. If you ask me, there's a bit more to it than that.'

'Anyway,' Jack Pettifer said, brushing aside Ivy Sweet and her problems, 'what us really wants to know is how Dottie's doing? Have you heard anything, Rose?'

The pub landlady shook her head. 'Not since yesterday evening, when Jeanie dropped in to tell us they'd been in to see her. I think the young vicar's going in this afternoon with Miss Simmons – Mrs

Copley, I mean. It's not easy for Jessie and Jeanie to go in during the day, with the shop to look after.'

The others nodded. It was always difficult to visit people in hospital when you lived in a village that was a mile or more off the main road. Buses went along there to Plymouth once an hour, but you had to walk to the stop, and at the other end you had to walk to catch another bus to the hospital. It wasn't an easy journey, especially for someone like Jeanie, who wasn't too steady on her pins.

'Perhaps they'll bring Dottie to Tavistock hospital once she gets a bit better,' someone suggested, and they all agreed that this would be a good thing. Better still, of course, if Dottie were to come home, but that might not be for weeks.

'It'll be the stairs that's the problem,' Jack said thoughtfully. 'Master steep, those cottage stairs be. Now if us could get her bed down to the front room ...'

'There'd be plenty willing to help with that,' Norman said. 'And plenty to go in every day and see her's comfortable and got everything to hand. The district nurse would be going in regular too. Look, when I finish me drink, I'll walk round to the shop and ask Jessie to find out if they'd let her home, knowing there'll be folk to look after her.' He turned to Jack. 'And what's this I hear about your Terry taking over Percy Shillabeer's place?'

Jack laughed. 'Don't talk so far back, Norman! Of course he's not taking over. Carrying on as an electrician with our Bob, he is, and just moving in to live there and give Ann a hand about the place. It's young Patsy who's going to be the farmer, I reckon. She've got a good head on her shoulders, that maid.'

The talk turned to other things, and soon the men had finished their drinks and departed. Most of them went home for their midday dinner and only called in for a beer on their way. If it was too far for them to go home, they might buy a couple of Rose's sandwiches or, if it was one of Dottie's days to work, the sausage rolls she brought. There wouldn't be any of those for a while, Rose thought with a sigh. She decided to go round to the shop herself later on, and offer to go in to see Dottie. The poor woman would need as many friendly faces to look at as she could get, once she started to sit up and take notice.

Chapter Twenty-One

Rehearsals for the children's play were now under way. Frances and James had decided in the end to give the part of Peter to Barry Sweet, who seemed to have an aptitude for getting some sense into his words instead of chanting them in a monotone as most of the children did, and let the Crocker twins play the dragon – it needed at least two people inside it, and since they each seemed to know instinctively what the other was thinking, they would work well together. Mabel Purdy, who often helped Dottie with costumes for the village pantomimes, was making the dragon out of old wartime camouflage material, but for rehearsals, George and Edward brought an old army blanket, which they held over their shoulders as they capered about in the playground.

'Well, their dragon is certainly different,' James observed as he and Frances watched. 'I just hope they don't come up with any more inventive schemes about how to breathe fire. That idea of rolling a newspaper tightly and setting a match to it so that it would smoulder was quite terrifying.'

'I know. You wonder how such young boys would think of a thing like that. I hope they don't try it at home.' Frances thought guiltily of the way she used just such tightly rolled newspaper to light her own fire. 'Come to think of it, that's probably where they learned it. But we still mustn't encourage it. And the plan of the one in front carrying a kettle of boiling water to make steam come out through the nostrils was even worse. I hope we're doing the right thing here, James. We don't want one of the children to end up with a serious injury.'

'They won't. I'll frisk them both for firecrackers or other incendiary devices before I allow them into their dragon skin. They hardly need them anyway – they've got enough steam of their own to let off. Which I think they've done quite enough of for the time being.' He blew his whistle. 'Come on, children, rehearsal's over. Line up, please.'

'You've got them very well trained,' Frances commented as the children obediently formed into lines, ready to walk through the doors in an orderly fashion rather than rush through in a crowd as they were otherwise apt to do. 'You're very good for our children, James.'

He turned and smiled at her. 'Thank you. I think we make a good team, don't you? Almost as good as George and Edward!' He paused, watching the children as they stood in their lines waiting for permission to go inside. 'I'd like to think I was good for you too,' he added quietly.

Frances felt her face grow warm. 'Of course you are, James. You're a tremendous help.'

He kept his eyes on her face and seemed about to say something else, then turned away as Janice Ruddicombe let out a squeal and turned to glare at Billy Culliford, standing behind her. 'You pulled my pigtails. Mr Raynor, Billy Culliford pulled my pigtails!'

James gave Frances a wry grin. 'That's just how good I am for the children! Billy – stop that at once. Janice, lead your line into the classroom, please, and when I come in, I want to see you all sitting quietly at your desks. No pushing, now. That's better ...' He turned back, but Frances was already moving away to deal with her own class. James watched her for a moment, then followed the infants inside.

Val was walking past the school with Christopher in his pushchair as the children filed inside. She lifted her hand to wave to her nephew Robin and strolled on towards the ford, thinking of the birthday she had just had and all that had happened in the past year.

She'd been really upset this time last year, she remembered, because Luke had been talking about giving up his teaching job in Tavistock and moving to London to paint seriously for a living. She'd thought they were going to have to go and live in the middle of a big city, with nothing but streets and traffic and noise. Nothing but a park for Christopher to play in, and perhaps even that miles away by bus or Underground. No moors or woods or fields, no tumbling streams or bridges or fords such as the one they were walking towards now; no sheep, no wild ponies, no village community with all its shared griefs and joys, all its gossip. She'd feared they were going to have to give all that up.

But after a lot of soul-searching, they had come to a compromise that both could accept. Luke now spent one week a month in London, where he rented a studio. He was able to visit the gallery where his paintings were shown, and he could work on the few portraits he still undertook. His first love was for landscape painting, and the other three weeks, at home in Burracombe, were spent either on the moors or in the charcoal burner's cottage where he had lived when he had first come to the village.

Today he had decided to paint another view of the little humpbacked bridge by the ford. It was a favourite scene, never quite the same twice, and although he pretended to disparage it as a chocolate-box or postcard view, Val knew he had a special love for it. As she passed the school playground and came within view of the ford, she saw him sitting on his folding chair, his easel set up before him, narrowing his eyes to gaze at the curved stonework and the glittering river, reaching out his hand to touch his brush to exactly the right shade of paint already mixed on his palette.

She paused to watch him before he noticed her. This was Luke as he was meant to be, she thought. Not the war artist recording scenes of destruction and torment that he had been when she'd first met him in Egypt; not the society portrait painter she'd once feared he might be tempted to become; but the dark, almost wild-looking Luke she loved most, with a lock of black hair falling over his forehead, his thin face tense as he concentrated, his whole being taut with the passion that brought his work to life, attracting the attention of the London gallery.

He was right to give up teaching, she thought. He was never able to paint so well while all his energies were taken up by the school.

'Daddy!' Christopher cried, and Luke glanced round. In an instant, the tension left him; his face cleared and broke into a broad smile, and he jumped up, laying his brush on the palette, and splashed across the ford towards them.

'Luke, honestly!' Val scolded him. 'Your shoes will be soaked.'

'They're only my plimsolls.' He kissed her, then stooped and unbuckled Christopher from his pushchair, swinging him high in the air. 'You'd like a paddle too, wouldn't you, Kes?' He had taken lately to calling Christopher Kes, or Kester, following the little boy's own pronunciation of his name, and it looked as if it might stick. Val had to admit she rather liked it herself. 'It's a hot day. Let's take all your clothes off and douse you properly.'

'Luke, you can't do that!'

'Of course I can. You don't think some prim spinster lady is going to come along and be shocked, do you? He's only a baby.' He gave her a wicked grin. 'Now, if *I* were to take all my clothes off ...'

'Don't you dare!' She watched as Luke stripped the toddler's romper suit and nappy off, laying them on a dry rock, and then carried him into the water. Christopher squealed in pretended terror as his father held him high above a still pool, then swept him downwards and plunged him into the cool water, taking care to keep his head above the surface. His squeals turned into a shriek of surprise as he felt the coldness against his skin, but he was laughing still, and Val smiled and sat on a rock to take off her own shoes. The bed of the stream was mostly large flat pebbles or slabs of rock, and not at all uncomfortable to walk on. She could remember many childhood days spent here, playing in the water with her brothers and their friends. She had brought Jackie too, when her younger sister wasn't much older than Christopher was now, and faced her mother's annoyance when they'd returned home soaked. Not that Alice had ever been very annoyed. You didn't live in the country, on the edge of Dartmoor, and not expect your children to get wet and dirty when they went out.

'Someone's having fun.'

Val turned quickly at the sound of the gruff voice. 'Miss Bellamy! How are you?'

'Well enough, thank you.' The old lady came to sit on a large rock near Val. 'Go on in with them. Don't let me stop you.'

Val shook her head. 'As you say, they're having fun.' She trailed

166

her bare feet in the water. 'Have you come out for a walk? I thought you spent every spare minute in your garden.'

'I do, but I like to have a dander round the village at some point during the day, to keep up with the news. Sorry to hear about Dottie. Have you heard any more today?'

Val shook her head. 'Only that she seems to have had a fairly slight stroke and should make a good recovery. With any luck she'll be back at home, bright as a button, before the summer holidays are over.'

Constance Bellamy frowned. 'Let's hope so. It's worrying when a young thing like Dottie gets struck down and old stagers like me and your grandmother keep plodding on.'

Val smiled to hear Dottie described as young. But Miss Bellamy must be nearly twenty years older, and Minnie Tozer was almost ninety. To them, Dottie probably did seem quite young.

'You don't seem like old stagers to me,' she said. 'Although I do think Granny is slowing down a bit. Mother does manage to get her to rest in the afternoons now. She wouldn't hear of it until a few months ago.'

'You need to take care of her,' Miss Bellamy said abruptly. 'I'll call in to say hello one day. That's a fine little boy you've got there.'

Her change of subject didn't surprise Val. She knew the two old ladies were firm friends and whichever one died first would be sorely missed by the other. Miss Bellamy probably didn't want to think about it. She looked across at Christopher, now knee-deep at the edge of the water, bending over to look at something, his little bottom presented towards the two women like a baby moon, and laughed, remembering Luke's comment about a spinster lady seeing him naked. Miss Bellamy was indeed a spinster lady, but the sight of Christopher's nakedness didn't seem to upset her.

'He's a little savage! I think that's long enough now, Luke,' she called. 'I don't want him to get cold. Bring him over here – I've got a towel.'

Luke swung the little boy into his arms and carried him across, nodding hello to Miss Bellamy, and deposited him on the towel Val had spread across her lap. She wrapped him in it and cuddled him dry, feeling a sudden surge of love for the firm, wriggling body and for the husband who stood beside her.

This was what life was meant to be, for herself and her family, she thought, in the place where she had grown up, the place where she wanted to bring up her son. They had been right not to move to London. This was where they were destined to be.

'What d'you reckon?' Alice Tozer asked her husband as she served meat pie, spring greens and mashed potatoes for the family dinner. 'Did us ought to let Joe know about Dottie?'

Ted poured extra gravy on to his plate. 'I dunno. Did us? I haven't thought about it, to tell you the truth.'

Alice looked at him, exasperated. 'Honestly, Ted! He's *your* brother.'

'I know that. But I dunno as it's up to me to tell him Dottie's private business. They'm only friends, after all.'

'Pretty special friends,' Tom observed. 'She's not long come back from staying with him in America. I reckon he'd want to be told.'

'Well, can't Dottie tell him herself, if she wants him to know?'

'I'm not sure she can,' Joanna said, feeding spoonfuls of mashed potato and gravy into Heather's open mouth. 'Val says she's pretty weak – nearly paralysed down one side. She might not be able to write. Anyway, she's not fit to do anything yet. She might be glad to have someone do it for her.'

'She could ask—' Ted began, but Alice cut him off.

'She's not even talking much yet, Ted! I know it's not a bad stroke, from what the doctor says, but it was a stroke just the same. Any stroke is serious. I think us ought to let Joe know. He'd be upset if us didn't and ... well, if anything happened. Like another stroke.'

Ted put a forkful of meat and pastry into his mouth and considered. After a few moments he nodded slowly. 'You'm right, Alice. The thing is, who's going to do it? You know I'm not much of a hand at writing letters; it's usually you or Mother that writes to him and our Jackie. If he gets a letter from me about Dottie, he's bound to think the worst.'

'I'm not suggesting you should write it. Just that someone ought to, so he knows what's up. Either me or Mother, it don't matter which.'

'Why don't I do it then?' Minnie said. 'I'll get down to it this afternoon. Or do you think us ought to wait a day or two, see how she gets on?'

'Maybe a couple of days,' Joanna said. 'We'll know a bit more then. It won't take long to reach him by airmail.'

'You don't think us ought to send a cable?' Alice asked.

Ted stared at her. 'Send a cable? He'll think her's at death's door. No, an airmail letter's the best thing. We'll find out how she is and write accordingly.'

'Tell you what,' Joanna said. 'I've got to take Robin to the doctor after school about that earache he's been getting lately. I'll ask him what news there is then.'

'He might not tell you,' Alice said dubiously. 'You know what he's like about discussing his patients.'

'He won't mind saying if she's getting better.' Joanna got up and began to collect the empty plates. 'Is it rhubarb and custard for afters, Mother?'

'Yes, it's over there. Has Robin been keeping you awake at night with that earache, poor little toad?'

'Not too much. It isn't a bad one, only Dr Latimer said last time he had it to take him back if he got it again. It's just a childhood thing.'

Alice nodded. It was good to see Joanna being so matter-of-fact about one of the children. She'd been so anxious about both Robin and Heather after the death of little Suzanne, and it had seemed for a time that she would wrap them both in cotton wool and be afraid to let them lead normal lives. Now, it looked as if she was feeling more relaxed, and Alice was glad to see it. She knew just how difficult it was to strike the right balance between caring for your children and letting them learn to stretch their wings.

As her own daughter Jackie was doing now. Alice only hoped she wasn't stretching them too far.

Chapter Twenty-Two

'I've been thinking,' Ivy Sweet said to the landlord of the Horrabridge Inn that evening. 'It's getting a bit much for me, traipsing in here three nights a week for what you pay me. Half of it goes on bus fares anyway. It's time I give in me notice.'

Lennie Yeo narrowed his glance. He was a thin, shortish man with sparse grey hair and pale blue eyes. 'Is this a roundabout way of asking me for a pay rise?'

'No, it's not, though it wouldn't be before time,' Ivy retorted. 'I've just had enough of standing behind a bar pulling pints and listening to other folk's troubles, that's all. We all comes to it sometime, Lennie.'

'Didn't realise you were old enough to retire,' he observed, turning away to pick up a glass and polish it. 'Though now I come to look at you proper ...'

Ivy flushed. 'I'm not talking about retiring, as such. I've had enough, that's all. I got plenty to do at home, what with Barry going up to the big school in Tavistock after the summer holidays. He'll have a lot more homework then and someone's got to see he does it. And George could do with a hand. I can't see that's so unreasonable.'

He shrugged. 'It's up to you. I hope you'll be decent enough to give me time to find another barmaid, that's all. I'll need to look for someone a bit younger and more friendly, like. Some of the chaps been saying you got a bit sharp lately.'

'Sharp?' she said indignantly. 'Pub banter, that's all that is, unless they gets above themselves. I got a right to put them in their place then.'

'Yes, well some of 'em think you'm a bit too quick with your tongue. There's one or two told me they're thinking of drinking up at the London Inn, and I can't afford to lose trade because my barmaid takes the huff. So maybe you'm right, Ivy, and it's time for the parting of the ways.'

Ivy didn't reply. She felt somewhat aggrieved because he hadn't tried to persuade her to stay, and even more affronted by his reference to looking for someone younger to replace her. She went to hang up her raincoat and looked in the tiny mirror in the cloakroom to touch up her lipstick and brush her hair. I'll be glad to leave the place anyway, she thought, and knew it was nothing to do with the bus fares.

When she went back to the bar, Lennie said, 'That feller was in here again asking for you.'

Ivy felt her heart thump. 'What feller? The same one as came in before?'

'The one what was in here last Tuesday *and* the Friday before that,' he said impatiently. 'How many blokes have you got after you, Ivy? I thought them days was past.'

Ivy knew her face was turning scarlet. 'I don't know what you mean.'

'Well if you don't, there's plenty could tell you. You were friendly enough with those airmen who were up at Harrowbeer during the war. Specially one or two of they Polish and Czechoslovakian ones,' he added, turning away almost as if speaking to himself.

Ivy drew in a sharp breath. Her heart was beating like a drum and she felt like turning on her heel and walking out there and then, but she had to know for sure. She asked in a trembling voice, 'Who is it that's been in here asking about me, Lennie? I got a right to know.'

He turned back and faced her, seeming to realise that this was more serious than a bad-tempered spat, and they looked at each other. He wasn't a bad sort really, Ivy thought. They'd rubbed along well enough all these years, and he'd been pleased enough during the war that her bright, flirting ways brought the airmen flocking. And if she'd got a bit more friendly with one or two of them, where was the harm in that? She'd always known where to draw the line.

Until ...

'Well?' she asked again, aware of an edge to her voice.

'Look, he didn't give me no name. Just said he was an old friend of yours and asked when your next shift was, that's all.'

'And you *told* him?'

'No, I never.' He faced her. 'I didn't see what business it was of his. If he weren't prepared to tell me his name, I wasn't going to tell him when you'd be in. Not that it'll be any problem for him to find out. He's only got to hang about for a few nights.' He looked at her under his scanty brows. 'Look, Ive, if you're in any sort of trouble ... well, you only got to say the word if anyone's bothering you. I can ban him easy as pie.'

'I'd just like to find out who he is,' she said. 'I can't think of anyone who'd want to know about me.' She paused, then said, 'He wasn't local, then, I take it?'

Lennie gave a short laugh. 'Not with an accent like that!'

'Like what?' She waited a minute or so, then asked reluctantly, 'You mean he's not English? You – you don't reckon he was some-one from Harrowbeer, do you?'

'How could he be? They closed the airfield the minute the war ended.'

'I don't mean up there *now*. I mean – you know, from back in those days. One of the pilots. A Pole, or a Czech. Not that there's any reason any of them would be looking for me,' she added hastily.

'Isn't there?' Lennie let his eyes linger on her hair for a moment, and Ivy turned abruptly away. 'I dunno what he was, to tell you the truth,' he went on. 'He was foreign, that's all I know, and if you'll take my advice, you'll be careful going home. In fact you can go twenty minutes early if you want, so you can catch the bus before it gets dark.'

'Why, what d'you think he'd do?' she asked, her heart hammer-ing again.

'I dunno as he'd do anything. I just didn't like the way he come in here, asking after you and not telling me his name. I didn't like the look of him.'

'What did he look like, then?'

'Oh, you know – tall, rangy sort of individual, black hair going back a bit, beaky sort of nose—'

'*Black* hair?' Ivy asked before she could stop herself.

'That's right,' Lennie said, his eyes once more on her own hair, which was looking particularly red today. 'Black.'

There was a short silence. Then Ivy turned abruptly.

'I'll go and make sure everything's all right in the snug. I dunno what the dinner-time drinkers was up to, but it was a proper mess yesterday evening.'

She shut the door between the two bars and leaned against it for a moment, her eyes closed. It hadn't been him, then. She knew it couldn't have been, but all the same ... She put a hand to her thin chest, still able to feel the thumping of her heart.

If it wasn't him, who was it?

Ivy was on tenterhooks all evening, serving drinks with one eye on the door, her replies to the customers' chaffing vague and abstracted, but the man didn't come in. She took Lennie up on his offer of leaving early, though, and by twenty to ten she was on her way over the little bridge across the bubbling waters of the Walkham and up to the Tavistock road to catch the bus. She walked quickly, glancing from side to side in case he should suddenly appear from between the houses, but there were few people about now. One or two men emerged from the London Inn as she passed, and she crossed to the other side of the road, but their faces were all familiar to her and they took little notice. She was relieved to see the bus coming as she turned the corner, and she scrambled aboard feeling as if she'd been in some way saved.

There was still a mile to go to Burracombe when she got off again, but although it was now almost dark, she had no fears about walking the quiet lane. She knew every turn, every hedgerow, every high bank and every field gate. No harm would come to her here.

The thought startled her. What harm was she expecting? A man had been in Lennie's pub, asking about her – a man with a foreign accent. It wasn't really so strange. The pub had been popular with the pilots and aircraft mechanics who had been stationed at Harrowbeer during the war. There had been plenty of pubs for them to drink in – the Who'd Have Thought It at Milton Combe, the Drake Manor in Buckland Monachorum, the Leg O' Mutton on the very edge of the airfield itself, the inns in Horrabridge – all within walking distance. Some had visited a different one each evening; some had stayed loyal to just one. Ivy had known most of the men by sight and quite a few to banter and flirt with. It wasn't really that unusual for one to come back to the area and drop in to say hello to the innkeeper and barmaids they'd known in those days. Not all of them had even gone back to their home country after the war; there was a Czechoslovakian living in Horrabridge itself at this very minute, married to a local girl and bringing up a family.

There really wasn't anything to worry about. And yet something in Lennie's manner, in the way he'd said he hadn't liked the look of the chap, gave her an uneasy feeling. It wasn't the first odd thing that had happened lately, either. For instance, there was that—

'Ivy?'

Ivy's heart kicked. She gasped and leapt back a step or two, her hand on her chest as she peered into the deepening twilight at the dark shape before her. 'Who's that?'

'Why, 'tis only me.' The shape became more distinct, and she realised that the voice was familiar. 'Sorry, maid, did I startle you?'

'You gave me the fright of my life,' she said crossly. Her breath was still coming quickly. 'Whatever are you doing, Jacob Prout, walking the roads at this time of night? I nearly jumped out of me skin.'

'It's not that late. I was just taking Scruff out for his last walk, and seeing as it's such a nice night, we strayed a bit further than us usually do.' The old man took his pipe from his mouth and looked closely at her. 'I didn't mean to frighten you.'

'I don't suppose you did, but you ought to be a bit more careful, springing out of the shadows like that.' She began to walk on and he fell into step beside her, his rough-haired Jack Russell trotting at his heels.

'I suppose you'm on your way home from Horrabridge,' he remarked after a moment. 'Bit early, aren't you? Don't you usually stop on and help clear up?'

'As a rule, I do, not that it's any business of yours,' she replied tartly. 'Lennie let me go a bit sooner tonight, that's all.'

He nodded and they said nothing for a few minutes. Then he

said, 'How are you doing these days, Ivy? I thought when I saw you in the shop the other day you was looking a bit peaky.'

'I'm all right.' But her voice quivered slightly. She and Jacob seldom had much to say to each other, and the gruff, unexpected concern in his voice brought a sudden lump to her throat. 'It's a busy time of year, that's all, what with holidaymakers about, and it'll be worse when the schools break up in a couple of weeks' time.'

'I don't suppose Lennie'll complain. He'll be pleased with the extra business. He'll be wanting you to work extra hours.'

'Well I won't be. I give in me notice this evening.' She bit her lip. She hadn't meant to tell anyone that, not until she'd told George, and least of all Jacob Prout, who looked at her sometimes as if she was a nasty smell. But there was something about the darkness of the quiet lane, lit only by a three-quarters moon, and the way he'd asked after her that made a difference. He wasn't the critical, sometimes surly Jacob Prout of the daytime. He was the Jacob she'd known as a child – a young man then, with a smile on his face and a pocketful of boiled sweets or toffees to hand out to the children he encountered. It struck her that his concern tonight was the grown-up version of a handful of toffees.

Jacob stopped dead and stared at her through the gathering dusk. 'You give in your notice? You'm leaving the pub?'

'That's what I said.' She walked on, annoyed with herself. It would be all round the village first thing, and Ivy liked to keep her business to herself. 'You don't have to spread it about,' she added.

'That's all right, he said in an affronted tone. 'I'm not one to gossip, as well you know. Not that I can see why it's got to be a secret. 'Tis no shame to give up work, specially when it's nights and you got a tacker to think about.'

Ivy stopped and turned on him. 'Are you saying I'm a bad mother, Jacob Prout – been neglecting my Barry?'

'No, of course not. It's not as if you were leaving him by hisself – George is there with him. Here ...' he paused and felt in his pocket, 'have a fag. They're Player's.'

'I thought you smoked either your pipe or Woodbines,' she said, taking a cigarette from the packet he held out.

'I stick to Woodbines during the day, when I'm working – a

'fag's easier than a pipe then. I got these for a change. Here, I got a match.'

They stood together while he lit her cigarette. Ivy drew on it and felt herself calming a little. After a moment, they began to walk on. 'I'm sorry I was a bit sharp, Jacob,' she said. 'Only things have got a bit on top of me lately. That's why I give up the pub, to be honest.'

He nodded. He didn't have a lot of time for Ivy Sweet, but she hadn't been a bad kid, and he'd quite liked her saucy ways when she'd been a girl. He could understand George marrying her. It was only later that she'd become the bitter woman she now was. Something must have happened to change her, but nobody knew what it was – except that if you tried to put your finger on it, you had to conclude that it was something to do with Barry, and the reason for that wasn't hard to figure out at all.

'You been working there a long time,' he said at last. 'We all needs a break from time to time. Maybe Bernie'll give you some work in the Bell while Dottie's poorly.'

'I never thought of that,' Ivy said. 'I'm not sure, though. I reckon I've had enough of bar work, and George could do with a hand. Anyway, there's Barry. I don't want anyone else hinting I'm a bad mother.'

'I never said ...' Jacob began, then stopped. You couldn't shift Ivy once she'd made up her mind to be offended, and he didn't want to spoil a walk through the lanes on a moonlit night with arguments. He smiled to himself. It came to something when he was taking a moonlight walk with Ivy Sweet! 'You'm probably right,' he said peaceably. 'Better to be helping George out. I dare say Bernie and Rose will rub along all right. They can easy find someone else while Dottie's out of action. And if you need a bit of a rest yourself, you don't want to be looking for another job.' It occurred to him that the sight of Ivy Sweet behind the bar of the Bell Inn would be more likely to drive customers away than bring them in, but he didn't say that. No need to be nasty.

Ivy searched his words for offence and decided there probably wasn't any. The warm night air and the glimmering moon were having their effect on her too. She debated whether to say any more, then asked tentatively, 'You're round the lanes a lot, Jacob, doing your hedging and that. There ... there hasn't been anyone asking about me, has there?'

Jacob turned his head towards her. 'Asking about you, maid? Why, no, not that I know of. A stranger, you mean? Someone from outside the village?'

'No one in particular. Just anyone,' she said evasively, trying to be offhand and wishing she hadn't asked. Jacob was bound to wonder. She was aware of an expectant silence and knew she'd have to give some sort of explanation. 'Only Lennie said there'd been a chap in the pub, and I can't think who it would be. It's probably some holidaymaker been in the area a year or two back. I don't suppose it's anything important.'

'No, I don't suppose it is,' Jacob said, eyeing her. 'Anyway, if it was someone knew you from Horrabridge, they wouldn't be looking for you here. I don't expect you give out your address to all and sundry.'

They came into the village. Most of the cottage lights were out by now and the street was dark. Ivy paused outside the bakery.

'Well, good night, Jacob. Thanks for walking with me.'

He nodded. 'Pleasure. You go in and make yourself a nice cup of tea, maid. And I won't say nothing about what we been talking about. You don't need to worry about that.'

Ivy nodded and went inside. Jacob waited until she had closed the door, then proceeded towards his own cottage, drawing thoughtfully on his pipe.

There was something going on with Ivy Sweet. He'd thought so more than once lately, but now he knew for sure. Giving in her notice at the pub in Horrabridge, where she'd worked for years? And a stranger, asking about her? No doubt about it, there was something happening, and whatever it was, Ivy was upset about it – upset enough to be frightened out of her skin by the appearance of someone she'd known all her life, walking in familiar lanes when it wasn't even properly dark.

Maybe us ought to go a bit easier on her, he thought, opening his garden gate and sniffing the scent of his roses. They were all a bit too ready to be sharp with Ivy – not that she didn't ask for it, but if something was worrying her so much she'd throw up her job for it, she needed a bit of leeway.

'Come on, Scruff,' he said to the dog, who was snuffling under the bushes. 'Time for bed. And you leave Floss alone,' he added as the Jack Russell shoved his nose against the cat, sleeping peacefully on Jacob's chair. 'It behoves us all to show each other a bit of kindness in this world, and that goes for cats and dogs just as much as it do for humans.'

Chapter Twenty-Three

Dottie continued to improve, and by the end of the first week was able to take a slow, shuffling walk as far as the hospital toilets, aided by a nurse on each side. She could talk, although her voice was somewhat slurred, and what she said made sense. It looked as if she would make a complete recovery.

'There's always the danger of a second stroke,' David told Hilary as they set off for an early-morning ride. He had got into the habit of borrowing Travis's bay mare, Lightning, who was so like Hilary's gelding Beau, even down to the width of the white nose stripe, that they could have been twins. 'But it's by no means inevitable. Dottie could get back to normal and go on for years without any more trouble.'

'I do hope so,' Hilary said feelingly. 'People like Dottie and Jacob Prout are such an important part of village life. That whole generation – Dottie, Jacob, Constance Bellamy, Minnie Tozer – they seem to be a special breed, somehow. Perhaps it's because they lived through two world wars and a depression in between. They're made of tough stuff.'

'Dottie and Jacob are younger than Miss Bellamy and old Mrs Tozer, though,' David pointed out. 'There must be a good twenty years between them. More, in Mrs Tozer's case.'

'Yes, that's true. It's just that they've been around all my life so I've always seen them as old. And Jacob is so weather-beaten he could be anything from sixty to eighty-five.'

'A pretty hale eighty-five!' David laughed as they swung out through the yard gate and on to the track leading to the slopes of the moor. 'Anyway, you've got other things to think about today – the grand opening of the new kitchen!'

'I know. I can hardly believe it.' She lifted her face to the rising sun. 'After all this time, we'll have a proper kitchen again! Mrs Curnow and Patsy and Brenda have been slaving all week carrying things through from the breakfast room and putting them in the new cupboards. It's so smart! And the new Aga is like something out of Hollywood.'

'Do they have Agas in Hollywood?' he enquired, his face deadpan.

'I don't know, but if they did, they'd be like ours. I'm really pleased we decided to have it. I know the old range survived the fire quite well, but it *was* old and would have looked very old-fashioned with the new dresser and everything. I'm glad we managed to rescue the big table, though.'

'Yes, the carpenters did a really good job on that. Oak's difficult to burn, it's true, but in honesty when I saw it the day after the fire I thought it was too charred to save. But it seems to have done no more than add to its character. And we'll be able to sit round it with our children and grandchildren and tell them about the fire. It's going to be a piece of history.'

'Our history,' she said, and smiled at him. 'Oh, David – children and grandchildren. It sounds too wonderful to be true.'

'It's going to be true,' he said seriously, and then grinned. 'But before it does come true, there's something else quite important to do – our wedding. When should we start to send out invitations?'

'As soon as we get the list finalised and stop adding people we'd forgotten we should invite! By the end of this month, anyway. That gives them six weeks to reply.' She gave a little yelp of dismay. 'Six weeks! That's no time at all for all we've got to do.'

'It's six weeks from the end of the month, but over eight from now. Plenty of time.'

'*You* might think so. You don't have to get a wedding dress made, not to mention the bridesmaids' outfits. It's a shame Stella can't be sure of having had her baby by then, not that she'd be fit to be a bridesmaid even if she has. There's an awful lot of standing about. But Val's really pleased to be my matron of honour – she missed Stella's wedding, you know, having her own baby – and my two cousins, Elaine and Catherine, from the South Hams, are getting their dresses made now that they've got the patterns and material. It'll be nice to see them and their families again – we don't see them anything like often enough.' She sighed. 'I just wish Maddy and Stephen could be here. She did say she'd try to come back for it, and with the situation in Cyprus as it is, Father and I would both like her home anyway. But there's no chance of Stephen coming.'

'Has Stella heard from her since she wrote to tell her about Dottie?'

'Shouldn't think so.' They reached the open moor and Hilary leaned over to unfasten the big gate by the cattle grid. 'There's not really been time.' She waited until David was through and the gate fastened again and then straightened up and smiled at him. 'Come on. Let's have a really good gallop – I'm looking forward to my first breakfast cooked in the new kitchen!'

Stella too was preparing breakfast. Felix declared that he could not possibly minister without a proper cooked breakfast inside him – except during Lent, when he gave up eggs – and she was slicing tomatoes to fry with bacon, eggs and a slice of bread when the post-man came to the open back door with a pile of letters. She wiped her hands on a tea towel and took them with a smile.

'Thank you, Ernie.' She glanced at the bundle. 'Mostly diocesan, I expect.'

'There's one you might be interested in.' Ernie Endacott took a lively interest in the people on his round and could be relied upon to give you your own news. Postcards especially were fair game, and anyone who went on holiday had learned to be careful about what they wrote home. 'Airmail, it is, from Cyprus. Reckon it's that sister of yours.'

'Maddy!' Stella scrabbled through the pile and found the pale blue airmail letter. 'Oh, thank you!' She went back to the kitchen and dropped the rest of the pile on the table while she found a thin knife to open the letter, which was one sheet of flimsy paper folded into three to form its own envelope. The inside was covered with Maddy's sprawling writing, and she was scanning it eagerly when Felix came in.

'Hullo, what have you got there?' He sniffed and went over to the cooker. 'You do realise you're about to set fire to the whole house, don't you? I can understand that you're jealous of Hilary's new kitchen, but there are less drastic ways of making a point, and if—'

'Do shut up, Felix.' Stella waved the letter at him. 'Look! It's from Maddy – and she's coming home!'

'Really?' He moved the big frying pan from the heat. 'Oh, that *is* good news. When?'

'As soon as she can get a flight. They'll squeeze her on to one of the RAF planes as soon as they can find room. She wants to see Dottie, of course, but she says once she's home she may as well stay until the baby's born and then until Hilary's wedding. Isn't that marvellous?'

'That's several weeks,' he said, slicing the last of the tomatoes. 'I didn't think it was possible to unglue her from Stephen's side for as long as that.'

'Well, there's a lot to be here for – she'll want to be with Dottie as much as possible, and the baby will probably come in the second half of August, and Hilary's wedding will be only two or three weeks after that. She won't want to miss any of those. And with all the trouble they're having in Cyprus, she might not even be able to go back for a while.'

'She'll stay here, of course,' Felix said, moving the frying pan back to the heat and laying the bacon slices side by side. Stella looked up from the letter to see what he was doing and moved as hastily as her bulk would allow to push him aside.

'I'll do that. You look through your letters – there's a whole mountain of them this morning. Yes, of course I want her to stay here, although if Dottie's back home by then, she might decide to stay there and look after her. But it would be lovely to have her here when the baby's born. She'll get to know her little niece or nephew right from the start.'

'I'll tell you another thing,' Felix said, coming back to the stove with half his attention on a letter from the archdeacon. 'Hilary told me the other day that she was really sad Maddy couldn't be one of her bridesmaids. But if she's going to be here after all ...'

'She could be!' Stella's eyes shone. 'Oh that would be perfect. We must let Hilary know at once.'

'She probably knows already. I expect Maddy's written to her as well.'

'Yes, I expect so. All the same, it wouldn't hurt to go over and see her. I could go this morning.'

'And have a look at this famous new kitchen of hers,' he said with a grin.

'It might be a good idea,' Stella said, moving the frying pan again. 'Because if you stand there much longer with that letter so close to the heat, you'll be the one setting fire to the house and then we *shall* need a new kitchen of our own!'

'Seems like old Dottie's world-famous,' Tom Tozer said when he came into the farm kitchen later that morning for a cup of tea. 'I ran into Stella Simmons just now—'

'Stella *Copley*,' his mother corrected him. 'She's been wed long enough now for folk to remember to use her married name.'

'Stella Copley, then. Anyway, she told me they'd heard from Maddy and she's coming home as soon as she can wangle a flight. Stopping a few weeks too, Stella said. She was some delighted.'

'She would be.' Alice beamed. 'I know she was upset to think her sister might not even see her baby till it was a toddler. And how's Stella keeping? It can't be more than a month till the baby's due.'

'Could be any minute, by the look of her,' he observed. 'I was surprised she'd walked over on her own, but she swears she's fine, and anyway, if anything did happen, there's plenty of folk handy to help. I told her she didn't want to be giving birth in a field, but she just laughed at me. She was coming over to see if Hilary Napier had heard from Maddy too.'

'Did you mention we'd sent a cable to your Uncle Joe?'

'No, I thought I'd save that until we hear from him. I just hope Dottie's up to getting all these visitors. Stella didn't seem to know if there were any plans to bring her up to Tavi or let her come home.'

'She'll be pleased to know folk care, even if she's still in Plymouth.' Alice took a cake tin from the cupboard. 'There's a few bits of my date cake left, if you'd like a bite with your tea.'

'Need you ask!' he grinned. 'I've got to go into town, so I might be late for dinner. Got to feed the inner man. Where's everyone else?'

'Your gran's out in the garden shelling peas and Joanna's taken Heather round to Maggie Culliford's.' Alice looked down her nose. 'They've been getting quite thick lately.'

'I know,' Tom said. 'It's because of Maggie losing those twins – Jo's got a fellow feeling for her. They sort of hold each other up.'

'As long as they don't make each other miserable,' Alice said. 'That can happen, you know, when people get talking about what they've been through. And Maggie's never been a shining example in the village.'

'I thought we'd got over all that,' Tom said, taking a bite of cake. 'You were as ready as anyone to help her when she had all that trouble last year. And you've got to admit, she does seem to have pulled her socks up since then. So has Arthur, come to that.'

'Well, maybe.' Alice picked up the cake tin and stood with it held against her pinafore. 'And I don't want to be uncharitable. I know the Cullifords have never had it easy, but then they haven't always made the best of the chances they did have. And it don't seem to matter how hard up they are, they still seem to be able to afford a packet of Woodbines. You never see her without a cigarette hanging off her lip, and if there's one thing I don't like to see, it's a woman smoking out of doors.'

'I don't think you need worry about Jo. She's not going to take up smoking. She's trying to get me to pack it up, you know. She's got this idea it's bad for your lungs.'

'I'm sure it is. Look at that smoker's cough they talk about. Stands to reason if it gives you something like that it's not doing you any good. I just wish your dad would give up his pipe, though they do say that's not as bad for you as cigarettes, for some reason. Anyway, we can't spend the morning chattering, I've got the dinner to cook and you're supposed to be halfway to Tavistock by now.'

'You're right, I am.' Tom gulped down the last of his tea and swiped another piece of cake from the tin just as his mother put the lid on. 'Keep my dinner hot if I'm not back, will you? I've got to go out to Mill Hill as well.' He opened the back door. 'Hullo! There's someone coming through the yard. It's a telegraph boy.'

'A telegraph boy?' Alice came swiftly to the door, staring past him at the fresh-faced boy dressed in a dark blue uniform pushing a red bike through the gate. 'Oh don't say it's bad news about Jackie!'

'Of course it's not.' Tom went forward and took the brown envelope from the boy, ripping it open and scanning the single page. 'It's Uncle Joe.' He turned to his mother, his face split by a beam of excitement. 'You'll never guess! He's coming over again. He's coming to see Dottie!'

Chapter Twenty-Four

It seemed as if half the world was on its way to Burracombe to see Dottie Friend.

Stella, walking through the village towards the Barton, was stopped half a dozen times by people who wanted to enquire after her own health, and glean any further information about Dottie. The news that Maddy was coming home sent them all hurrying off, beaming, to pass it on, so that it was soon all round the village.

'I can't say I'm altogether surprised,' Jessie Friend remarked as she served Jacob Prout with his morning packet of Woodbines. 'Dottie looked after her like a mother. Those two sisters have got a lot to thank her for.'

'It'll do her a power of good to see young Maddy again,' Jacob said. 'Set her right back on the road to recovery, that will.'

'What's that?' asked Val, coming through the shop door just as he was speaking. 'Is Maddy coming home?'

'So young Stella just told me. On her way to Miss Hilary, to see if they've heard too. I wonder you didn't bump into her.'

Val laughed. 'I'm glad I didn't! Stella's quite something to bump into now, the size she is. But that's lovely news. And it's not all, either.' She waited as Jessie gave Jacob his change, their faces turned expectantly towards her. 'I'll have a quarter of mixed toffees and two ounces of dolly mixtures, please, Jessie.'

'Well, come on, out with it,' Jacob urged. 'Us can tell you got summat you'm bursting to tell us. Is the Queen herself coming to visit our Dottie?'

Val laughed again, enjoying the moment of suspense she had

created. 'No, though I don't think Dottie could be any more pleased if it was. It's my Uncle Joe – he's coming over to see her. I just went up to the farm and Mother told me. She's thrilled to bits.'

'Your Joe! Well, I'll go to sea.' Jacob opened his packet of cigarettes and took one out. 'Coming all this way just to see Dottie? He must be even sweeter on her than us thought.'

'I hope he don't have no ideas about taking her back to America with him this time,' Jessie said. 'I hardly expected her to come home again when she went over there before. And I'd rather you didn't light up in here, Jacob. The smoke gets into the food.'

'Sorry. I wasn't thinking.' He put the cigarette back. 'Anyway, I'd better get back to work. I'm doing all the hedges round Mrs Warren's garden today, and if you stretched 'em all out in one length, I reckon they'd get nearly as far as Tavistock. And the amount they've grown since the spring don't bear thinking about.'

He went out, pausing to light the forbidden cigarette, and then set off, pushing his wheelbarrow. Val waited while Jessie weighed out the sweets and made blue paper cones for them, then said, 'How's your Billy? Someone told me he had a bad cold.'

'He did have, but he's nearly over it now, thank goodness. You know how they go to his chest, and I always think a summer cold's worse than a winter one. To tell you the truth, me and Jeanie's a bit worried about him. He don't seem to bounce back like he used to. He didn't even want to go to the cinema last Saturday, and you know how he enjoys the pictures.'

'I'm sorry to hear that.' Val knew that Billy had already lived longer than many people born with his condition did. With his short, thickset figure and flat, smiling face with its button nose and slanting eyes, he was a familiar sight in the village as he helped Bert Foster heave meat carcasses into the butcher's shop. He was proud of his strength, but it seemed as if each cold he suffered weakened him a little more. 'I hope he's better soon. The warm weather will help.'

'Oh yes, he'll soon be out and about again.' Jessie turned to serve the next customer and Val stepped out into the sunshine, where Christopher waited in his pram. She decided to walk down to the ford so that he could have a paddle, then head towards the school, where the children might be outside. They would be breaking up for their summer holiday at the end of the week, and then the play-ground would be silent again.

By the time Christopher had been persuaded to come out of the water and was back in his pram, the children were pouring out through the doors for a quarter of an hour's rushing about and screaming before those who stayed for dinner went inside again. Those who went home, including Val's nephew Robin, were being met by mothers or were in the charge of older brothers or sisters. Joanna was at the gates, talking to Maggie Culliford.

'Hello, Val. I was just telling Maggie about Uncle Joe. It's good news, isn't it. Mother's in a tizzy already, thinking about bedrooms and meals!'

'I don't know why she should be. At least the spare bedroom's been redecorated now – Joe and Russell did it themselves last time they were over. Is Russell coming too? I didn't think to ask.'

'The cable didn't say. I shouldn't think so. He'll be looking after the business now. Of course, you know who Mum and Dad would really like him to bring with him.'

Val nodded. 'Jackie. But I don't think that's very likely. She's taken to America too well. I don't think she'll ever come home to live again.' She turned to Maggie. 'And how are you getting along now? You've had good news too, haven't you?'

'My Arthur, you mean? Yes, a proper full-time job over at the Shillabeers' place. He's a good worker, my Arthur,' she added a little defiantly, as if expecting them to challenge her. 'He's just never been given a proper chance before.'

'I'm sure he'll do well,' Joanna said reassuringly. 'He's a country-man – he can turn his hand to anything. He'll be a real help to Mrs Shillabeer.'

Maggie nodded and turned to walk home with her children tagging along beside her. Joanna set off back to the Tozers' farm, and Val was about to cross the road to her own cottage when Miss Kemp came out to call the children in and saw her. Val waved and waited while the teacher ushered the children inside then came across to the gate.

'I don't suppose you've heard the news. Stella came over this morning to tell us that Maddy's coming back to see Dottie Friend.'

'Oh, that *is* good. She'll be a wonderful tonic for poor Dottie. And for Stella, too. Will Maddy be able to stay for the baby's arrival?'

'I think so, and maybe even for Hilary's wedding. And that's not all. Uncle Joe's coming too – they had a cable at the farm this morning.'

'Goodness! There's going to be a real crush around Dottie's bed. The rest of us won't be able to get a look-in.' Miss Kemp hesitated, then said, 'He certainly seemed very fond of Dottie when he was here before. It seemed almost as if romance was in the air then.'

'He'd like to marry her,' Val said. 'He asked her before they went to America but she wouldn't hear of it. She said they were too old and one of them would have to move and leave everything behind, and whichever one it was, it would be too much. If they lived in the same area to start with, it would be different.'

'But your uncle did live here as a young man. It might not be quite so hard for him to come back.'

'He's got family in Corning,' Val pointed out. 'Russell, and the two daughters and their families. And Dottie considers the whole of Burracombe her family. I don't think she could uproot herself now. I'm afraid they've left it too late.'

'No, I don't think she could.' Miss Kemp smiled at Val. 'Well, it will do her good to see him, and Maddy too. I'll look forward to seeing her again myself.' She turned back towards the school. 'I'd better go and see what those young scallywags are doing now. Mr Raynor is very good with them, but it's really my turn for dinner duty today.'

Frances Kemp went inside, thoughtful. The story of Dottie and Joe was, as she had suggested, quite romantic, but it was a poignant tale with no traditionally happy ending. Not that either of them was actually *un*happy, as far as anyone could tell, but Dottie was right – the hurdles were too high for them to jump now, and perhaps Val was right too, in saying they had left it too late. She felt a little sad.

The dinner children were sitting at the long table eating the food Mrs Purdy had set before them. Today it was shepherd's pie with fresh peas, followed by rhubarb crumble and custard. James was already in his place at one end and Frances took her seat at the other. He caught her eye and smiled, lifting his water glass a little, and Frances smiled back.

How did you know when it might be too late? How did you know when a vow you had made years ago could never be fulfilled? How could you tell when the right moment had come to make a change in your life – to take that final, heart-stopping leap into a different future?

Perhaps, she thought, Dottie and Joe would still be able to grasp at their own chance of happiness. Perhaps, after all, it was never really too late.

Stella was staying for lunch at the Barton with Hilary and her father. Felix had gone to a meeting in Tavistock, so she hadn't needed much persuading, and she sat at the old oak table, so miraculously saved from the fire, and gazed around.

'It's just beautiful. You must be thrilled with it.'

'We are. At least, I am – I think to Father a kitchen is just a kitchen. And he's not quite sure about the pale green cupboard doors, or the Formica worktops. But Mrs Curnow and Patsy and Brenda and I all love it!'

'It's good to get out of the breakfast room, too,' the housekeeper agreed, taking a pie out of the new Aga. 'It was all a bit ramshackle in there and you couldn't keep it properly tidy, not with the best will in the world. But in here – well, us've got a place for everything.'

'And everything in its place,' Hilary added with a grin. 'Mrs Ellis always used to say that too.'

'It's a good way to live. Now, if you'd like to go and tell the Colonel that lunch is ready, I'll start bringing it through.'

'I'll take the pie,' Hilary said. 'You can bring the beans, Stella.' She went through the kitchen door towards the dining room and tapped on her father's study door. 'Lunch is ready, and we've got a visitor, with news.'

'News?' Gilbert Napier enquired, emerging and following them to the dining room. 'Why, it's young Stella. Good to see you, my dear. And what's this news you've brought us? Good, I hope.'

'Very good.' Stella eased her bulk on to a chair at the table as Mrs Curnow came in with a dish of new potatoes and a jug of gravy. 'Maddy's coming home.'

'Is she indeed? They're sending the wives back, then? Not that I'm surprised; the situation with EOKA's no better, getting a lot worse, in fact.'

Stella and Hilary looked at each other blankly. Then Stella said, 'No, it's not because of EOKA. It's Dottie. Maddy's coming home to see Dottie. And it looks as if she'll stay until Hilary's wedding.'

'So she can be one of my bridesmaids!' Hilary added, her eyes shining. 'Isn't that wonderful? If only Steve could get back too – but I don't suppose they'll let him.'

'Not just for a wedding, I'm afraid,' Gilbert said. 'Still, it'll be a relief to have Maddy safe home, at least.'

Hilary said doubtfully, 'Do you really think it's that bad, Father? Steve's not going to be in any danger, is he?'

Her father gave her a look. 'He's serving in the armed forces, girl, and the conflict is building up. Of course there's danger.'

There was a small silence. Stella said, 'But the RAF don't actually fight. They're just on patrol, surely. It won't be like during the war.'

Gilbert glanced at her. There had been a faint quiver of fear in her voice, and as Hilary watched him, she hoped that he would remember that Stella was Maddy's sister and not far from her time with the baby. Don't upset her now, she begged silently. Not before it's really necessary. She felt her own fear too, for her younger brother, who might very well be in danger far from home, but thrust it down out of sight.

'Have some potatoes, Father. They're out of our own garden, and so are the runner beans. Patsy picked them this morning. Stella, how much pie do you want?'

'Just a small piece, please. I'll be cooking Felix a meal later.' Stella's voice was quiet and Hilary thought she looked pale. Her bubbling joy that her sister was coming home seemed to have evaporated.

'Dottie's going to be so pleased to see Maddy. I wonder if they'll let her come home soon – Dottie, I mean. They'll want her to have someone to look after her for a while, I should think.'

'Maddy will probably do that,' Stella said. 'She won't come all this way, leaving Stephen, and not do as much as she can. She really thinks of Dottie as a second mother, you know, more than Fenella Forsyth, even though Fenella adopted her. She was away so much during the war, entertaining troops and so on.' Her voice faded and Hilary saw her blink away a tear before turning to Gilbert.

'Colonel Napier, do you really think there's going to be fighting in Cyprus? I don't know what Maddy would do if anything happened to Stephen.'

'Nothing's going to happen to Steve—' Hilary began, but Stella lifted a hand and she fell silent.

'I'd rather know the truth,' Stella said quietly.

Gilbert gave her a steady look, then nodded. 'You're right. It's better to face facts.' He cleared his throat. 'You see, the trouble in Cyprus started in a rather unusual way. It began when we started to withdraw our troops from Egypt and set up our Middle East HQ in Cyprus. The Green Howards went first, last August, and then the Royal Inniskilling Fusiliers. That's when the Enosis movement was set up, and things have got steadily worse. And will continue to do so as long as we're there.'

Stella didn't ask why the British didn't simply leave Cyprus if they were so unwelcome. That wasn't the sort of question you asked a soldier. She sighed, and said, 'So there will be fighting, and even though Stephen isn't in the army, he'll be involved.' She laid down her knife and fork and rested her head on her hand for a moment. 'As if we haven't had enough war,' she said in a tired voice. 'The Second World War, taking both our parents and separating Maddy and me so that we thought we'd never find each other again, then the Korean War, and now this ... It seems as if it will never end.' She looked at Hilary. 'I'm sorry. I don't think I can eat any more. I'll go home.'

'Not on your own, you won't.' Hilary was on her feet. 'I'll drive you round. I'm not having you walk back all by yourself, over the Clam and up that steep rocky track. But why not wait and have a coffee first? Or a cup of tea?'

'I don't want to spoil your lunch ...'

'You're not spoiling it. We're the ones who are spoiling the day for you.' Hilary cast an annoyed glance at her father. 'Stella came here so happy and excited, and now look what we've done, putting ideas into her head. You should never have mentioned it.'

'Don't be absurd! She asked to know the truth. She's not a child.'

'No, but she needs looking after.' Hilary caught herself up and turned back to Stella. 'Darling, I'm sorry, we're arguing over you as if you're not here. Now look, I've just about finished my meal and I don't want any pudding. Why don't we go into the drawing room and have a pot of tea, and then I'll take you home? Felix will be back soon, won't he?'

'Yes, probably around three o'clock. But I'm all right, really.' She turned to Gilbert and attempted a smile. 'You didn't upset me at all – I felt a little off-colour anyway. But I'm perfectly all right now and I can walk back. The fresh air will do me good.' She stood up and put her hand to her head again. 'I'd quite like a cup of tea, though.'

Hilary looked at her in some alarm and moved to put her arm around the slight shoulders. 'Come along now. Let's get you comfortable and I'll go and make a pot. I'll tell Mrs Curnow you're ready for your pudding, Father.'

Gilbert nodded, but Hilary's concern was reflected in his face. 'D'you want me to telephone Charles?'

Hilary hesitated and Stella looked up. 'No! There's no need to bother him – I told you, I'm quite all right. It was just rather a shock, talking about Cyprus. I don't think I'd realised ...' Her voice faded a little. 'I was so excited about Maddy coming home ...'

'And so are we,' Gilbert said more gently. 'I'm sorry, my dear. I didn't mean to frighten you. I should have been more tactful.'

'Well there's something new,' Hilary said with a little laugh. 'You, admitting to being tactless! Come on, Stella. You'll be as right as rain after a cup of tea. But I'm still taking you home, and I'm not leaving you until Felix is back.'

Chapter Twenty-Five

'So that's that,' Frances Kemp said with a little sigh of relief as the last of the children departed from the playground, burdened with pictures they had drawn and painted, Plasticine models they had squashed and pummelled into shapes that – in some cases, anyway – almost resembled real animals, and various other bits and pieces accumulated during the term. 'Six weeks of bliss.'

It was the end of the third week in July, and school had broken up for the holidays. The children had been let out early, as was tradition, and rushed off screaming with excitement along the village street. Frances felt almost like screaming and rushing with them.

James Raynor smiled down at her. 'Not quite. We still have the play to perform at the summer fair on August Bank Holiday, and at least three more rehearsals before then, if the children remember to come.'

'They'll remember to come all right. Especially George and Edward. You had quite a job to persuade them that they couldn't take their dragon home with them.'

'They swore they only wanted to rehearse in it,' he said. 'But I know that gleam in their eyes by now. We'd have had that dragon capering up and down the village street frightening old ladies before we could blink. I'm still not convinced they haven't got their own plans for breathing fire.'

Frances laughed. 'You underestimate the old ladies of Burra-combe! They're not likely to be frightened of a dragon made out of camouflage material with a few splodges of yellow paint daubed on it. Anyway, it's not finished yet and we don't want it damaged before the big day, so I think it's better in your keeping than in the not-so-gentle hands of the Crocker twins. Although I really think this play has been very good for them. It's taught them some discipline.'

'They enjoy it, that's why. I'm not sure the discipline, such as it is, extends to activities they're not so keen on. Learning to read and write, for example. Or anything that involves sitting still for more than five minutes. The Crocker twins are all for action.'

'I'm sure that can be put to good use.' She hesitated, and James glanced at her.

'So what are your plans for the holidays? We've both been so busy during the past two or three weeks, we've not had much chance to talk. Are you going away?'

'Only to stay with my cousin Iris. I usually go to her in the summer. She used to come here – this is where she lived as a girl – but she's not very mobile now. But that won't be until after the summer fair, and my most immediate plan is to go home and celebrate the end of term with a cup of tea.' She returned his glance. 'Will you join me?'

He followed her into the school house and leaned against the door jamb while she filled the kettle and got out a tin of biscuits. 'And are you going away?' she enquired after a moment.

'No. I want to enjoy my second summer in Burracombe. Last year was all very new and we were so busy with the Culliford camp, I barely had time to take it all in.'

'The Culliford camp! What a success that was. I'm surprised we haven't had requests to repeat it.'

'There have been a few hints dropped in my hearing, but I declined to rise to the bait,' he grinned. 'Not that it might not be quite a good idea to have a village camp for the children each year. Most of them don't get a real holiday – they all seem to work harder on the farms than they do at school, what with harvest and so on. We might think about it next year, perhaps – take them all away somewhere for a week.'

'That sounds rather ambitious,' Frances remarked. 'Where would you think of going?'

'Oh, I don't know – somewhere near the sea, perhaps. Bigbury Bay, or Blackpool Sands near Dartmouth. We could hire a chara-banc and find some more tents. It would do the children so much good.'

'It would.' She turned to him. 'You're really a very kind man, James.'

He flushed a little. 'I just enjoy my job, that's all. I like seeing the children grow and flourish. Dorothy and I wanted a big family, so I suppose I see them as substitutes, in a way.'

'Yes.' She gazed at the kettle without really seeing it. 'It's rather the same for me. I love the peace and freedom of the holidays, but I'm always even more pleased when term begins again and the children come back.'

There was a short pause. Then James said gently, 'It's boiling, Frances,' and she came out of her thoughts with a start and poured hot water into the teapot.

'Sorry – I was miles away.' She put the kettle back to boil again, tipped out the pot and spooned in tea before filling it with water. James had already set cups and saucers on the old wooden tray, and Frances took a jug of milk from the pantry to add to it. Once loaded with the pot and a plate of biscuits, he picked it up and carried it out to the garden.

The azaleas were over now and the hedge was a patchwork of greens. A potentilla bush was covered in yellow flowers and a bud-dleia was sending long spires of lilac like rockets towards the sky. A cloud of butterflies rose at their approach, but soon settled back to their job of harvesting nectar alongside a hum of bees. The voices of the children had long faded and the garden was very peaceful.

Frances was silent. She had a feeling that an important moment was approaching and she didn't know quite how to deal with it. She had had this sensation several times before, but always it had been averted, either by some small crisis with the children or by some other interruption. Once or twice she had even managed to divert it herself. But she was aware that she could not keep doing this, and by allowing her friendship with James to develop after all, despite her attempts to prevent it, she had brought the moment closer. It was not going to go away.

She slanted a look at him from beneath her lashes and found that he was watching her. Her colour rose and she said quickly, 'The tea must be brewed now,' and leaned forward to pour milk into the cups.

James said nothing. He waited until the tea was poured and he had taken a biscuit from the plate she offered him. Then he said quietly, 'We need to talk, Frances, you and I.'

'I know.' She couldn't look at him. She stared into her cup instead, feeling her heart rate increase. She knew that she couldn't turn away any longer from the issue that lay between them.

James set down his cup. He leaned across and touched her wrist. She glanced up at him and felt herself blush at the look in his eyes. She wanted to get up, to run indoors, but her body refused to move. I'm behaving like a coward, she thought. Whatever would Ralph say?

The thought of Ralph seemed to strike at her heart. It was so long since she had seen him, so many years, and a lifetime had been lived since then, yet he seemed so close to her at that moment that she felt she could reach out and touch him. And here she was, with another man's fingers on her wrist ...

'Please, James,' she said in a low voice. 'Please don't say whatever it is you want to say.'

'And how do you know what I want to say?'

She shook her head. 'I do know. I *think* I know. But ...'

'You don't want to hear it?' he said after a pause.

'It's not that. It's more that I *can't* hear it.' She raised her eyes to look at him. 'I – I'm not ready. I don't know if I'll ever be ready.'

He was silent again. Gently she withdrew her hand, and he let go of her wrist. They sat, not looking at each other, as a robin sang a sudden trill in the hedge and their tea grew cold.

'Was it in the first war?' he asked at last, and she nodded.

'My cousin – my second cousin – Ralph. He lived here then – his father was the pharmacist in Tavistock – and we used to come down, my brother Johnny and I, to spend our holidays with him and his sister Iris. We'd known each other all our lives, of course, but that summer – the summer the war started – we were growing up and we fell in love.'

'You were very young then.'

'I know. But it was still love, James – not puppy love, as they call it. Ralph joined up and went away, and we wrote to each other every

197

day. His letters only came occasionally and he didn't always have time to write much, but I posted mine every morning. I wanted to go too, I wanted to help, to be a VAD nurse or something, but I was too young. I had to stay at home and *knit*.'

'Knit?'

'Balaclavas,' she said bitterly. 'And socks and gloves. For the men. I could at least comfort myself that they kept some poor soldier's hands and feet warm. It was all I could do, all I was allowed to do, all those years.'

He waited, but she had fallen silent, remembering those endless, frustrating evenings of knitting. 'And in the end?' he prompted at last.

'In the end, he died, of course. Died of his wounds, they said, whatever that might have meant. We never found out.' She turned and looked him in the eyes. 'You can see his name on the village war memorial. *Ralph Stannard. Died 1918*. It was all my uncle and aunt would allow to be put there.'

'And your brother? Johnny?' he asked after a few moments.

'Influenza,' she said with a short laugh. 'He didn't even go to war – he was rejected for poor eyesight. He was studying to become a doctor in the hope that he could go in that way. It all seemed so cruel, so pointless.'

'Yes,' he said quietly. 'I felt that too, rather.'

'Oh James.' She turned to him swiftly. 'I'm sorry. You lost your wife and all your hopes and dreams too. And we're only two. Two – out of millions.'

He leaned forward again. 'And don't you think that perhaps there may be more hopes and dreams for people like us? For the millions who seemed to lose everything? Our lives have gone on, and we've made something of them. We've found pleasures and fulfilments. We've found laughter and even happiness. Don't you think we may find even more?'

Frances looked at him. His eyes were dark and steady, the creases in his brow drawn deeper by the strength of his emotion. She longed to say yes, to see those creases grow smooth, to see the warmth in his eyes and to feel it in the strength of his hands. But deep within her, like a heartbeat, she could still feel the echoes of her first love's name. Ralph – Ralph – *Ralph* …

'I don't know,' she said at last, turning away. 'I'm sorry, James. I just don't know ...'

There was another moment of silence, and then he sat back, and she knew that if she looked at him, she would see disappointment in every line. Eventually, he spoke again.

'I'm sorry, Frances. We agreed a little while ago just to be friends and I don't want to spoil that. I hope we will always be friends.'

In relief, she looked up at him at last, and her taut mouth relaxed to a smile, even though there were tears on her cheeks that she could not remember shedding.

'Of course we will, James. Always.'

He got up soon after that and left, and she knew that when they met again he would behave as if the last half-hour had never happened. But as she stood at the gate, watching him limp slowly away, she knew it could not be as easily forgotten.

She went back into the garden and tidied away the cold tea and the untouched biscuits.

Chapter Twenty-Six

'I see Bernie got Ivy Sweet working behind the bar now,' Jack Pettifer commented to Norman Tozer as they met in the village street on their way to the Bell Inn. 'I didn't know she'd left the pub in Horrabridge, did you?'

'I did hear about it. Jacob Prout told me. Met her walking home one night, he said, and she told him then she'd give in her notice. He didn't know no more than that. Handy for Bernie and Rose, with Dottie being poorly. Not that Ivy's much of an asset – her face is enough to turn the beer sour.'

'You don't know why she left Horrabridge? Only, she've been there for years. I thought she was a fixture.'

Norman shrugged. 'You know Ivy. Shuts up like a clam if you ask her questions. Mind you, I got a cousin over Horrabridge way, and he reckons there was a spot of trouble. Chap been asking round the village about her, and Ivy didn't like it.'

Jack shot him a look. 'Stranger, you mean?'

'Bit more than that. Foreign, my cousin said. Spoke good English, mind. He wondered if it was someone who knew her back along – in the war, maybe.'

They glanced at each other. After a moment, Jack said, 'A lot of funny things went on during the war, specially with that airfield up to Harrowbeer and all they Polish and Czech airmen stationed there. Not that it'd be a good idea to mention it to Ivy.'

'Not if you don't want your beer poisoned!' Norman said with a laugh.

They pushed the door open and went inside.

*

Ivy hadn't intended to work in the pub, but when Bernie had found out that she had left her job, he'd called round one morning to ask her to help him and Rose out while Dottie was off sick.

'It might be quite a while, depending how she gets on,' he'd said cautiously, not at all sure he wanted Ivy as a permanent barmaid. She knew the work all right, but you couldn't pretend she was a popular figure in the village. 'But maybe you're not looking for anything long-term.'

'To tell you the truth, I'm not looking for a job at all,' Ivy told him. 'Reckon I deserve a bit of a rest after all these years, and I'm usually in the shop helping George out during the day anyway. I couldn't do dinner times, if that's what you want.'

'No, me and Rose can manage then. It's only a few farmhands and such that likes a pint with their crib. Evenings are what we're looking for.'

'I don't want to work early evening. I got Barry to think about too.'

'Eight o'clock?' he asked, feeling a little desperate. 'Till ten thirty, so we can clean up and do the money after we close? Just a few days a week would be a real help while Dottie's off.'

Ivy chewed her lip. 'All right, then,' she said at last. 'I'll do four nights a week – Wednesday till Saturday. You'll have to manage the others yourselves, or get someone else in. How long d'you reckon Dottie's going to be off?'

Bernie shrugged. 'I don't think even the doctors know that. But if you don't want it to be permanent, we'll start looking for someone else straight away. Put an advert in the *Tavistock Gazette* and the *Times*. It's just to help us out in the meantime, Ive, what with it being summer and all.'

'Give it a month or so,' Ivy said. 'You'll have a better idea how Dottie's getting on then, and I might decide to stop on after all. I'll start tomorrow.'

Bernie went off, partly relieved and partly apprehensive, wondering if he would be able to get rid of Ivy if she decided to stay on. It ought to be my decision, he thought ruefully, but he had never been much good at dealing with strong women. Still, Rose was strong enough for both of them – she'd be able to handle the situation if it came to the point.

Now that she was working in the village, Ivy felt easier in her own mind. The black-haired man who had been asking about her in Horrabridge wasn't likely to track her down here. Lennie wouldn't give her away, and as far as she was aware, none of the customers in his pub knew exactly where she lived. Whoever the man was, and whatever he wanted, she felt safe for the first time in months.

Whoever he was ... whatever he wanted ...

Ivy had racked her brains to think who he might be. She had known plenty of airmen during the war, of course. She had known their names and what beers they liked, looked at photographs of their families, listened to their troubles. She had exchanged the usual flirtatious banter expected of a barmaid and had always known where to draw the line.

Except in one case.

But it couldn't have been him, she told herself. Not with black hair. Unconsciously she touched her own ginger frizz and thought of Barry's bright curls. And he hadn't even known. Even George didn't know – not for certain. He might have suspected, but he'd put his suspicions away and never asked her outright, and she had never told him. There were times when she'd even managed to persuade herself that there was nothing to tell. Why cause upset when there was no need?

So if it wasn't him ... who was it?.

Now she was working at the Bell she felt more settled. She had money in her pocket again – she'd always hated having to ask George for every penny – and she was away from the bakery for a few hours but she was still there for Barry before he went to bed. Really, everything had worked out for the best after all, and when Jack and Norman pushed open the door and came in, she greeted them with a smile that made them blink.

Dottie was making good progress, and when Felix and Stella went to the hospital to see her, she was sitting up in bed reading *Woman* magazine.

'Telling you how to make scones, they are,' she said as they greeted her. 'Just as if everyone don't learn that at their mother's knee. But there, I suppose these folk as lives in big cities don't know nothing about baking, get all their cakes and scones from the shop.'

'So do a lot of people in the country,' Stella said with a smile, settling herself on the chair beside Dottie's bed. 'Or you and George Sweet wouldn't be able to make a living.'

Dottie opened her mouth and closed it again. Felix laughed. 'She's got you there, Dottie. Mind you, if city folk have bakeries like George's to go to, with scones like yours, it's no wonder they don't bother to bake for themselves. You'd better move to London when you get out of here, and make your fortune.'

'Fortune!' she snorted. 'Who wants a fortune when they've got a place like Burracombe to live? Anyway, I'm forgetting my manners.' She lifted her face for a kiss. 'It's good to see you both – not that you wouldn't be better off at home with your feet up,' she added to Stella. 'I suppose you'm still running about like a two-year-old.'

'Well, not exactly,' Stella said, thinking of the way Hilary had insisted on taking her home when she had walked to Burracombe Barton with her news about Maddy. 'They won't let me now.'

'And quite right too,' Dottie said. 'You got to take care of yourself. You got a babby to think about.'

'I can tell you're better,' Felix teased her. 'Sitting there like the Queen of England, giving your orders. When are they sending you home to boss us about?'

Dottie pulled down the corners of her mouth. It was still a little lopsided, Stella thought, but not nearly as bad as it had been at first. And there were roses in the cheeks that had been so pale. She was definitely on the mend.

'They told me today I've got to go to Tavi first, and then they'll see after a few days. It'd be sooner if there was someone there to look after me, but there isn't, so that's that. I reckon I could manage all right by myself if someone brought a bed into the front room, but the doctor won't have it, and once they get you in here, you don't seem to have no say in your own life.' She moved restlessly in the bed and Stella glanced at Felix and then leaned towards her, smiling.

'Well, we may be able to do something about that, Dottie. You could have someone staying with you by next week, if you want them. Of course, you might say you don't, you'd rather be in hospital, but …'

Dottie stared at her. 'Whatever be you rambling on about now, maid? Who is it that I might have staying with me? Doesn't sound as if it's anyone I really want, the way you'm talking. I hope you'm not thinking of one of they Culliford girls.'

Stella giggled. 'Well, Maggie did offer, but—'

'*Maggie Culliford?*' Dottie exploded, and Felix stepped forward and laid his hand on her shoulder. He shook his head at his wife.

'You'll give her another stroke if you're not careful. No, Dottie, it's not Maggie, nor one of her girls. They're too young anyway, except for Brenda, and even she shouldn't be given the responsibility of looking after an invalid, especially one as precious as you. No, it's somebody you'll be pleased to have with you. Tell her, darling, before she bursts into flames.'

Dottie looked from him to Stella. 'You'm both acting like a pair of children yourselves. For pity's sake, put me out of my misery.'

'It's *Maddy*!' Stella said, her face wreathed in smiles. 'Maddy's coming home especially to be with you. We knew a few days ago but we didn't want to tell you until it was absolutely certain – but she sent a telegram today to say she'll be here on Tuesday. Isn't it wonderful?'

Dottie gaped at her. She turned to look at Felix, as if asking him if it could possibly be true. He grinned and nodded.

'Stella's quite right. Maddy will be here next Tuesday and she'll certainly want to stay with you. So you can tell your doctor that from then on, you'll be well looked after. Why, you'll probably be begging to come back after a day or two for some peace and quiet – the whole village will be beating a path to your door.'

'Maddy,' Dottie said wonderingly. 'My Maddy, coming back here just for me. But what about Stephen? He don't want to let her go, surely? It'll be only for a week or so, won't it?'

'No, she says once she's back she may as well stay until our baby's born, and even for Hilary's wedding. She's going to be a bridesmaid, after all.' Stella beamed at her. Then her smile faded a little. 'Actually, Hilary's father thinks she might have been sent home anyway. With all the trouble going on out in Cyprus now, he says they'll be sending all the wives home.'

Dottie nodded. 'I saw something about it in the *Daily Express* yesterday. It don't look too good, do it? Tell you the truth, I been worrying a bit about Maddy, so it'll be good to have her back here safe. She's bound to miss her man, though. We'll all have to be careful not to upset her.'

Felix smiled. 'Dottie, she's coming home to look after *you*, not the other way about! But you're right, she's sure to miss him and be anxious about him. I'm sure you'll keep her busy, though, and when the baby comes, we shall be competing for attention. Now then, let's see what we've got in this bag for you.' He lifted the shopping bag they had brought with them and started to take out gifts. 'A bunch of roses from Jacob – we ought to have found a vase and put them in water as soon as we came in – some Cadbury's Milk Tray from Joyce Warren, a nice romantic novel from Aggie Madge, and an *Amateur Gardening* magazine from Miss Bellamy. And we're to tell you that Ted and Alice Tozer are coming to see you tomorrow and they may have some news for you too, only we're not allowed to say what it is.'

'I'm not even sure we were allowed to say that much,' Stella remarked. 'So pretend you didn't hear it, Dottie.'

'Hear what?' Dottie said innocently, and they all laughed. 'And what other news is there from the village? How are Bernie and Rose getting on without me?'

Stella and Felix glanced at each other. 'I suppose you'll have to know sometime,' Stella said. 'They've asked Ivy Sweet to help out behind the bar while you're away.'

'*Ivy Sweet?*' For the second time, Dottie looked ready to explode, and Stella took hold of her hand. 'Behind my bar? But what about her job in Horrabridge?'

'She's given it up,' Felix said apologetically, feeling like a messenger about to be shot for bringing bad news. 'And Bernie needed someone, so he asked her. It's only until you're ready to go back.'

'That's if there's a pub to go back to,' Dottie said ungraciously. 'It'll probably have closed by then. The customers will have all gone across to the Standard in Little Burracombe.'

'Now don't be like that,' Felix chided her. 'They had to do something, and she knows the work. She didn't go after your job deliberately, Dottie. Bernie said she wasn't all that keen when he first asked her.'

Dottie sighed grumpily and Stella glanced at her husband.

'I think you're getting tired,' she said softly to the older woman.

'Why don't you have a rest now? We'll put your roses in a vase and leave you. You're probably ready for a sleep.'

'Just look forward to Maddy coming home,' Felix advised. 'That's a much nicer thought to go to sleep with.'

Dottie nodded. She looked at them both and smiled, holding out a hand to Felix.

'You'm right. I shouldn't be so bad-tempered. It's just being stuck here in this hospital bed, not knowing when I'll get back to my own cottage again – well, it do get me down a bit. But I know I'm a lucky woman to have so many good friends, and there's plenty in here worse off than me – plenty that'll never see their homes again. You just tell everyone I'm doing well and thank them for the lovely things they keep sending. And tell Alice I'm looking forward to hearing her news – though it can't be anything as good as the news you brought me.'

'I wonder if she'll still think that when she hears what it is,' Stella said to Felix as they left the ward. 'If you ask me, it'll be a close call between Maddy and Joe Tozer. Except that he won't be able to stay in the cottage with her, of course.'

'It would raise a few eyebrows if he did,' Felix chuckled. 'But I'm pretty sure Dottie will get better very quickly indeed when she knows what a welcome home she's going to get!'

Chapter Twenty-Seven

Maddy arrived tired and rather wan after the long journey home. Hilary drove to Tavistock to meet her train, pointing out that the big Armstrong Siddeley was more comfortable than the little Austin she had given on permanent loan to Felix, and Stella would be able to go too. 'I don't suppose we'd fit all Maddy's luggage into the Austin anyway,' she added, and Felix grinned and agreed.

'Take care of my two girls,' he said, tucking Stella into the front seat. 'I wish I could come with you, but I've got a funeral to conduct. It's old Josiah Wedderburn, from Ants Farm,' he added to Hilary. 'He was ninety-five, so it wasn't unexpected.'

'Yes, I'd heard he'd died. I remember him from when I was a child. He used to bring plums round in his horse and cart. They'd be sent down by train to Tavistock from some fruit farm up the line, and he'd load up and hawk them round all the villages. You could hear him shouting "Plums!" from miles away.'

'I don't think I've ever seen him,' Stella said.

'No, he was bedridden for years, poor old man. I should think it's been a happy release for him.'

'For his family too, I think,' Felix remarked. 'He was a cantankerous old ... Well, I suppose I shouldn't say that now he's dead, especially as I have to say nice things about him later! I'll talk about the plums instead.' He bent to give Stella a kiss. 'See you later, darling. And Maddy too, of course.'

The big grey car slid away from the vicarage. Stella leaned back in her seat and stretched luxuriously.

'It's lovely to have so much room. I can hardly get into the Austin now. And I'm sure even Maddy won't be able to fill all that space you've got in the boot.'

Hilary laughed. 'She won't be bringing everything she possesses. After all, she's only staying a few weeks.'

'I suppose so. But you know what Maddy's like. She needs a choice of three outfits for every occasion, including breakfast. I'll be surprised if she doesn't have at least three suitcases.'

In fact, she had five. Hilary blinked as her sister-in-law stepped down from the train at Tavistock station, and even Stella was startled, though as much by the cluster of hefty young men who passed the luggage down from the carriage to the platform as by the seemingly endless succession of cases and bags. Maddy herself directed operations and then thanked her assistants with a dazzling smile before turning to fling her arms around her sister.

'Stella, you're enormous! I can hardly reach round you. And Hilary, thank you so much for coming to meet me. I thought I'd have to get a taxi, and a taxi might not have been able to carry all my luggage.'

'I'm not so sure *we* can,' Hilary observed, giving her a hug. 'We may have to leave some of it here and make two trips.'

Maddy stared at her and then broke into a laugh. 'You're teasing me, and it's not fair, because I'm too tired to be teased. I'm absolutely exhausted.' She linked her arm through Stella's as a porter arrived and started to load the cases on to his trolley. They followed him outside to where Hilary had parked the car, and he stacked them in the boot. Maddy rewarded him with the same dazzling smile she had given her young men and pressed a few coins into his palm.

'You don't have to do that, maid,' he said. ''Tis my pleasure.' But he grinned and touched his cap and took them anyway, before returning to the station.

'You haven't changed,' Hilary observed. 'You still have all the men at your feet. I don't know how you do it.'

'I'll give you lessons sometime,' Maddy answered cheekily as she helped Stella into the front seat and then scrambled into the back. 'Not that you need them, now you've got your lovely fiancé. How are the wedding preparations going?'

'Not quickly enough.' Hilary got into the driving seat. 'There seems to be so much to do and never enough time to do it all. And Dottie's illness hasn't helped, with all the sewing she would have been doing.'

'Well I can lend a hand now I'm here. Don't forget, Dottie brought me up – I can't sew as well as she can, but I'm not bad. And I'm good at weddings, too. I've already organised two – mine and Stella's.'

'I wouldn't say you exactly organised it,' Stella said. 'Took over on the day, perhaps.'

'Well, I can help while I'm here. Until Dottie comes home, of course, and then I'll want to be with her, but I daresay I can still manage a bit of sewing or writing invitations and things like that. And how *is* Dottie? I ought to have asked that first. She's the main reason I'm here, after all.'

'And that puts us in our place,' Stella told Hilary. 'Weddings and new babies pale into insignificance beside Dottie. Which is just how it should be, of course. She's getting on very well,' she answered her sister. 'They've moved her to Tavistock hospital now, which makes it easier for people to visit her, and she'll be able to go home as soon as they're satisfied with her progress and she's got someone to look after her.'

'Which is me,' Maddy said as they drove down the twisting road towards Bedford Square. 'I suppose we can't pop in to see her now? It's only just up the road.'

'It's not visiting time. They only allow people in at three in the afternoon or seven in the evening. Anyway, Ted and Alice Tozer are going to see her this evening. They've got news for her as well. We'll go tomorrow and you can talk to the doctor then, too.'

'Ted and Alice have got news for her? What's that?'

Stella and Hilary looked at each other, and Maddy squirmed with impatience. '*Tell* me!'

'Joe Tozer's coming over from America,' Stella said. 'They heard last week – the same day as we heard about you – but they didn't want to tell her until they were certain he was on his way. But they got a cable yesterday to say he'd got a passage and he'll be in Southampton by the weekend. Dottie's going to be so thrilled.'

'Yes, I expect she will be,' Maddy said, but her voice sounded flatter than it had before. Stella turned her head and glanced at her, but Maddy was looking out of the window. Stella sighed a little and turned back.

They drove in silence for a few minutes, then Hilary said, 'You haven't told us anything about Stephen. How is he? Did he mind very much that you were coming home for several weeks?'

'Of course he minded. But he could see that I had to come, if Dottie needed me. Not that I'm really sure she does, with everyone rallying round as they seem to be, and Joe Tozer coming.'

'Don't be such a goose,' Stella said. 'Joe can't stay in the cottage with her and do all the things you can. Of course she needs you. You should have seen her face when Felix and I told her you were coming. It was as if someone had switched on a light inside her.'

'Was it really? She was really pleased?'

'Of course she was, idiot. You know how much she thinks of you. You were like a daughter to her – you still are.'

'She was certainly like a mother to me,' Maddy said in a wobbly voice. 'More than Fenella was, really. Fenella was always kind to me and gave me all she could, but she was away so much. It was Dottie who looked after me.'

'You were lucky to have her,' Stella said quietly, and Maddy gave a little cry.

'Oh, there I go again, being selfish! I had so much, after we lost our own mother and father, and *you* – you spent your whole life till you were grown up in a children's home. You didn't have any of the lovely family life I had.'

'No, but I've had it since. Dottie didn't know I was your sister when I first came to Burracombe, but she treated me just like a daughter rather than a lodger. Anyway, she was delighted to know you were coming and you'll be able to take care of her now. But until she comes home, you'll be staying with us. Felix is really looking forward to seeing you.'

'And you still haven't said much about Stephen,' Hilary remarked. 'Is he really all right, Maddy?'

'Yes, he is, but he's terribly busy. I hated leaving him, even though he hardly ever seemed to get home, but he wanted me to come. It's not very nice there now, you know. They've been attacking police stations – EOKA, I mean – and the wives and other civilians haven't been allowed into town for weeks. Everyone thinks they'll start on the air stations next. Stephen said that if I hadn't been coming home anyway, I'd probably have had to soon.' Her voice shook again.

'That's what Father's been saying,' Hilary agreed. 'It doesn't look very good.'

'I just hate being away from him when he's in danger,' Maddy said, sounding ready to cry. 'I ought to be *there*.'

'Darling, you mustn't worry too much,' Stella said quickly. 'He's not in danger now, and he may not be at all. It's not as if he's a soldier and has to fight. They're only patrolling, aren't they?'

'At the moment, yes. Well, I think so, but how do I know he tells me everything? They're not really supposed to talk about it at all, not even to their wives. And I feel so far away.' She glanced restlessly out of the window. 'If it hadn't been for Dottie being ill – and your baby coming so soon – I would never have come. They'd have had to force me.'

'Well, you're here now,' Hilary said, swinging the car off the main road and down the narrow lane leading to Little Burracombe. 'And you're almost at the vicarage. Felix will be home again by now and I'm sure he'll have the kettle on for a cup of tea the minute you get in. And Mrs Curnow has made some scones, and Alice Tozer sent over some cream, so that you can have a proper Devonshire tea.'

'With Dottie's strawberry jam,' Stella added. 'She gave me half a dozen pots and I managed to hide them from Felix. Here we are.'

They turned into the vicarage driveway and Hilary brought the car to a gentle halt. They sat for a moment in the silence. Then Maddy got out slowly and stood looking about her at the rhododendron bushes that lined the drive, and the sunlit lawn beyond.

'Thank you, Hilary,' she said in a small voice. 'It really is good to be here, and it was nice of you to meet me. I'm sorry I was so selfish. It's just that Cyprus and Stephen suddenly seem so very far away.'

Hilary got out and gave her a hug, while Stella followed more slowly. 'You weren't selfish at all. You've had a long journey and you're tired. Now, you go inside and see if you can find a strong young man to help us with these cases. And no, Stella, you are *not* to try lifting them out. Much as I want this baby to be born soon, I'd rather it wasn't here and now on the driveway!'

'I'll go inside and look for the strong young man, then,' Stella said, making for the house. 'Although I'm afraid it will only be Felix! And here he is. He must have heard the car.'

Felix appeared at the front door and stood at the top of the steps. He held his arms wide and Maddy gave a stifled cry and ran into them. Stella and Hilary watched as he enfolded her in a giant hug.

'He's always been good for her,' Stella said quietly, ignoring Hilary's admonishment and lifting a small overnight case. 'She'll be all right now. But she's obviously very upset at leaving Stephen, and very worried about him too. I really do hope he's going to be all right ...'

Dottie was so stunned when Alice and Ted gave her their news that they were afraid for a moment that she would have a second stroke.

'Your Joe coming here?' she said at last, staring at them with wide eyes. Her cheeks, which had gone quite pale for a moment, blazed with rosy colour. 'Well, that's just plain ridiculous!'

'Ridiculous?' Alice echoed. 'Us thought you'd be pleased.'

'Pleased?' Dottie's hands fidgeted with the bag of barley sugar Ted had dumped on her lap. 'Well, I'll be pleased enough to see him, I dare say, but to come all this way on a wild goose chase just because I had a bit of a turn – well, that's outlandish. Whatever must it be costing him?'

'I don't think you need worry about that,' Ted said. 'Joe's worth a bob or two in anyone's book. Anyway, he must think you'm worth it, Dottie.'

'I don't know what he'm thinking, and that's the truth,' Dottie retorted. 'I just hope he doesn't think he'll catch me in a weak moment and get me to marry him. I made it plain enough when I was over there that it wasn't on the cards. We'm too old and settled in our ways, and neither of us wants to leave our home.'

'I don't think he's thinking of that,' Alice said, although she wasn't entirely sure this was true. 'He just wants to see you and help you get better. He really does care about you, Dottie.'

'I know that.' The little woman was silent for a moment, then she sighed and said, 'I'm being ungrateful, I know. It's something to have a chap so caring he'll come halfway across the world to do a bit of sick visiting. It just came as a bit of a shock, that's all. I'll be glad to see him.'

'Of course you will.' Alice smiled. 'We weren't going to tell you at all, you know – we were just going to bring him in as a surprise. But Val thought it might be too much for you, and I think she was probably right.'

'I should say she was!' Dottie exclaimed. 'I reckon I'd have died right here in this bed if Joe had walked in unexpected. When is he coming, anyway?'

'We're hoping by the weekend, or soon after. He couldn't get a passage on one of the *Queens* so he's coming on one of the slower liners.'

'It'll be good to see him,' Dottie admitted, getting used to the idea. 'How long is he coming for? He'll be stopping with you, I take it?'

'Should think so,' Ted said. 'Can't think of anyone else who'd put up with him. And he hasn't said how long he'll be here, but now that he's pretty well retired and has handed over the business to Russell, he's a free man to do what he likes. Not like us farmers, working all hours till us drops,' he added in a gloomy tone that made both women laugh.

'Go on with you,' Alice said, poking him with her elbow. 'You know you'll never hand over to our Tom till you're in your box, and even then us'll probably hear you issuing instructions about the cows as they lowers you into the ground. Mind you,' she added to Dottie, 'I have got him to agree to take me away on holiday once harvest's over – what do you think of that?'

'Holiday?' Dottie said. 'Where to?'

'Perranporth,' Alice said in a pleased tone. 'Us went there years ago on a day trip and I always wanted to go back. Pretty little place, right by the sea, and we'm going to stop at a cottage that does bed and breakfast and evening meal, and just sit by the beach every day and watch the waves. I can't wait!'

'Can't imagine you two just sitting about all day,' Dottie said, but there was a wistful note in her voice. 'Perhaps 'tis different by the sea, with different things to look at.'

'Here!' Alice said, struck by a bright idea. 'Why don't you come with us, if you'm out of here by then? A few days with all that sea air and ozone would do you a power of good, set you right back on your feet. I dare say the cottage got room for you.'

'Me?' Dottie's face brightened for a moment. 'Oh, I don't know ... And what about your Joe if he's still around?'

'Nothing to stop him coming too,' Ted said robustly. 'I reckon it's a good idea, Dottie. You think about it. Harvest's still a little way off and you're sure to be home again by then. The doctor'll be all for it, if you asks him.'

'But it'll be getting near Hilary's wedding, and I promised—'

'You're doing nothing,' Alice said firmly. 'She's getting all that sorted out and all you got to do is be there to enjoy it. Told me that herself, she did. And we've fixed to go the week before, so you'll be back in good time. What d'you think, Dottie? Shall we write to the cottage and ask if they got room for you – and Joe, if he's still here?'

'You'd better ask Joe about that. I can't answer for him. But – well, yes, if the doctor thinks it would be all right, I'd like to. It will be something to really look forward to.' She gave them both a beaming smile. 'Seems to me I got a lot to look forward to, and there was me a few days ago thinking my life was taking a proper downward turn.'

'Don't talk so daft,' Alice said, giving her a kiss. 'You got too many people who love and care about you to think that. Now I think us had better be going. You just lay here and think about all the good things that's come out of this turn you had – Maddy coming home from Cyprus, Joe all the way from America, and a holiday by the sea! Seems to me your bit of a cloud don't just have a silver lining, it's pretty well silver all over!'

Dottie returned her kiss and watched them go, still smiling. Then she settled back against her pillows, waiting for the cocoa that would come round the ward soon before the patients went to sleep. Alice is right, she thought. I'm a very lucky woman. Though I'm sure I don't know what I ever did to deserve it all.

Chapter Twenty-Eight

Ivy heard all about Dottie's progress from the Nethercotts and their customers, as well as from people she encountered in the village street and shops. Sometimes, she thought a little bitterly, it seemed as if Dottie Friend was all people could talk about. It was as if there was nothing else going on in the world.

Not that Ivy took much account of the news of the day. She and George had the wireless on at six o'clock in the evening, after Barry had listened to *Children's Hour*, but they were usually too busy having their tea then to pay much attention, and by nine o'clock George was in the bakery making next day's bread, Barry was in bed and Ivy was in the pub. She knew, of course, that the Conservatives had won the general election a few weeks back – you couldn't not know that – and that a woman called Ruth Ellis had been hanged for murder; there'd been a lot of talk about that in the newspapers, and George, who followed motor racing, had told her that Stirling Moss had become the first English winner of the British Grand Prix, but most of the news passed over her head. There was quite enough happening in the village to occupy her mind.

This evening, Jack Pettifer was in, with his son Bob, and they had Terry with them. Bernie looked over the top of his glasses as they came in and frowned sternly.

'Now then, what are you doing in here, young man? And you, Jack, you ought to know better than to bring young children into a pub. Put the little tacker outside with a bag of crisps and a glass of lemonade.'

'Not so much of the tacker,' Jack said, grinning. 'He's a man now, our Terry, passed his eighteenth birthday yesterday and as entitled as anyone else to come in and have a drink. As well you know, Bernie Nethercott, so pull him his first pint unless you wants to turn away good custom, and have one yourself to help celebrate. You too, Ivy.'

'A married man and a father too,' Bob added. 'It's a funny world, when a chap can get married, have a family and fight for his country but can't go into a pub for a drink, but there you are. He's legal now, anyway.'

'Congratulations to you,' Bernie said, filling a tankard and handing it across the bar. 'Same for you too, Jack? And Bob? Not but that there's still a lot of things you're not allowed to do until you're twenty-one, but I don't suppose you care too much about those. And how d'you like living over to Little Burracombe, then? It's not everyone would want to move in with the mother-in-law!'

Terry grinned and accepted his pint. The three men lifted their glasses and Bernie thanked Jack and said he'd have his later. He gave Ivy a few coins and she slipped them into her pocket.

'Thanks, Jack.' She looked at Terry. 'I hope Patsy and the baby are going on well.'

'We're getting on handsome, thanks,' Terry answered them both. 'Mrs Shillabeer's made us proper welcome and they all treat little Rosie like a princess. Patsy likes being back on the farm, too. It's what her was brought up to, after all.'

Jacob Prout came in then with Norman and Ted Tozer and they all pretended to faint at the sight of Terry with a pint tankard in his hand. They were followed by several more of the bell-ringers, who had just come from their Friday evening practice. Ted still insisted that they follow the Devon tradition of ringing the bells up, then a peal of call changes before lowering them again, with no pause to stand them in between. Three such peals in an evening were enough to set a thirst going in anyone's language, Jacob said, swallowing half his first pint of cider almost without stopping.

'It's a pity young Henry and Micky can't come in,' Travis Kellaway remarked, buying two glasses of lemonade and a couple of bags of crisps to take outside to the boys. 'They're doing well and deserve to share in the talk afterwards.'

'They'm not so bad,' Jacob allowed. 'To be honest, I thought you'd spoil their ringing, teaching 'em that there scientific stuff, but it don't seem to have done them no harm. And that visiting team from up country what came here the other week and rung – what d'you call it, method ringing? – well, they made it sound quite pretty, once you got used to listening to it.'

Travis grinned and took the lemonade outside. When he came back, he said, 'We'll be able to ring a bit of Grandsire for Hilary's wedding, if Ted doesn't object. Vic and Roy are getting on well, too, and if Norman can bring himself to ring the tenor for us, which he did very well last week, we'll really make Burracombe sit up.'

'For the Napier wedding?' Ted frowned. 'I dunno about that. There'll be a lot of folk here that knows what good call changes sound like and won't understand the music changing every stroke the way it do in method ringing. They might think we're just making a mess of it.'

'There'll be people from up country as well,' Travis pointed out. 'All Dr Hunter's friends and so on. They'll be used to it.'

'They won't know the difference,' Jacob said. 'You know that. People that aren't ringers can't tell what we'm ringing; all they know is when us goes wrong and makes a clash. And if scientific goes wrong, it sounds worse than call changes. It fair hurts your ears.'

'Well, we'll see how we go,' Travis said peaceably. 'There are a few weeks to practise in yet. We've got the summer fair before that and Mrs Warren wants us to ring to start that off. Where are Roy and Vic anyway? They're usually first up at the bar.'

'Last I saw, they was heading off down the other end of the village,' Norman said. 'Said something about Jack's shed.'

'My shed?' Jack exclaimed, and looked accusingly at Bob. 'Is this your doing?'

'Oh my stars!' Bob swallowed the rest of his drink hastily. 'We're supposed to be having a special rehearsal of the skiffle group. We'm practising "Rock Around the Clock" – it's been top of the charts for weeks now.' He set his tankard on the bar and loped out, while the others laughed.

'"Rock Around the Clock" at the summer fair!' Norman chuckled. 'That'll make Mrs Warren's hair stand on end!'

Ivy took some glasses out to the little kitchen to wash them. Rose was there, boiling ham for next day's sandwiches, which she and Bernie liked to have available at lunchtimes, especially at this time of year when there were likely to be visitors about too.

'Have you heard anything about that caravan park Jem Barrow's opened up?' she asked as Ivy turned on the tap. 'I thought we might be getting a few holidaymakers along from there.'

'I don't know nothing about it. In one of his fields, is it?'

'That's right, the one beside the river where he lets the Scouts and Guides camp. He've joined up with the Caravan Club so people can bring their own caravans and stop there. It's only a mile or so away, so I reckon we'll get folk walking down of an evening, or maybe calling in at dinner time when they're out on the moors. I was wondering about making a few more sandwiches. I might even put out a few meat pies if your George would make some.'

'If you order them, he'll make them,' Ivy said, plunging glasses into the hot water. 'None of us is going to turn away business.' She swilled the water about. 'I suppose that means we might get a few more strangers around the village.'

'There's been a few already, now that the school holidays have started. And that reminds me – there was one here asking about you the other day, so Bernie told me. Tall gentleman, sounded a bit foreign, Bernie said. Who would that have been, d'you reckon?'

Ivy stopped and stared at her. 'Asking about me? In here? When was that?'

'Let's see, was it yesterday, or the day before? I'm not sure now. Oh, here's Bernie.' Rose lifted the ham out of the pan and turned to her husband as he came through the door. 'When was it that man was in here asking about Ivy?'

He frowned. 'I think it was Wednesday. Yes, it was, because we changed the barrels over and I saw him as I was coming up from the cellar. Wednesday, that's right.'

'Wednesday?' Ivy repeated, panic rising in her breast. 'And you never thought to tell me?'

'Sorry, it slipped me mind. Didn't he come down to the bakery then?'

'No, he didn't,' Ivy snapped, and began to dry her hands on a towel. 'You don't mean to say you told him where I live?'

'Why shouldn't I?' Bernie asked, astonished. 'He'd find out soon enough. Here, Ivy, what's got into you? Who was he anyway? Not got the police after you, have you?'

Ivy glared at him. 'Of course I haven't got the police after me! I don't know how you dare suggest such a thing. I just don't like the idea of strangers asking my business, that's all, and I'd be grateful if you don't answer any more questions about me. I like to keep my privacy.'

'All right, no need to get your rag out.' Bernie picked up a tray of clean glasses and turned to go back to the bar. 'And if you don't mind, we got customers waiting to be served, and as far as I can see, none of them's the slightest bit interested in you. All they want you to do is pull them a pint, so I'd be pleased if you'd come out and do it, seeing as it's what we pay you for.'

Ivy's cheeks flared with colour. She glanced at Rose, who was staring at her in amazement, and then drew in a breath and shrugged.

'I don't suppose it was anything important anyway,' she muttered, and followed Bernie back to the bar.

The stranger was not mentioned again. But Ivy kept a sharp eye on the door, and every time it opened, she held her breath until she saw who it was. When the inn finally closed, she helped clear up without speaking to either Rose or Bernie, and then hurried out with her head down.

She walked rapidly along the village street, glancing from left to right all the way as if she expected someone to leap out from behind a bush. So he'd tracked her down to Burracombe. If he hadn't been to the bakery already, perhaps even while she'd been at the pub tonight, he'd be coming in soon. He'd found out where she lived, and probably a lot more about her, and soon he would confront her.

But why? she asked herself desperately. And who was he?

And what was she to say to George?

She reached the bakery without meeting anyone apart from Henry Bennetts' father giving his dog a late walk, and almost ran the last few steps. She pushed open the back door and scurried through, slamming it behind her. George, who was at the kitchen table having a bite of supper and reading the *Daily Sketch* while waiting for next day's bread dough to prove, stared at her in astonishment.

'Whatever be the matter, Ivy? You came in then as if all the wolves of hell were behind you.'

'There's no call for that sort of language,' she retorted, breathing rather quickly as she took off her coat and hung it behind the door. 'And there's nothing the matter. I don't know why you should think there is.'

He looked at her more closely. 'I reckon there is, all the same. You look proper flustered. And you haven't been yourself for weeks now. Come on, Ivy, out with it. Someone been bothering you?'

Ivy caught her breath. 'What d'you mean? Who d'you think would be bothering me? What have you heard?'

'I haven't heard nothing, but I've lived with you long enough to know when you got summat on your mind. You might as well tell me. You know what they say – a trouble shared is a trouble halved.'

'I don't know why you should think I got any troubles,' Ivy muttered, turning away from him and putting her hands on the teapot. 'I told you, everything's all right. How long's this tea been made? I could do with a cup.'

'Not that long.' He watched her as she fetched milk from the larder and poured herself a cup. 'You can put a drop more in my cup too, while you got the pot in your hand. Now come on, Ive. Stop trying to pull the wool over my eyes. There's something the matter and I want to know what it is.'

'I told you—'

'And I'm telling you!' George Sweet rarely raised his voice, but he was beginning to sound annoyed. 'I'm not a fool, you know. I can see when something's going on. First you up and leave your job at Horrabridge after I don't know how many years and say you don't want to do bar work no more, then you go down the Bell three or four nights a week –'

'That's just to help out while Dottie's laid up.'

'– and then you come pelting through the door like there's a pack of wolves at your heels and try to tell me there's nothing wrong. Now either someone's been bothering you, or there's summat else on your mind, and I want to know what it is. So are you going to tell me?'

'Haven't you got bread to see to?' she asked desperately, but he folded his arms and sat back more firmly in his chair.

'It'll be all right for a good half-hour yet. Come on, Ive. Sit down here. What is it?'

She stared at him, her mind in a whirl, then sat slowly down at the table opposite him. At last she said feebly, 'It's Barry.'

George's brows came together in a frown. 'Barry? What about him? Not ill, is he? He looked all right at teatime.'

'No, he's not ill, he—'

'In some sort of trouble? He's not got the village bobby after him, I hope? What's he been up to?'

'It's nothing like that,' Ivy snapped. 'If you'd just let me *tell* you . . .' In truth, she was thankful for George's interruptions, which gave her a few precious seconds to think what to say next, and now she burst out, 'I think he needs a holiday!'

'A *holiday*?' George stared at her. 'What d'you mean, a holiday? He's on holiday now, isn't he? School broke up last week.'

'I mean, I think he needs to go away for a holiday.' The idea began to take shape in her mind. 'Somewhere out of Burracombe. So that he can see a bit more of the world. I could take him.'

'See more of the world? What on earth are you on about, Ivy? You're not thinking of going *abroad*, I hope!'

'No, of course not. I just meant – well, London, perhaps. We could stay with my cousin Flo. She's always on at us to go up for a visit. I could take him to see Buckingham Palace and the Tower of London. Things like that. It'd be good for him.'

George gazed at her. 'What's brought this on? You never said nothing before.'

'I'm saying it now. Why shouldn't we have a holiday? You can't because of the bakery, but that don't have to stop me and Barry.' The more she thought about it, the better it seemed. Get out of Burracombe while this stranger was hanging about, and he'd get tired of it and go away. And then it would all be over, whatever it was, and she could settle down again. Maybe work at the Bell permanently, if Dottie wasn't up to bar work any more. 'It'd be educational,' she added, hoping this would clinch it. George was very keen on Barry's education.

George chewed his upper lip. He stared at the tablecloth for a minute or so, then looked up at her. 'And are you telling me this is what's been biting you for the past month or more? You've been working up the nerve to ask me to let you take our Barry to London for a holiday?'

Ivy stared at him helplessly. 'Well ...'

'Because I don't believe it,' he stated. 'You never been frightened of me, Ivy, never had no cause to be, and if you decided to take Barry off to London, or America, or even Timbuktu, you'd have just done it. I'm not saying it's a bad idea, mind,' he added, as Ivy began to speak, 'but what I am saying is that you're still hiding summat from me, and that's what I don't like.' He stood up. 'You take Barry away for a few days and welcome, but before you go, you tell me the truth about what's really on your mind, and we'll see if we can sort it out together. All right? And now I got me bread to see to.' He turned towards the door leading through to the bakery, then looked back over his shoulder. 'You just think about it. Husbands and wives don't have secrets from each other – or shouldn't have. But it seems to me you do, and I'm not standing for it.'

He went through and closed the door. Ivy sat with her hands folded round her cup of tea, staring after him. She became aware that she was trembling, and felt tears burn in her eyes.

She put the cup down before the tea spilled and wondered what he would do if she told him the truth – the whole truth. It was something she'd longed to do but never dared. But now it seemed as though it was going to come out whether she liked it or not, and she groaned and buried her face in her hands.

Who was this stranger, looking for her, asking questions about her? And what in the name of heaven did he want from her?

Chapter Twenty-Nine

Joe Tozer arrived in the village unannounced, just as he had the first time he had returned to Burracombe after almost a lifetime in America. He drove up the farm track in a hired car and stopped beside Ted's battered truck. Minnie, who was in the garden, taking in some washing, gave a cry of joy when she saw him and ran to the gate, where he caught her in a huge bear hug.

'Joe! Why didn't you let us know?'

'I did. I sent a cable.'

'That only told us you were on your way. Us didn't know when to expect you. There might not have been enough dinner!'

'That'll be the day,' he laughed, and held her at arm's length to inspect her. 'You're looking well, Ma.'

'You'm not looking so dusty yourself. And how's all the family?'

'They're fine. They all send their love.'

'I wish I could see them too,' she said wistfully. 'It was grand to see Russell last time you came, but I'd like to see the girls too, and their little ones. You'll have to try to bring them over, Joe, before it's too late.'

'Too late! Don't talk so silly, Ma. You've got years in you yet.'

'Yes, but the children are getting bigger all the time. I want to see them while they're little. But I suppose it would be too expensive. Maybe I'll just go back with you after you've seen Dottie.'

Joe grinned at her. 'That's an idea, Ma! We'll bear it in mind. And how is Dottie now? It's over a week since I heard, so I hope she's on the mend.'

'She's doing well, by all accounts. They've moved her into

Tavistock now and she hopes to be back home in a few days. You know young Maddy's come over to look after her?'

'She's arrived, has she? That's good.' He followed her into the farmhouse, where Alice and Joanna were putting the dinner dishes on to the table. They looked round in surprise as he came in, bending his head under the low doorway, and Alice hastily set down the bowl of potatoes she was holding.

'Joe! My stars, you gave me such a shock! Why ever didn't you let us know?'

'I asked him that,' Minnie said. 'But you know what he is, likes to arrive out of the blue. I told him there might not be enough dinner to go round.'

'There isn't,' Alice said. 'It's sausages, and you know Ted and Tom always has four each, and you and me and Joanna has two, and Robin can manage one now as well as half of Heather's, and we'll want some cold—'

'There's plenty!' Joe said, laughing. 'I've never sat down to a meal in this kitchen without there being enough for at least three extra.' He gave Alice and Joanna a kiss. 'Say, you're all looking blooming.'

Ted was in now, shucking off his boots on the doormat before he realised his brother was in the room. 'Well I'll be blowed, if it's not our Joe. Why didn't you—'

'Let you know I was coming?' Joe finished for him. 'It's all right, Ted, everyone's asked that. But you should have known. You didn't think I was going to sit at home and wait for news, did you? Not when my Dottie's been so ill.'

'Oh, Joe ... *Joe* ...' Dottie said as Joe came into the ward carrying a huge bunch of roses. She pulled a hanky from the sleeve of her nightdress and wiped her eyes. 'Look at me, silly old woman, piping my eye over nothing. It's weakness after the turn I had, that's all. Don't take no notice.' She put her hanky away again. 'And whatever have you been doing, spending money on all they flowers when you could have picked a bunch in my own garden?'

'These *are* from your garden,' he said, grinning as he bent to kiss her. 'Don't you recognise your own roses? I thought you'd rather have them than some bought from a florist. How are you, my dear?

You're looking better than I expected.' He held her close for a moment or two, knowing just how afraid he had been.

'All the better for seeing you,' she admitted, her lips trembling again. 'But you shouldn't have come all this way just because I had a funny turn. I'm sure you got better things to do at home.'

'None better than seeing you,' he said, drawing a chair close to the bed. 'I was real scared when I got the cable from Ted saying you'd had a stroke. Thought I'd lost you.'

'Don't be daft. I'm not ready to go just yet, and the good Lord's not ready to take me, as far as I know. I'll be around for a while to come.'

'You better had be,' he said seriously. 'We can't do without you, Dottie, and I can't keep on dashing across the Atlantic like this. We've got to do something about it.'

'About what?' She had buried her face in the roses, drawing their scent into her lungs, but she looked up then. 'Please, Joe, don't start that the minute you arrive. I might be better, but I'm not well enough to be plagued.'

'I don't want to plague you, Dottie,' he said quietly. 'But you know how I feel about you and I'm pretty sure I know how you feel about me. It's just daft for us to go on being apart when we don't have to be.' He took the flowers and laid them on the bedside cabinet, then held both her hands in his. 'I've missed you, Dottie. The place doesn't seem the same without you now. I want to come home knowing you'll be there waiting for me. I want to take you about with me, enjoy just being with you. I feel only half alive when we're not together, and the thought of you being ill and me not there to take care of you – well, it's more than I can bear.' He paused, but Dottie was looking down at their clasped hands and would not meet his eyes. 'Sweetheart,' he said, his voice rough now with the force of his feeling, 'you know as well as I do, we should have been together all our lives. I know I was lucky to have a good marriage and you say you've had a good life too, but – well, now we've got a second chance and I don't want to throw it away.'

Dottie looked up at last, her eyes brimming with tears. 'I've missed you too, Joe,' she said in a quivering voice. 'When I first started to think about things after I was took bad, I knew it was you I wanted to see here beside me. And I can't tell you how pleased I was when Alice and Ted told me you were coming over. But the way things are, I don't see what us can do about it.'

'Well, I've got one or two ideas about that,' Joe said. He patted her hands. 'But I won't trouble you with them now. You're not strong enough to be worrying about ways and means. Your job is to get better and come back to Burracombe. That's what everyone in the village is waiting for.' He smiled at her and she nodded, brushing away her tears and feeling for her hanky again. She tried a little laugh.

'Maybe. I don't reckon they'll all be pleased to see me, though. I hear Ivy Sweet's took over my job in the Bell.'

'Yes, Alice told me that. She doesn't like Ivy any better than you do.'

'I don't reckon many do. Bitter old harridan. I'm surprised Bernie and Rose took her on. Her face is enough to turn the beer sour.'

'Maybe she's different in the pub. She worked long enough in Horrabridge, didn't she? I guess she must put on a smile for the customers, or the landlord there would have given her the push years ago.'

'Oh, she can put on a smile, right enough, when it suits her. A bit more than that too, so I've heard. You know what they say about her Barry, don't you?'

'Now then, Dottie,' he reproved her, taking her hands again and giving them a little shake. 'That's gossip and it's not worthy of you. I think there's been things happen in Ivy's life that nobody knows about. She was bright and cheerful enough as a young girl, as I recall.'

'Oh yes. But she always acted like she was a cut above the rest of us. Had her eye on your brother for a time, didn't she, until Alice came along. You don't have to look far to see why they two don't get on. Anyway, you didn't come all this way to talk about Ivy Sweet. Tell me about things back in Corning. How are the girls and Russell? And have that couple next door made up their differences yet? Oh, and how's the widow down the road – is she still asking you over for drinks on the veranda?'

'She is, and I go now and then,' he answered with a grin. 'I could have my feet under her table in no time at all if I wanted. You'd better come back and keep me in order or I might lose my head.'

'I might come back, just to encourage her,' she retorted. 'It would stop all this plaguing you promised you wouldn't do.'

'Go on, that's not plaguing. You'll know soon enough when I think you're well enough to be plagued.' He looked at her for a moment and she met his gaze. 'It really is good to see you, Dottie,' he said quietly. 'I meant it when I said I was scared of losing you.'

She nodded. 'I know, Joe. I really appreciate you coming all this way. It's done me a power of good to see you.'

'You'll be seeing a lot more of me from now on,' he said. 'I mean to stay until you're properly back on your feet. And then we're going to have a good long talk.'

Dottie said nothing. After a moment, she drew in a long, tremulous breath and a tear fell upon their joined hands. He loosened his hold and gathered her against him and she wept for a moment or two on his shoulder.

'I'm sorry, Joe. I'm just being a silly old woman. It's like I said – it's because I'm a bit weak, that's all.'

'I know, Dottie. I know.' He held her close and rested his cheek on her white hair.

They sat like that, quietly together, for several minutes, and Dottie never saw the tears in Joe's eyes.

Chapter Thirty

The day of the summer fair was less than a week away, and the children were gathering in the school playground every day to rehearse *The Dragon Who Was Different*. Mabel Purdy had finished the dragon costume, and on Friday evening she brought it along for the dress rehearsal.

'Coo,' breathed one of the Crocker twins, gazing at it with rapt eyes. 'It's smashing. Look, Eddie, it's got holes for its eyes, and huge teeth. Can us try it on, miss?'

'Of course you can. That's why Mrs Purdy has brought it along. But take care – that camouflage material's made out of netting and will catch on anything.' Miss Kemp watched as the two boys scrambled into the long, sinuous costume, helped by Mrs Purdy and James Raynor. It was certainly very effective, she thought, with the green and black of the camouflage material enlivened by splashes of gold and silver paint. Luke Ferris had painted scarlet flames all along its jaws, and there were threatening red rims round its eyeholes. George Crocker's own eyes peering out took on quite an alarming glitter.

'I hope we don't frighten the smaller children,' she said to James when he stood back to admire the effect.

'Not at all. They all love monsters. This is going to look wonderful in the parade, capering through the village.' He turned to smile at her. 'You've put a lot of work into this. You're going to be exhausted afterwards.'

'No more than you. And I am going away on holiday a couple of days afterwards, you know. Not that it will be much of a rest – Iris

228

needs a lot of help, so I do most of the cooking – but we do manage to get out and about quite a bit, by taxi. She's used the same one so much that the driver's become a real friend and will take us out all day if we want to go somewhere special. He took us to a beautiful garden once, and pushed Iris's wheelchair around all afternoon. And it's always good to see her. We spent a lot of time together as children.' She paused for a moment. 'She lived in Burracombe. She was Ralph's sister.'

'I see.' He was silent for a moment. Then he glanced at her and said, 'You've shared a great loss, then.'

'Yes. It was a very long time ago, but we talk about those times and reminisce, and we think about Ralph. I suppose you think it's time we put it behind us.'

'Not at all,' he said quietly. 'We all have to manage these things in our own way, and it's a relief to be able to share such memories. There probably aren't many who can, now.'

'No. Our parents are all dead, of course, and Johnny, and our friend Herbert. I suppose there are other people still alive who knew them and might remember, but I don't know them. So I'm afraid Iris and I wallow a little.'

'And you're going on Wednesday?'

'Yes, I need Tuesday to recover from the fair and get ready, and I'll be catching the train from Tavistock on Wednesday morning. Iris lives in Great Malvern, so it's quite a journey.'

'Will you have supper with me on Tuesday?' he asked. 'It will be one less thing to bother about, getting yourself a meal that evening. And we can enjoy ourselves without any more rehearsals hanging over our heads, and have a good laugh at whatever went wrong.'

'James!' she exclaimed. 'You're not expecting anything to go *wrong*, surely!'

'I'm certainly not expecting everything to go right,' he returned with a grin. 'This is a primary school production, remember – and the Crocker twins are playing a dragon. Speaking of which . . .' He started across the playground to where the dragon was wrapping itself sinuously around a squealing infant. 'Stop that at once, you two! You'll crush poor little Billy to death!'

The dragon unwound itself reluctantly and a Crocker twin poked out his head. 'It's what pythons do, sir. They winds themselves up tight and then squeeze …' He elongated the word and took a step or two towards Billy Culliford, who squealed again and backed away. 'And when they stops breathing, they swallows them whole.'

'Maybe so, but you are not a python, you're a dragon.' He was about to add information as to how dragons killed their prey, but thought better of it. These two probably knew all about that anyway. 'And nobody in this playground is going to have their breath squeezed out of them or be swallowed whole. Remember, our dragon just breathes peppermint over people. Now, come out of that costume, both of you.' The two boys emerged reluctantly and stood holding the empty folds of camouflage material. 'Do you want to be the dragon, or don't you?' he enquired sternly.

'Oh yes, sir, please, sir, we do, we been practising.' They emitted a series of noises that might, at a stretch, be imagined to be those a dragon would make. 'Please, sir, we'm sorry. We won't do it again.'

'Very well.' James tightened his lips to stop them twitching. 'We'd better start the rehearsal. All of you who are in the first scene, come over here. The rest of you group together in the corner. And remember, this is the very last rehearsal we'll have, so we must get every word right.'

The children scurried to their places and James turned back to Frances. He cast his eyes upwards and shook his head.

'It doesn't matter what those two do, or how cross I ought to be with them,' he admitted, 'they always make me want to laugh!'

Barry Sweet had been working hard in the school production too, a fact that Ivy had overlooked when she had come up with her plan for getting him and herself out of the village. She tried to persuade him to give up his part, but he was unexpectedly stubborn.

'It's my last chance. I'll be going to big school after the holidays and I don't suppose I'll ever be able to be in anything there.'

'You don't know that. They probably put on all sorts of plays and things. You'll have plenty of chances.'

'I've got a chance now. It's the main part in the whole play and Mr Raynor says I'm really good. I might even be an actor when I'm older.'

'An actor!' Ivy laughed scornfully. 'Don't be silly. People from Burracombe don't go and be actors. If that's the sort of idea you're getting into your head, I think it'll be a good thing if you aren't in the play.'

Barry scowled. 'Well I *am* in it, so there. Anyway, I'd be letting Miss Kemp and Mr Raynor down if I went away now. You're always telling me not to let people down.'

'He's right, Ive,' George said, coming in at that point. 'We've always brought him up to stick to his promises. Anyway,' he gave her a suspicious look, 'why are you so keen to go on this holiday in such a rush? Why not wait till next week? The Bank Holiday'll be over then and Barry will have been in his play and we'll have been able to enjoy the summer fair together like we always do.'

'Yes, let's do that, Mum,' Barry agreed. He put his head on one side and looked at her cajolingly. 'It's not that I don't want to go to London, but I don't want to miss the best bit of the holidays here.'

Ivy looked at them helplessly. She felt as if control were slipping away from her. Everything they said made sense, yet she felt that every moment spent in Burracombe was a moment nearer to a danger she still didn't understand. And she didn't like the way George was looking at her. She hadn't forgotten his words about secrets, and she knew he hadn't either. He was still waiting to be told the truth and she wasn't at all sure how long his patience would last.

'Don't you want to go to the Tower of London?' she asked Barry desperately. 'And London Zoo, and Buckingham Palace and Trafalgar Square? Don't you want to see all them places?'

'They'll still be there next week,' George said before Barry could answer. 'At least, I haven't heard they won't be. Calm down a bit, Ivy. Our Barry's been learning his words for weeks. You can't take him away now. And I'll tell you what,' he went on, beginning to sound quite enthusiastic, 'if you wait till next week, I'll shut the bakery and come too! How about that?'

Ivy stared at him. 'Shut the bakery? Whatever will folk do about their bread?'

'They'll manage for a couple of days. I might get Ellis's to come out from Tavi and make a few deliveries.'

'And suppose all your customers decide they'd rather go on having Ellis's bread and cakes after we come back?' Ivy demanded. 'That's our livelihood gone.'

'It won't be. Everyone knows Ellis's is at the top of West Street.

They could go there now if they'd a mind to. Some of 'em do already, for a change. A few days won't make no difference. We could go Wednesday, stop till next Saturday.'

'I dunno. I just thought it'd be nice to go now, being a holiday weekend.' She tried once more. 'You'll be shut on Monday anyway. If we just went for the weekend, you could come without closing the bakery specially.'

'But I want to be in the *play*,' Barry wailed, sounding close to tears, and Ivy gave in.

'All right, don't start piping your eye. We'll go next week. I'll let Flo know we're coming. And you'd better start making your own arrangements,' she added to George. 'Like deciding what we're to live on when we come back and find we got no business any more.'

'So what exactly happens at the summer fair?' David asked as he and Hilary sat with her father after dinner that night.

Hilary set down a tray bearing a whisky decanter, glasses and a siphon of soda water. Gilbert glanced at David and raised his eyebrows.

'Just a small one, please,' David said. 'That was a very good dinner, darling.'

'Thank you. I don't do so badly when it's Mrs Curnow's day off, do I? Mind you, Patsy made the gooseberry fool. We're going to miss her when she leaves at the end of the month.'

'I didn't think she'd stay long once she and young Pettifer had moved over to the farm,' Gilbert observed. 'She'll have too much to do there. Pity – she's a nice little thing to have around the house.'

'Brenda's shaping up very well, though,' Hilary said. 'And she gets on famously with Mrs Curnow.' She poured herself a liqueur and sat down beside David. 'You'll be well looked after when you're living here.'

'I'm well looked after already,' he said, taking her hand. 'Charles and Mary treat me like a long-lost son. But it's not quite the same as it will be here, being married to you!'

'I should hope not indeed,' she laughed. 'I won't be treating you like a son, for a start.'

David returned to his question. 'This summer fair – what happens exactly?'

'Oh, all kinds of things. Practically everyone in the village takes part and people come from miles around to enjoy it. The money we raise is going to the church organ fund this year. Basil's hoping we'll get enough to be able to make a start on its refurbishment. Not before time, either. You must have noticed how it—'

'But what *happens*?' he persisted.

'Well, it squeaks a lot, and wheezes, and sometimes it makes quite a rude noise ...' She caught his look and laughed again. 'Sorry! I'm in a silly mood tonight. Well, as I said, nearly everyone takes part in some way. It starts with the bells being rung, and a parade through the village. We have a village princess – it's Jenny Gribble this year – and her two attendants, arrayed in bridesmaids' dresses that weren't wanted after various weddings. They lead the parade on a farm cart all decked out in garlands, and then the village organisations follow. There aren't all that many, of course – just the whist club, the WI, the Mothers' Union, the Brownies and Guides and Boy Scouts, the drama group, and anyone else who wants to dress up and march through the village. And the school, of course, in the costumes of whatever production they're going to enact later. They did the forest scene from *A Midsummer Night's Dream* one year. It was rather sweet. I believe it's something to do with dragons this year.'

'Sounds quite a parade,' David said. 'Don't you have a band? There ought to be music.'

'No, we've never had a village band, but the handbell ringers will be ringing two or three times during the afternoon. Oh, and the skiffle group's going to be there. You remember them from the Christmas extravaganza last year!'

'Will I ever forget that night?' David said, shaking his head. 'Birth and death in the same family within a few hours. It was certainly a different introduction to village life than the one I'd expected.'

Gilbert stirred in his chair. 'I thought you two were going to discuss wedding plans. There's still a lot to decide.'

'Not really, Father. We're getting replies to the invitations now, although we can't confirm with the caterers until we know for certain how many will be here. Marianne and Rob are coming over. The cake's made and ready to be decorated. The flowers are organised. My dress is ready, and as far as I know, the bridesmaids' dresses are on schedule. Your suit's ready – and I assume David's is.' She cocked an eye at her fiancé, and he grinned and pretended panic. Ignoring him, she continued, 'The marquee will be coming two days beforehand so that it can be erected and the flowers arranged and the tables set. The church is ready – apart from the wheezing organ – and I don't know what else there is to do, really. Honestly, it's all in hand.' She laughed. 'There's a lot still to happen in this village before our wedding!'

'Maybe so,' Gilbert said. 'But there's just one thing you haven't mentioned. I'm not sure you've even thought about it.'

'Is there?' She looked at him in surprise. 'What's that, then? The honeymoon? That's all organised too. Venice and Verona!' She closed her eyes dreamily. 'It's going to be so wonderful.'

'No,' her father said. 'Not the honeymoon. It's something that's been troubling me and it doesn't even seem to have crossed your mind.'

'What?' Hilary's eyes opened again. 'What are you talking about?'

'Your name,' he said flatly. 'I didn't want to bring it up. I hoped you'd realise for yourself. Once you're married, you won't be a Napier any more. You'll be a Hunter. At least, I assume that's how you'll be known. And so will any children you may have.'

Hilary's brows came together in a frown. 'Well, yes, of course. That's what normally happens, isn't it? The bride takes her husband's name. So naturally I'll be Mrs ...' Her voice faded as she met her father's eyes. There was a moment of silence and then she said, 'Oh. Yes, I see what you mean.'

'There'll be no more Napiers at Burracombe,' he said, and turned his head away.

'He's right,' Hilary said later as she walked down the drive arm in arm with David. 'I never gave it a thought. He's wanted an heir so badly, and every time he thinks he's got one, it's snatched away. Baden, Rob – and now me. He must feel so let down.'

'But he wanted you to get married. He must have known you'd change your name.'

'I don't suppose he thought about it either. He was just anxious that I should be married. You know how it is – we can get our minds fixed on one idea and never actually realise the implications.

And he always hoped that Stephen would take on the estate.'

'Well, he and Maddy will probably have children. He'll have his little Napiers then.'

'But not at the Barton. Stephen doesn't want it. And he plans to go to Canada. Father will hardly ever see any children he and Maddy have.' She stopped and turned to him. 'David, it took him a long time to accept that I was the one who would be taking on the estate, and he obviously thought that my children, if I ever had any, would carry on from me. And perhaps they will. But they won't be Napiers, and that's what he's suddenly realised. That's what's hurting him.'

David said nothing for a moment or two. The darkness was settling around them. A pale moon showed fleetingly through the branches of the tall beeches that lined their way, and somewhere nearby an owl hooted. At last he said, 'Are you saying that you don't want to take my name? You're not asking me to change mine to Napier? Because—'

Hilary gripped his arms tightly. 'No! Of *course* I want to take your name. I want to be your wife in every way – and that includes being Mrs Hunter. But I understand how Father feels too, and I don't want to hurt him.'

He sighed. 'We can't live our whole lives according to other people's wishes, darling. Sometimes others have to accept what *we* want for a change.'

'I've always tried so hard to be and do whatever he expected of me,' she said in a low voice. 'Coming home to look after Mother when she was ill – staying after she died. I thought of being an airline stewardess once, but that would have meant leaving home, and he was going to be so lonely. And then his heart attacks … How could I leave him then? He really did need me, David.'

David slipped his arms around her. 'You've been a good daughter to him. In fact, I might even venture to suggest that you've spoiled him!'

She smiled a little. 'Well, it hasn't always been selfless, you know. Once I realised I could manage the estate, I wanted that more than anything. And I had to fight him for it. I didn't want a manager at all. It took me quite a while to accept Travis. And we've had our arguments, Father and I. I don't always give in.'

'But if you'd married earlier – if Henry hadn't been killed, or you'd met someone else, or if we'd been able to marry when we first knew each other …' He tightened his grasp. 'You would have left home then, lived your own life. Your children would not have been Napiers, but nobody would have thought anything of it.'

'I know. It doesn't really make sense, does it. But none of that happened, and this is how things are now. We have to deal with it as it is, not as it might have been.'

David kissed her, and she rested her head against his shoulder. 'Let's not worry any more about it now, sweetheart. We'll sleep on it, all of us. Maybe he'll come round to the idea anyway, now that he's brought it out into the open. He may realise there's nothing to be done.'

'And if he doesn't?' she asked wryly, and he kissed her again.

'Then we'll think again. But it may be that he just has to accept it, like it or not.' David looked down at her seriously. 'Because I share his feelings, in a way – I want my children to bear my name. I'm sure that when he considers it, he'll understand that. And there *is* Stephen – there really will be Napiers to carry on the name.'

'If they're boys,' she pointed out. 'Oh, I don't know, David – I could have done without this, to be honest. It's casting a shadow over everything.'

'We won't let it,' he said firmly. 'Our wedding is going to be a happy day for everyone. Including your father. He'll come round to the idea, you'll see.'

'Yes,' she said, lifting her face to his. 'He probably will.'

But as she walked back to the house, with the moon rising higher in the darkening sky and the bats busy in the air, she felt her doubts return. Gilbert was, she knew, of the old school. He set great store by the family name, by the inheritance of the Burracombe estate, by the fact that there had been Napiers in the village for hundreds of years. To be the last of the name, as he might well be, would be a heavy blow to his pride.

The fact that neither she nor Stephen might have sons would not be taken into account. The name must be there in place for any sons that did arrive, ready for them to carry along with their inheritance – and the responsibilities that went with it. And much as he liked and respected David, much as he welcomed him as a son-in-law, Gilbert would not be happy to know that the name Hunter would take the place of Napier on the title deeds. To him, that would be a blow almost as cruel as the loss of his elder son and heir, Baden, in the war.

There had to be some way round it, she thought as she let herself into the house and went up to her bedroom. There had to be some way that would satisfy them all.

Chapter Thirty-One

August Bank Holiday dawned with a grey sky. All over Burracombe, people craned their necks to look upwards and remind each other of fragments of folklore.

'Pink all over last night, shepherd's delight, that is' ... 'No shepherd's warning anyway, with all that cloud' ... 'They do say mackerel sky, twelve hours dry' ... 'Yes, but that's not mackerel, it's just plain grey' ... 'Listen, Burracombe always has good weather for the summer fair, and today won't be no different. Now stop staring at they clouds as if you'm trying to hypnotise them and come and have your breakfast.'

The Crocker family was up earlier than anyone. George and Edward, having slept the sleep of the just until five o'clock, could not stay any longer in bed once their eyes were open, and crept quietly downstairs and out of the house to look at their dragon costume, hanging up in their father's shed. They fingered its folds, thinking of the day ahead and the fun they would have capering down the village street, breathing fire – peppermint, anyway – and frightening children and old ladies. Mr Raynor had told them nobody would be frightened, but this they could not believe. They would make sure of it.

'All we got to do,' Edward said, 'is take Dad's old pipe and stuff it with tobacco and get it lit just before the parade starts. We'll be in front, so nobody'll be looking at us then – they'll be making sure all the other children and the rest of the parade is ready to go. Then when Mrs Warren gives the word, we dance off down the street and you start puffing away at that old pipe and breathe out the smoke. Easy as winking.'

'I've never smoked a pipe before,' George said dubiously. 'I tried those cigarette ends we picked up in the street that time, and they made me feel a bit sick.' In fact he'd been quite a lot sick, but Edward did not remind him of that.

'A pipe's easier than fags,' he said instead. 'All you got to do is suck in and then blow out. It's a pity us didn't think to bring it out with us now, us could have had a practice. Tell you what, I'll go and get it.'

George began to protest, but his twin had already gone, creeping through the back door like a burglar. He emerged a few moments later with their father's best pipe and a box of matches.

'I couldn't find the old one. Anyway, he never smokes it during the day, so he won't miss it. Us'll put it back and get the old one for this afternoon. Let's get the skin down.' They both flatly refused to call it a costume. It was a dragon's skin, as real as could be.

Carefully they lifted the drapes of camouflage material from its hook and carried it out to the yard.

'Better not put it on out here. Someone might look out of a window. Let's go out in the lane.'

The Crocker cottage was in one of the little back lanes that wound their way through the village. The two boys crept between the high Devon banks that bordered the gardens and paused in a nook. Between them, they got the dragon skin unwound and wriggled into it. George shifted the head about until the old cap Mabel Purdy had sewn into it fitted over his ears, and peered out through the eyeholes.

'I bet if anyone came round the corner now they'd get the fright of their lives,' he said, and began to skip about, almost pulling Edward off his feet.

'Here, be careful. You'll tear it, going on like that. You got to say when you'm starting off, and then I can keep in time like teacher told us.'

George stopped and adjusted the skin around his shoulders. 'All right, then. Go.'

'Not till you've got the pipe going, though,' Edward objected. 'That's what we'm meant to be practising.'

George wasn't really very keen on the pipe. He remembered how he had felt after smoking the cigarette ends, and whatever Edward said, he didn't believe a pipe would be any better. But if he refused to smoke it, Edward would claim his position at the head of the dragon, and George had won this hard, with much argument and a few lucky punches. He wasn't going to give it up now. Besides, he liked the idea of breathing fire – dragons weren't dragons if they didn't breathe fire – and he thought this was the best idea they'd had yet.

Edward passed him the pipe and a lump of sweet-smelling tobacco. George stuffed it into the bowl and then took the matches. Fumbling in the darkness under the head, he slid the box open and most of them fell out and scattered on the ground.

'Whatever be you doing?' Edward asked impatiently from within the depths of the dragon's body.

'The box was upside down.' George rescued a few and struck one. It went out and he tried again. The third one stayed alight, and he jabbed it at the pipe and sucked hard. Hot air touched his tongue and the match burned his fingers at the same moment. He squealed and dropped everything.

'Oh, you stupid fool!' Edward stormed, bending to help pick up the debris. 'You'll have half the village out to see what's up.'

'Well it's you doing all the shouting.' George scrabbled for the pipe and matches. 'It's all right. It's still got some baccy in. I'll have another go.'

This time he was more successful and the tobacco caught. He drew in a deep breath, more of relief than to keep it going, and blew out a cloud of smoke.

'We're breathing fire!' Edward cried, skipping with excitement. 'We're really breathing fire! Let's do a few steps to make sure it don't go out when us moves.' He began to jump forward, almost pushing George over.

'We'll be out in the street if you keeps on shoving like that.' George struggled to keep his footing and hold on to the head at the same time as he puffed on the pipe. 'I can't hold on with both hands, I got to have one for the pipe. And I feel – I feel a bit sick ...'

'Go on,' Edward urged, too carried away by the excitement of being a real, fire-breathing dragon to take notice of his brother's predicament. 'Keep going!' He pushed harder and George stumbled.

The dragon lurched out of the narrow back lane and into the main street. Bob Pettifer, on his way to meet Terry at the field to make sure the loudspeaker system was working, came round the corner just in time to see it emerge. He stopped and stared, then roared with laughter. At the same moment Ted Tozer came from the other direction driving his cows, who were going to a new field about a hundred yards down the lane. The leading cows saw the dragon and stopped dead. They started to retreat, almost trampling on those behind, while Ted, who could not see what the obstruction was, shouted and smacked the rumps of those at the back. George, whose eyes were now streaming from the smoke, could see nothing in front and could only hear a terror-stricken bellowing and clatter of hooves, while Edward had no idea at all what was going on and was beginning to panic in his turn. The dragon twisted and turned more effectively than it ever had in rehearsals as both boys tried to get out from the clinging folds of netting, which seemed determined to catch in their fingers, elbows and clothes, and the pipe rubbed against one of the newly painted scales and caught it alight. The smoke that rose from the head now had nothing to do with tobacco.

'Get me out!' George screamed. 'I'm on fire! Help! I'm burning to death! Get me out!'

'What in the name of all that's wonderful ...' Ted exclaimed, trying to push past the rearing beasts. 'Bob, what the hell's going on?'

'It's those Crockers,' Bob shouted. He got hold of the skin and pulled it aside, getting caught in the netting in his turn. 'Come on out of here, you daft toads. My stars, George, what's that you got? One of your dad's pipes? Do he know you'm out here smoking?' He dragged the boys clear and beat at the dragon's head to put out the flame that had begun to lick around its jaws. 'Are you all right? You're not really burned, are you?' He shook out the dragon skin. 'It don't look as if you've done too much damage to this, anyway.'

George shook his head and was suddenly sick on the ground. His twin looked up at the two men. He was shaking.

'We didn't mean it to catch fire,' he said in a wobbly voice.

'I don't suppose you did,' Ted said grimly. 'Anyway, we'll sort that out later. I got me beasts to catch now, and just look what they'm up to – rampaging round half the gardens in the village. Bob, you better give me a hand.' He gave the boys a ferocious look. 'And you two better get off home and tell your mother and father I'll be round later to talk about this. There'll be no summer fair for you – not if I have anything to do with it!'

By the time Ted and Bob had got the cows under control and into their new field, with the dependable help of Ted's two collies and the enthusiastic but rather less dependable help of a number of village dogs who had been attracted by the noise, Ted had calmed down a bit and even managed to see the funny side. Bob, who had never seen any other side at all, kept bursting into peals of laughter, interspersed with choked-out phrases such as 'Those boys ... nearly set fire ... that dragon ... whatever will they get up to next?'

'That's just it,' Ted said, still a trifle grimly as he closed the gate on the grumbling cows. 'What *will* they get up to next? I used to think young Micky Coker and Henry Bennetts were bad enough for mischief, but these two is ten times worse and they'm barely seven years old. They'll be setting fire to the whole village before they'm finished.'

'Oh, come on,' Bob said, shooing away half a dozen disappointed village dogs. 'There's always a couple of tackers around who seem to attract trouble. I bet you weren't a saint when you were a boy, Mr Tozer. I know I wasn't.'

'Well, maybe,' Ted allowed with a small grin as he recalled a few of his and his brother Joe's exploits. 'And it's not as if Ernie Crocker and his missus don't do their best to keep 'em in hand. They got a proper job on with they two. I don't reckon I'll bother going round to see them after all. They'll have enough to do getting ready for the fair as it is, and I wouldn't like to be in those boys' shoes when Ernie finds out they've been playing about with his pipe.'

Bob smiled. He knew that Ted Tozer harboured a soft heart under his gruff exterior and wouldn't have wanted to spoil the twins' moment of glory at the fair. He said goodbye at the end of the track to the farm and went on his way to the field attached to the village hall, whistling.

*

The rest of the Tozers were up and about by the time Ted got back, and there was an air of celebration in the kitchen that had nothing to do with the village fair. Dottie had been allowed home from hospital the day before, and Joe had managed to borrow a wheelchair from Dr Latimer, who kept one for emergencies, and proposed taking her along to see the fun.

'You mustn't let her overdo it, mind,' Alice warned him. 'She's still an invalid, don't forget, and a lot of excitement won't do her any good. She needs plenty of rest.'

'I'll take good care of her,' he promised. 'And Maddy's like a mother hen with her – she'll hardly let Dottie out of her sight. Anyway, there won't be much excitement at the village fair.'

'Don't you be too sure of that,' Ted grunted, sitting down to his breakfast. 'Those Crocker boys have already tried to set fire to the village with that dragon of theirs. My cows were all over the road in panic – the milk yield will be right down by this afternoon's milking, that's if it hasn't turned to butter by then.'

'Sounds like it's going to be fun,' Joe said, helping himself to crisply fried bacon. 'What's a dragon got to do with Burracombe anyway? Are they acting out the story of St George?'

'No, it's a children's play they're doing,' Joanna said. 'Robin's one of the courtiers, aren't you, Rob?' She poured warm milk on his Weetabix. 'All the children have got to be at the school early to get ready and have a final rehearsal. Mother's judging the baking at the village hall, where all the competitions are being displayed, and I've got to be at the chapel by eleven to get the tables set out for tea and put all the cakes and scones and sandwiches on plates ready for opening at two.'

'So you two will stay here with Great-Granny,' Alice told Robin and Heather.

'They can help me make some extra cakes,' Minnie said. 'You can never have too many cakes.'

'Oh Gran!' Joanna said with a laugh. 'You know we always have enough to sell off afterwards.'

'And since that raises more money, it's not too many, is it?' Minnie replied. 'It would only be too many if us were bringing them home unwanted.'

'And that wouldn't be too many either,' Tom observed, wiping egg yolk from his plate with a slice of bread. 'There's always some-one here to finish up a bit of cake.'

'You, mostly,' Alice told him. 'I never knew such a boy for cake!' She turned to Joe. 'I had to hide all the tins when he was a tacker or there was never any for anyone else.'

'That's because they were always so good.' Tom grinned and got up from the table. 'I'll be going now anyway. I said I'd help set out the stalls in the field, and I've got to go into Tavi at eleven to collect the coconuts from Roland Bailey's. They didn't have enough on Friday and I didn't have time to go on Saturday.'

'But it's August Bank Holiday!' Alice exclaimed in consterna-tion. 'They won't be open.'

'Mr Bailey said he'd come in specially. That's why I got to be there at eleven.' He pulled on his boots at the door. 'Tell you what, Robin could come with me if he likes. You'd like that, wouldn't you, Rob? Help Daddy collect the coconuts?'

'Can I have one?' Robin asked eagerly, and they all laughed.

'Only if you can knock it off its stick.' Tom opened the back door. 'I'll pick you up when I come back for the truck. See you later!'

'Is Tom doing the coconut shy, then?' Joe asked.

'No, old Bert Luscombe does it, but he don't have a car so Tom's helping out. I think he's hoping to take over when Bert gives up, but that won't be yet awhile, if Bert has anything to do with it. He's not going to give up his coconuts in a hurry.'

'Bert Luscombe? Is he still about?' Joe asked in astonishment. 'Why, I remember him doing the coconut shy when I was a boy! You're sure this is the same one? It's not his son?'

'It's the same one,' Alice said, laughing. 'He's a fixture in the village. I'm surprised you haven't run across him before this; he's always out and about in the lanes.'

'He must be getting on for ninety,' Joe marvelled, and caught his mother's eye. 'Not that that's particularly old, of course,' he added hastily.

'Ninety?' Minnie snorted. 'Bert Luscombe's nowhere near ninety. He'm only just past eighty. Plenty of life left in him yet. If our Tom wants to run the coconut shy, he's got a long wait ahead of him.'

'What time are you going to collect Dottie?' Alice asked as Joe spread home-made marmalade on the last slice of toast.

'Half past one. Maddy won't let me across the doorstep before that. She's taken Dottie over as if she was a new baby. We're not even going to need to queue at the gate like everybody else – we've got special dispensation to go straight through the crowd and get in first.' He grinned. 'I think Dottie's going to get quite a reception.'

'She will, since it's the first time she've been in the village since her stroke. I can easy make some more toast if you want it, Joe. We'm only having a scratch dinner, so you want to make sure you've got plenty inside you.'

'Scratch dinner!' he laughed. 'Shepherd's pie is what I heard. And knowing you, there'll be enough to feed half the village too.'

'Well, 'tis easy, and everyone can help themselves as and when they're ready. What I mean is, us won't be sitting down together like civilised folk, and there's always one or two extra dropping in on fair day. Now, does anyone want more toast or not?' She held up the big wire toast holder, but they all shook their heads.

'I must get started,' Joanna said, gathering up plates. 'I'll wash these dishes first, Mother, and then I've got to put a stitch in Robin's tunic. I noticed last night it was a bit loose round the waist. And if there's nothing else you need doing here, I'll start taking cakes and scones down to the chapel.'

'Will you see if I've got a prize for my garden?' Robin asked, and Heather chimed in, 'Mine too! Mine too!'

'They won't be saying who's won until this afternoon,' Joanna told them. 'But I'll make sure both your gardens are there.' She went to the sink to start washing up. Both children had made miniature gardens for the competition – Heather's a simple arrangement of a small square of grass bordered by tiny flowers from her grand-mother's rockery, and Robin's a more ambitious affair representing a vegetable patch, with spring onion and carrot tops planted in neat rows and a few small tomatoes which, if they had been in proportion, would have been the size of footballs, together with a scarecrow made from a wooden peg and a tiny gardener borrowed from Joanna's old dolls' house and furnished with a spade made by Tom from a scrap of wood.

'Mine might need watering,' Robin said anxiously, and Joanna promised to take the little spray with her, at which Heather immediately said, 'Mine too!'

'That's her favourite thing to say at the moment,' Joanna said wryly. 'It's surprisingly useful, too – can be used on all occasions, from holding out a plate for more food to having her shoes put on. She'll probably never need to say anything else in her whole life.'

The family began to bustle about, helping to clear the table for Minnie to start baking the extra cakes she believed to be essential and then going off on their own concerns. Ted still had a few jobs to do outside, and Joe went to help him.

'It looks as if the weather's going to clear up,' he remarked, looking at the sky. The clouds of the morning had lifted and parted to reveal blue sky, and the sun was slanting down between them and lighting the fields and hills with bright colour. On the moors, the heather was a coverlet of glowing amethyst against which the gorse shone with a gold so brash and gaudy it almost made your eyes ache. 'It's going to be hot later.'

'It always is for Burracombe summer fair,' Ted said. 'The rest of the country might grumble about bank holiday weather, but 'tis always fine here. Not that us'd notice if it wasn't. We're all too busy once it gets started to look at the sky.'

'It's going to be grand,' Joe declared. 'My first summer fair since I was a young chap, and I'll have Dottie with me. It'll be like stepping into the past. And this time, she won't be able to run away!'

Chapter Thirty-Two

Ted didn't have a word with Ernie Crocker, surmising – correctly, as it happened – that he would find out that his best pipe had been borrowed and deal with the culprits accordingly. But even Ernie didn't have the heart to ban the twins from the fair, and contented himself with telling them they would not be able to go out to play for the rest of the week. They accepted this with relief, knowing how much worse their punishment could have been, and set out to enjoy their moment of glory.

'You're quite sure you haven't got any matches in your pockets? Or any other way to start a fire?' James asked them sternly as they stood in the playground with the dragon skin draped across their arms. 'And when I say pockets, I mean anywhere on you at all.'

They shook their heads, not entirely sure whether he had heard about their early-morning exploit. In fact, he had – Tom had encountered him in the field while he was delivering the coconuts to Bert Luscombe – but James thought it better to keep his own counsel, partly because the story had made him laugh so much that he wasn't sure he'd be able to keep from smiling if he did mention it.

'But that's awful!' Frances had exclaimed when he told her. 'They could have really injured themselves. And what about Mr Tozer's cows?'

'I think they're recovering from the shock,' he said solemnly. 'Come on, Frances, I admit it could have been nasty, but it ended well and I think the boys frightened themselves even more than the cows. They're quite subdued now.'

'Are they? I hadn't noticed.' They both looked across the playground to where the twins were now in their skin and chasing the girls around the playground, snarling and roaring loudly. 'Well, I suppose it *was* rather funny,' she agreed. 'But we really will have to keep an eye on those two. We don't want them burning down the school one day.'

They called the children into order and got them lined up. The signal for the parade to start was when the church bells began to ring, and the cavalcade was to wind its way round all the little back ways and finally up the main village street to the field behind the hall. The village princess, Jenny Gribble, a rather lumpy girl of fourteen who had been passed over three times and whose last chance this was, was to ride in Ted Tozer's hay cart with her two attendants, each arrayed in whichever frock from the village's store of bridesmaids' dresses fitted them best. They also wore headdresses made of flowers, with Jenny's the most elaborate, as befitted the chief princess.

The dragon was to follow immediately behind the cart, with the rest of the children in their costumes next, and then the representatives of all the village organisations, some on decorated carts and some walking. This wasn't easy to arrange, as a lot of people belonged to more than one organisation, but it usually got sorted out to everyone's satisfaction. The only potential problem was that so many of the village people would be in the parade that there would be hardly anybody left to watch it go by, but the Burracombe summer fair attracted visitors from villages for miles around – even Little Burracombe – so there was always a good crowd lining the main street to cheer them on.

At last everything was ready. The Tozers' farm horse Barley was in position, harnessed to the hay cart with Val at his head, and the three princesses were helped up on to their bales of hay, their satin dresses arrayed around them and their flowers tucked into place. The dragon was shifting impatiently from foot to foot, and the other children, with Barry Sweet at their head, were whispering and giggling. Behind them, the rest of the parade waited for the first sound of the bells.

'It's half past one,' Frances said anxiously. 'They ought to be—' But her words were lost as the bells rang out, their clamour drowning all the muttering, and a great cheer went up. Val gave Barley's leading rein a twitch, and he neighed loudly and began to lumber forward. The princesses squealed as their cart began to rock, and the dragon gave a huge snort and leapt into the air with all four feet off the ground. The following children shouted with excitement, and the representatives of the various village organisations moved on with all the dignity their own delight and pride could muster.

The summer fair had begun!

Joe had brought Dottie's wheelchair to her gate in good time to see the parade pass by on its way to the field. Maddy had helped her dress in her best blue summer frock, with her white cardigan in case it turned chilly, and had decorated her straw hat with roses from the garden. Dottie had shaken her head when she saw it and objected that she didn't want to look as if she was setting herself up to be a part of the parade, but Maddy had put it on her head and held a hand mirror up, and she'd had to admit it looked very pretty. 'And you've made a lovely job of the flowers,' she added. 'I didn't mean to be ungracious. I just don't want to look as if I'm making myself out to be someone special.'

'But you *are* someone special,' Joe said, coming in at that moment. 'Special to me and special to the whole village. You must know that, Dottie.'

'Oh, you,' she said, but her face was pink and her eyes bright. He bent to kiss her and she lifted her face to his, and they looked at each other for a moment.

Maddy turned away quickly, feeling a twinge of pleasure followed swiftly by a stab of pain. She had been missing Stephen badly in the past few days. Being here with Dottie in the cottage where she had spent so much of her childhood, it had seemed almost as if she were indeed a child again, and that none of her life with Sammy or Stephen had ever happened. She felt as if she had dreamed it all. And now, seeing the feelings that these two older people clearly had for each other, knowing that they had spent so many years apart, the pang drove even deeper. I want to be with him, she thought. I want him here with me now, in Burracombe, where we belong ...

But almost as soon as the thought had entered her mind, she

thrust it away. She had come back to look after Dottie, and she had promised to stay until after Stella's baby was born and Hilary was married. She would carry out all those promises, and she would do it with a smile on her face, and it was that smile that she gave to Dottie and Joe now.

'Stop canoodling, you two,' she commanded. 'It's time to be at the gate to see the parade go by. The bells have been ringing for nearly a quarter of an hour – it must be almost here. Hurry up.'

By the time the hay cart reached the village street, Dottie was in position by her gate, beaming, with Joe standing proudly at one side and Maddy at the other. They waved as the cavalcade approached, and Val saw them and waved back. The princesses, who, like everyone else, knew Dottie and were pleased to see her home again, gave cries of excitement.

Barley had never seen a wheelchair before. He was accustomed to large carts, to wheelbarrows, to all manner of farm equipment, but he had never actually seen a wheelchair with a person sitting inside it. He had also already been subjected to clusters of school-children in peculiar costumes, and to some rather hefty princesses in frilly satin dresses that were, in Jenny's case at least, rather too tight. Worst of all, he had a suspicion that there was somewhere behind him an animal the like of which he had never encountered and hoped never to encounter again. It reminded him a little of an adder he had once almost trodden on, only several hundred times larger.

When Dottie waved back to Val, the princesses squealed and the dragon roared and stamped its feet. Startled and confused, Barley stopped dead for a moment. The hay cart rocked and the princesses fell against each other in a tumble of pink and blue satin frills. The dragon, caught in mid-caper, twisted round the cart to avoid crashing into its wheels and appeared suddenly beside the horse, just at the edge of his vision. George, making the most of the moment, scuttled in front of him, narrowly missing a pair of stamping hooves, and dragged his twin in corkscrew fashion into the lead position where they had both felt all along that they ought to be. Unable to see exactly where they were going through the eyeholes of the dragon's head, which had come loose from the cap and fallen down over George's eyes, they collided with each other and fell in a heap of green and gold camouflage netting, which immediately draped itself over them and tangled itself around their struggling arms and legs.

Barley had had enough and made what he felt to be the only appropriate response. He neighed loudly, reared up on his hind legs, almost pulling Val off her feet, and set off at a trot along the street, dragging the cart with its now screaming bundle of princesses behind him.

'Oh my dear Lord!' Frances Kemp exclaimed from somewhere amidst the group of diminutive courtiers now surging forward to see what was going on. 'Stop, all of you! Come back! Stand still! James, whatever's happening? What are those boys up to now? Is anyone hurt?' Torn between hurrying forward herself and trying to get the children into some sort of order, while the rest of the procession came to a straggling halt behind her with what sounded like further collisions, she craned her head and saw to her horror that Dottie's wheelchair seemed to be in the middle of the chaos, although apparently still upright, and its occupant having some kind of seizure. 'Oh no! Dottie – *Dottie*! James, are you there? Mr Tozer – Maddy! Whatever's happening? Is Dottie all right?'

But gazing in dismay at the mayhem before her, Frances Kemp was very much afraid that she was not.

'Oh my stars,' Dottie wept, as Joe stood beside her with his arm around her shaking shoulders, and James and Frances between them quelled the throng and brought back some semblance of order. 'Oh my goodness gracious me! I never in all my born days saw anything so funny! Those poor girls up on that cart, all flung about like fancy dolls, and that great big snake—'

'It's a *dragon*,' said George indignantly from his position by Dottie's fence, where James had stood the twins with the direst of threats as to what would happen if they dared move an inch. 'It's *The Dragon Who Was Different*.'

'I'll say it's different,' Joe said, grinning. 'I've never seen anything like it, even on a Fourth of July parade in the States.'

'We shouldn't laugh,' Dottie said, tears of merriment pouring down her crimson cheeks. 'Those girls have had their day proper spoiled. But – oh, you got to admit …' and she was off again, shaking with laughter so that all those about her were infected with her mirth, and Barley, hauled back into his place by Val, gave them a sidelong glance and seemed to shrug his big shoulders, as if to say he never had understood humans and wasn't likely to begin now.

'Come on,' James said at last. 'Let's get you all sorted out and back on your way. The bells stopped ringing five minutes ago – people will be wondering where we are. We don't want them coming to look for us, or worse still, thinking the fair's off and going away!'

Frances turned to Maddy. 'Maddy, are you sure Miss Friend's all right? She doesn't need to rest after all the excitement?'

'I'm perfectly all right, thank you,' Dottie said a little waspishly. 'And I can answer for myself. I've got myself all dressed up to go to this fair and I'm not missing it now. If the rest of it is as good as this bit's been, it'll be the best ever!'

'And now that we have stopped,' Val said, satisfied that Barley had recovered from his fright and could be trusted to remain calm provided the dragon stayed out of his sight, 'I think you should go on ahead. Go on, Uncle Joe – push her out in front of Barley. He won't mind as long as he can see where she is and what she's doing, and I know Jenny and the girls won't – will you?' She looked up at the princesses, who were back in place with their dresses more or less tidy apart from the loss of one or two frills, and with only a few bits of hay stuck amongst their flowery head garlands, and they smiled back – a somewhat tremulous smile, perhaps, in the case of Jenny Gribble, who had been looking forward to her triumphal progress for weeks, but a smile none the less.

Barley was not asked if he would mind. But he was used to his opinions being unsought and did no more than heave a deep sigh of resignation as he thrust his bulk once more into the harness and followed the wheelchair along the street. His attitude seemed to be that if there was no choice in the matter, it was best to get it over with as soon as possible, and although the wheelchair prevented him from setting as spanking a pace as he would have liked, his clattering hooves were perilously close to Joe's heels all the way to the field.

*

'Here they are at last. Whatever happened to you?' Jacob Prout, who had hurried down from the church to take the entrance money at the gate, didn't wait for an answer. He waved the procession through, to the cheers of the waiting queue, and once they were safely inside and the hay cart was in position for its other duties of the afternoon, he began to allow the paying visitors in.

'That's sixpence each, threepence for tackers still at school, or old folk. And nothing for wheelchairs,' he added, beaming as Dottie appeared, having hung back from the throng. 'It's real good to see you back with us, Dottie. Us've missed you summat awful.'

'Go on with you, Jacob. I don't suppose you even noticed I wasn't there. But thank you for feeding Albert. I was a bit worried about him while I was in hospital.'

'You didn't need to worry about he. And I watered your vegetables and picked a few gooseberries that were going ripe. Mabel Purdy made jam with 'em, to save them being wasted. Her'll pass it on to you now you're home.'

Dottie's eyes filled with tears at this kindness, and Joe pushed her further into the field. She rubbed her eyes fiercely with her handkerchief and said, 'I dunno what's the matter with me lately. I seem to cry at every little thing. Fancy shedding tears over a few jars of jam!'

'It's because you're not very strong yet,' Joe said. 'We've got to look after you. And I don't think we'd better stop here the whole afternoon. We'll just have a look round, and then slip back home.'

'And miss the prize giving?' she asked, outraged. 'And the kiddies' play? I've been looking forward to that, and if that dragon's half as good in the play as it was in the procession, it'll be talked about for years to come!'

Frances Kemp came up beside them and heard the last few words. 'I think the Crocker twins are going to provide gossip for several decades to come,' she said wryly. 'This is just the start of their exploits. Dottie, it's so good to see you. And Mr Tozer, too. I hope you're looking after her.'

'Call me Joe, please – we Americans don't take as much account of ceremony as folk here. And sure I'm looking after her – got her wrapped up in cotton wool. Maddy and me don't intend taking any risks with our Dottie.'

Americans didn't take much account of English grammar either, Frances thought, but she was too accustomed to the vagaries of the Devon dialect to correct him. In any case, it would have been rude. Frances might never quite be able to forget she was a teacher, but she did try to remind herself that not everyone was a pupil.

'Well, I hope you don't get too tired this afternoon,' she said to the invalid. 'Everyone is going to want to come and speak to you.'

'We'll charge them sixpence each then,' Dottie said. 'Might as well make myself useful, since I've done nothing else towards the fair.'

Frances laughed and moved away. There was already a line of people queuing to wish Dottie well, and she was pleased to see that Ivy Sweet was amongst them. She glanced around for Barry and the rest of the courtiers, who were milling about and trying their hand at the various games set up in different places – roll a penny, giant snakes and ladders, the coconut shy – and getting ever more excited about their play, which had been scheduled for two forty-five. That would give them time to enjoy the fair first, although they'd been forbidden to eat ice cream or anything sticky until afterwards, when they could indulge to their hearts' content.

'Although why we should expect townspeople of whatever medieval period the story is set in to be spick and span, I'm not sure,' James had commented. 'They were more likely to have been dressed in rags and stained with all sorts of things.'

'They were dressed in their best on this occasion,' Frances had retorted firmly. 'Anyway, these aren't the common townsfolk; these are the burghers and the members of the king's court. Of course they would be finely arrayed.'

'In which case, we seem to have fallen between two stools,' he remarked, and she shook her head at him.

She found Barry Sweet sitting on a bench in a corner, poring over his script and muttering to himself.

'Barry, why are you doing this? You know all your words. You were excellent at the dress rehearsal. Go and enjoy yourself until it's time.'

He looked up at her, his face white. 'I can't remember any of them, miss. I feel sick.'

'You'll be perfectly all right once you start. Even famous actors feel like this when they're just about to go on.'

'I can't do it,' he whispered. 'Can't Billy Madge do it instead? He was ever so good as Joseph at Christmas and he's learned all the words.'

Frances gazed at him. There had been considerable rivalry between the two boys for this part and Billy would indeed have been very good – she could still hardly suppress a smile at the memory of him haranguing Basil during the nativity procession last Christmas over his refusal to allow Mary to give birth in the vicarage drawing room – but she and James had decided to give it to Barry because it would be his last chance before leaving for the secondary school in Tavistock.

'You really will be quite all right,' she said. 'Look, there's Maddy Forsyth – Mrs Napier, I mean. She knows all about it from her mother, Fenella Forsyth. She's a famous actress, you know.' She raised her voice and called Maddy over. 'Barry's having a bad attack of stage fright. I wondered if you could reassure him.'

'Why, of course.' Maddy sat down beside him. 'There really isn't any need to worry. Almost all actors feel just the same. Some really are sick before they go on. And the worse they feel, the better they are. In fact, if you feel like this now, it means you really are a good actor. Didn't you know that?'

He gazed at her. 'Billy Madge never feels scared. He told me.'

'Billy Madge is quite good,' Maddy said fairly, 'but he's not a *real* actor like I think you are. I saw a bit of the dress rehearsal, you know. You really seemed to *be* Peter, not just act him. Do you know what I mean?'

'I felt as if it was true,' he admitted. 'I forgot it was just George and Edward Crocker in that skin. It seemed like a real dragon.'

'There you are, then,' she said triumphantly. 'That proves it. Now, I'm going to sit here with you until it's time, and I'll come with you when you have to start. All you need remember is your first words, and then everything will happen just as it should. You'll see.'

'But I can't remember the first words!' he wailed, panic setting in again as he fumbled for the front of the script. 'I'm going to spoil it all, I know I am!'

'You are not going to spoil anything,' Maddy said firmly. 'The

255

words will come back as soon as you begin. They always do. You've learned them, so they're inside here' – she tapped the side of his head – 'and once you start, it will all come true again. You'll be Peter, and George and Edward will be a dragon, and the whole story will just *happen*. I promise you it will.'

Frances left them to it. She had no doubt that it would all transpire just as Maddy foretold. She went to the area set aside for the play and found spectators already gathering there, although the cast were nowhere to be seen – either enjoying their freedom, she thought, or, like Barry, suffering from varying degrees of stage fright.

Many of the visitors to the fair came from outside the village. Quite a lot, who came every year, were vaguely familiar, but others were complete strangers – people on holiday or from other localities, even a few from Okehampton or Plymouth. Once again the sun had obliged and shone warmly enough to keep Jeanie and Jessie Friend busy selling their ice cream, while others filed into the chapel, which was accessible from the village hall field, for tea and cakes. The village hall was also full of those who wanted to admire the competition displays or see if they had won a prize or certificate.

'I've got a first prize!' Robin Tozer cried in excitement, spotting the certificate by his miniature vegetable garden. 'And Heather's got a – what's that, Mummy?'

'A highly commended. It means the judge thought it was very good.'

'But not as good as mine.'

'No, but you're a lot older than Heather. You both did very well.'

They browsed around the rest of the displays. Jacob Prout had won prizes as usual for his vegetable marrow, plate of four perfect tomatoes, and runner beans, while Dottie had been awarded a second for the roses he had picked from her garden that morning and arranged to his own satisfaction, if not the judge's, in a china vase that had belonged to his mother. Minnie Tozer had won a prize for her Victoria sponge, and Alice one for her cherry cake and another for a plate of scones. Mabel Purdy had a prize for an embroidered baby's frock, which she intended to present to Stella when the fair was over, and Micky Coker, who had been given a Brownie box camera for his birthday, had been awarded a second prize for his photograph of the old oak tree on the village green in the new photography competition. Henry Warren, who was also a keen photographer and had won first prize for his photograph of the standing stones at sunset, looked at it with interest.

'It may be just luck, but he seems to have a good eye for composition,' he remarked to Joyce. 'Pity he's not old enough to join the Tavistock Camera Club.'

'He'll probably have other interests by the time he is,' she said. 'You know what these boys are.'

Henry, having been one himself once, smiled and suggested going for a cup of tea before the play started. When they came out of the chapel again, the cast was assembled and most of the chairs, set out in rows, were taken. The latecomers stood around at the back, with small children hoisted on to fathers' shoulders so that they could get a good view, and after a short announcement by Frances Kemp, the play began.

Barry Sweet was word perfect. He faced the greedy king boldly, and when given the choice between going to prison or seeking out the dragon, chose to hunt the beast who had, according to the king, been terrorising the country. His encounter with the fearsome dragon, played by the Crocker twins with even more enthusiasm than usual to make up for their lack of real fire, had all the smallest children squealing and the adults laughing, and when the dragon was revealed to be as friendly as a puppy and as cuddly as a teddy bear, there was a chorus of ohs and aahs. When Peter returned to the king's court and was condemned to be executed, there was real tension and calls for the dragon to come to his rescue, and the Crockers enjoyed their final moment of glory as they danced triumphantly onstage, breathing peppermint fumes over the entire cast, who all fainted dramatically away.

The applause afterwards would have raised the roof, had the makeshift theatre had a roof, and Ivy, standing at one side, felt herself swell with pride at her son's performance. She turned to her husband, her face glowing with pleasure, and found that he had already gone to congratulate the star of the show. Instead, she found herself looking at a stranger.

He was tall, with black hair and dark, deep-set eyes. She stared up at him and felt her heart thud painfully in her breast. She opened

257

her mouth a little, then turned away as if to escape, but he reached out and took her elbow in a firm, strong grip.

'You are Ivy Sweet, yes?' His voice was deep, tinged with an accent she knew well. 'And the boy with red hair, who played Peter so well – he is your son?'

There was no point in denying it. With a sense of doom and a recognition that this meeting had been inevitable for weeks, if not years, she nodded.

'Then I must talk to you,' the stranger said. 'I have much I wish to say.'

Chapter Thirty-Three

Ivy allowed herself to be led away like a lamb to the slaughter. She had no will to resist, and besides that, she dared not cause a scene here, in front of the whole village. There was still, she hoped, a chance of hiding the shame she had kept concealed for so long.

They went out of the side gate and along the tree-lined banks of the brook that flowed down from the old mill. Ivy's heart was thumping. Suppose someone had seen them slip away? What would they think? And how could she explain why she hadn't immediately gone to congratulate her son, as all the other mothers had done?

'I ought to go and see Barry,' she said weakly, making a token show of pulling her arm away. 'He'll be expecting me.'

The stranger regarded her for a moment, then nodded. 'But you will come back here after you have told him how good he was.'

It wasn't a question. There was, she knew, no escaping him now. He had found her, and if he didn't know by this time where she lived, he could quickly find out. She ducked her head in acquiescence and he let her go, to hurry back through the gate and over the field to where the children were being fussed over and praised by their families. She pushed through to Barry, who was looking flushed and excited.

'Mum! Did you see me? Was I all right?' His beaming smile told her that he knew very well how good he had been.

'You were a proper little star. I nearly cried when the king said you were going to be executed. *Everyone* was good,' she added in a burst of generosity that might, she hoped, divert attention from her late arrival. 'Weren't they, George? I reckon it was the best little play the school's ever done. Why don't we give them all free cakes? You come along to the bakery tomorrow afternoon,' she said to the open-mouthed children, 'and we'll give you all a cake, won't us, George?'

'If you say so, Ive,' he said, almost too astonished to speak. 'But I hope you'll give me a hand with the baking.'

'Of course I will.' She glanced over his head and caught the eye of the stranger, watching her from the back of the crowd. Feeling suddenly sick, she swallowed and said quickly, 'I got to go now. I promised to give a hand with the ... with the ...' But what she had promised to give a hand with, nobody could hear, for the last few words were mumbled as she turned and hastened away.

'Well!' Ted Tozer exclaimed from where he and Alice had been congratulating Robin on his performance as a courtier. 'If that don't beat the band! Ivy Sweet giving away free cakes!'

'She's always treated Barry like a little prince,' Alice said, making sure that George Sweet couldn't hear her. 'I suppose she got a bit carried away with him acting like one. Mind you, I got to admit he was good, got quite a way with him.' She glanced round at the crowd now making for the chapel. 'I'm going back to help with the teas now, and you ought to be getting ready for your sheep-shearing demonstration. Those poor creatures have been waiting since Whitsun to have their coats cut off; they must be almost roasting in this hot sun.'

They went their separate ways, forgetting about Ivy Sweet, as did almost everyone else there as they made for sideshows, ice cream, teas and various demonstrations. The skiffle group began to play in one corner and the Morris dancers were getting ready in another. Ivy slipped out of the side gate unnoticed and made her way back along the path by the millstream. Her heart was beating hard.

She still had no idea who he was, but it was clear that he knew her. And what was worse, he knew Barry.

'Well, I think that went off very well,' Frances said to James as they cleared up after the children and their parents had dispersed. The discarded costumes had been gathered up and the small tent that had been used as a dressing room was being transformed for use by a fortune-teller (whose identity was known only to Jack Pettifer, because he'd had to get his own dinner). The Crocker twins had refused to part from their dragon skin and were now to be seen cavorting all over the field, roaring and breathing peppermint at anyone who got in their way. Since the field was still crowded, this was almost everyone, but luckily all the visitors were in a holiday mood and a few enterprising youths lured the dragon into a corner, where they began to teach it tricks.

'Very well indeed,' James agreed, almost hidden behind a huge armful of costumes. 'Where are these going?'

'There's a small room in the chapel – we can just dump them there for the time being. And while we're there, we can have some tea. I think we deserve it.'

Together they carried the costumes through the gate to the chapel and dropped them in a pile on a bench in the anteroom. The main body of the chapel, now a temporary tea room, was thronged with people, and the two teachers were besieged by thirsty theatregoers. It was the best play ever, they declared, but as Frances remarked to James as they stood in the queue, they said that every year so it didn't necessarily mean much.

'You certainly know how to make a man feel good,' he said ruefully, and she laughed. 'Still, it must have been at least *one* of the best. I can't see how even *Dream* could surpass our dragon.'

'I think he will be remembered for a very long time to come,' she agreed.

'What are you going to have?' asked James as they reached the front of the queue. 'I want as many scones and cakes as my plate will hold, starting with those little chocolate things made with cornflakes.'

'James! They're meant for the children.'

'And are not all men little boys at heart?' he enquired, adding two jam and cream scones and a rock bun to the pile already on his plate. 'Anyway, it's hungry work keeping twenty children and a dragon under control. Have a slice of that lemon cake, it looks delicious.'

They carried their tea to a free table in the corner and sat down. There was a sudden silence between them. Feeling oddly awkward, Frances drank some tea and then concentrated on the lemon cake.

After a moment or two, they both began to speak together, then laughed.

'You first,' James said.

'No – you.' As soon as she had said it, she wished she hadn't, knowing that her chance to deflect the conversation had gone. She glanced up at his face and saw that his dark eyes were fixed on her in a steady gaze. 'James ...'

'It's all right,' he said quickly. 'This isn't the time or the place, I know that. But Frances ... about our pact.'

'Friends,' she said. 'True, simple friendship. That's what we said.'

'I know. But we both know, don't we, that it can't stay like that.'

'I don't see why ...'

'Because things change,' he said quietly. 'Or they develop. We don't always have the control that we think. And our friendship *has* changed and developed. We both know it.' He waited a moment. 'True, simple friendship. *True.*'

Frances gazed down at the crumbs on her plate. 'James, I—'

'Please,' he said. 'I'm not asking you to say anything now. But you're going away on Wednesday, to stay with your cousin.' She looked up and he met her eyes again. 'Talk to Iris,' he said quietly. 'Tell her what's happening here, and when you come home again, talk to me. Will you do that, Frances?'

'Yes,' she said in a low voice. 'Yes, James. I'll do that.'

Hilary and David were in the queue as well. They had watched the play, laughing at the dragon's antics and marvelling at the touching performance by Barry Sweet, and then joined the crowd making their way into the chapel. As David picked up their tray of tea and cakes, he spotted Frances and James and started to make his way towards them, but Hilary touched his arm.

'They look rather deep in conversation. Let's take it outside. There are two or three tables with sun umbrellas.'

David followed her obediently and they found a table just about to be vacated by Val and Luke Ferris and baby Christopher. They sat down and breathed sighs of relief.

'The fair only last two hours, but an awful lot gets packed in,' Hilary said. 'Mind you, it's the culmination of weeks of planning

262

and several days of last-minute frenzy, so I suppose that's why we're all so exhausted afterwards.' She grinned at him. 'It's a sort of rehearsal for our wedding, in a way!'

'You're not telling me we're having that dragon in it!' David exclaimed. 'I know the bride likes to spring a few surprises, but a dragon following you up the aisle as well as half a dozen bridesmaids might be a bit too much even for me!'

Hilary laughed and thumped her fist on the table. 'Bother! You've guessed. Now I'll have to think of something else.' Her face grew more serious. 'But now that the fair's over, we really will have to start making serious arrangements. Accommodation, for a start. We need to know who'll have to be put up and decide where they're to go.'

'Charles and Mary have already said they'd like to have my parents to stay. They all got on very well at Easter. Like a house on fire, in fact,' he added wickedly, and Hilary closed her eyes and shuddered.

'Don't remind me. What about your other relatives? There's the Bedford, of course, and the Two Bridges Hotel. Would those be suitable?'

'Eminently, I should think. But do we need to discuss this now? Let's just enjoy the rest of today and think about it when it's all over. None of it is that urgent.'

'I suppose not.' She fiddled with her teaspoon. 'There is one thing we have to decide, though, and the sooner the better. We both know it's been on my father's mind, but I have to admit it's been bothering me too.' She looked up at him. 'This question of my name.'

David said nothing for a moment. Then, meeting her eyes, he said quietly, 'I'm afraid I'm not prepared to change mine, darling. Not unless there's no other choice. Can't your father accept that it's bound to be this way?'

'I think he could, if he absolutely had to. But I don't want either of you to feel forced into accepting something you don't want. I think there is a solution.'

'Yes?'

'Why don't I keep both names?' she said. 'Why don't I simply become Hilary Napier Hunter?'

*

'Who are you?' Ivy asked. She and the stranger were sitting on a fallen log, staring at the tumbling mill stream. The sounds of the summer fair made a background to the rushing water and the whispering leaves above. Somewhere nearby a chaffinch was uttering its warning *spink*, and there was a clap of wings as a pigeon took off. 'Why have you been following me about?'

'I was looking for you. I went to the pub in Horrabridge and thought I had found you, but the landlord would tell me nothing. And I was looking for a woman with brown hair, not red.'

Ivy flushed. 'Lennie knew you meant me but he didn't like you sneaking round. And it's nothing to do with you what colour my hair is.'

'No?' he said. 'But it is to do with me what colour your son's hair is.'

Ivy caught her breath. She started to get up but he caught her wrist and pulled her down again. She turned on him furiously.

'Let me go! I've nothing to say to you! I don't know who you are or why you're pestering me like this, but if you don't let me go this minute, I'll shout for help. I'll scream!'

'I think not,' he said quietly. 'It is true you don't know me, but you knew my brother.' He paused, and she stared at him. 'Does the name Igor mean nothing to you, even after nearly twelve years?'

Ivy sank back on to the tree trunk. 'Igor?' she whispered. 'You're Igor's brother? But you're nothing like him. You're dark and he ... he—'

'He had red hair,' he finished for her. 'Just as your son Barry has.'

Ivy stared at him. 'What ... what are you saying? What do you want? Why have you come here after all this time? And where's Igor? I thought ... I thought he was dead.' Her words ended in a little sob, and as he let go of her wrist, she covered her face with her hands.

'Yes,' he said after a pause. 'Igor is dead. He was killed fighting for his country – and for your country.' He looked around at the softly moving trees, cocking his head to listen to the laughter and the music coming from the fair. 'So that we could enjoy such simple pleasures together,' he said quietly.

Ivy felt the tears brim from her eyes. There was a pain in her heart that she had thought healed, an ache for a love gone for ever. She stared at the mossy path and wondered what came next, knowing that the consequences of what had happened years ago could no longer be buried. The world had shifted beneath her feet and she had lost control.

'Why have you come?' she asked in a whisper. 'After all this time ... Me and Barry ... and George ... we'm a *family*. Why have you come to spoil it?'

'I have not come to spoil it. I didn't know how you were placed – what your life was. For all I knew, you might be alone and in difficulty.'

'Well you left it long enough to find out!' she flashed. 'Suppose us had been? Suppose George had thrown me out when he found out I was expecting? Suppose I'd been on me own with Barry all this time, maybe not even in Burracombe any more? Don't tell me you've spent the last twelve years looking – so why start now?'

'Because I didn't know until now,' he said, and she stopped abruptly and stared at him. 'And even then I might not have come if there had not been my mother to consider.'

'Your *mother*?' Ivy rubbed a hand across her forehead. 'I don't understand ... And you still haven't told me your name,' she added.

He held out his hand in an oddly formal gesture. 'I am Konrad.'

Ivy caught her breath. '*Konrad*? So you – you really are—'

He nodded. 'I am Igor's brother. His younger brother.' He paused. 'There were just the two of us, and we were young when Hitler invaded Poland. We left at once to fight – our parents were both alive then and insisted that we go, although we were afraid for them. As you know, Igor came to England as a pilot and was killed a little while later, and I did not know until after the war ended what had happened to my parents. Then I found out that my father had been taken to a concentration camp and died there. My mother had been left behind, and survived. She is still alive now, but very old and very frail.'

Ivy could not speak. The story, so baldly and quietly told, caught at her heart. She had known a little of it, of course – that Igor and his brother had left Poland to train as pilots, leaving their parents behind. She had known nothing of their fate, and little of Igor's

– only that he had disappeared from her life at the worst possible moment. It was through other airmen coming into the pub that she had heard he was missing, believed killed, and for months she had harboured a hope that he would return. Later, she had even tried to find him through RAF records kept at St Clement Dane's church in London, but without going there herself it had been difficult. She was afraid to attract attention by getting post sent to the pub, and she certainly couldn't have risked it arriving in Burracombe.

'I'm sorry to hear that,' she said at last. 'She must have had a terrible time.'

'She did. She lost her husband and one of her sons. And she lost all the other members of our family in the Jedwabne pogrom of 1941. You probably have not heard of this. Over three hundred people were killed. My mother was the only one of her family to survive.'

Ivy's head swam. She looked into his face and felt the bitterness of years fall away as she began to realise how this woman, whom she had never met, had suffered. How so many hundreds, thousands, even millions of people like her had suffered.

'I don't have no right to complain at all,' she said. 'I've had it all so easy compared with your mother.'

'Yes,' he said. 'I believe you have. Your husband – he knows about the boy?'

'He's never asked me and I've never told him. He always took him for his own. He's been a good father and a good husband.' She paused. 'Better than I deserve, I reckon.' She was silent for a few moments, then turned to him and said, 'You still haven't told me why you've come. And how is it you didn't know about us till lately?'

'I found Igor's diary, and some letters. They were amongst the papers my mother had been sent after the war. She had never looked at them – she was too distraught after all that had happened, and put them away. But just lately she has been sorting out all her belongings and she found them again. He had written of you and in his last entry he said that he believed you might be expecting his child.'

Ivy felt her colour rise. 'I was. I wrote and told him but I never had an answer. It was months before I knew he'd been killed, and by that time I'd told George I was expecting and he took it for granted it was his.'

'Your letters were there too,' Konrad said. 'I know you loved him.'

Ivy's tears came again. 'I did,' she whispered. 'We loved each other. But I was married and people would have thought it was all so sordid ... It wasn't at all. It was wartime, and things happened. They happened to a lot of people.'

'I know.' There was a short pause. At last he said, 'When I read Igor's diary and your letters, I didn't know quite what to do. At first I thought I would leave things as they are. What use to bring it all up again, to bring trouble to you? But then ...'

'But then what? Why *did* you come? Why didn't you leave well alone? We're all right, me and George and Barry. Why can't you go away and leave us alone?'

'I had first to assure myself that you and your son – Igor's son – were provided for.'

'Well we are. We're all right, thank you very much. You saw Barry in that play. You can see I've been a good mother to him, and George has been a good father.'

'I can see that, and I am happy for it to be so. But there is another thing. A thing you have not thought of.' He looked at her with great seriousness. 'Barry is not just your son. He is my nephew. And my mother – *Igor's* mother – is his grandmother. Your Barry is her grandson, the only grandchild she will ever have, for I will never have children. She is an old woman, with not long to live, and she has a right to know about him. She did not even know, until I began my search, if the baby had been born; if it was a boy or a girl. She cannot put it out of her mind. She thinks about it day and night. She longs to see him.' His dark eyes were intent upon Ivy's face. 'That is the reason I have come.'

Chapter Thirty-Four

'It were a lovely afternoon,' Dottie said, sinking on to the bed that had been brought down into her living room and lying back against a pile of pillows. 'Thank you, my dear. And if you haven't forgot how to do it after all those years in America, you can make me a cup of tea.'

'You know very well I haven't forgotten,' Joe said, filling the kettle. 'And Maddy's left a plate of her own scones and cakes on the table under that tea cloth, so you can see how well you've taught her to bake. You're not too tired, are you? I can soon run back to the field and bring her home if you want to go to bed. Or I could help you myself,' he added with a sidelong glance.

'Joseph Tozer! How dare you suggest such a thing!' She lay back and closed her eyes. 'I do feel a bit done in, to be honest, but I'll be all right here for a bit. I'll see how I feel after I've had some tea.'

Joe looked at her carefully, a little worried to see that she was looking rather pale. I should have brought her back sooner, he thought, or not taken her at all, just let her see the procession go by.

Still, he had brought her home again soon after the play. She had been round all the stalls and seen and spoken to almost everyone there, and he thought that was enough, especially after all the excitement of the parade. She needed a good rest now and a quiet day tomorrow, or they'd have her back in hospital again.

He made the tea and left it at the side of the range to brew while he removed the tea cloth from the plate of cakes and scones. Maddy had left Dottie's second best tea service on the table as well, and he filled the little jug with fresh milk from the larder and brought out some clotted cream to put on the scones with some of Dottie's own strawberry jam. When the tea was ready, he brought the pot to the table and poured a cup just as he knew Dottie liked it.

Dottie was watching him, her eyes half closed. She had regained a little colour, and as she sipped her tea he saw the roses return to her cheeks. He handed her a plate with a scone and a small fairy cake on it.

'You can have more if you want, but I don't want to overface you.'

Dottie took a bite of the cake. 'That's nice. Maddy's done a good job, and she's looking after me like an angel. I don't know what I'd have done without her.'

'You'd still be in hospital. They only let you out because she was here to look after you.' He waited while she ate some more. He could almost see the strength returning to her. 'It's what you'll do without her when she goes back that worries me, Dot.'

'Go on with you, I'll be right as rain by then. Her's not going back till after Miss Hilary's wedding, and it's not even certain she'll go back then. Colonel thinks all the wives will be sent home because of this EOKA business.'

'So you reckon you'll have Maddy as a full-time nurse, then?' He spoke casually, knowing how Dottie would react to this, and saw her head come up with a jerk.

'Full-time nurse? Why of course not! She won't even be here by then anyway – her'll be over with Stella, helping with the new baby.' She saw the trap he had led her into. 'Not that I'll need any sort of nurse – I told you, I'll be right as rain. You don't need to worry about me, Joe.'

'But I do,' he said. 'And nothing you say is going to make any difference to that. You're my woman, Dottie. You always were back in the days when we were young, and you are again now. We went our separate ways for a long time, and I won't say I didn't have a good wife and some happy years, because I did, but now we're back where we started, you and me. Like I said the day I came back, we've got a second chance, Dottie, and I don't want to throw it away.'

There was a long silence. Dottie met his eyes and he saw that hers were full of tears. The blue that had once been so bright was faded now, and the hair that had been golden had turned to silver, but she was the same Dottie she had always been, and as beautiful to him now as she had been as a girl. He leaned forward and took both her hands in his.

'Remember when we used to meet down at the bridge, all boys and girls growing up together, sizing each other up and flirting a bit? You were the one that first caught my eye, and I never looked at another girl. It nearly broke my heart when you refused to come to America with me.'

'It nearly broke mine too,' she said. 'I can't tell you how many times I regretted that, Joe. But you found your Eleanor over there and got married and had your family, so there was nothing to be done about it. I'd let you go and I had to get on with it.' She paused. 'There was never anyone else for me, though. Never.'

They gripped each other's hands tightly. Then he said, 'So can't we take our second chance, now it's been handed to us? Don't you think this is a sort of sign – telling us we're meant to be together?'

She turned her face away and he saw the tears on her cheeks. He pulled one of his hands free and wiped them away gently with the tea cloth.

'Dottie … Dottie … Don't cry, my sweetheart. Don't cry.' And then, 'I'll not bother you again – not if it upsets you.'

'It's not that,' she said, and turned back to him. 'Oh Joe! I know you'm right. We'm meant to be together. I just can't see how, with me here and everyone who's part of my life, and you over there in America with your family and friends. How can we ever be together? And it's all my fault, for sending you away all those years ago.'

'No,' he said, catching her hands again. 'No, you must never think that. We've lived good lives, both of us, and we must never regret what's past. But now we've got the chance to make a future together, and there is a way, if only you can see it.'

Dottie gazed at him. 'What is it, then? What way is there? Because I *can't* see it – not just at the moment. I can't see any way at all.'

'Napier-Hunter,' David said thoughtfully. 'With a hyphen, you mean?'

'Well, I suppose so. I don't know if it's obligatory. I'd be quite happy without one, so that people could just call me Mrs Hunter if they want to, but the point is that as far as Father is concerned, I'd still be a Napier.' She paused. 'And so would our children.'

'You mean they'd be called Napier-Hunter?'

'Well, that's the thing: if I didn't have a hyphen, neither need they. We'd just use Napier as a middle Christian name – John Napier Hunter, for instance. And if any of them …' She laughed suddenly. 'Listen to me, talking as if we're going to have dozens! But if one does take over the estate, as my father would be hoping, the name Napier would still be there.'

'But it would be their choice. They wouldn't have to use it. Will your father accept that, do you think?'

Hilary met his eyes. 'Darling, he won't even know. We're talking twenty, perhaps thirty years in the future. A lot can change in that time. Estates like Burracombe may not even exist. It's happening already – farms and land being sold to pay death duties, families unable to afford the upkeep of the house and gardens. Everything's changing.'

He stared at her. 'You mean you think it will be split up? But your father would be devastated. It would kill him.'

'Oh, it won't happen yet – not for years, with any luck. You know we're always fifty years behind everyone else down here anyway! It may not even happen at all. What I'm saying is that we can't take anything for granted.' She took his hand. 'Are you worried that there won't be anything for our children to inherit?'

David shook his head. 'No. I never thought my children would inherit anything anyway, except the capacity for hard work and to make the best of their lives. I don't want any of them to feel they have to run the estate, as you do, as your father obviously thinks his children and grandchildren should. I want them to be free to follow their own paths. We'll make sure they're well educated and equipped to do that, and then leave it to them.' He was silent for a moment. 'We've come a long way from a decision about the Napier name, but it's all a part of it, isn't it. If it's important to you that our children take on this responsibility, it's something we need to discuss.'

'What's important to me,' she said quietly, 'is that you and I marry and take what comes. We may not even have any children.

But if we do, I agree with you. We won't force any burdens upon them. They'll make their own choices just as I have, just as Stephen has. And if you don't want them to carry the name Napier, then so be it. I shan't force that on you or them.'

'Oh, I don't mind that,' he said with a laugh. 'It seems a very small concession to make. And I'm happy for you to be Napier Hunter as well. So long as the whole world knows you're my wife – that's all that matters!'

'She wants to *see* him?' Ivy exclaimed. 'She never even knew he existed until you told her. Igor told me he couldn't write home because of the war.'

'That was true. We knew nothing of our family during that time.' His dark gaze was steady. 'But think, Ivy – I may call you Ivy, please? – what it is like for her. She lost her whole family – her husband, her father and mother, all her relatives – during a war so horrific I don't think you can understand it, here in your quiet English village. And when it was all over, she found she had lost one of her sons as well. I am all she has left, and all she will ever have.' He paused. 'Except for Barry.'

'Why? Why can't you have children yourself?'

'I did not come through the war unscathed,' he said quietly. 'I was shot down and wounded. I will never be able to father another grandchild for her. Barry is the only one she will ever have.'

Ivy stirred restlessly on the tree trunk. 'But lots of people don't have children, or grandchildren. What was the point of telling her now? All you've done is upset her because she can't see him.'

'But I want her to see him. I want her to know. She has suffered so much, Ivy – you can have no idea. I want to give her this one small happiness in her last days.'

'We had a bad time here too, you know,' she said sullenly. 'Plymouth was smashed to pieces by bombs. Hundreds of people were killed. You could see the light of the flames right out here. It wasn't no picnic.'

'I know that. I was here during the war, remember, and so was Igor. But you were not invaded. You did not wake to hear the tramp of enemy jackboots marching down your streets and through your lanes. You did not hear the smashing of glass and the firing of guns as your neighbours were shot down in their own gardens just for daring to be there. You did not have your children snatched away, your young women raped, your men—'

'All right!' she cried, covering her ears. 'All right, I know how much worse it must have been. But I still can't see why you're here now – why you want my Barry. What happened between me and Igor was twelve years ago – it's over. Barry's got his own grandma and grandad here. He don't need one hundreds of miles away who can't even speak English!'

'He may not have the need now,' Konrad said, 'but he may wonder later about his father and his family in Poland. He may wish then that he had had the chance to meet his grandmother.'

'He won't even know,' Ivy retorted. 'I haven't ever told him about that and I don't mean to now. George is his father and that's all there is to it. And now, if you've said all you want to say, I'm going back to the fair. We're going on holiday on Wednesday and I got a lot to do.'

'Oh yes,' he said. 'You have to make cakes for all the children.'

Ivy, half on her feet, turned and looked at him. 'You *are* going away now, aren't you?' she asked uncertainly. 'You won't come bothering me again?'

Konrad stood up. He was a full head taller than her, and he looked down, unsmiling, into her eyes.

'I did not come all this way to be refused,' he said, and his voice was quiet but with a steely undertone that made her shiver. 'I believe that it was right that my mother should know about Barry, and it is right that he should know about her, and about his true father. Igor was a hero. Doesn't every boy wish for his father to be a hero?'

'And my George wasn't?' Ivy flashed. 'You don't know nothing about it! I'll tell you this, Konrad – I knew them both, George and Igor. Yes, I'd have left George for Igor if I could have done, if he hadn't been killed, but when he was, I had the sense to stay. And although I never treated him right, I know my George is a fine man. He took my Barry on without question, though he must have known in his heart that he wasn't his. He worked all hours to keep us both, and he joined the Home Guard and worked as a fire-watcher as well. He might have stopped here in Burracombe, where you think we hardly knew there was a war on, but only because he was past the age to go and fight, and he was a hero to me. It wasn't only you pilots that were so brave. It was those who stayed at home and kept things going too.'

She turned away, breathing rapidly, her colour high, but before she could move, Konrad reached out and gripped her arm. Furious, Ivy wheeled back.

'Let me go!'

'Only when you have given me your promise,' he said. 'Only when you have agreed that you will tell your hero the truth – yes, and your son too – and that you will let me take the boy back to Poland to meet his grandmother and make her happy at last.'

Chapter Thirty-Five

The summer fair was over. The stalls had all been cleared away from the field, the washing-up done in the little kitchen in the chapel; the coconuts had all been won and the competition prizes distributed. Sunburned, tired and looking forward to a quiet evening listening to the wireless or playing a game of cards, the residents of Burracombe made their way home.

'It's been a grand day,' Tom Tozer observed. He had been let off milking tonight so that he and his little family could enjoy the festivities together. Ted and Norman had left early to do the work, and Alice had gone home with Minnie, so she would manage the poultry. As on Easter Monday, the farm work was kept to a minimum on the day of the summer fair. 'The school play was really good.'

'Was *I* good?' asked Robin for probably the twentieth time. 'Miss Kemp said I was good and so did Mr Raynor.'

'You were very good,' Joanna assured him, as she had done each time he asked. 'Everybody was good.'

'I wish I could have been in the dragon,' he grumbled. 'It's not fair, George and Edward being the dragon just because they're twins. Me and Billy Culliford would have been just as good.'

'Perhaps,' said Tom, who was getting tired of this complaint. 'But you weren't, and it's all over now, and perhaps you'll get a chance next year. Everybody can't have the best part, you know.'

This argument didn't seem to weigh much with Robin, who frowned and stuck out his lower lip. Tom decided to ignore him and turned to Joanna.

'Are you all right, love? Not feeling too tired?'

'I'm fine. You don't have to worry about me. Strong as an ox.'

'That's useful,' he said with a grin. 'You can pull the wagon when we bring in the corn harvest. That reminds me, whatever happened to old Barley in the parade? I was up in the church, ringing, and then I was busy helping on the coconut shy, so I never got the full story. Nobody seemed to know what it was all about, but somebody told me Dottie Friend was nearly killed.'

'Of course she wasn't,' Joanna said, laughing. 'It was just a bit of panic, that's all. Barley caught sight of that dragon twisting about, and you know what he's like, you think he's bombproof and then he spots a paper bag in the hedge and he's all over the place. I don't blame him this afternoon, though. That dragon was enough to scare anyone to death.'

'Me and Billy Culliford are going to be the dragon next year,' Robin stated. 'George and Edward can be courtiers. And Barry Sweet won't be there so someone else can do Peter, and—'

'It won't be the same play next year,' Tom broke in. 'You know that. The school does a different play every year. There probably won't even be a dragon in it.'

Robin stared at him. 'No dragon?'

'Probably not,' Tom said bluntly. 'There might not even be any courtiers. It'll be a *different play*.'

'But that's not fair!' Robin cried. His face turned scarlet and his mouth opened in a big square. 'I want to be a dragon! *I want to be a dragon*!'

'Oh for goodness' sake,' Joanna said in exasperation. 'Robin, you should be ashamed of yourself, a great big boy of five like you behaving like a baby. Whatever did you want to say that for, Tom? Let's get him home and he can have a bath and a quiet hour or so with his jigsaw. It's all been too exciting – he's over-tired.'

'Come on, Robbie,' Tom said, lifting the howling boy on to his shoulders. 'Let's pretend we're a dragon now, shall we? You do the roar, and we'll see if we can frighten Grandad when he comes in from milking.'

He set off along the village street, weaving and snaking as the real dragon had done earlier, and ran straight into the cows being brought back from their field for milking. At the same moment,

Robin let out a roar that would have been quite creditable in a dragon-infested jungle. The lead cow, who had not yet forgotten her earlier experiences, bellowed and took several steps backwards, cannoning into the beasts immediately behind her. In another moment, the chaos of the morning was repeated and Joanna, who was more tired than she had wanted to admit, sat down on a garden wall and covered her face with her hands.

She wasn't quite sure whether to laugh or cry. But in the end, when order had been restored and Tom was beside her, shaking with mirth, she decided that laughter would make a more fitting end to the day.

Felix and Stella left as soon as the fair ended. In previous years they had stayed to help clear up, but Stella's size made her less welcome now in the tiny kitchen, and she had been told to go home and put her feet up. Felix and Maddy had both agreed that this was the best thing for her, and Maddy said she would come too and see to their evening meal.

'Don't you want to go back to Dottie?' Stella asked, but her sister smiled and shook her head.

'Joe's taken her back. He had a rather determined look on his face – I think he wanted to have her to himself for a while. I rather gathered I'd be playing gooseberry!'

'Maddy!' Stella protested. 'Whatever do you mean? Dottie and Joe are nearly in their sixties.'

'That doesn't mean they're too old for a bit of canoodling,' Maddy said with a grin. '*I've* seen the look on Joe's face.'

Stella shook her head at her and Felix held the car door open for her to clamber in. 'I think this will be the last trip I do in this car until after the baby's born,' she remarked ruefully. 'I'm wearing it rather than riding in it! I shan't be able to get in at all if I get any bigger.'

'It won't be long now,' Maddy said, making sure Stella was well tucked in. 'Another two or three weeks and you'll have a darling little baby to look after. I'm really glad I came home now,' she chattered on as she tipped the driver's seat forward and climbed into the back. 'I'd have hated to miss the baby's first few weeks. And Hilary's wedding too, of course. It's really quite lucky that it all comes so close. And with Dottie being poorly too, I just had to— Why, Stella – whatever's the matter?'

Stella groaned. She was lying back as far as the limited space would allow her, with one hand pressed into the small of her back. Maddy leaned forward and Felix, about to get in, gave her a swift look and ran round the car to Stella's door.

'Darling, what is it? What's the matter? Is it the baby?'

'I think it must be,' she gasped. Her face was white and there were beads of sweat on her forehead. 'Felix ...' She reached out one hand.

He gripped her fingers and laid his other arm round her shoulders, holding her firmly until the spasm passed. She lay back, panting a little, and looked up at him with frightened eyes.

'It must have started. Felix, it's nearly two weeks early!'

'We'd better go to the maternity home straight away,' he said, releasing her hands and drawing back.

'But my bag ... I packed it a few days ago, it's got all the things I need ...'

'You won't need them today. Anyway, I can bring them in later – the important thing is to get you there as soon as possible.'

'It's probably just a false alarm,' she said, her colour returning. 'The midwife said they can happen. I feel better now. Let's just go home.'

Felix hesitated. He glanced at Maddy, who shook her head.

'I'm sorry, Felix, I don't know anything about it.'

'Please,' Stella said. 'Let's just go home. I'll go to bed and I'm sure I'll be all right. I don't want to make a fuss.'

He hesitated again, then went round the car to get back into the driving seat. Carefully, as if driving a cargo of very fragile and very valuable eggs, he started the car and set off slowly along the village street. Maddy sat tensely in the back, her eyes fixed on her sister, wincing at every small dip and bump in the road.

'You're all right?' Felix asked anxiously, and Stella nodded. But Maddy could see that her eyes were closed and her colour was fading again. They came to the main road and Felix looked to right and left, preparing to make the turn towards Little Burracombe. He waited for a couple of cars filled with laughing holidaymakers to go past, then inched across the road.

'Oh!' Stella gasped, and then again, more loudly, '*Oh!* Felix – it's starting again – oh my goodness, oh, oh, *oh*!'

'Stella!' Maddy exclaimed, reaching forwards towards her sister. 'Felix, it's really hurting her!'

'I know.' He twisted the wheel in his hands and turned the car in the opposite direction. 'I'm taking her straight to the maternity home. Hold on, darling – we won't be long.'

Joe and Dottie heard the car go by but took no notice of it. Quite a few visitors had come by car, and now that the fair was over, there was a steady stream of them driving through the village. They were too engrossed in each other to bother about who was passing by.

'So what is this idea of yours?' Dottie asked. Joe had insisted on pouring them both a fresh cup of tea before he told her any more, and she had managed to nibble at one of Maddy's fairy cakes to give her a bit of strength. 'You'd better tell me, now you've started.'

Joe set down his cup. 'I've been thinking about it a lot. You're right when you say we've both got our own home and the place where we live, and neither of us wants to give it up. That's natural. I suppose a lot of people would say I should be the one to move, since Burracombe's where I came from in the first place, and I've still got family here. I know my mother would be delighted if I came back. But I've got family in the States too – daughters and grandchildren. We live close and we see a lot of each other. It would take a lot of doing to give them up.'

'I wouldn't ask you to,' Dottie said. 'You'd be miserable and so would they.' She looked at him. 'But it's the same for me. There's too much here in Burracombe for me to say goodbye to it all. Even if we came back for visits every few years – is that what you were going to suggest? Because I can't see it working, Joe. I'm sorry to say it, but I just can't.'

'No. That's not what I was going to suggest.' He took another sip of tea. 'What I thought was this: how about if we spend half the year in each place? Summers in Burracombe, winters in America – or the other way about if you'd rather. Keep your cottage here to come back to, and my house in Corning. We'd keep up with all our families and friends, and be a part of both places. What do you think about that?'

There was a long pause. Dottie stared at him, a small frown gathering between her brows as she took in his suggestion and thought it over. At last she said, a little feebly, 'But what about Alfred?'

Joe roared with laughter. He looked at the big black cat, slumbering like a furry black cushion on the small armchair, and said, 'What do you say, Alfred? D'you fancy a trip in an ocean liner twice a year? We could hang a line over the side to catch you some fish.'

'Don't be a fool, Joe. You know I wouldn't take him with me. I was just thinking about when we'm not here. I'd have to get someone to look after him.'

'I'm sure that wouldn't be too difficult. Who looked after him when you came over before?'

'Val did, but she might not want ...'

'Dottie,' he said, taking her hands. 'I know you think a lot of Alfred and he's a lovely cat, but he is getting on a bit – what is he, thirteen, fourteen?'

'Fifteen,' she said proudly. 'I had him as a kitten off Alice Tozer when her Maisie had a litter, the day us heard about Dunkirk. Nineteen forty, that was, and he've been with me ever since, and good for a few more years yet.'

'Yes, but he *is* an old cat,' Joe said. 'He sleeps most of the time now. He wouldn't be any trouble to anyone. I'm sure Val or Jacob Prout or even Miss Bellamy ...'

'Jacob's already got a cat, his Floss, and Miss Bellamy's got that little sausage dog Rupert, and he hates cats, chases every one he sees. And—'

'Dottie,' he said firmly, 'we're getting off the subject. Much as I know you love Alfred, this is *us* we're talking about – you and me. We'll find someone to look after Alfred and he'll be perfectly all right. But what do you think about my plan? If the only objection you can find is what happens to Alfred, it sounds to me as if you like it. Am I right?'

She looked at him, then slid her eyes away. 'I don't know, Joe. There's a lot to think about.' But her voice seemed less firm and he felt a quick twinge of hope.

'You're not saying no out of hand, then?'

'No, I'm not,' she said slowly. 'It wouldn't be right to do that. I know it means a lot to you. And I got to be honest, Joe – it means a lot to me too.' She looked at their clasped hands, then raised her eyes to his. 'I had a bit of time to think while I was in hospital. I realised none of us goes on for ever – we all know that, but we don't want to think about it. If George Sweet hadn't found me that day, I could have died. But he and Val got me to the hospital and they saved me. They gave me my second chance. I don't want to be foolish and throw it away like I did the first time. Not after you dropped everything and come all this way to say goodbye.'

'Not goodbye, Dottie! I came to see you live, not die.'

'You must have thought that's what it might be. But I didn't die, and I'm not going to for a while, God willing, and the way I see it is us has got to make the most of whatever time us has left.'

He stared at her, light and hope dawning together in his eyes. 'Are you saying what I think you're saying?' he asked, his voice husky.

'I suppose I am.' She smiled suddenly and reached up to his shoulder, drawing him towards her. 'I'll marry you, Joe, and us'll do what you said – spend half our time in Corning and half here in Burracombe. And I don't reckon Alfred will mind at all where he lives, so long as he has a comfortable chair to sleep on and a full belly!'

Chapter Thirty-Six

Stella's son was born late that night. It was very quick for a first baby, Felix told Dottie and Joe when he and Maddy finally came back from the maternity home in Tavistock, but everything had gone smoothly and mother and baby were both doing well, as the saying went. 'Nobody ever asks if the father's doing well too,' he said, rubbing a hand across his tired face. 'But just in case you're interested, I think I am.'

'Of course we're not interested in you!' Maddy said brutally. 'Stella's the one who's done all the hard work. She really is all right?' she asked anxiously. 'It seemed terribly painful when they wheeled her away.'

'You saw her just now.' The nursing staff had allowed them both in for a quick peep once Stella and the baby had been washed and put into fresh nightclothes. 'She looked very tired but I think a good rest is all she needs now. I wish she didn't have to stay in for a whole fortnight,' he added fretfully. 'You and I could look after her perfectly well at home.'

'I think they're afraid she'd be getting up to look after you,' Maddy told him. 'But I'll come over every day to make sure you're properly fed, and I'm sure Joe will help me take care of Dottie. Who ought to be fast asleep at this late hour,' she added severely, looking at the invalid now tucked up in her bed by the window. 'When we telephoned Dr Latimer to tell him about Stella and ask how you were, we thought he'd insist on that.'

'He tried,' Joe said apologetically. 'And I tried too, but I couldn't leave her alone and she refused to go to sleep before we got any news, so we've been listening to the radio and playing cards. And making a few plans,' he added casually.

'Plans?' Maddy enquired, diverted, but then a huge yawn caught her and she shook her head. 'No, don't tell us now. I can't take any more in. It's been such a long day. I can't believe it's only a few hours since the fair. But you really should have gone to sleep, Dottie. It could have been hours yet before there was any news.'

'I wanted to hear about the baby. And I still do,' Dottie retorted, looking at Felix. 'You've told us nothing. How big is he, who do he look like and what's his name? I hope you haven't chosen anything too outlandish.'

'Of course we haven't,' Felix said with dignity. 'As a matter of fact, we haven't made our minds up yet. We've got it down to about six, but we can't decide which we like best. We're going to wait a day or two until we know which one suits him best. And he weighed just seven pounds, by the way – a good weight, the midwife said, considering he's nearly two weeks early.' He turned to Joe. 'I'm sorry, but I really must go home and get some sleep now, and I'm sure Maddy must be nearly dead on her feet. Can I drop you off at the Tozers' on my way past the farm?'

'Sure,' Joe said, and grinned. 'To tell the truth, I was kinda hoping you wouldn't be back till morning. You know how hard I've been trying to persuade this lady here to marry me. If we'd spent a night together under the same roof with no one to keep an eye on us, I guess that might have clinched it!'

'Joe!' Maddy and Dottie exclaimed together, and he laughed. He bent over the woman in the bed and kissed her cheek.

'Good night, sweetheart,' he said. 'You have a good sleep now and I'll see you in the morning. And maybe by then folk will be a bit more interested in our plans. But I dare say the new baby will still be what they want to hear about most.'

The two men went out and Maddy looked down at Dottie.

'Just what is all this about?' she demanded. 'You might as well tell me now. Are you thinking of going to America again? Because I'm not sure I shall allow it. You're nowhere near well enough to do that, and won't be for months.'

'Then us can wait months to talk about it,' Dottie said serenely. 'Now you take yourself off to bed, my bird. There's nothing more

I need tonight, and if there is, I'll ring my little bell.' She picked up the bell standing on the low table beside her bed and tinkled it. 'You can tell me all about the baby tomorrow. Joe's right – that's all anyone will want to hear about now.'

'That's marvellous news!' Hilary exclaimed, beaming, when David called in next morning to tell her about the baby. 'A little boy! They must be thrilled.'

'I gather so, from Felix's behaviour when he telephoned Charles,' David said. 'Apparently he made almost no sense at all for the first three minutes. But it seems that it was very quick – she started as they left the fair and there wasn't even time to take her home to collect her suitcase. The baby was born at ten past eleven.'

'About seven hours, then,' Hilary remarked. 'It doesn't seem very quick to me.'

'Believe me, for a first, it's quite quick enough. But all went well and she'll be home in a fortnight with young Master Copley.'

Gilbert came out of the breakfast room and Hilary turned to him. 'Did you hear that, Father? Stella's had her baby and it's a boy.'

His face brightened. 'Excellent. And they're both well?' He looked at David. 'Pity it's too early to wet the baby's head, but you'll stay for coffee, won't you? I want to run over one or two of the wedding arrangements with you. Some old friends I ought to invite.'

David nodded. 'We're not very busy today. There were only a few people at morning surgery and I've just a short round.' He turned to Hilary. 'Perhaps it's a good time to tell your father what we were discussing yesterday.'

'Oh, what's that? Hilary, will you see to the coffee?'

'I've a better idea,' she said, slightly nettled and wondering if her father would ever learn not to exclude her from his discussions with other men. It was a habit of his generation, she knew, but really – this was her wedding! She had no intention of being elbowed aside, and from the amused expression on David's face she knew that he was well aware of what was happening. 'We'll all go into the kitchen. We're on our own today so we can talk while I make coffee, and it's so nice and new out there now, I'm quite reluctant to be anywhere else.'

Gilbert grunted, but led the way along the passage and seated himself at the table while Hilary busied herself with the coffee. His concerns about the guest list were quickly dealt with, and when they each had a cup of coffee before them, he lowered his brows and looked from Hilary to David.

'So what was this discussion about, then?'

'It's about my name,' Hilary said. 'We both understand how you feel about losing the name Napier from the family, so we've thought of a solution.'

'*You've* thought of it,' David said. 'I have to admit it would never have occurred to me.'

'David doesn't want to change his name,' Hilary went on, 'and I think that's quite reasonable. And I do want to be Mrs Hunter. I'm proud of our name, of course, but if I'd married years ago I would have changed it and you would never even have blinked. It's only because of the situation we're in now that the question has arisen.'

'Nevertheless—' Gilbert began, but Hilary held up a hand and he fell silent.

'This is what I thought,' she said, 'and David agrees it's a good way out. I take the name Hunter, as I should, but I keep Napier. So I'll be known as Hilary Napier Hunter. And any children we have will have Napier as their second name – or the last of their middle names – and if they want to, they can use it as part of their surname.'

There was a pause. Gilbert's brows came down once more and Hilary was conscious of a quickening of her heart. Please don't object, she thought anxiously. Just let it go. Please ...

'Can you do that?' he asked at last. 'Legally, I mean?'

'I don't see why not, but we can ask John Wolstencroft. There's plenty of time, after all – it will be quite a while before we have any children.'

'Not too long, I hope,' he said abruptly. 'You're not a young woman, Hilary. You don't have time to waste.'

Hilary flushed and felt a spark of anger. She strove to keep her voice level. 'We're not rushing into anything, Father. But we are trying to address the concerns you have. If you can think of a better way, perhaps you'd let us know.'

She was conscious of David's glance. Her father too recognised the note in her voice. He said in a more conciliatory tone, 'Well, it sounds a reasonable idea since there seems to be no other way. But there is one thing I'd ask.' He paused, and when he spoke again, his voice was gruff. 'Name your first son Baden, will you? I'd like to think of a Baden Napier taking over here after I'm gone. It would bring the inheritance back to where it should be.'

Hilary did not reply. She drank her coffee quickly and turned to David. 'I expect you'll need to be going now, won't you? And I know you're going to be busy this evening, so we probably won't see each other again till tomorrow. I'll come to the door with you.'

Outside in the passage, he looked at her with some anxiety. 'Darling, what's the matter? Don't you want to do as he asks?'

'No, I don't!' she answered angrily. 'And I'm going to tell him so, too. It's all right, David – we often have these spats and sometimes I give in. But not this time!'

She went back to the kitchen and faced her father, who was pouring himself another cup of coffee. For a moment or two he didn't look up. Instead he said mildly, 'You know, the more I think about it, the more it seems like the ideal solution. Napier Hunter – and a Baden Napier here after all. It's a good notion, Hilary.'

'Oh is it?' she asked tightly, and he looked up in surprise. She glowered down at him. 'Do you know, Father, I wish I'd never thought of it. I wish I'd never tried to find a way round it and just told you I'd be Mrs David Hunter, like it or lump it. But as always, all you're concerned about is the estate and the family name. It was the same when you found out about Rob – he had to become a Napier, to suit your pride and ego. And now this. You always have to take things one step further, don't you. You always want that extra pound of flesh!'

'Hilary!' he remonstrated. 'What in heaven's name are you talking about? What's brought this on? Pound of flesh? I don't know what you mean.'

'No, you don't,' she said bitterly, sitting down suddenly. 'You don't even begin to know because you never think about how things seem to other people. You've never given a thought to David's feelings.'

'David's feelings? But you said he'd agreed to you keeping your name. You said he'd agreed to your children being called by it too. What else is there to think about?'

'Only your demand for a choice in the name for our first son, if we have one. Only you wanting our child to be called Baden Napier Hunter – and don't tell me you wouldn't want him to drop the name Hunter and just be Baden Napier, because I won't believe you.' She faced him with angry eyes. 'Can't you see what it must be like for David to come here to marry me? He won't be providing his family with a home, because it's all here. He won't even be providing an income and living, because the estate does that. He may not even be able to provide an education without you wanting a say in it, and our son, or perhaps our daughter, won't be allowed to choose their own way of earning their living – which we are determined they will, by the way – because you'll expect them to take over the estate. If you have your way, David won't have any of those things most men take for granted. And now – *now* – you want to tell him what to call his own children.' She ran her fingers fiercely through her tumbling hair. 'I wouldn't be at all surprised if he decided to back out of the entire wedding, because once he's married to me, he could lose all his self-respect. And it would be all your doing!'

Chapter Thirty-Seven

I vy was up by six that morning and in the kitchen baking the cakes she had so rashly offered the children. She'd decided to make rock buns – they were easy, and the kiddies liked their crisp, knobbly surface and the currants that made little pockets of sweetness. She rubbed butter into flour until her fingers ached, stirred in sugar, fruit and nutmeg and then mixed it all up with beaten eggs and milk until she had a stiff consistency that would rest in lumpy piles on the baking trays.

She was just taking out the last batch when George came through from the bakery. He had been up even earlier, making loaves from the dough he had set to prove before going to bed. The smell of fresh bread wafted through the door with him. He stopped and looked at Ivy.

'You was up with the lark. Didn't get much sleep, neither. You were tossing and turning all night.'

'What if I was?' Ivy turned her face away from him as she slid a knife under the cakes and turned them over to prevent their bases from softening. 'I got a lot to do today if we're to be going to London tomorrow. And I hope you've made some extra bread to tide people over while we're away.'

'I told you, Ellis's are going to bring some round in their van on Thursday. Folk'll go into Tavi anyway on Friday and we'll be back on Saturday.' He gave her a narrow look. 'Don't tell me you were awake all night worrying about bread.'

'I never said that. I just want to get all me jobs done in good time today, and I had to make an early start to get these cakes made.' She put the buns with the rest on wire trays and turned to the larder. 'I suppose you want your breakfast now.'

'It's what usually happens around now. Our Barry up yet?'

'No, I let him sleep in. He was worn out last night with all the excitement yesterday. Still going on about being an actor when he grows up, if you ever heard of such a thing.' She came out of the larder with some rashers of bacon on an enamel plate. 'I don't know what puts these ideas into his head.'

'A few days in London will give him different ones. He'll want to be a Yeoman of the Guard by the time we've taken him to the Tower of London. Or are they the ones outside Buckingham Palace?'

'I don't know, I'm sure.' Ivy laid the rashers in the big frying pan. 'Pass me those eggs. And don't stand in the way! Did you bring me a bit of day-old bread for toast?'

'Here you are.' George handed over half a loaf kept from yesterday. 'Well, if Barry's not up yet, that gives us a chance to talk, doesn't it.'

'Talk?' Ivy's heart sank. She kept her face averted. 'What have we got to talk about?'

'About why you've been so upset these last few weeks. It's not just about going on holiday, I know that. There's something else been worrying you, and I want to know what it is.' He sat down at the kitchen table, watching as she fried bacon and eggs. After a few moments' silence, he added firmly, 'I want to know now.'

'George, this isn't the time ...'

'It's as good a time as any. Barry's in bed asleep, you've done your cakes, I don't have to do anything to the bread for the next half-hour. When will we get a better chance?'

'I told you, I've got a lot to do.'

'But before you do it, you're going to sit down to your breakfast with me. And you're going to tell me what's on your mind.' He picked up his knife and fork as Ivy set his plate on the table. 'Come on – out with it.'

Ivy picked up her own knife and fork and stared at them as if she had never seen such things before, then laid them down again. The plate seemed to shimmer and shift before her eyes. A tear fell on to her breakfast, followed by another and another.

George put down his knife and reached across the table. He laid his hand on her wrist.

'Come on, Ive,' he said, his voice more gentle now. 'Tell me all about it. It can't be that bad.' He hesitated, then added with a note of anxiety, 'You're not ill, are you? It's been at the back of me mind it might be something like that.'

She shook her head. 'I'm not ill, George. In a way, I wish I was. It wouldn't be my fault then – not like this is.' Tears were falling steadily now, and she rested her elbows on the table, leaned her head on her hands and gave way to them. 'Oh George, I don't know what to do. I just don't know what to do ...'

George stared at her. He put down his fork, still bearing a load of bacon, and took both her hands in his, lifting them away from her face. She raised her head and he looked into her streaming eyes.

'Ivy,' he said quietly, 'you got to tell me what all this is about. You got to.'

She nodded. 'I know. I just don't know where to start.'

'You know what they say.' He gave her a small grin. 'Start at the beginning – whenever that was.' He waited a moment, then said quietly, 'Right back in the war, I reckon. Sometime around 1943 ... 44?'

She made one last attempt to deny it, as she had denied it for so many years, then gave in. She nodded and said, 'It's our Barry.'

George nodded too. 'I thought it was. You had a bit of a fling, didn't you?'

'I suppose you could call it that,' She spoke drearily, each word an effort. 'It was one of the Polish pilots that came to Harrowbeer. I never meant it to go that far. It was just – you know, pub banter. A bit of flirting, nothing more than that. The customers expect it of a barmaid. *Lennie* expected it. And there they were, miles from home, not knowing what was happening to their families – you had to give them a bit of comfort. Not that I gave them more than I should,' she added swiftly. 'Not until ... not until Igor, anyway.'

'Igor?'

'We just seemed to get on,' she said. 'He was different from the others. Quieter. He just wanted to talk. About his family – his mother and father. His uncles and aunts, his cousins ...' She met his eyes. 'He didn't know what was happening to them. He wouldn't know until the war was over, and of course we didn't know when that would be. Anyway, as it turned out, he never did know, because he was killed.'

'And Barry?'

'I never really knew for sure,' she said quietly. 'But I reckoned the baby was his.'

'And Igor had red hair?'

She nodded. 'That's why I started dyeing mine. I don't suppose I fooled anyone – you knew, for a start. I just didn't want other children asking Barry about his ginger hair. Mind, I didn't know for sure that the baby would *have* red hair – I just couldn't take the chance. Oh George, I was so frightened!'

'Frightened?'

'I thought you'd throw me out,' she said in a low voice. 'I thought you'd know straight away. But you never even asked. You never said a word.'

George was silent for a moment. Then he said, 'I wanted it to come from you, Ive. You see, I was frightened too.'

'*You* were frightened? What were *you* frightened of?'

'I thought I was going to lose you,' he said. 'I thought you'd leave me and go off with – with whoever this man was. And the baby – it *could* have been mine. I wanted it to be mine. I thought we weren't ever going to have kiddies, and I couldn't let this one go. I suppose to be honest I didn't really want to know the truth, so I shut me eyes to it.'

There was a short silence. Ivy looked down at her plate. 'We can't shut our eyes any longer, George.'

'I can see that. But what's happened, Ive? Why's it all come up again now? What have you been worrying about all these weeks?'

She looked up at him.

'I told you about Igor's family. He never knew what happened, but they were all killed – his father died in a concentration camp, the others died in the pogroms. All except his mother. And his brother that got away when he did and became a pilot too.' She took a breath. 'Konrad his name is, and he's been looking for me. He found me yesterday, at the fair.'

'At the fair?'

'Yes. He wanted to talk to me. I had to go with him, George. People would have seen – they'd have wondered. So I went down to the mill stream and we talked there.'

'But what did he *want*, for pity's sake? Why's he been looking for you?' A thought struck him. 'Is that why you left the pub? He'd been asking round Horrabridge?'

She nodded. 'I didn't think he'd track me down – Lennie swore he'd never tell anyone – but someone must have said something, because he turned up yesterday.' Her voice rose a little. 'I *said* we ought to go away over the weekend! I knew something would happen if we stayed here.'

'He'd have found you when we came back,' George said. 'It sounds like he was determined. He wouldn't have let the summer fair stop him. But what I want to know is *why* did he come? What does he want?'

'He wants Barry,' she said flatly. 'Oh, not to keep – at least I don't think so – but he wants to take him to Poland. To see his grandmother.'

'His *grandmother*?'

'He says she's very old and frail. She don't have no other grandchildren and she won't ever have, because he was wounded in the war and can't have children. He says if she can just see our Barry and know he's her grandson, she'll be able to die happy. And she hasn't had much in her life to make her happy.'

There was another silence. Then George said, slowly and carefully, 'Let me get this right, Ive. This man – Konrad, did you say? – is our Barry's uncle and he wants to take him away from us, all the way to Poland, to see a granny he never knew he had? And what happens then? Because it'll change everything, you know. Nothing's going to be the same for us after that. And whatever anyone else says, Barry's *my* son. Legally, he's mine. He's got my name on his birth certificate.'

A sound at the door made them both start. They turned quickly and saw Barry himself standing there in his pyjamas, his red hair tousled and a frightened look on his face. He stared from one to the other and spoke in a shrill, terrified voice.

'What are you talking about? Who's my uncle? And why is he going to take me to Poland to see my granny? What granny? My granny lives in the village – she was at the fair yesterday, I saw her!' He took three steps across the kitchen and clutched his mother's arm. 'Don't make me go, Mum! *Please* don't send me away to Poland!'

Chapter Thirty-Eight

News of Stella's baby spread swiftly through the village. Maddy had run round to the school house as soon as she had taken Dottie an early-morning cup of tea and made sure she was comfortable, passing Mabel Purdy, who was at her door shaking crumbs from a tablecloth. She called out the tidings and hurried past, knowing that Mrs Purdy would be lying in wait for more details as she returned and then straight off to the village shop, hoping to be first with the information.

Frances Kemp was already putting away her breakfast things in readiness for an early departure to stay with her cousin Iris. She opened the door to Maddy's knock.

'Is it Dottie? She's not had another stroke?'

'No, nothing like that. It's the baby – Stella's had her baby! I wanted to let you know first. Mrs Purdy caught me as I came past so the whole village will know in half an hour, but I had to tell you myself.'

'Oh, how lovely. So you're an auntie now! But isn't it rather early? I hope they're both all right.'

'Yes, they are. He's absolutely bouncing! Well, not exactly bouncing – he was all wrapped up in a shawl fast asleep when I saw him – but they always say that about baby boys, don't they. Did I tell you it was a boy? Seven pounds and looks just like a coconut.'

Frances laughed. 'I'm sure he doesn't. No more than any other baby, anyway. That's wonderful news, Maddy, I'm so pleased. Do give them both my love and congratulations. But when did it happen? I saw Stella at the fair yesterday afternoon.'

'She started on the way home. Felix took her straight round to the maternity home and the baby was born at eleven o'clock. You should see Felix – he's like a dog with two tails! It's a good job it wasn't a Saturday night, because he would never have been fit to take a service next morning.' She caught sight of the suitcase standing in a corner of the kitchen. 'Oh my goodness – are you going away? I'm not making you late, am I?'

'No, I'm in good time. I'm catching the morning bus into Tavistock and then going on by train to stay with my cousin. You just caught me.'

'I'll go now and leave you to get ready,' Maddy said. 'I've got to get Dottie's breakfast. Felix is coming over for me later on and we'll go in to see Stella, but I want to go to the shops first. I daren't admit it to Dottie, but we've run out of flour!'

'It's good that she's got you to look after her. And I gather Joe Tozer is spending quite a lot of time with her too.'

'Yes. They're hatching up some plan between them.' Maddy frowned. 'I hope he's not intending to take her away again. Burra–combe needs Dottie!'

She whisked out of the door and, as she had expected, found Mabel Purdy at her gate, waiting to catch her. Maddy stopped and gave her what details she could, then returned to Dottie's cottage, knowing that the grapevine had now been set safely in motion. To her surprise, she found Joe already there, making toast.

'My goodness, you're an early bird.'

'Sorry.' He turned from the stove. 'I woke up early and thought it would be nice to help you with breakfast. Dottie said you'd made her tea and gone to see Miss Kemp.'

'Yes, I thought she ought to hear it from me before the rest of the village knew. Lucky I went then, too, because she's going away for a few days.'

'They're pleased as Punch up at the farm,' he said. 'There was nobody up when I went back last night, so I had to wait till this morning to break the news. You should have seen Alice's face light up. They're all real fond of Stella.'

'Everybody is,' Maddy said, putting together a tray for Dottie. 'There you are, Joe, you can take this in to her. A boiled egg, toast, butter and marmalade, and tea in her favourite bone-china cup. Are you having breakfast here too?'

He shook his head. 'Alice is expecting me back and I don't want to get into trouble! I just wanted to see Dottie this morning – we had something to talk about.' He winked at her, and Maddy shook her head at him, laughing.

'You two and your secrets! I hope you're going to tell us what they are soon. As long as you're not going to take Dottie away from us. The village won't stand for that, you know.'

Joe grinned and looked mysterious. He picked up the tray and carried it into the next room, where Dottie was sitting up in bed with her best lace bedjacket on.

'You look as fresh and lovely as the day you first caught my eye,' he told her, laying the tray across her knees. 'Now, you're sure you're not regretting saying you'll marry me? Because as far as I'm concerned, we're engaged now, and I want to start telling people!'

'Engaged? That's for young folk, not old codgers like us. And I don't know as I want it spread around too quick. We'll be the talk of the village.'

'We're engaged,' he said firmly. 'And we can't keep it a secret. I want it in the Tavi *Times* and the *Gazette*, so that everyone knows. The quicker they do, the harder you'll find it to wriggle out of it.'

'Oh Joe!' Then her face grew serious and she said quietly, 'I'm not going to wriggle out of it. I give you my word and that's final. And I don't mind telling you, I've been thanking the dear Lord all night for letting me have this second chance, because I don't reckon I deserve it.'

He took her hand. 'You deserve all the happiness in the world, Dottie, and I'm going to try to give it to you. I promise you'll never have cause to regret it. And now you eat your breakfast before it goes cold. I'm going back to the farm, and this afternoon I'm coming to take you out for a walk in that wheelchair we've borrowed. We're going down to the bridge to pretend we're young again.'

'You're an old fool, Joe,' she said affectionately. 'But before you go, ask Maddy to come in here, will you? I'd like her to hear the news first. She's the nearest I've got to a daughter, and she's already half guessed it anyway.'

*

Joe was late for breakfast at the farm after all, but nobody told him off. They were all still full of the news of Stella's baby and deep in conjecture as to its name. Ted was of the opinion that it would be a good, steady name like John or Andrew, which were both saints' names too, as befitted the son of a clergyman. Alice wasn't so sure. Felix was inclined to be rather unconventional, for a vicar, and might well choose a more unusual name. His own name wasn't all that common, after all.

'Stella may have a say in it too, by the way,' Joanna pointed out. 'She does happen to be the baby's mother!'

Joe ate his breakfast quickly and went upstairs. He always made his own bed and tidied his room himself, not wanting to give Alice extra work, and when he had done that, he took three airmail letters from the stock he had bought at the post office, sat down on the old kitchen chair by the bed and started to write to his son and daughters. They would, he knew, be both pleased and a little saddened by his news, as he expected all his and Dottie's friends would be. Half the year absent wasn't going to suit anyone's plans. But they would soon get used to it, and the important thing was that he knew it would suit himself and Dottie.

Later on, he went downstairs and found his mother alone in the kitchen, knitting something small and blue.

'Everyone else gone out?' he asked hopefully, and she nodded.

'The men are busy catching up with the jobs that didn't get done yesterday, and Alice and Joanna have gone into Tavi on the bus. Joanna's going to take the children to the meadows to play on the swings while their granny does the shopping.'

Joe drew a chair close beside her and sat down. He took the knitting from her hands. 'I guess this is for Stella. Well, for her baby, anyway.'

'Us couldn't do colours until us knew what 'twas going to be,' Minnie explained. 'So I got some pink and some blue wool laid by, waiting. It's second size – they grow out of first in three weeks, and I know she's got plenty to see her through that time. She won't even be out of hospital for a fortnight.'

She reached to take the knitting back, but Joe held on to it. She looked up at him in surprise. 'What is it, Joe?'

'I've got something to tell you, Mother,' he said. 'I'm glad you're

297

here by yourself, because I wanted you to be the first in the family to know. Dottie and me – we're getting married.'

Minnie stared at him. Then her wrinkled face flushed and her faded eyes lit up. She gripped both his hands in hers.

'Oh Joe! That *is* good news! And not before time either – you should have done that nearly forty years ago! Oh, my handsome, let me give you a kiss.'

Joe laughed and bent his face closer so that she could press her crinkled lips to his cheek. Then she drew back.

'But where be you going to live? Have Dottie persuaded you to come back here, or are you going to whisk her off to the other side of the world? Because Burracombe won't like that, you know.'

'That's just what Maddy said. And it's been the stumbling block ever since I first came back to the village. She didn't want to leave here, and I can't leave Corning – not for good. But we reckon we can live in both – half a year each. You'll hardly have time to miss us before we're back again.'

She looked at him, chewing her top lip a little. 'It means a deal of travelling, and neither of you's getting any younger.'

'That won't be a problem, Mother. The big liners are so comfortable now, you could live on them – I wouldn't be surprised if some people don't already just stay aboard and go backwards and forwards between England and the States all the time. They're like huge floating hotels. And the trip itself is only five days – we can leave here on a Monday and be in Corning the following Monday, and the same coming back here. And a home in both places.'

She thought about it, then nodded. 'It sounds a nice way to live, if you can afford it.'

'I can afford it, Mother. But I'd spend my last penny on Dottie anyway. I've waited for her all my life. Oh, I was happy with Eleanor – she was a good wife and we loved each other – but Dottie was always there in a corner of my heart. And now she's come out of the corner and filled it up again.' He grinned self-consciously. 'You don't have to tell anyone else I said that. I don't want them thinking I've gone soft.'

'I don't think it's soft at all,' she said, patting his hand. 'And now I want you to do something for me. Go up to my bedroom and open the top drawer of my dressing table. There's a little box in the corner. Bring it down to me, will you?'

He looked at her quizzically, but she folded her lips and indicated the door to the stairs. Doing as he had been bid, he went out and returned a few minutes later with a small leather box in his hand.

'Is this the one, Mother?'

'That's it.' She took it from him and opened it. Inside was a small ring, with a half-hoop of five tiny diamonds. She took it out and held it for him to see.

'This was your granny's engagement ring, Joe. My mother's. She left it to me when she died and I always wanted to pass it on. I thought of giving it to you when you told us about Eleanor, but I guessed you'd got her a ring by the time us knew about that, and to tell the truth I didn't want it to go to America, not permanent. I would have given it to Ted for Alice, but I could see her fingers were too big – my mother had tiny hands and feet. Then there was Val, but I didn't think it was her taste, and young Jackie's already flashing her big diamond. So I've never really had anyone to pass it on to. But now ... You see, if you and Dottie had wed all those years ago, she'd have had it then, and I know her fingers are still small enough to take it, so if you'd like to give it to her ... You don't have to,' she added with sudden anxiety. 'If you want to buy her summat big and shiny like our Jackie's wearing, you do that. But you could have it anyway, and if I know Dottie, it's what she'd rather have.'

Joe took the ring and held it, turning it so that the diamonds caught the light and flashed their rainbow colours. He looked at his mother and knew that his eyes were as bright as the precious stones with the tears that had come to them.

'That's real nice, Mother,' he said. 'Thank you. I'll give it to her this afternoon. I'm taking her down to the old bridge, where us used to meet as youngsters, and I'll put in on her finger then. I know she'll value it, and she'll pass it on to someone else who will too.'

'That won't be for a long time yet,' Minnie told him. 'You and Dottie got a good many years ahead of you, and I wish you happiness in every one of them. Now, give me my knitting back. You took it when I was in the middle of a row, and I never like leaving it like that. It spoils the tension.' She glanced at the clock. 'Not that I got time to do any more now. The bus will be arriving soon, and I told Alice I'd have the potatoes done. It's cold meat and pickles today for dinner.'

'I'll do the spuds,' he offered. 'You carry on with your knitting.' He gave her a wicked glance. 'You never know, you may be knitting for another little stranger when Dottie and me have been married a few months!'

'Joe Tozer!' she exclaimed in a scandalised tone. 'What a thing to say! You'd better not let Dottie hear you speak like that, or she'll be turning you down flat.'

'Not this time,' he said more seriously. 'I let her slip through my fingers once. I'm not letting it happen again.'

Chapter Thirty-Nine

Frances arrived at Great Malvern late that afternoon and took a taxi to her cousin's house, looking out across the broad plain of the Severn Valley towards Bredon Hill. Iris greeted her with delight and took her at once to the sitting room, settling her on a chaise longue facing the window with its wide sunlit view while she went to the kitchen to make tea.

'It's so good to be here,' Frances said, leaning her head back. 'Life in Burracombe seems to get busier all the time. You really ought to come and stay sometime, Iris. You've never been in all the years I've lived there. We could revisit all our old haunts together.'

'It would be lovely,' Iris said wistfully. 'But I can hardly walk any distance at all now. My neighbour kindly takes me down to town in his car, and I can walk along Belle Vue Terrace or in the Winter Gardens, but the hills defeat me. I can't see how I could manage in Burracombe.'

Frances thought of James, who had decided to buy a small car. 'I'm sure there would be people all too ready to help. There are still those who would remember you, you know – Miss Bellamy, Minnie Tozer, Dottie Friend, Jacob Prout. I didn't know the village people as well as you, since Johnny and I only came for holidays, and I'm not sure they even connect me with those times, but you actually lived there and they'd be pleased to see you again.'

'We didn't know them all that well. Ralph and I were away at school, and we kept ourselves more or less to ourselves when you and Johnny came to stay. And if you weren't with us, we were up in

Portsmouth with you. And after Ralph died ... well, you know what happened. Mother and Father were so heartbroken, they decided to make a fresh start and we all came up to Malvern to live. And then I met Richard and we seldom visited Burracombe after that. I don't think anyone is likely to remember me.' She paused, thinking about it, then added, 'But I have been thinking about it just lately. Thinking about Ralph, mostly. He never had a gravestone, not even in France, and the only memorial to his name is in Burracombe, on the churchyard cross.'

'Yes,' Frances said quietly. 'I look at it every week.'

Iris looked at her. 'Do you? You haven't forgotten him, then?'

'How could I? He was the love of my life. My only love. At least ...' She hesitated, and Iris's glance sharpened.

'Was there someone else? You never said.'

'No, there wasn't.' Again Frances paused. Then she said, 'There's something I want to talk to you about, Iris. Later on, when I've unpacked and had a bath – I always feel so grubby after being on the train – and we've had something to eat. We'll talk then.'

As usual, Iris had given her the best bedroom, immediately above the sitting room. Frances took up her suitcase and unpacked it, then wandered on to the balcony and gazed out at the great tower of the priory, built in a stone the colour of richest Devonshire cream, and across the chequered plain. I wonder if Lewis Carroll ever came here, she thought. Surely this was the landscape he saw when he was planning *Through the Looking Glass*. She imagined the Red Queen racing madly across the flat, square fields, panting, 'Faster! Faster!' and demanding that Alice do three impossible things before breakfast. After all, there had been plenty of other artistic people here – George Bernard Shaw, Elgar, even Wordsworth. Why not Carroll as well?

She turned away from the view and went along the short passage to run a bath. Iris had put a chicken casserole in the oven earlier, and the rich smell wafted up the stairs. There was a quality about Malvern, she thought, that was timeless, a quality that set you at your ease and softened the sharp edges of anxiety. Iris could no longer walk on the hills, but she liked Frances to go out through the gate at the top of the garden and on to the path contouring round to West Malvern, taking her little West Highland terrier Bruce with her. Frances could walk for miles on those hills, breathing air as fresh and invigorating as cold wine and watching the ever-changing landscape – the great sweeping panorama of Worcestershire, with the tower of Worcester Cathedral rising in grandeur from the tangle of streets surrounding it, the Clee Hills to the north, and then, as you came to the summit of North Hill and looked west, the entirely different landscape of Herefordshire, with its fields bordered by knitted hedgerows and the distant shadowed shapes of the Black Mountains across the Welsh border.

If there were anywhere I could live that wasn't Burracombe, she thought, planning her first walk with little Bruce next morning, it would be here in Great Malvern.

'His name is James,' she told Iris later as they shared a small brandy after their meal. Iris was limited in her mobility, but the kitchen was small and she could move around it without much trouble. She had always been a good cook and enjoyed preparing meals for her cousin. Later in the week they would ask a few friends in, and Frances would do the shopping, and lay the table while Iris cooked, but for tonight it was just the two of them and Bruce, lying stretched out on the sofa beside her, his head in her lap. 'He's our new teacher. I told you about him in my letters.'

'You did, and I had the impression that you liked him. A retired major, I think you said.'

'That's right. He doesn't use his rank, though – he says he only joined up because of the war and became a major by default, through better men dying. I don't think that's entirely true, but like a lot of men he doesn't talk much about his war experiences. He lost a leg, though.'

'Lost a leg? But how does he manage to teach?'

'Well, we don't do it by waving our feet at the children,' Frances said, amused. 'He's an excellent teacher, as it happens. He takes the infants' class and they obviously adore him. They're quite reluctant to come up into my class after the end of the holidays. He lost it below the knee,' she added. 'He has an artificial leg, but apart from a limp you wouldn't know there was anything wrong.'

Iris was silent for a moment. She was a plump woman, with hair turning white. After a few moments she said, 'Well go on. Tell me more. Has he ever been married?'

'He's a widower.' Frances told her cousin how James had lost his wife in the Blitz. 'He doesn't seem to have thought of marrying again. But ...' She let her voice drift into silence.

'But now you think he might be.'

Frances nodded, then hesitated. 'I don't really know. I don't know what to think. But ... he did suggest I talk to you.'

'To me? But why?'

'About Ralph. He thinks I need to talk about Ralph. Maybe to sort out my own feelings – I don't really know.'

There was another silence. Iris finished her brandy. She looked at Frances and said, 'And what are those feelings?'

Frances lifted her hands and let them fall back. Bruce raised his head and she began to rub his ears. 'I don't really know. I haven't thought about them for so long. I've thought about Ralph – of course I have; I think about him every day. His photograph's on my dressing table and I look at it every evening and – and wish him good night. But I haven't actually thought about how I feel now. I've never needed to – I've always known how I felt. Just as I felt when I heard he'd died. I don't think I've ever changed.'

Iris regarded her. 'You mean you've stayed in that one place all your life. You've never let yourself move away.'

'I don't know what you mean.'

Iris got up stiffly. She poured a little more brandy into both glasses.

'Things change,' she said, sitting down again. 'Time goes by and things happen. *We* change. Even if nothing happened at all, if we sat in the same room all our lives with not even a window to look out of, we'd change inside.'

'I should think we would!' Frances said. 'We'd go completely mad.'

Iris smiled. 'Well, yes, we probably would, but it would still be a change, wouldn't it! But what I'm saying is that as we go on, growing older, living our lives, meeting different people and having different experiences, we're bound to change. Our thoughts and opinions change. And so do our feelings.'

Frances was silent. She sipped her drink thoughtfully, then said, 'Yes, I can see that. But not everything changes, Iris. I still feel the same about the people I used to know – my parents, for instance, and Johnny.'

'Do you? Do you still feel as irritated with your mother and father as you did during the Great War, when you wanted so badly to do something more than knit balaclavas? Do you still feel as exasperated by Herbert and his silly jokes?'

Frances looked at her sharply. 'Well of course I don't. Those were just passing things. Every girl feels annoyed by her parents, and mine were less annoying than most. They did at least make sure I had a good education. They really wanted me to go to Oxford, you know, but I couldn't see the point when women could do all the work yet not be awarded a degree at that time. And Herbert – well, he was just a boy and liked to tease, but you saw more in him than that silliness of his.'

'Yes, I did,' Iris said quietly. 'And if he had survived, I believe we would have married and had a good life together. But it wasn't to be, and I met Richard and our marriage was a happy one.' She glanced at Frances. 'I was always sorry that you didn't meet anyone else.'

'I never wanted to. I never wanted anyone after Ralph. I just wanted to be back in Burracombe, where we'd been so happy and carefree together. We always said we'd go back, you know. We said we'd make our home there. And it's been a good home and a good life, even without him.' She looked down into her glass.

'You know,' Iris said carefully, 'you wouldn't be betraying him if you loved someone else.'

Frances's head came up. 'I never thought that!'

'Are you sure? Are you sure this hasn't held you back? Is it holding you back now?'

Frances shifted in her chair. She turned her head and gazed out of the window. The shadow of the Malvern Hills was beginning to fall across the landscape, and the distant bulk of Bredon Hill was like a beached whale on the plain, lit by the evening sun.

'You were lucky,' she said. 'You were old enough to volunteer as a VAD. You could do something. I just had to knit socks and gloves and those eternal balaclavas.' She turned back to her cousin. 'You could move away and have different experiences, meet different people. You even carried on nursing after the war; you had quite a high position in the Worcester Royal Infirmary before you met Richard. I just seemed to be stuck where I was, in a groove.'

'And that's where you've stayed,' Iris said. 'You went back to Burracombe, and you've stayed there, in your groove. You've never allowed yourself to climb out of it.'

'Are you saying that what I've done wasn't worthwhile? The children ...'

Iris flipped her fingers. 'No, of course I'm not saying that. You've lived a valuable life and you must have set hundreds of children on the path to valuable lives of their own. I don't decry that at all. But you haven't lived for *yourself*.'

'I have!' Frances protested. 'I always wanted to teach. I've enjoyed it, every minute of it. Well, almost every minute,' she amended, thinking of the unpleasant Miss Watkins and the havoc she had wreaked. 'Isn't that living for myself?'

'Not when the rest of your life is empty,' Iris said.

There was a small silence. Bruce stirred beside her and she rubbed his ears again. He snored a little, and she smiled. 'Maybe I should have got a dog.'

'Yes, perhaps,' Iris said. 'But a husband would have been even better.'

Frances laughed. 'I'm not sure everyone would agree with you there!' She thought of Ann Shillabeer and her brutal husband. 'In any case, if I'd married, I wouldn't have been able to go on teaching.' A thought struck her then and she bent her head to hide the sudden colour in her cheeks. 'I would have missed years of fulfilment.'

'Except for possibly having children of your own,' Iris pointed out. Then she added, 'But you're right – there are more ways of finding fulfilment than in marriage. And if you really did never meet anyone else you felt you could marry ...' She shot Frances a look. 'But that's not quite the case now, is it? You *have* met someone you feel you could marry. So things *have* changed. And so have you.'

Frances looked up again and met her cousin's eyes. 'I'm not sure. To tell you the truth, I feel rather confused – and a little afraid.'

'Afraid,' Iris said thoughtfully. 'Yes, I suppose you would feel that.'

'But why? Why should I feel afraid? James is the kindest man you could ever hope to meet. He's wonderful with the children. He's fitted into Burracombe as if he's always been there. And he's such good company – we can talk about anything and everything, we can laugh or we can just be quiet. We share so many of the same tastes in books and music. What is there to be afraid of?'

'Marriage,' Iris said. 'Marriage can change things beyond all recognition.'

Frances stared at her. 'What do you mean?'

'It's hard to say. Everyone's marriage is different, just as every person is different. All those things you talk about – they're important, of course they are. Married people need to be able to share things. But something else happens when two people become husband and wife rather than just friends, something at a much deeper level. That's what's making you afraid, my dear.'

'So how does anyone ever have the courage to get married?' Frances asked.

Iris smiled. 'I think there's a moment where your love for the other person overcomes the fear, and then you won't feel the need to talk to me or to anyone else about it. You'll just know what you want to do, and you'll do it.'

Frances looked out of the window again. The sunlight had gone and the deep shadow of the hills was now a part of the dusk creeping across the plain. 'I think James has already reached that moment,' she said quietly. 'He's told me that after he lost his wife, he thought he would never marry again. But lately ... I've felt several times that we were about to cross the line between friendship and – and something more. But I've always drawn back, and I know he's been disappointed. He's been very patient, but how long can I expect him to go on waiting for me to make up my mind?'

She shifted Bruce gently from her lap and stood up. 'I think I'll go to bed now. We had a busy weekend and I'm tired. Thank you for the talk, Iris. I'll take Bruce for a long walk on the hills tomorrow, and perhaps the Malvern air will help to clear my mind.'

'Not too long,' Iris said, also getting up. 'In human terms, he's about ten years older than me! But not quite so arthritic, I'm glad to say.'

Frances went to bed and lay for a little while watching the moonlight illuminate the wide, flat fields. Her window was open and the soft night air drifted across her face like a balm. She turned with a sigh and fell asleep.

Chapter Forty

'You don't have to go to Poland,' Ivy said for the twentieth time, tucking her son into bed. He was almost too old now to be tucked in like this, but he'd been in such a state all day, he seemed to have reverted to being a three-year-old. 'I've told you, it's nothing for you to worry about. Nobody's going to make you go anywhere.'

'You said we were going on holiday. You said we were going to London to stay with Auntie Flo.' He stared at her with huge dark eyes, and she was reminded sharply of his father, the Polish airman who had briefly stolen her heart. I did love you, Igor, she thought sadly; for those few weeks I really did love you, but then you went away and never came back and I had to shift for myself ... 'Aren't we going to London after all?'

'Your dad and I have been talking about it.' They'd hardly had time to talk properly, what with George being so busy baking extra bread and Iris herself getting the washing and ironing done and Barry pestering her with questions, and all the time the worry of it all hanging over her head. But they had agreed that they would still go to London, if only to take their minds off what had happened. 'Of course we're going. We're catching the train first thing in the morning. The early one stops at the halt, so we won't even have to go into Tavistock. We'll be there by dinner time.' She patted his cheek, then bent and kissed him. 'Go to sleep, Barry, and stop worrying.'

He turned over and closed his eyes. Ivy sat beside the bed for a few minutes, watching to make sure he was asleep. Her heart ached with love for him. She had thought, after several years of marriage, that she and George were never to have children, and although she had known that George might have disowned her when he discovered she was carrying another man's child, she could not help feeling the joy of knowing she was to become a mother after all. But George had never known – or never mentioned it, anyway – and had seemed as pleased as she was. He had taken Barry for his own son. It had seemed as if she had got away with it.

Yet as the years passed, she had felt her joy dwindle. It had happened wrongly. She had betrayed the man who had proved himself to be such a good and faithful husband. She had broken her marriage vows. She had felt an increasing shadow of guilt, a shadow that had grown to a burden and weighed her down with a bitterness she could not explain. And always there was the fear that her shame would come to light, that George would know, the whole of Burracombe would know. That Barry himself would know.

It was as if she had always known it would happen, and now it had.

Barry was asleep. Ivy got up and moved silently from the room, and went downstairs to face her husband again.

'I told you, Ive, I always took him for mine, and that's not going to change now. I left him more to you to bring up than maybe a father should, because that's the way you seemed to want it, but I always felt a father to him. And I'm not going to see another man take him off us now, not if he's got twenty grandmothers in Poland.'

Ivy sat opposite George at the table. She had come down to find him with a pot of tea made and the cups set out on the table. It seemed easier to talk that way, even if they let the tea go cold. She took a biscuit and broke it in half.

'I can see how she feels, though. They had such a terrible time over there and she's got no one else except Konrad. And to know she's got a grandson – that Igor had a little boy ...'

'But he didn't, did he? He never even knew.'

'I don't know as that makes much difference to her,' Ivy said. 'It's a bit like that grandson Colonel Napier suddenly found he had, coming from France. His boy Baden's son. Baden never knew about him, but that didn't make any difference to the Squire. It was his blood.'

'But they're landed gentry. It matters more to them.'

Ivy stirred her tea. 'I don't know that it does. Anyway, the thing is it *does* matter to this old lady, and it matters to Igor's brother too, and he's not going to let it rest. We've got to make a decision, George.'

'I've made mine,' he said tersely. 'Barry's not going to Poland, and that's final.'

'Suppose Konrad don't accept that?'

'What choice has he got? Like I said, Barry's legally my son as well as yours, and nobody can take him away. It's not even as if Igor was English. He don't have a leg to stand on, Ive.'

'But—'

'But nothing. I've had my say and that's it. He can argue all he likes, but there's nothing he can do. He might as well go straight back to Poland now. How is it he keeps coming here anyway? Doesn't he have a job?'

'He lives here,' Ivy said. 'In England, I mean. Somewhere up country – Northampton or Nottingham, I forget which. He's been coming down every chance he got, looking for me. He's going back today, but he says he'll be back next week and he wants an answer then.'

'He could have it now, if he cared to knock on the door,' George said grimly. 'Barry's not going anywhere.'

Ivy was silent for a moment. Then she said, 'I can't help feeling sorry for her, though. She's old and ill and got no family nearby. If only it wasn't so far away ... I don't think I could face a journey like that, George.'

He stared at her. 'Well of course you couldn't! You don't even have a passport, and where would we find the money anyway? But I've already said – there's no question of it, sorry for her or not. It isn't your fault, Ive.'

'It is, in a way. If I hadn't given in ... I didn't mean to, George. I just felt sorry for him and I was a bit swept away, but I never meant anything like this to happen. I was nearly out of my mind for a while when I found out I was expecting. But I was sort of excited too – I'd thought it was never going to happen. And when you seemed so pleased, I thought maybe it was going to be all right after all.'

'I tried to make it all right,' he said. 'I thought he could be mine. Even the red hair – my great-grandad on my mother's side had ginger hair, so it could easy have come down through the family.'

She stared at him. 'You never told me that.'

'I thought that if I did, you'd know I was suspicious,' he said. 'I *wanted* him to be mine, see? I didn't want you to know I even wondered.'

The silence stretched between them. Ivy reached across the table and took his hand. 'You're a good man, George. I've never treated you the way I should.'

'Well that's as maybe, and there's a lot of water flowed under the bridge since us first got wed. What we got to decide now is what to do about this Konrad, and what to tell our Barry.' He turned her hand over in his and looked at the palm. 'I tell you what I think. I think us ought to go away tomorrow and have our holiday and not talk about it again for a few days. Let it settle in our minds. By the time we come back, we might have some idea how we wants to go on.'

Ivy nodded. 'I reckon that's the best thing, George. Give ourselves a bit of breathing space and give our Barry a good time up in London. We could take him to the zoo. He'd like that.'

George gave her his slow smile. 'Our Barry,' he repeated. 'That sounds good, Ive, don't you reckon? Our Barry ...'

'It sounds right,' she said, and gave him a kiss before she put the kettle on again.

Chapter Forty-One

'**R**eally, Hilary,' Gilbert Napier said testily as they ate their dinner. 'There's no need to get on your high horse about it. I'm not making any demands.'

Hilary stared at him. 'But you said—'

'I asked you if you'd name your first son Baden. *Asked*, Hilary. I didn't demand it. I admit it would give me a great deal of pleasure if you did, but I'm fully aware that you have the right to name your own children. And I realise it's a considerable concession for you to keep the Napier name in the family as you suggest. Not every young woman would have done that, and not every young man would have agreed to it.' He paused. 'It would make me very happy if you gave your son, if you have one, the name Baden, but it doesn't have to be his first name and I shall never expect him to become Baden Napier. I'm sorry if what I said made you think that.'

Hilary looked at the tablecloth, then said in a low voice, 'I'm sorry too, Dad. I shouldn't have flown off the handle. I suppose things have been getting on top of me a bit – all the wedding arrangements, the situation in Cyprus getting so dangerous, then Dottie Friend's stroke and being extra busy on the estate just now . . . But I still shouldn't have lost my temper like that.'

He smiled. 'You wouldn't be my daughter if you didn't explode every now and again. We're rather alike, you and I. All the same, what you said does worry me a bit.' He frowned. 'Am I really taking over? I don't want David to feel he doesn't have a proper place here. He's a good man – I don't want to demean him in any way.'

'I don't think he feels that. Not at present, anyway. But you can see how it could happen, can't you? We run the house and estate between us, you, me and Travis, so he's not needed in that way. He won't even have a say in any changes we make – in maintenance or repairs, for instance, or even redecoration. We know almost without thinking about it what needs to be done. And he's never going to help manage the estate either – he's got his own profession. He'll be busy enough being the village doctor. I don't want him to feel like an outsider, Dad.'

'I can see that,' he said thoughtfully. 'You're right, it's something to be aware of. David can't come here solely as your husband, a sort of appendage. He's got to have his own place, his own rights.' He paused. 'We're becoming a complicated family, Hilary – what with Baden's son Rob appearing out of the blue and then going back to France, and now David ... I can see we must tread carefully, all of us.' He shot her a glance from under his heavy brows. 'Has he said anything to you about how he feels?'

'No, he hasn't. Only about where he's to have his surgery when Charles retires, since it's unlikely it will carry on in the Latimers' house. He doesn't think you'll want it here. But we've shelved that for the time being. We can't solve every problem before it arises.'

'No, we can't. It's another point to consider, though.' He thought again, then said, 'Let's turn all these things over in our minds, my dear. As you say, they don't all need to be dealt with immediately, and we may find they solve themselves anyway if left to it.'

'If in doubt, do nowt – the problem may disappear!' she said with a grin. 'One of our teachers used to say that at school. But I only remember after I've jumped in feet first and created even more problems.' She smiled at him. 'Thanks, Dad. I deserved to be sent to my room and fed on bread and water for the rest of the day after blazing away at you like that.'

'Not at all. You've given me food for thought, and a good explosion often clears the air.' He returned her smile. 'I'm pleased to see you happy at last, Hilary. You've been alone too long. And you may feel a little overwhelmed at present, but that will soon pass. You've found yourself a good man and you're going to have a good life together.'

'Thank you, Father,' she murmured, looking down to hide her sudden tears. 'I believe we are.'

'Well thank heaven you've patched that up,' David said when she told him. He had walked up to the Barton an hour or so later and they were taking a last stroll through the grounds in the dusk. 'It turned out to be just a storm in a teacup after all.'

'It could have been more than that, though,' she argued. She hadn't told him all that she had said to her father. 'He can't be allowed to run our lives just because we live in the same house. Even if it is his house.' She looked at him uncertainly. 'Are you sure you don't mind that, David? So much of your life is going to be taken over as it is.'

'Is it?' He sounded surprised. 'I'm still going to be doing my own work. I won't be a kept man, if that's what you're afraid of!'

'No, of course you won't.' But the fear that he might feel that way had touched her mind more than once. 'And we can have our own part of the house, you know. There are enough rooms – we could make an apartment of the west wing, which will be just ours.'

'That will be good,' he said. 'But it's your father's house. We can't just shut him out of parts of it. And I don't think we'll need to anyway. He has more sensitivity than you give him credit for. He won't come barging in, and we'll spend more of our time in the main part than by ourselves. I think we really must do that.'

'Yes, perhaps.'

They walked a little further. Hilary opened her mouth again, but before she could speak, David gripped her arm. 'Look! Isn't that Maddy running up the drive?'

Hilary turned her head. 'So it is. I wonder what— Oh David! It must be Dottie! Oh *please* don't say she's had another stroke ...'

'It's not Dottie.' Maddy turned a tear-blotched face towards them as they met. 'She's in bed asleep – all the Tozers have been down at the cottage this evening celebrating the engagement and she was worn out. It's—'

'Engagement?' Hilary interrupted. 'What engagement? Who ...'

'Joe and Dottie, of course. They told me at teatime, and then Joe went back and told them at the farm and the Tozers came straight down, all of them, even Minnie and the children.' Maddy brushed the news aside. 'It's not that. It's Stephen. I've had a telegram.' She burst into fresh tears, and David moved swiftly to comfort her. She turned her face against his chest and wept, her slight body shaking.

Hilary felt a stab of fear. 'Steve? What's happened? Is ... is he ...' She could not say the word that was like a blood-red shadow in her mind.

It was several minutes before Maddy could speak. At last she fumbled in her pocket and dragged out a scrap of paper. Hilary took it, feeling a strange sense of déjà vu. So many people had received such telegrams during the war, but that was over now and should be a thing of the past. Was it all about to happen again?

'I can't read it,' she said shakily. 'It's too dark. Maddy, please tell us what's happened.'

'I don't know very much. Only what it says there. *Wounded while flying*. What does that mean? It doesn't say how it happened, or how badly he's hurt, or anything like that. Just *Wounded while flying*. It could mean anything. And I'm not there with him! Hilary, I *ought* to be with him.'

'I know, darling. I know.' Hilary looked at David. 'Let's take her up to the house. She's only come out in a thin cardigan – look, she's shivering. Come on, Maddy, we'll get you indoors and make you a hot drink. Are you sure Dottie's all right on her own?'

Maddy sniffed and nodded. 'Mrs Purdy's keeping an eye on her.' She allowed them to lead her towards the house. The lights were on in several rooms and it looked welcoming and warm. 'I thought I should come and tell you now, though, not leave it till tomorrow.'

'Of course you should. You couldn't bear that all night by yourself.' Hilary could feel her own body begin to tremble too. Stephen hurt ... She shared Maddy's fears about how serious his injuries might be. A flying accident – how had it happened? He was a good pilot. Or had he been shot down? We're not told everything, she thought with increasing dread. The situation in Cyprus might be much graver than they knew. There could be fighting. Planes could be shot down ... Whatever had happened, he was hurt, and it must be serious for a telegram to have been sent to his wife.

She felt suddenly sick and swayed a little.

'Hilary?' David's voice seemed to come from a long way off. 'Hilary, are you all right?' She felt his arm around her shoulders and gave a little gasp. 'Put your head down between your knees.'

316

Hilary stared at him blankly and found herself, without any memory of having sat down, crouching on one of the rocks that had been put along the drive to prevent vehicles driving on to the lawns. David was kneeling before her, holding her steady, and Maddy was hovering nearby.

'What happened?'

'You fainted. It was only for a moment – you'll be all right in a minute or two. Just stay quiet.'

'It's all my fault,' Maddy said remorsefully. 'Blurting it out like that. I'm sorry.'

'Nonsense, it's not your fault at all. You're upset, and no wonder.' David brushed Hilary's hair back from her forehead, then asked gently, 'Better now? Do you think you can walk the rest of the way up the drive?'

'Yes, I'm OK.' Hilary stood up, still a little shaky, and put her hand on his arm. 'Just let's get indoors. I hope Father's gone to bed – although he'll have to know sometime. Oh David, what can have happened?'

'We'll find out soon,' he said, guiding them both up the steps to the front door. 'There's bound to be more information tomorrow. You've got addresses, Maddy, haven't you?'

'Yes.' The younger woman's voice was steadier now, but still tearful. 'I can write – or send a telegram, I suppose. There's a place in London. And our friends in Cyprus, I could contact them. Someone will know.'

'You'll be told when there's some more news,' David said, opening the door. 'Let's go straight through to the kitchen. It'll be warm in there – you're both shivering. I'll make a hot drink.'

But before they could reach the kitchen, the door to the study opened and Gilbert stood there, a glass of whisky in his hand, staring at them in dismay as he took in Hilary's white face and the tears still on Maddy's cheeks.

'What is it?' he demanded harshly. 'What's happened? It's Stephen, isn't it?' He staggered slightly and David moved quickly to support him. 'Oh my God – don't tell me he's been killed. Don't tell me I've lost another son...'

*

317

It was one of the longest nights Hilary could remember. There was almost nothing they could do until morning, and none of them could stop their imagination running riot with the little information they had been given. *Wounded while flying* ... What did it mean? What could possibly have happened?

'He's still alive,' David said, trying to reassure them. 'Wounded could mean no more than ... than a slight flesh wound. Nothing to worry about at all.'

'Then why send me a telegram?' Maddy flashed. 'And if a telegram had to be sent, why couldn't he do it himself? It must be worse than that, it must! And just because he was still alive when the telegram was sent doesn't mean that ... that ...' She broke down in fresh tears and Hilary pulled her close. 'I can't lose him,' she sobbed. 'I can't lose him as well.'

'As well as who?' Gilbert asked, his voice ragged, and Hilary frowned at him.

'She's thinking of Sammy, Father. Have you forgotten she was engaged to him before Stephen?'

Gilbert grunted. She knew he had forgotten, if he had ever taken proper account of it in the first place. Sammy Hodges hadn't been a Burracombe boy, hadn't even visited the place – why should he remember? He had been a part of Maddy's life that had nothing to do with the village.

'We'll start making enquiries first thing in the morning,' he said. 'There must be people who can find out what's happened. People at the air station that Maddy knows – there may even be a few strings I can pull myself. We can't be left up in the air like this.'

Hilary bit her lip. He could scarcely have used a more unfortunate term, but there was no point in remonstrating any further. He hadn't meant to be tactless. And he was right – there was nothing to be done tonight. She turned back to the exhausted girl beside her.

'Darling, why don't you go to bed? You can use one of our spare rooms. You're worn out. I'll bring you some hot milk and an aspirin to help you sleep.'

'I can't. I ought to go back to Dottie. I told Mrs Purdy I wouldn't be long.'

'I'll go to Dottie,' David said. 'She's probably all right to be on her own anyway, but I'll ask Mrs Purdy to stay overnight. You two girls can look after each other, and I'll be back first thing to do whatever I can.' He glanced at the Colonel. 'How about you, sir? Are you feeling all right? It's been a nasty shock.'

'I'll manage,' the older man said brusquely. 'Survived enough shocks in my life to cope with another one. And I agree with you – "wounded" might not mean too much at all. We're bound to find out in the morning, and the best way to get through the night is to sleep.'

'I won't sleep a wink,' Maddy whispered, and Hilary felt inclined to say the same. Neither did she think her father would sleep much. But at least if they all went to bed they would be resting, and it was clear that they would receive no further news that night. She turned back to David.

'All right. You go down to Dottie's, but don't frighten her. With any luck she'll be asleep now anyway.'

'She was when I came out,' Maddy said. 'She doesn't usually wake in the night.' She looked at Hilary. 'Could I have a hot-water bottle?'

'Of course you can! There's one in every bedroom. Come on – we'll put the kettle on and I'll come and find you a nightie and toothbrush. We've always got some spares. And then I'll bring you that hot milk. Father, would you like some as well?'

'Whisky and hot water would suit me better,' he growled, and Hilary smiled despite her anxiety.

'That sounds much more like you! You go up and I'll see to it.' She turned to David. 'You'd better go now. I can manage here.'

'Are you sure?' he asked anxiously. 'You were pretty shaky just now.'

'I'm all right. I'm better if I've got something to do.' She went with him to the front door and he held her close for a moment. 'Oh David, what do you think has happened? I don't want to frighten Maddy, but it must be serious, surely, for them to have sent a telegram.'

'I'm afraid it must,' he said soberly. 'But we must just hope that "wounded" means just what it says, and no more. And I'm sure we'll find out in the morning.'

'I wish you didn't have to go back to the Latimers tonight,' she said. 'Come back as early as you can, won't you?'

'I will. Charles will take surgery tomorrow if I ask him. He'll want me to be here with you and your father and Maddy.'

'Poor Dad,' she said. 'My heart went out to him when he said that about losing another son. It really would break his heart, you know.'

'Let's hope it won't come to that,' he said quietly, and gave her a swift, firm kiss. 'Goodnight, my love, and try to get some sleep. We may have a long day ahead of us tomorrow.'

And perhaps more bad news to face, she thought, closing the door behind him. How would Maddy, and her father, ever be able to cope with it?

It was past midday before the news finally came. All morning Maddy, her face pale and her eyes swollen but her mouth firmly set, had been busy sending and receiving telegrams. David and Hilary too had been in touch with all the people they could think of who might be able to help; even Gilbert had tried to call in favours from a few old friends. But in the end it was Stephen's second-in-command who gave them the most important information, in the longest telegram Hilary had ever seen.

'He's going to be all right,' Maddy said. 'At least, he's not going to die. Nothing else really matters beside that, does it?' She looked at them a little woefully and Hilary knew there must be more.

'What happened?' Gilbert asked, his voice still roughened by fear. 'Was it in action? Was he shot down?'

'Nobody will say. They were patrolling. I suppose they don't want anyone to know what's happening.' Maddy sounded bewildered, but Hilary understood, and knew that her father would too. You never knew who might see whatever information was given. In times of conflict, everything was secret. 'But Andy says the plane came down quite close to the air station, so they were able to send help very quickly. Stephen was hurt, but they got him out and took him to the hospital and he ...' her voice quivered, 'he was operated on almost immediately. But ...' Her voice shook again, and Gilbert broke in, apparently not noticing.

'Operated on? Why? What had happened?'

Hilary saw Maddy's throat move as she swallowed. 'The ... the plane was badly damaged. They had some difficulty getting him out and they were afraid it was going to explode at any moment.' She looked round the table at their anxious faces. 'They're heroes, you know. They could all have been killed if it had gone up but they kept at it and got Stephen out. But there was nothing they could do about ... about ...' Her voice faded once more, and Hilary glanced at her father, afraid he would interrupt again. But this time he seemed to realise Maddy's distress and kept silent. After a moment or two the shaky little voice went on. 'About his arm,' she said at last, quite flatly.

Hilary was the first to break the shocked silence. 'His arm? You don't mean he's ... lost his arm?'

Maddy nodded. 'Yes,' she said in a whisper. 'They had to take it off. In fact, I think it may have happened in the crash. Andy doesn't quite say, but ... but ...' She raised her head and looked at them all, and Hilary could see that she was struggling in vain to keep her composure. 'It seems that Stephen has lost his left arm.' And then she put her head in her hands and broke into a storm of tears.

Chapter Forty-Two

By the end of the week, the various dust storms were beginning to settle, although it seemed that for several families in Burracombe, life would never again be quite the same.

The Tozers were still bemused by the news that Joe and Dottie were to be married and spend half their lives in Burracombe and half in America.

'Would you credit it,' Alice Tozer marvelled, shaking her head yet again as she started to serve out steak and kidney pie. 'To think that Dottie Friend is going to be my sister-in-law! It's a good job us have always got on well, that's all I can say.'

'Just as well it wasn't Ivy Sweet,' Tom remarked, helping himself to runner beans. 'I don't think you'd be so pleased about that.'

'That's just plain silly,' she retorted, slapping his wrist and causing him to drop a spoonful of beans on to the tablecloth. 'Now look what's happened! Really, Tom, if you can't find something more sensible to say than that, best not say anything at all.'

Tom grinned and winked at his wife, who frowned and shook her head at him. Unrepentant, he scooped up the beans and said, 'Well, she's going to be my auntie – that's even more incredible.' He looked at his uncle. 'I suppose that means you won't be stopping with us any more when you come over. You'll be in Dottie's cottage.'

'I guess we will,' Joe said, waiting his turn with the beans. 'It means some pretty big changes in some ways.'

'Mind you, I don't know as I like the idea of Dottie being out of the village for half of every year,' Alice went on. 'She was missed bad enough last time she went. Some of us wondered if she'd be coming back that time.'

'Well she'll always be coming back now,' he said comfortably, pouring extra gravy on his steak and kidney pie.

'And always going away again! And what about when you get older and can't do the travelling? Or if one of you gets ill?'

'We'll cross those bridges when we come to them,' Joe said. 'You can't plan everything, Alice. You got to take your life as it comes and do the best you can with it while you have it. None of us knows what's round the corner.'

'That's true enough,' Ted said. 'Look at what's happened in the village just over the past year or so. Hilary Napier getting engaged to the new doctor, Stephen getting married to young Maddy and going off to Cyprus, two new teachers at the school – and I wouldn't be surprised if there's not something going on between Miss Kemp and that Mr Raynor; they've been getting pretty friendly by all accounts – all that to-do with the Shillabeers, and now you and Dottie. Not to mention our Jackie swanning around all over America,' he added rather grimly.

'And this latest news from the Barton about poor Stephen,' Joanna said, putting Robin's plate in front of him and helping Heather with her spoon and pusher. 'Fancy losing an arm! It's dreadful.'

'He was lucky to come out of it alive, from what I heard,' Alice said soberly. 'It'll put paid to any plans he had about running a flying business over in Canada, that's certain. I feel sorry for Maddy. Her life's going to be a bit different from what she thought.'

'I don't see why,' Tom argued. 'Plenty of people manage with only one arm. He might still be able to fly – look at Douglas Bader and what he did without any legs. I don't see that it'll make any difference to Maddy anyway, except that she'll have to help him put on his socks.'

Minnie had been quietly getting on with her meal. Now she turned to her elder son and said, 'Let's get back to what we were talking about. Have you and Dottie set a date yet, Joe?'

'Oh my goodness, yes,' Joanna exclaimed. 'Another wedding! I hadn't thought about that.'

'Well it's to be hoped there'll be one,' Alice said tartly. 'You weren't planning to live in sin, I hope, Joe.'

He grinned. 'Would it matter if we were? All right, don't answer that! We thought something quiet, as soon as Dottie's well enough to walk up the aisle. Just the two families and a few friends, that's all, nothing fancy.'

'And that means most of Burracombe,' Ted observed. 'I don't know how you're going to decide who to invite and who not to invite out of all that lot. You might as well issue an open invitation to the whole village.'

Joe looked at him thoughtfully. 'That's not a bad idea. We could have it in the village hall – it doesn't have to be a formal sit-down meal. Everyone welcome for a drink and a bite to eat. I'll see what Dottie thinks.'

'Dottie will think she's got to make enough sausage rolls to feed the five thousand,' Tom said. He put his knife and fork together and started to get to his feet. 'Can you save me some pudding for later on, Mum? We've got the vet coming to look at that cow we're worried about, and he's just driving into the yard.'

He went out, whistling cheerfully, and Alice sighed. 'He doesn't make much of what's happened to poor Stephen Napier, but I reckon Tom'd find it hard enough to manage with only one arm. I don't care what anyone says, it's not going to be easy for those two.'

Maddy was too relieved that Stephen was alive to worry just yet about the future. She had heard more about his injury and had even received a scrawled note from Stephen himself. She produced it when Hilary came down to the cottage to see Dottie and hear if there had been any more news.

'He says he's getting on well and it doesn't hurt too much,' she told them. 'But that can't be true, can it? Think how much it hurts when you just cut your finger. To lose a whole arm ...' She shuddered. 'But he's still alive and he won't have to fly any more, so at least he's out of danger now – not that that will be much comfort to him. You know how he loves flying.'

'Will they send him home?' Hilary asked. 'Father thinks they may even discharge him from the RAF.'

'I don't know. He says something about "flying a desk", which I suppose means he'll just have to do ground duties in an office – he'll hate that. But they *are* sending him back to England, as soon as he's fit to leave the hospital there. He'll need quite a lot of care for a while. I don't know where he'll go – to some service hospital, I suppose. Wherever it is, I'll go and stay nearby, so that I can see him as much as possible.' She looked down again at the letter. 'I should be with him now,' she said miserably.

'And that's my doing,' Dottie said. 'If I hadn't been so silly and had that blessed stroke ...'

'No!' Maddy cried. 'I didn't mean that! Of course I had to come home to see you. It's just that everything seems to happen at once. And I wanted to be here for Stella, too. Oh – that means I probably won't be able to stay with her to help when she comes out of Chollacott with the baby!'

Hilary reached out to touch her hand. 'I'm sure Stella will be able to manage. Most mothers do, and she'll be quite strong again by then. She'll want you to go to Stephen – it will be good for him to have you near. But that probably won't be for a week or two at least. You'll have plenty of time to get to know your new nephew. Have they thought of a name yet, by the way?'

'Oh yes,' she said, brightening. 'They're going to call him Simon. And Thomas, after our baby brother who was killed in the Blitz,' she added in a low voice.

'Simon Copley,' Hilary said, trying it out. 'That's rather nice. And lovely to remember your little brother, too. Are you going in to see them today?'

'This afternoon,' Maddy said. 'Three o'clock. They're allowed two visitors then – you could come with me if you like.'

'I'd love to! I'll pick you up at two thirty, shall I? And now I must go back and tell Father the latest news about Stephen. I was really worried about him the other night. I thought he was going to have another heart attack.'

'I shouldn't have come rushing up to you like that. But Dottie was asleep and I had to tell someone, and I thought you ought to know as soon as possible.'

'You were quite right, and on any other night he'd have been in bed by that time. Now, I really am going.' Hilary kissed them both and departed, leaving Maddy to make the light lunch Dottie had been ordered to eat every day.

She made her way back to the Barton, more disturbed than she had let Maddy see. The loss of an arm was no small matter. It was fortunate that it wasn't his right arm, but life was certain to be more difficult for Stephen from now on, and, like Alice Tozer, Hilary thought his plans for a flying business in Canada must now surely be ruined. He and Maddy were going to have some hard decisions to make.

But not just yet, she thought, hurrying up the long drive. There'll be time for that later. Meanwhile, she and David had a wedding to plan, and it seemed to be getting nearer every minute.

Ivy and George Sweet had heard nothing of the new developments as they returned to the bakery that afternoon and dumped their suitcases on the floor with sighs of relief.

'I'll make a cup of tea,' Ivy said, making for the kitchen. The milk had been delivered that morning and put into the meat safe, which stood on a small table just outside the back door in the shade of an apple tree, and she went out to fetch it.

'Take these cases upstairs, Barry, will you?' George said. He followed Ivy out to the kitchen. 'That was a good holiday. I enjoyed it, and I know Barry did. How about you, Ive? Feel a bit better about things now, do you?'

She turned and faced him. 'I shan't feel properly better until I've seen Konrad again and cleared the air with him. But you're right, it did us all good to get away, and I think Barry's got over his upset. He really thought we were going to send him halfway across Europe all by himself, you know.'

George nodded. 'Well don't let's talk about it while he's in the house. He'll be off down the road to see Billy Madge as soon as he's had his tea, to tell him all about London. We can chew it over then.'

Sure enough, Barry swallowed his tea and a slab of fruit cake as quickly as he could before dashing out to see his friends. 'I'm going to tell them all about the zoo,' he said excitedly. 'I bet none of them's been on an elephant or a camel. And I can tell 'em I saw the Tower of London, too, where Henry the Eighth got his head chopped off.'

'It wasn't Henry, it was his wives,' George began, but Barry was gone and George turned back to Ivy. 'I just hope Miss Kemp don't hear him. She'll be keeping him back another year in the village school.'

'I wouldn't mind if she did,' Ivy said. 'At least I'd know he was in the village all day. Once he's away in Tavistock, I won't know what's going on. He could be kidnapped in broad daylight and I wouldn't know a thing about it until the youngsters get off the bus in the afternoon and him not there.'

George stared at her. 'Go on, Ive, you don't really think this Konrad will kidnap him, do you?'

She shrugged. 'I don't know, do I? I only met the man once. But he's spent enough time and money looking for me; he's not going to take no for an answer as easy as that.'

George didn't reply. At last he said, 'You'd better see him as quick as you can, then, and tell him plain what's what. Today's Saturday – didn't you say he'd be here this weekend sometime?'

She nodded. 'Said he'd come into the pub. He knows I work there.' She turned to him. 'I reckon I might as well go along this evening, George, and get it over with. If I don't, I'll spend all night worrying, and he's bound to be in tomorrow if he don't see me today.'

George nodded. Then he said firmly, 'And I'm coming with you. No ...' he held up his hand as she began to protest, 'I'm not leaving you to face him on your own. And it'll cause a lot less talk if us both goes than if you go on your own. If folk see you leaving the Bell Inn with a stranger all on your own, the news will be round the village in half an hour.'

'I don't want no trouble,' Ivy said nervously. 'He's a big man, George.'

'And I'm a baker, which means I got a lot of muscle. But I don't intend to get into a fight with the chap, Ivy. If anything like that starts, it'll be his doing, not mine. Anyway, I want to make sure he understands the situation. Barry's my son to all intents and purposes, and he'll not go anywhere without my say-so till he's old enough to decide for himself.'

'The old woman will be dead by then,' Ivy said a little sadly. 'But you're right, George. He's too young to have all this put on his shoulders. We'll give Konrad that shoebox and hope it's enough.'

Barry was back in time for a supper of toast and cocoa before he went to bed, and then George and Ivy set off for the Bell Inn. At nearly twelve, they considered him old enough to be left for a few hours, and it wasn't as if they were going to be out late. They'd see Konrad, if he came in, and sort things out once and for all, as George said, and then they'd come straight home.

They had only been in the pub for five minutes and were sitting at a table with the shoebox on the floor and drinks in front of them – a pint of ale for George and a port and lemon for Ivy – when the door opened and he came in.

There was a moment of silence as everyone turned to look at the stranger. Then Norman Tozer shuffled along a bit to make room for him at the bar and murmured a greeting. Konrad returned it politely, and at the sound of his voice, with its Polish accent, they all looked at him with renewed curiosity.

'On holiday, then?' Bernie asked, serving him with a pint.

'Something like that.' He glanced around, his eyes moving over George and Ivy as if they were of no more interest than anyone else in the bar. 'I was at Harrowbeer during the war.' He passed over his money.

'Pilot, were you?' Bernie pushed the coins back across the bar. 'Here – have this one on the house.'

'That's very kind of you. Thank you.'

'Don't mention it. Pleasure to serve you. You had a pretty rough time of it over there, and we were glad to have you with us. Come to think of it, there's someone here you might remember.' He called over to Ivy. 'Chap here served at Harrowbeer airfield during the war. I dare say he came into Lennie's place a time or two.' He turned back to the Pole. 'Nice little place down by the river. Ivy was barmaid there most of the war – only left a few weeks ago, as a matter of fact.'

'Indeed?' Konrad said, turning politely to look across at Ivy. 'Yes, I think I do recall her face. I'll go over and have a word.'

He carried his pint across to the table where the Sweets were sitting and bowed courteously. 'May I sit with you for a few minutes?'

Ivy was almost too confused to reply, but George inclined his head and Konrad sat down. They regarded each other in silence for a minute or two.

'We thought you might come in here tonight,' George said at last. 'We've been to London for a bit of a holiday, got back this afternoon.'

Konrad nodded. 'I hope you found time to discuss the situation concerning my nephew.'

Ivy opened her mouth indignantly, but George laid his big hand on hers and she closed it again, though her face was flushed and her eyes angry.

'Don't draw attention,' he said quietly. He looked at Konrad. 'I know what you said was right in your eyes, but Barry's *my* son and it's *my* brothers he calls uncle. Now, we got things to say to each other, but this ain't the place to say them. Too many ears. I dare say it's much the same where you come from, in small villages.'

'That's true,' the Pole said. 'So where shall we go? To your home?'

Ivy shook her head quickly, and George said, 'No. Barry's there. We don't want him hearing – he's heard too much already and it upset him. Thought he was going to be sent away, he did. It took all that time in London to get him over it.'

'I don't wish to frighten him,' Konrad said. 'Perhaps if we walk a little.' He finished his pint and spoke a little more loudly, so that others could hear. 'Why don't you show me this beautiful village of yours while we talk of old times?'

'Good idea.' George drained his glass and got to his feet. 'Come on, Ive, drink up. We won't take him away for long,' he said to Bernie. 'Just a quick look round while the light lasts and we'll bring him back for another drink.'

They walked across the green and away from the inn towards the old ford. There was nobody on the bridge, and they paused to look down at the chattering stream.

'So,' Konrad said at last, 'what have you decided?'

George faced him. 'Same as you were told in the first place. Barry's my boy and I don't want him gallivanting off to foreign places. He's too young to know what happened back in the war anyway. He heard us talking the other day and he was real upset, couldn't understand that he might have a granny he'd never seen thousands of miles away when he's already got two here. He's the sort that worries about things.'

'He is like his father then,' Konrad said. 'Igor was always too sensitive.'

'I told you, *I'm* his father,' George began, and then stopped and shook his head. 'All right, I know what you mean and I know this is important to you.'

'It is even more important to my mother. You can't imagine – how could you – what it is to lose almost your whole family, to know that there will never be anyone else of your blood to walk the paths you know, to bear the grandchildren you should have had and to hand on the traditions of your family. And to know that they died in such cruel and brutal ways ... you cannot know this. If you did, you would understand.'

George leaned on the stone parapet of the bridge, staring into the tumbling water. Beside him, Ivy was shivering as if she were cold, though the evening air was warm. He thought that she had been frozen inside all these years, her sorrow and guilt turning her heart to a bitter ice, which was now, perhaps, beginning to thaw.

'Us've tried to understand,' he said at last. 'Us went to war over it, after all. But you got to try to see our point of view as well.' He turned to the tall man beside him. 'Look, we've put together a few bits and pieces for you to take to your mother – photos of Barry that have been taken through the years. There's only one of him as a baby – we had it taken at the studio in Tavistock, because there wasn't any film to be had for ordinary folk then – but there are a few of him as a little tacker, taken at Christmas and in the summer. We took the negatives to London with us and got some prints made. And there are a few pictures he drew at school – Ivy kept all that sort of stuff – and a couple of little models him and me made last winter. That's supposed to be HMS *Victory*, Nelson's ship that's in Portsmouth dockyard now, and that's a Spitfire. Well, you'd know that – maybe you even flew one yourself.' He handed over the shoebox. 'Take those to your mother with our good wishes, and tell her we're sorry she can't see Barry but this is the best us can do.'

Konrad stared at the collection. For a moment or two Ivy feared he was about to explode with anger that this was all he was to be given. He looked up again and his eyes met hers.

'This is the best? When it is her own grandson she longs to see?'

'We can't help it,' Ivy said, near to tears. 'We can't let our boy go all that way by himself with strangers. You got to see that. And I can't go with him – I've never been further than the Isle of Wight. In any case, he doesn't know about it. How can I tell him? He wouldn't understand – he's barely twelve years old. You got to see it from his point of view – and ours.'

'I see it from my mother's point of view,' he began, but Ivy shook her head.

'I've been trying to do that too, and I'm sorry for her, I really am. I've been trying to imagine what it must be like for her. It's too awful for words. I'd want to see him too, if I was her. But I've got to think of my son. To me, he's the one who matters in all this, and I'm not having his life turned upside down because of what happened years ago between me and your brother.'

'His father,' Konrad said obstinately, and this time George stepped forward.

'Let's get this straight, once and for all. *I'm* Barry's father. I'm on his birth certificate and I've brought him up. And me and Ivy were wed before your brother ever come on the scene. What he did was wrong. I know there was a war on, and I know he was a long way from home and he needed some comfort, but he shouldn't have come looking for it from another man's wife. No, Ive,' he said as she began to interrupt, tears now pouring down her cheeks, 'I don't want to upset you, but it's got to be said, and maybe it should have been said sooner instead of me keeping it all bottled up inside. What happened was wrong on both your sides, but a lot of things happened wrong in those days, and who's to say any of us would have behaved any different if pushed? I'm not passing judgement on either of you. It happened, and what's done can't be undone. And nor would I want it to be. It's given me a son I'm proud to call my own.' He threw a challenging glance at the Pole. 'And who's to prove he's your brother's anyway? Like I told my Ivy the other day, one of my grandads had red hair. He could just as easy be mine, and there's no way of proving otherwise.'

There was a long silence. Ivy turned away and looked over the bridge into the darkened water, her hands gripping the rough stone. The two men faced each other, squared up almost as if ready to fight.

'Please,' she said at last, turning back. 'Please don't let's all fall out over this.' She looked up beseechingly at Konrad. 'Can't you take the photos and let her see them? Let her be happy just to think she has a grandson? Maybe one day, when he's older, maybe then we'll tell him, and he can decide for himself whether to go.'

'She will not live that long,' he said brusquely. He paused, then looked at George and added, 'But you are right. Wrong was done to you, and although I do believe that Barry is of my blood, I don't wish to make the wrong worse. I will not insist any more and I will take these photographs. I will do my best for my mother.' He took the box from Ivy's hands and she drew in a sigh of relief. 'But do not think I will simply go away and forget,' he added, and his voice was as cold and as hard as iron. 'Even if my mother dies without ever having seen her grandson, he will still be my nephew. And I have no other relatives. I will not forget.'

He gave them both a sharp nod, then turned and walked away into the gathering darkness. Ivy and George stood very still, close together, listening to his footsteps as they faded in the night. Ivy felt George's hand close around hers, and she clasped his fingers tightly.

'Oh George,' she whispered shakily. 'Is everything all right now, do you think? Will he really go away and leave us alone?'

'I dunno, maid,' he said. 'I dunno. Maybe for a while – maybe for a few years. Who knows? But at least we don't have to worry about him taking our Barry to Poland. And we don't have to tell him about it – not yet, anyway.'

A young couple came down the lane, their arms entwined about each other's waists, and George squeezed Ivy's hand.

'Time us was going home, Ive,' he said quietly, and as they walked slowly back along the village street, he slipped his own arm around her waist. It was something he had not done for years, but he sensed a new closeness between them, the closeness that could come only when there were no more secrets to be told.

'Well!' Frances Kemp said, leaning back in her chair. 'I can't believe it. I turn my back on Burracombe for five minutes and the place goes mad. Dottie Friend engaged to a rich American – poor Stephen Napier horribly injured and coming home. Whatever next?'

James smiled at her. He had known that Frances was home the evening before, but had restrained himself from knocking at the door until mid-morning, when he judged that she would be up and dressed. He found that he was her first visitor, so was able to impart all the news himself over coffee.

'I don't think there's anything else. Oh, the Sweets have been to London – they came back on Saturday – and Barry's been holding court at every opportunity, boasting about his adventures with camels and elephants. Lions, too, I wouldn't be surprised. His exploits seem more daring every time I hear about them.'

'Camels and elephants? Lions?' she echoed, and then laughed. 'Oh, I see – the zoo! I hope they took him somewhere educational as well.'

'I think so. He told me he'd been to the railway station where they had the Battle of Waterloo.'

'Surely not!' She caught his glance. 'You're pulling my leg. Well, perhaps I shouldn't expect too much – it was supposed to be a holiday, after all. And what have you been doing with yourself, James?'

'Oh, you know – pottering about, doing a little housework, a little gardening, reading, listening to music, going for the odd stroll on the moors. I've managed to pass the time.'

She tilted her head sideways. 'You sound as if you've been rather bored. I hope you're not regretting making Burracombe your home.'

'I don't regret it at all,' he said, looking across the room at her. 'Although there's one thing that would really make it home.' He paused, but Frances looked down and said nothing, and after a moment he said, 'Tell me about your stay in Malvern. Did you have a good time?'

She looked up, and he saw that her face was tinged with colour. 'I did, thank you. Iris and I always enjoy our time together. We visited Ledbury and Worcester and Hereford – did you know they have a wonderful chained library in the cathedral there? – and I went for some beautiful walks on the hills. I always think of Elgar when I'm there. He said, "There is music in the air, music all around us and you simply take as much as you require." Isn't that lovely?'

'It is,' he said, smiling. 'And did you do anything else?'

'We talked,' she said simply. 'We talked about life and ... and about love. We both lost sweethearts in the First World War, you know – hers was a friend called Herbert Turnbull, one of those facetious young men who never take anything seriously. He was one of the earliest to join up, and when he came back for his first leave, he was a different man. He never spoke of what he saw, but I've been able to guess a little since then. He used to joke about being a hero, and that's just what he was in the end.'

James nodded. She thought of his experiences and loss in the Second World War. What a violent century we live in, she thought, and yet we believe we have progressed with civilisation. After a few moments, she went on.

'Iris grieved for him for years. But then she met Richard, and they fell in love and married. He died ten years ago, but they had a very happy life together.'

'She was fortunate,' he said. 'Many young women never found another man.'

'I know. I was one of them.'

James stirred. 'Was it really that, Frances? Or was it that you didn't want to find one?'

Frances looked at him. 'Iris asked me something very like that. I think it was both. Perhaps I did turn away from all such thoughts, but who knows – if the right man had come along and I had been ready, I might have overcome my grief. Iris said I was like one of those birds you might see under glass in Victorian drawing rooms. Trapped behind an invisible wall.'

'And do you think you're still trapped?'

'No,' she said at last. 'It's taken me a long time, James, but I think I've managed to break free. I think if the right man comes to me now, I will be ready.'

There was a long silence. At last he reached across the space between them, and Frances reached out in her turn to him. Their hands touched and their fingers clasped.

'Am I the right man for you?' he asked in a low voice. 'I would like to think so – I believe I am. But what do you think?'

Frances raised her eyes and looked at him very directly. A thrill ran through her and his touch was suddenly like a flame, burning through her skin and up her arm to scald into life the heart that had been frozen for so long.

'I think you are the right man for me, James,' she said. 'I think it's time I let myself love again.'

Chapter Forty-Three

Stephen Napier came home the week before his sister's wedding. He was thin and pale, and the stump of his left arm was still swathed in dressings. As a special dispensation, he was under orders to report to the naval doctors at Devonport Hospital to have them changed and checked. After the wedding, he had to return to the RAF hospital at Halton, in Buckinghamshire.

Maddy moved back to the Barton to be with him. Dottie was almost able to manage on her own now, as long as she had someone there at night, so Mabel Purdy popped in to sleep, and in true Burracombe style a path was beaten to her door to offer help during the day. More often than not, Joe Tozer was already there, and most people stayed to hear about their own wedding plans. Their story was considered almost more romantic than that of Hilary and David.

'Us don't want to steal their thunder,' Dottie said firmly. 'Not that we could anyway, but we want to wait till all that excitement's over and they'm back from their honeymoon. So it'll be the first Saturday in October, and our honeymoon will be a trip to America on the *Queen Elizabeth*. Dr Latimer reckons I'll be fit to travel then, and Joe's got a good doctor in Corning.'

'And I shall be wrapping you up in cotton wool and cosseting you like a baby all the way across,' Joe said.

'A honeymoon on the *Queen Elizabeth*,' Aggie Madge marvelled. 'That's proper glamorous. You'll be going to Hollywood next, Dottie. Us'll see you at the pictures yet.'

Dottie laughed. 'Only in the one-and-ninepennies! If they tried to make a picture with me in it, I'd break the camera. Anyway, it's nearly as far from Corning to Hollywood as it is from here to Corning. America's a huge place.'

'I think you're really lucky,' sighed Brenda Culliford, who had brought down a basket of fresh tomatoes and a cucumber from the Barton's kitchen garden. 'I wish I could go to America.'

'It's not all that special,' Dottie said offhandedly. 'Just like England really, only American. The countryside even looks much the same.'

Brenda stared at her. 'But what about the Rocky Mountains and the Grand Canyon and the Great Lakes? We had to learn all their names at school.'

'They're in a different part. They're not even close to each other. You look in an atlas next time you get a chance and you'll see.'

Brenda finished arranging the tomatoes in a Pyrex bowl and took them into the larder. 'I'd like to go, all the same,' she said, coming back. 'Jackie Tozer went, and she seems to like it all right.'

'Yes, she settled in like a cat finding a new home.' Dottie looked at the girl. 'You're all right up at the Barton, though, aren't you? You'll get a good grounding there – don't forget, Jackie herself started off there and then went on to be a receptionist in one of the big hotels in Plymouth. You could do something like that.'

'I dunno. I reckon Mum's going to need help with the little 'uns for years, and by the time they're growed I shall be too old. I'll probably be married myself anyway. You were lucky, going off to London and working in the theatre, doing costumes and meeting all those famous people.'

'Only because I was fool enough to turn down Joe the first time he asked me. I didn't want to leave Burracombe, but I had to. Not that I didn't enjoy the costume work, but London was no place for me. I was glad to come home when Fenella Forsyth started to go abroad to entertain the troops in the war and asked me to look after Maddy for her. And that brings us back to Mr Stephen. How's he getting on? You must see quite a lot of him. I was hoping Maddy would bring him down to see me, but she hasn't so far.'

'He's not supposed to do too much. She told me to tell you that they'll come soon. Oh ...' She went to the window. 'There's a car outside. It looks as if you've got visitors after all.' She picked up her empty basket. 'I'll go now. It was nice to see you, Miss Friend.'

'Thanks for the tomatoes and cucumber.' Dottie watched her go, thinking what a transformation there had been in the girl. In the whole Culliford household, in fact. They would never be the pride of the village, but their cottage did look tidier now that Arthur was putting in a bit of time in the garden, and Maggie was managing to keep it cleaner indoors. She'd taken notice of Dottie's cookery lessons too, and at least the family had a proper meal together now after Arthur came home from work.

The door opened. Dottie looked round to see who the new visitors were, and gave a cry of delight.

'Stella! Felix! Oh, you've brought the baby to see me! Oh, how lovely!'

'We came straight from the maternity home,' Stella said, bending to kiss her. She held out the little shawl-wrapped bundle and Dottie looked down into the tiny face. 'Let me introduce you to Simon Copley. You can be the first to hold him.'

'Oh, my dear Lord.' Dottie took the baby in her arms and gazed at him. 'He's so beautiful. Look at those tiny fingernails. And those long eyelashes! He's going to be a real heartbreaker when he grows up.'

'So long as it's not too quick,' Stella said, sitting down beside her. 'I want him to stay like this for a while, but apparently he's insisting on growing. He's already back to his birth weight.'

'They lose a bit in the first week after they're born,' Felix put in helpfully, and both women gave him a look. 'Well *I* didn't know that before,' he added defensively.

'And no reason why you should,' Dottie said. 'Now, why don't you put the kettle on and make us all a nice cup of tea. I want to nurse this dear little chap for a bit longer. Unless you want to go straight back to Little Burracombe?' she asked. 'If you've only just come out of Chollacott, you'll be wanting to get home.'

'We can stay for a cup of tea.' Stella smiled at her. 'And how are you, Dottie? I've been worried about you while I've been imprisoned. I felt bad about not coming to see you.'

'Bless you, I'm almost well again now and would be up and about if Dr Latimer would let me. But he says I got to rest for a bit longer, just take little walks now and then, and Joe's here a lot of the time keeping me in line. He's turning into a proper bully.' The door opened again at that moment and Joe himself came in. 'I'm just telling them how you order me about, Joe.'

'It's about time someone did. And is this the vicar's new son?' He came over to look. 'Now that's what I call real handsome.' He looked at Dottie. 'I just ran into David Hunter. He asked me to tell you that Hilary's wedding dress has arrived and she wants to show it to you. How do you feel about a trip to the Barton this afternoon? I could take you in the wheelchair or we could go in the car.'

'Oh, let's use the wheelchair if 'tis not too much for you to push,' Dottie said. 'And I can walk a bit of the way too.' She looked around at them and then down at the baby in her arms. 'This fine young fellow here, and Hilary and David's wedding just round the corner! And then it's me and Joe. We've fixed it for the first Saturday in October, so they'll be back from their honeymoon. And ...' her eyes sparkled at the chance to pass on a little bit of gossip she'd heard from Mabel Purdy that morning, 'a little bird's been whispering in my ear about the two schoolteachers too. Seems they're pretty friendly now, *and* been seen in Tavistock looking in certain shop windows, and we all know what *that* means. If you ask me, we might be going to have another wedding in Burracombe!'

'There must be something in the air here,' Felix said. 'It makes people fall in love. Don't you think so?'

'I do,' Stella said. 'And ...' But her words were drowned by the whistling of the kettle and a sudden roar of indignation from Simon. Felix leapt to remove the whistle and make the tea, and Stella took the baby back from Dottie and began to soothe him.

Burracombe, she thought. A village of joy and tragedy, but mostly of love. A village where life might seem quiet but was never dull; where every day brought fresh news, fresh events and fresh surprises.

Surprises – yes, there were always a few surprises in Burracombe.